Tree-House Comix Proudly Presents

DOG MAN
GRIME AND PUNISHMENT

WRITTEN AND ILLUSTRATED BY DAV PILKEY
AS GEORGE BEARD AND HAROLD HUTCHINS
WITH COLOR BY JOSE GARIBALDI

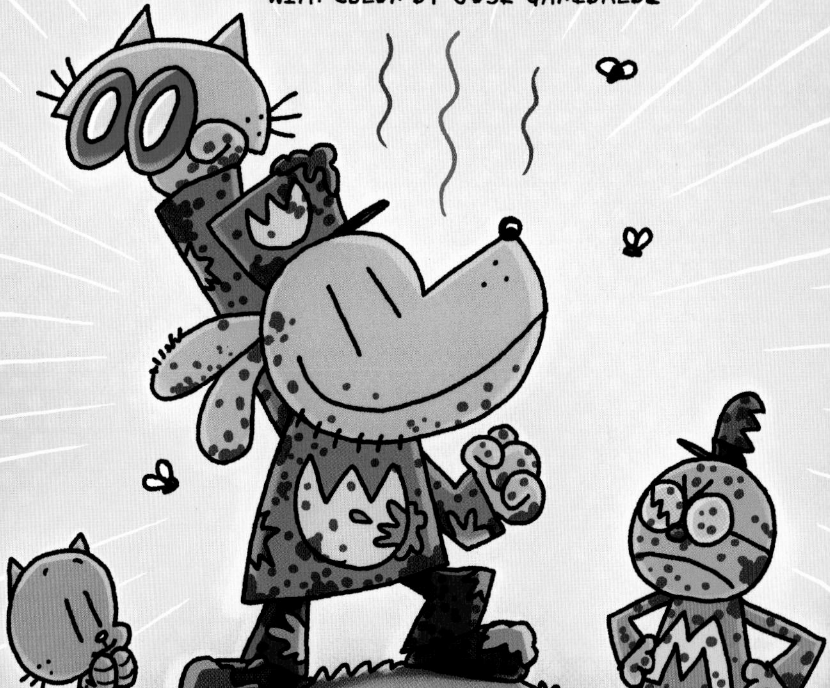

graphix
AN IMPRINT OF
SCHOLASTIC

TO AMY BERKOWER, WHO
ONCE TOLD ME, "WRITE THE BOOKS
THAT MAKE YOU HAPPY." THANK
YOU FOR BELIEVING IN ME.

Library of Congress Control Number 2020930257

978-1-338-53562-4 (POB)
978-1-338-53563-1 (Library)

10 9 8 7 6 5 4 3 2 1   20 21 22 23 24

Printed in China   62
First edition, September 2020

Edited by Ken Geist
Book design by Dav Pilkey and Phil Falco
Color by Jose Garibaldi
Color flatting by Aaron Polk
Publisher: David Saylor

CHAPTERS

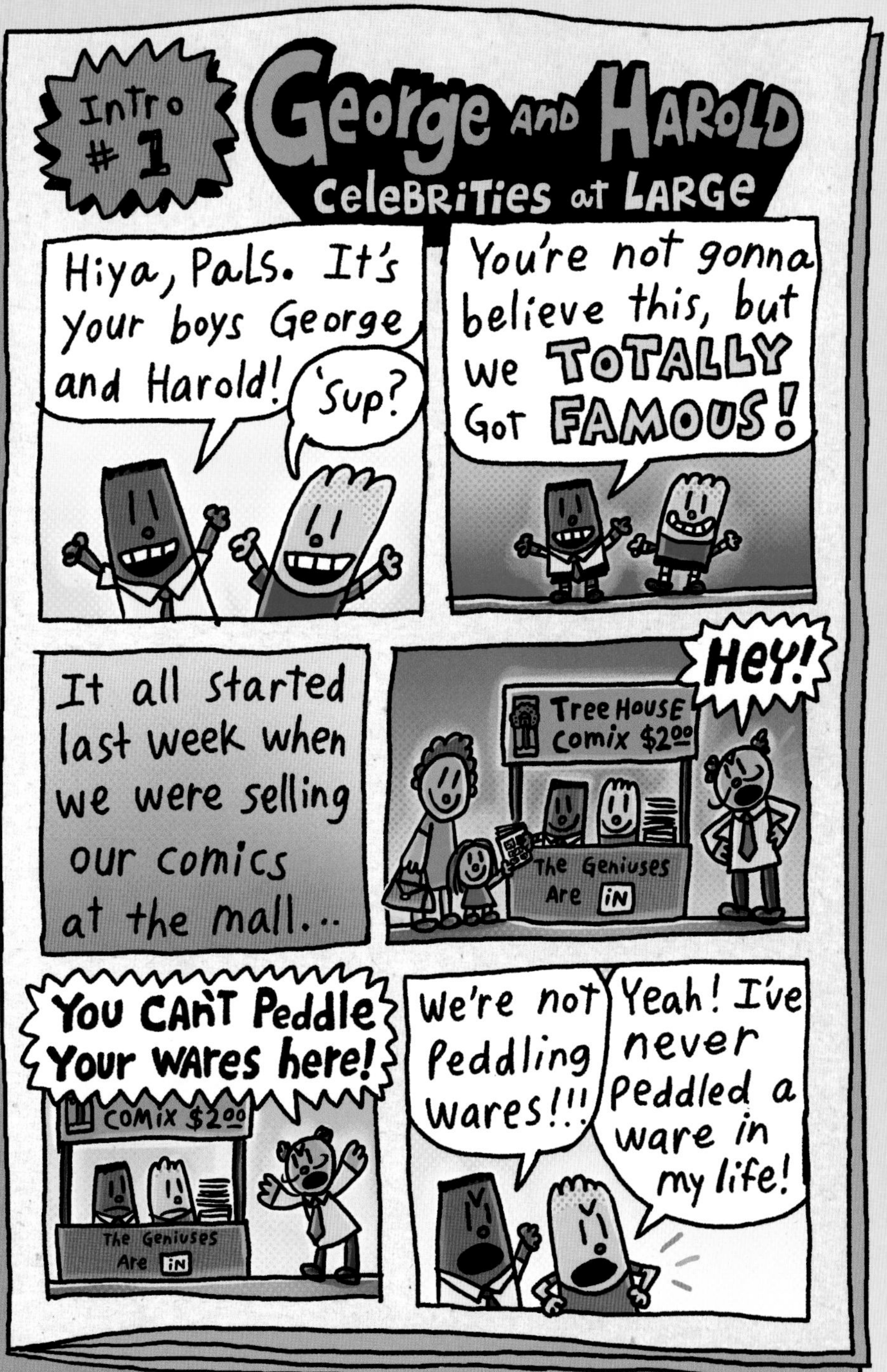
Intro #1
George and Harold
Celebrities at Large
Hiya, Pals. It's your boys George and Harold!
'Sup?
You're not gonna believe this, but we TOTALLY Got FAMOUS!
It all started last week when we were selling our comics at the mall...
Tree House Comix $2.00
The Geniuses Are iN
HEY!
You CAN'T Peddle Your wares here!
COMIX $2.00
The Geniuses Are iN
We're not Peddling wares!!!
Yeah! I've never Peddled a ware in my life!

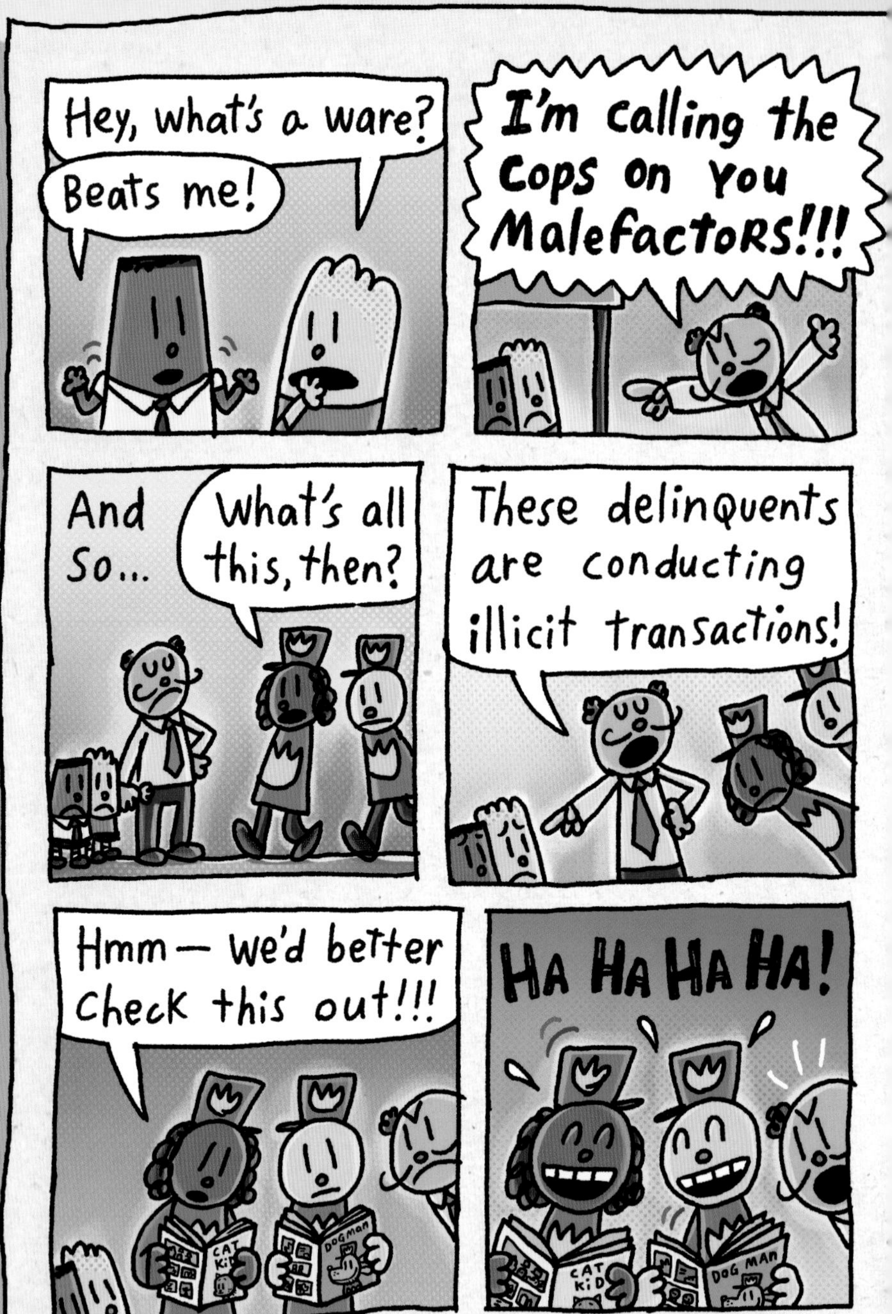
Hey, what's a ware?
Beats me!
I'm calling the Cops on you Malefactors!!!
And So...
What's all this, then?
These delinquents are conducting illicit transactions!
Hmm— We'd better check this out!!!
HA HA HA HA!

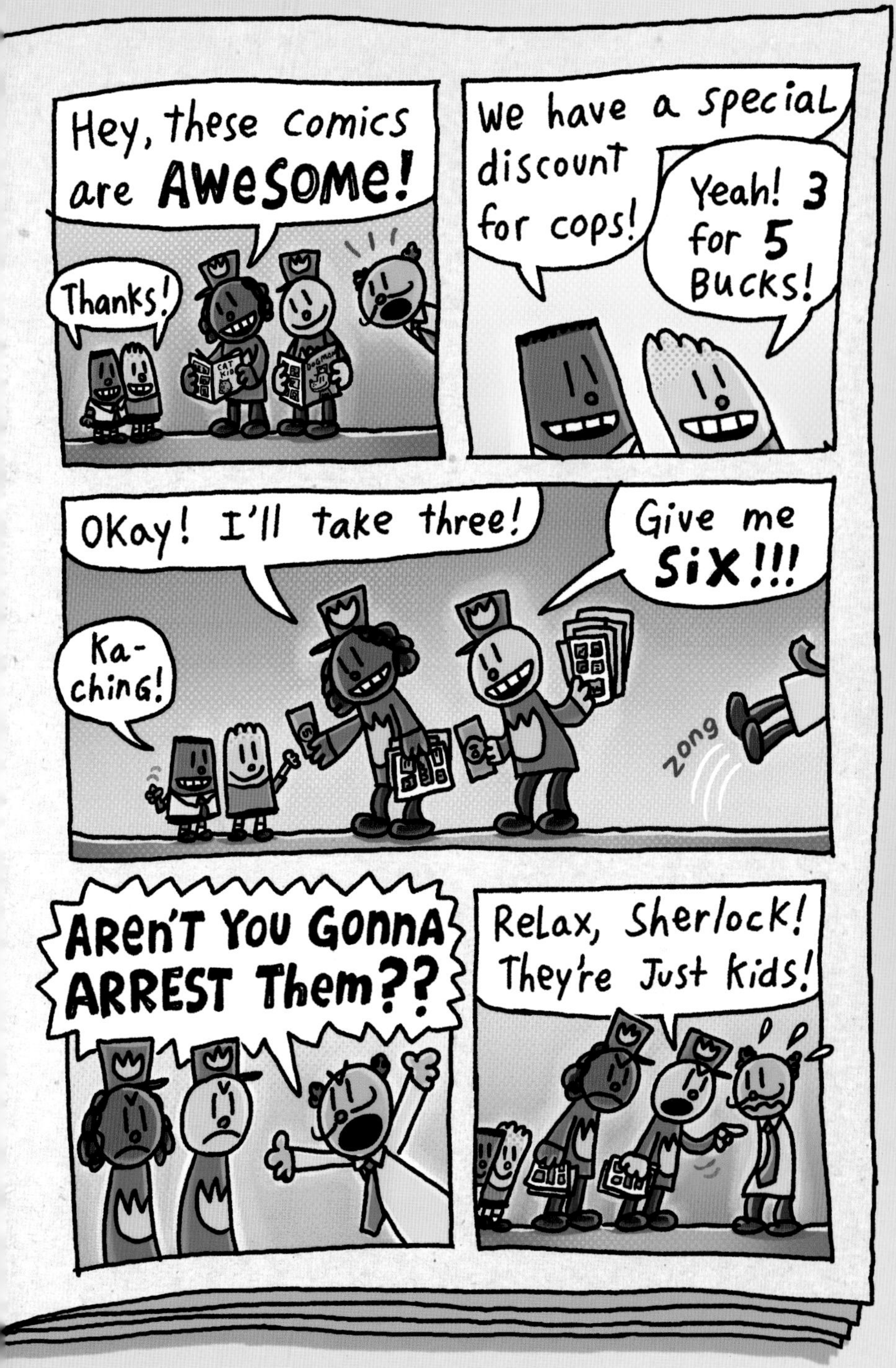
Hey, these comics are AWESOME!
Thanks!
We have a special discount for cops!
Yeah! 3 for 5 Bucks!
OKay! I'll take three!
Give me SIX!!!
Ka-chinG!
zong
AREN'T YOU GONNA ARREST Them??
ReLax, Sherlock! They're Just Kids!

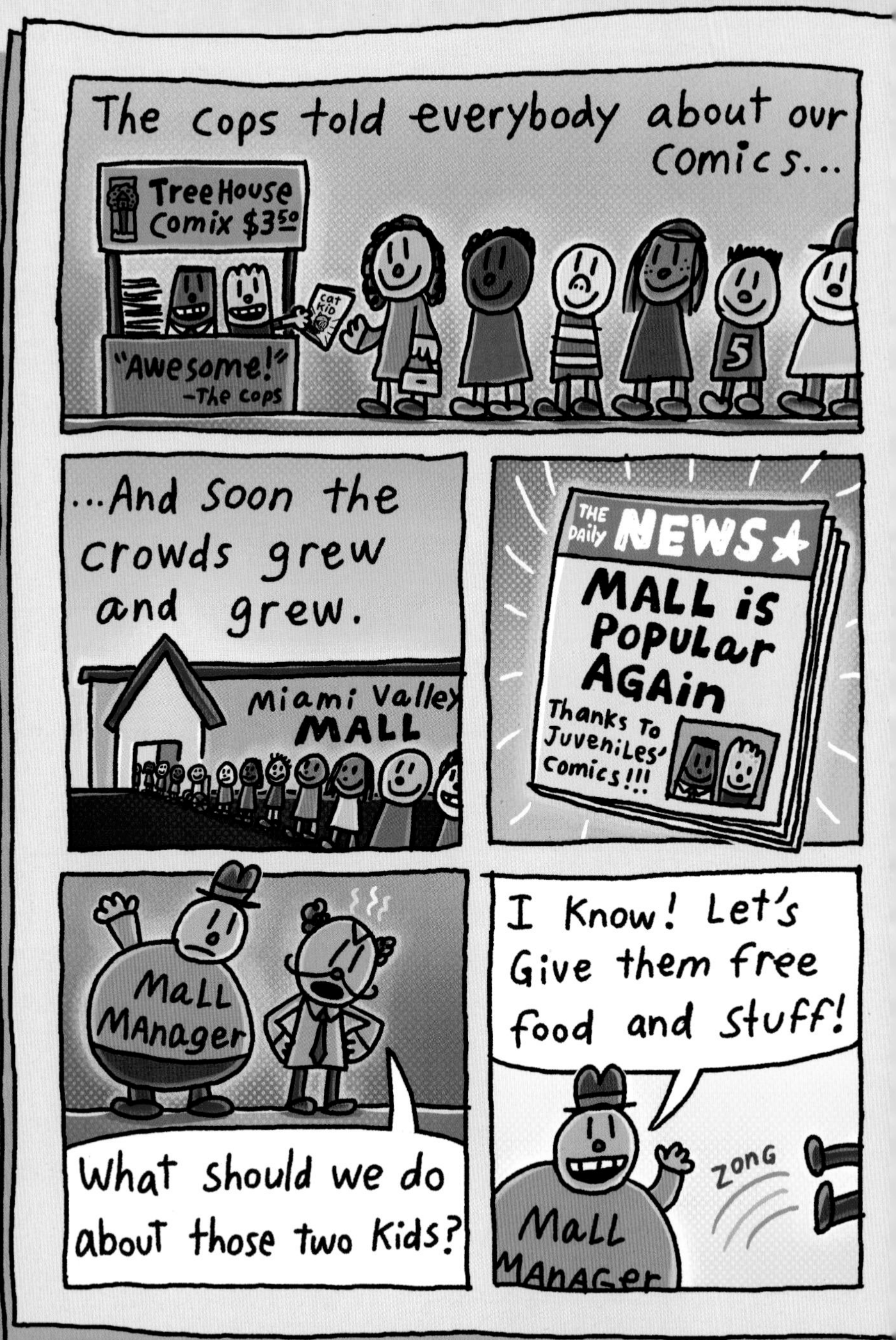
The cops told everybody about our comics...
Tree House Comix $3.50
Cat Kid
"Awesome!" —The cops
5
...And soon the crowds grew and grew.
Miami Valley MALL
THE DAILY NEWS
MALL is Popular AGAIN
Thanks To Juveniles' Comics!!!
Mall Manager
What should we do about those two kids?
I Know! Let's Give them free food and Stuff!
ZONG
Mall Manager

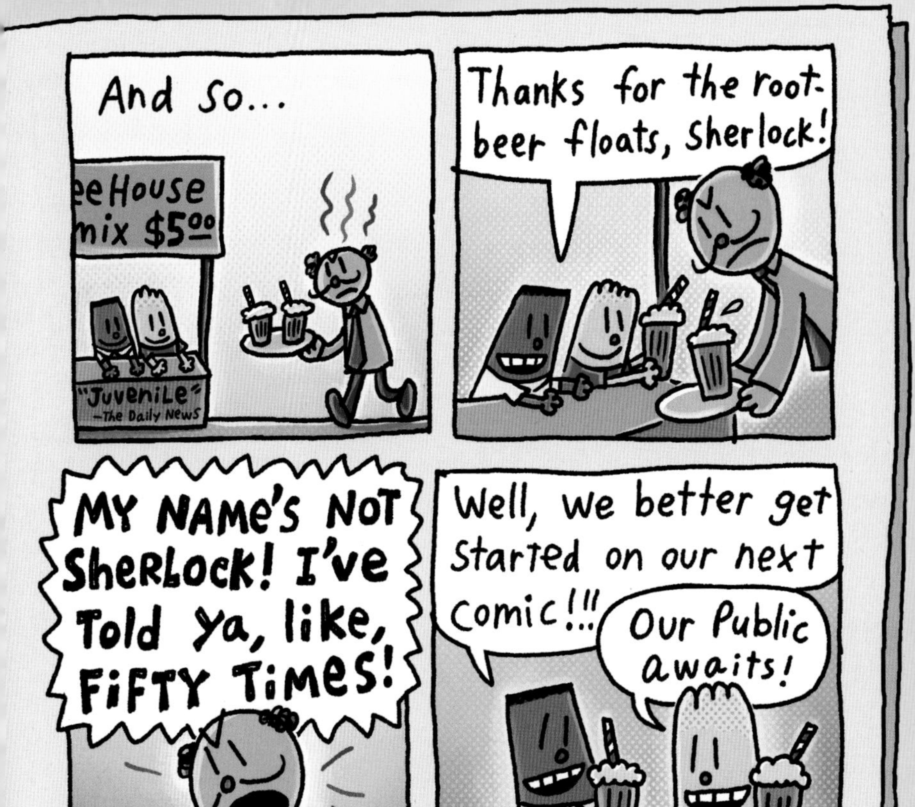
And so...
eeHouse
mix $5⁰⁰
"Juvenile"
—The Daily News
Thanks for the root-beer floats, Sherlock!
MY NAME'S NOT SHERLOCK! I'VE TOLD YA, LIKE, FIFTY TIMES!
Well, we better get started on our next comic!!!
Our public awaits!
While we work on our next tale of depth and maturity...
...check out our story thus far!!!
TURN

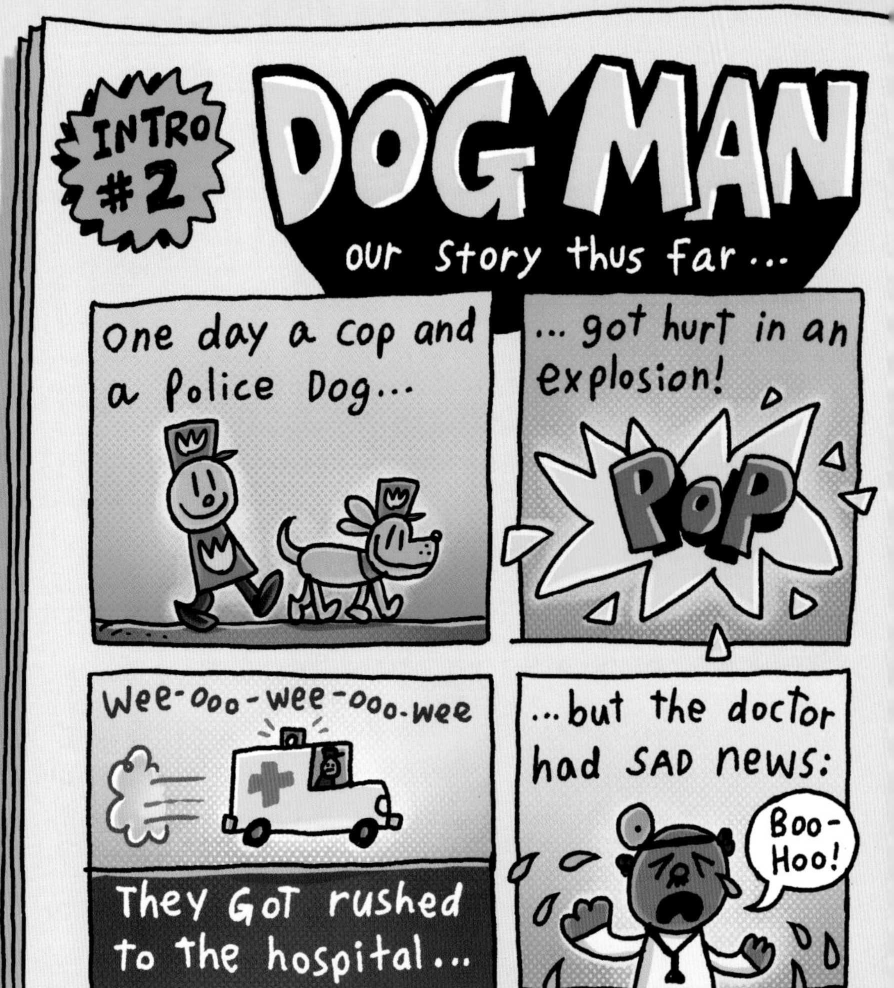
INTRO #2
DOG MAN
our Story thus far...
One day a cop and a Police Dog...
... got hurt in an explosion!
POP
Wee-ooo-wee-ooo-wee
They GoT rushed to the hospital...
...but the doctor had SAD news:
Boo-Hoo!
Sorry, cop Dude-but your head is dying!
aw, Darn it!!!

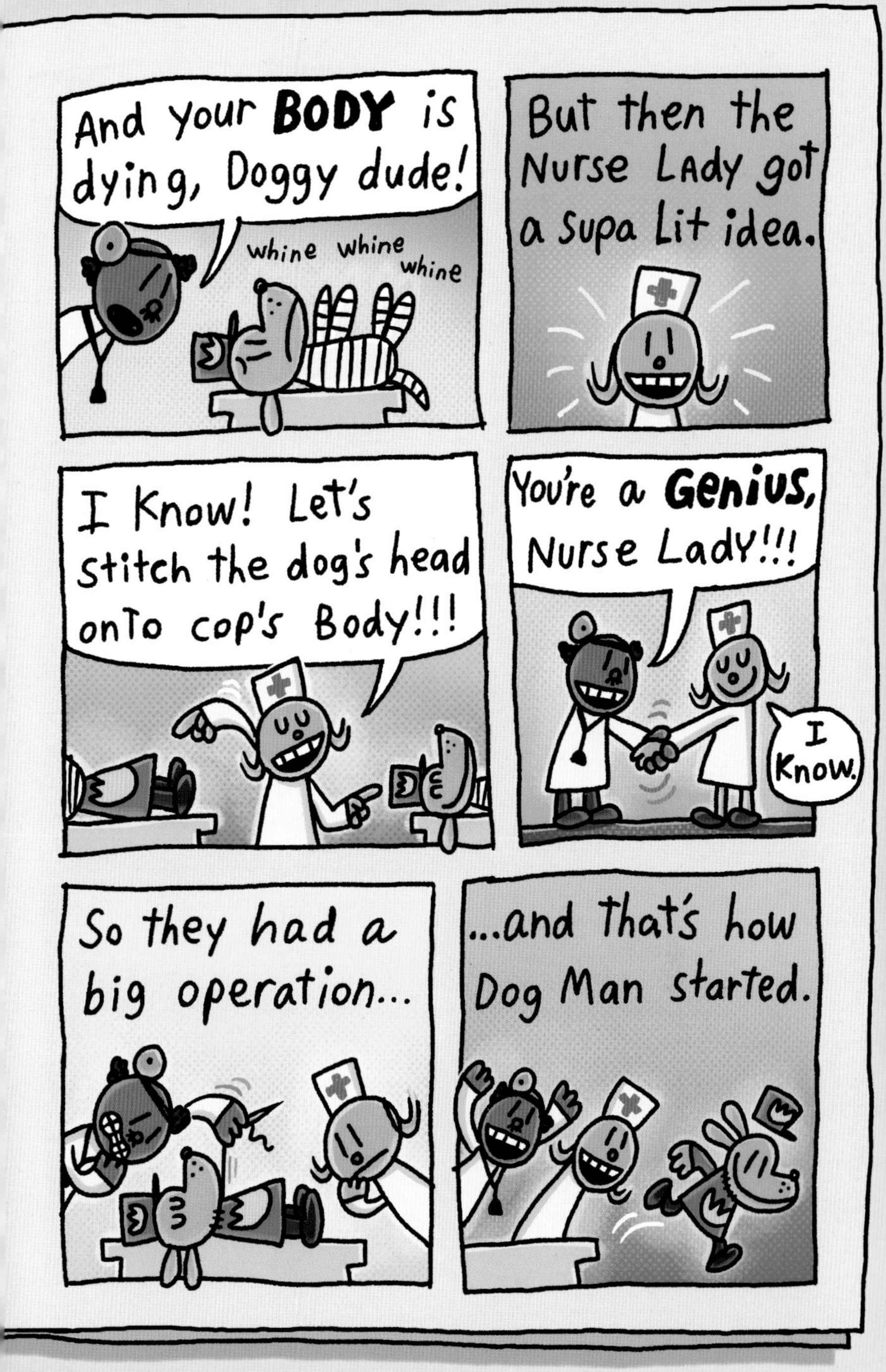
And your BODY is dying, Doggy dude!
whine whine whine
But then the Nurse Lady got a Supa Lit idea.
I Know! Let's stitch the dog's head onTo cop's Body!!!
You're a GENIUS, Nurse Lady!!!
I Know.
So they had a big operation...
...and that's how Dog Man started.

Dog Man Kept the city safe from evildoers...
RATS!
...until one day...
CLONING MACHINE
START
DNA
...when everything changed.
Hi, Papa!
Petey, the world's most evil cat...
...was trans-formed by Love...
...And now he's a GOOD GUY!

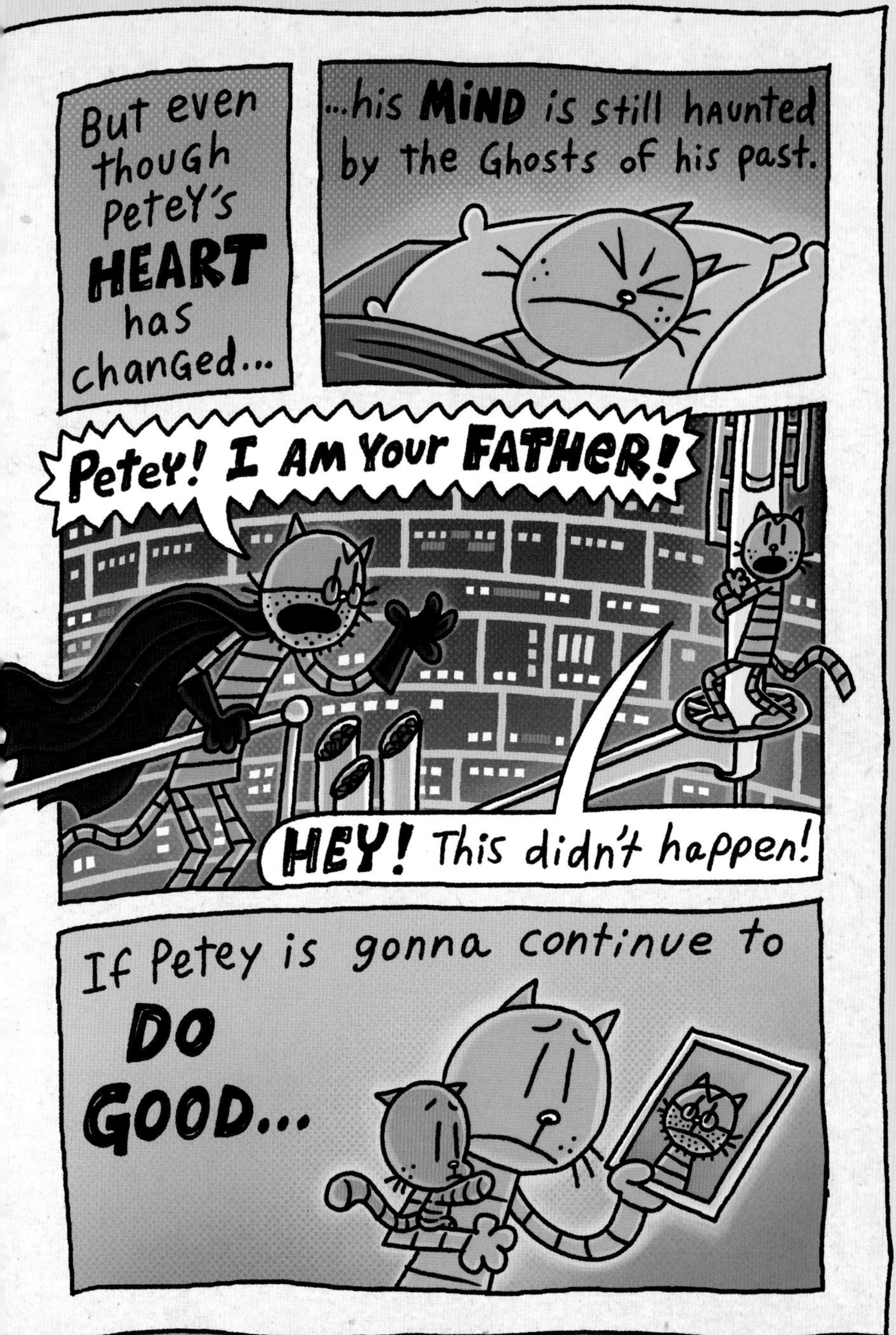
But even though Petey's HEART has changed...
...his MIND is still haunted by the Ghosts of his past.
Petey! I AM Your FATHER!
HEY! This didn't happen!
If Petey is gonna continue to DO GOOD...

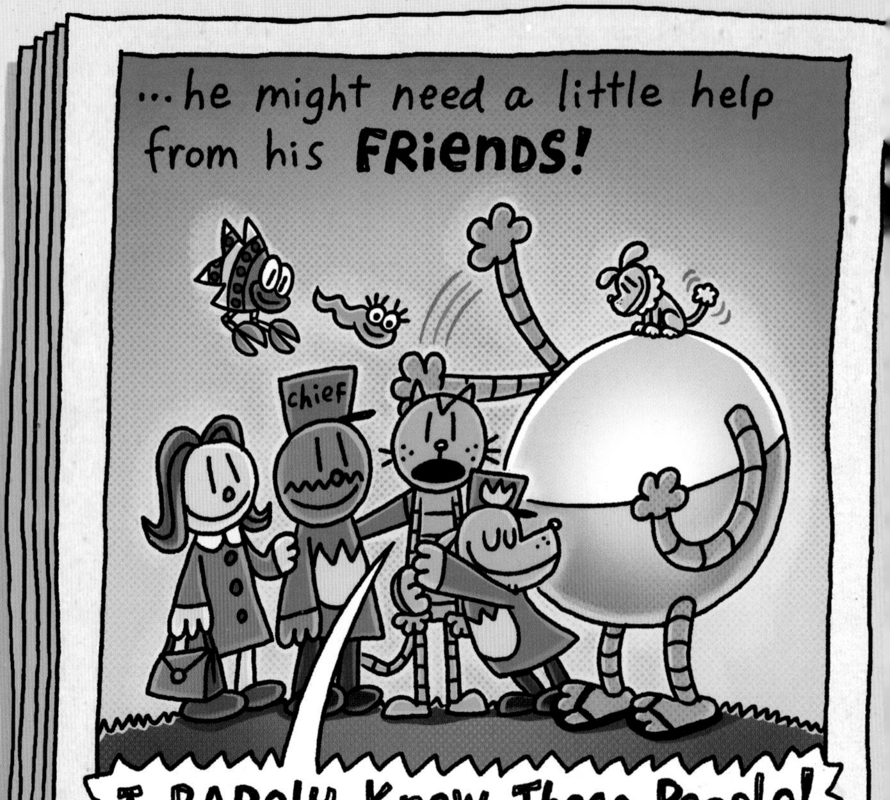

...he might need a little help from his FRIENDS!
chief
I BARELY Know These People!
So sit back and enjoy...
...our Newest Epic GRAPhic NOVEL!
IT'S ONLY A COMIC BOOK!

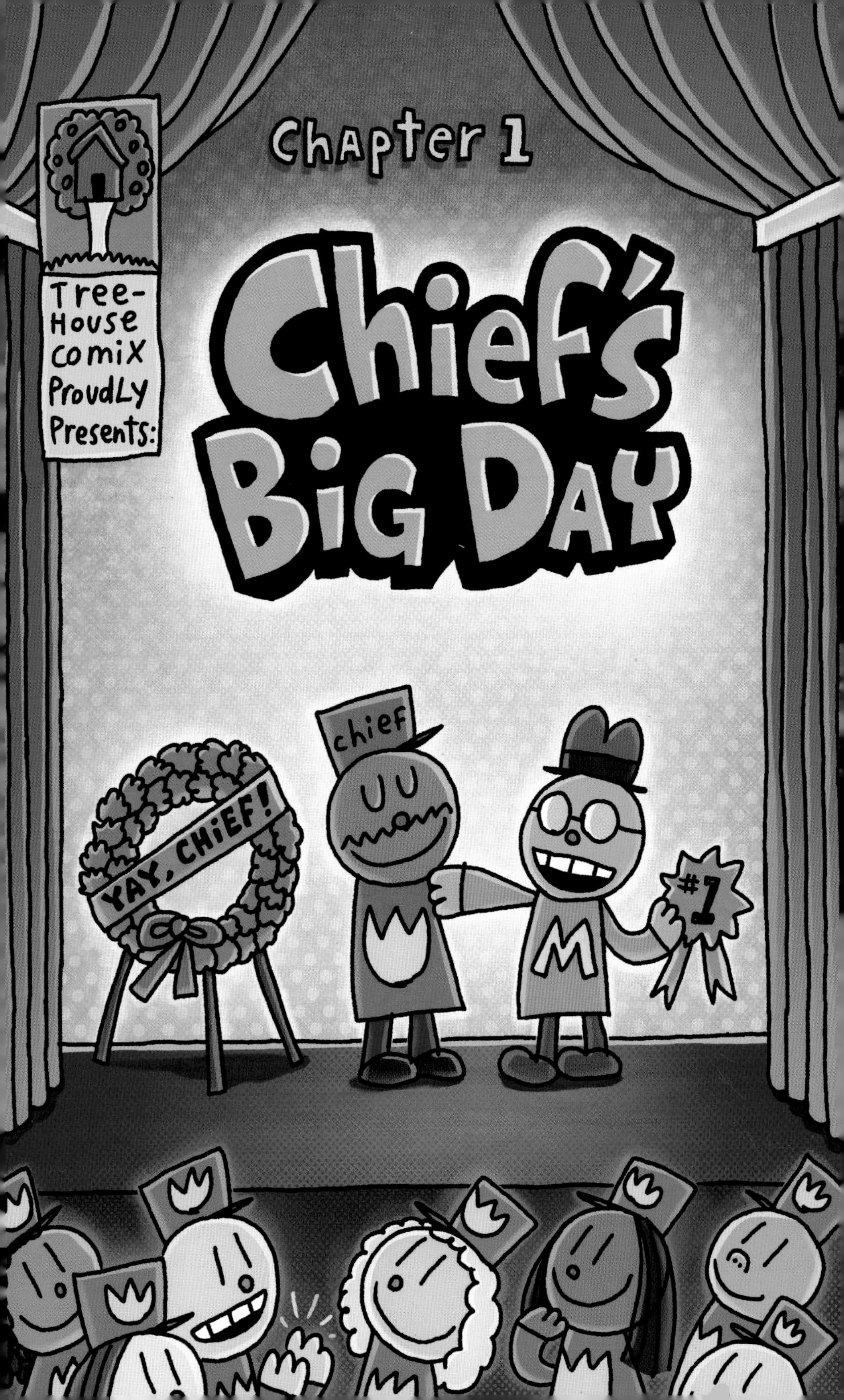
Tree-House Comix Proudly Presents:
Chapter 1
Chief's Big Day
chief
YAY, CHIEF!
M
#1

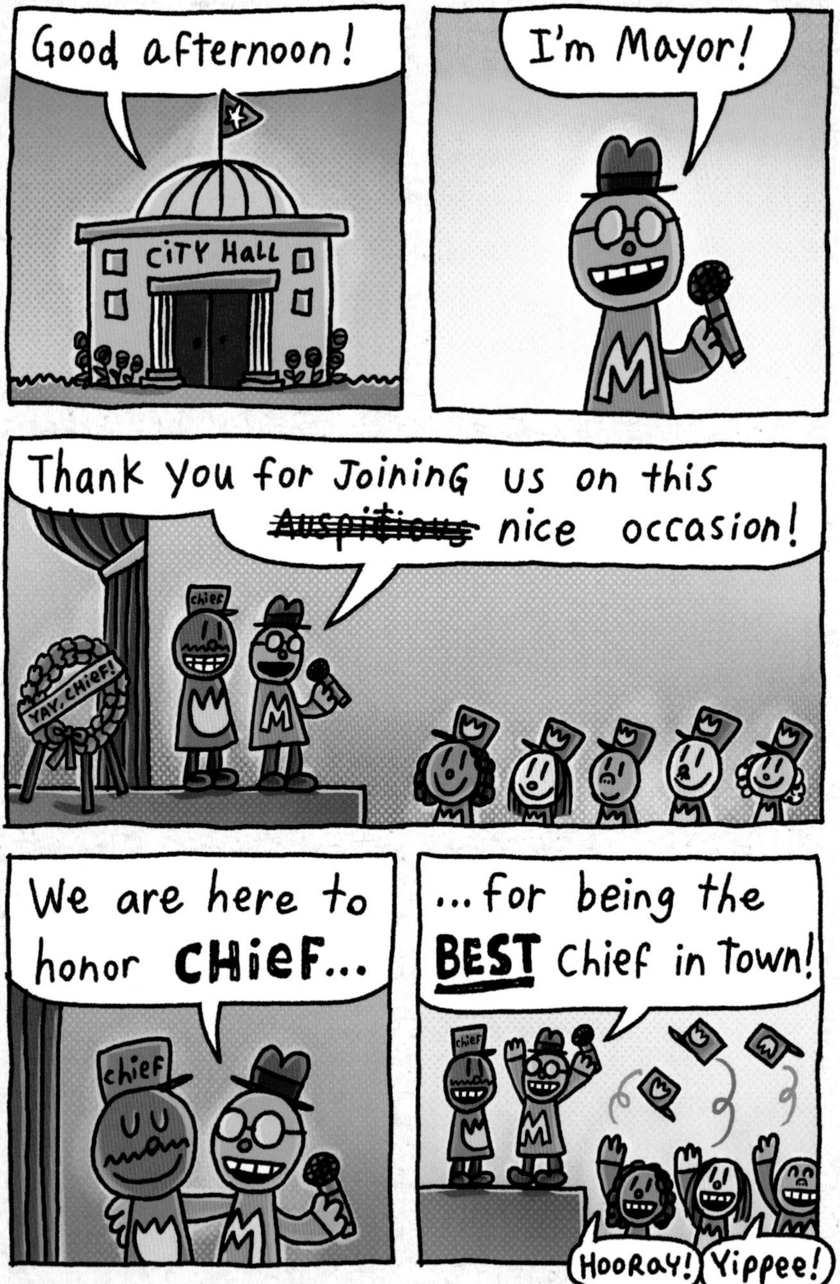
Good afternoon!
CITY HALL
I'm Mayor!
Thank you for Joining us on this ~~Auspitious~~ nice occasion!
chief
YAY, CHIEF!
We are here to honor CHIEF...
chief
...for being the BEST Chief in Town!
chief
HOORAY!
Yippee!

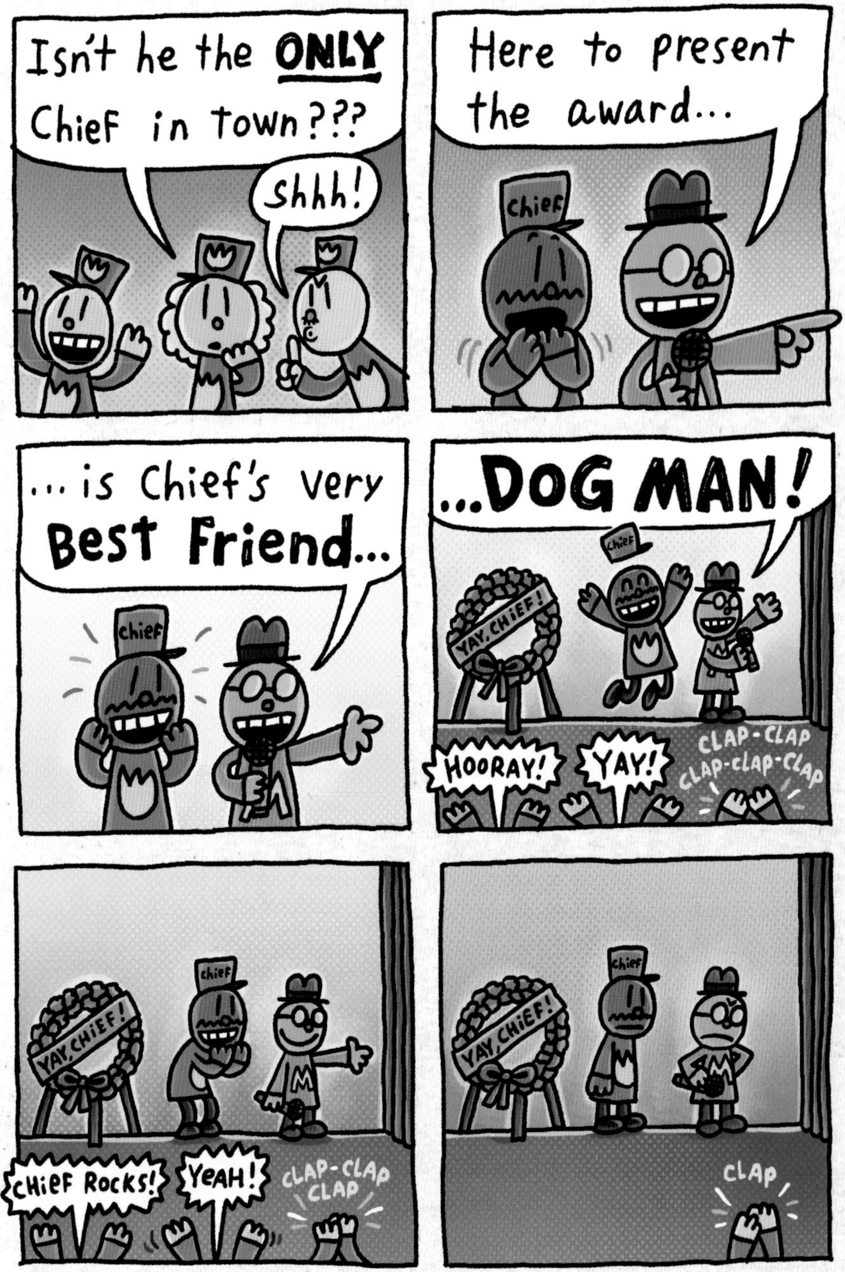

Isn't he the ONLY Chief in town???
Shhh!
Here to present the award...
chief
... is Chief's very Best Friend...
chief
...DOG MAN!
chief
YAY, CHIEF!
HOORAY!
YAY!
CLAP-CLAP CLAP-CLAP-CLAP
YAY, CHIEF!
chief
CHIEF ROCKS!
YEAH!
CLAP-CLAP CLAP
YAY, CHIEF!
chief
CLAP

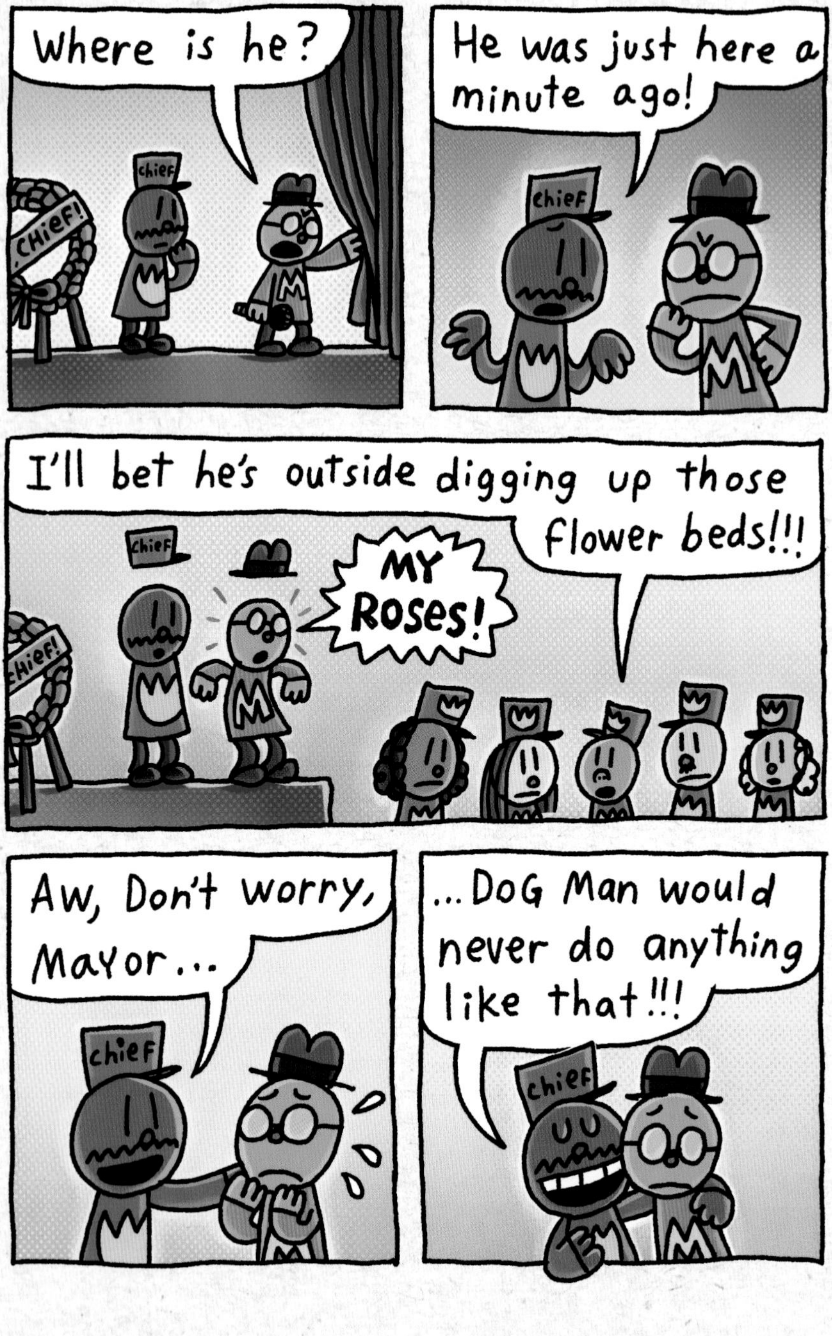
Where is he?
He was just here a minute ago!
I'll bet he's outside digging up those flower beds!!!
MY ROSES!
Aw, Don't worry, Mayor...
...DOG Man would never do anything like that!!!

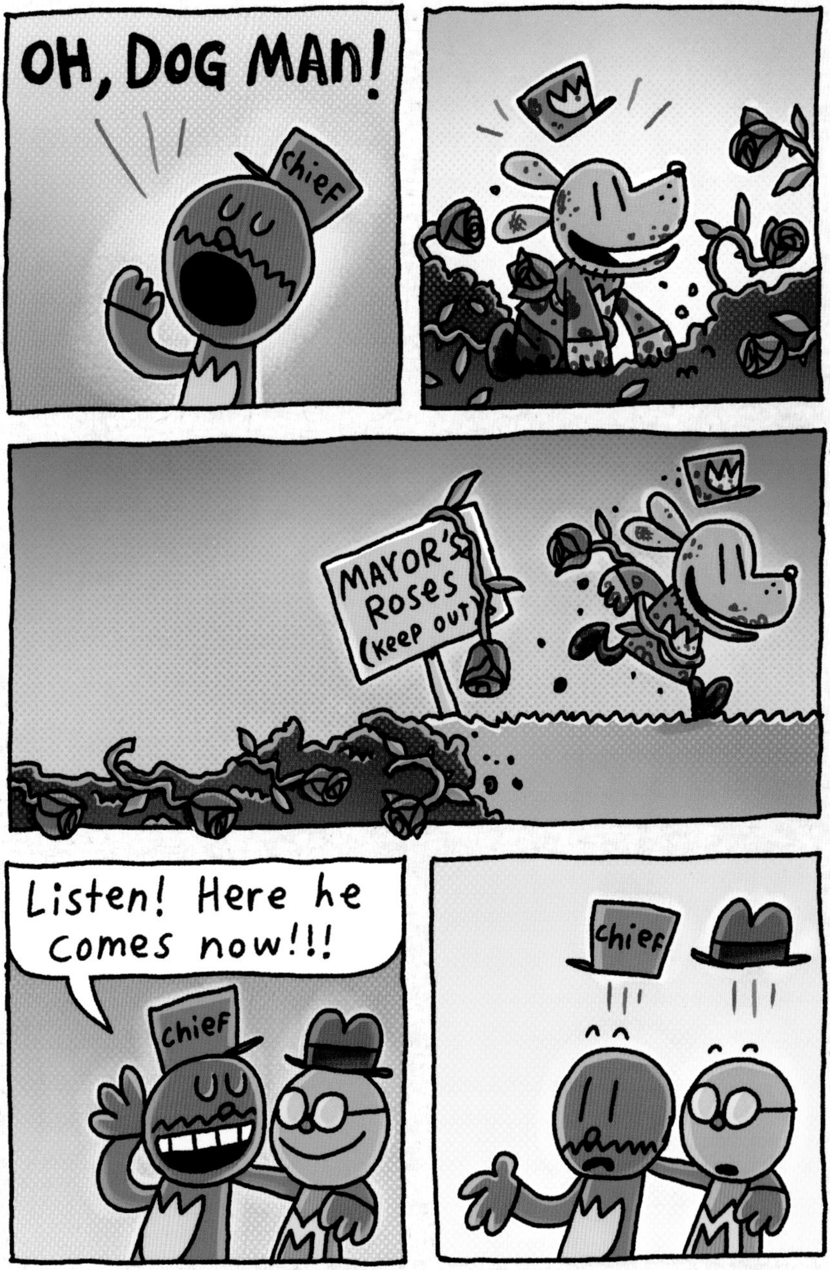
OH, DOG MAN!
chief
MAYOR'S ROSES (KEEP OUT)
Listen! Here he comes now!!!
chief
chief

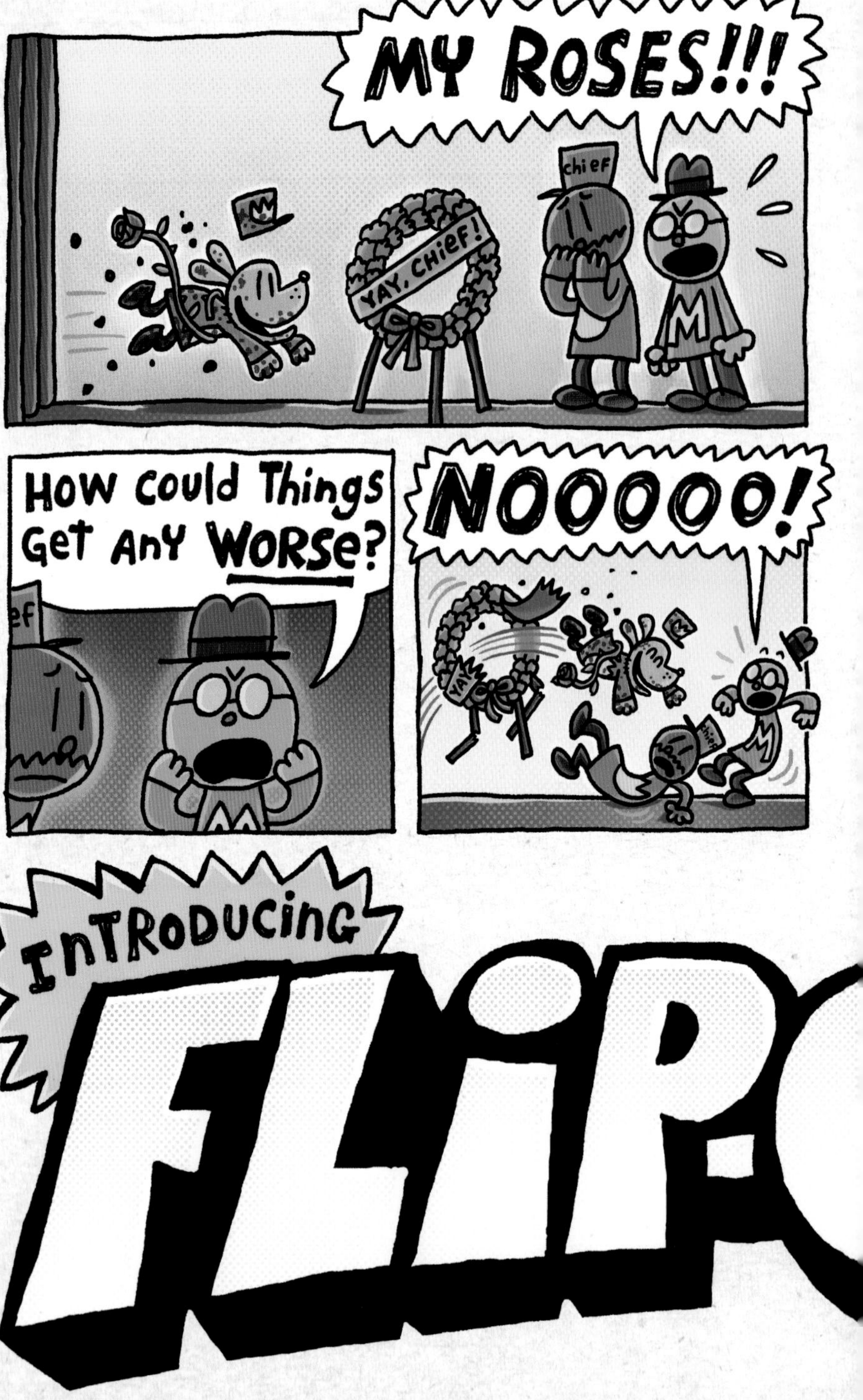
MY ROSES!!!
chief
YAY, CHIEF!
HOW COULD THINGS GET ANY WORSE?
NOOOOO!
INTRODUCING
FLIP

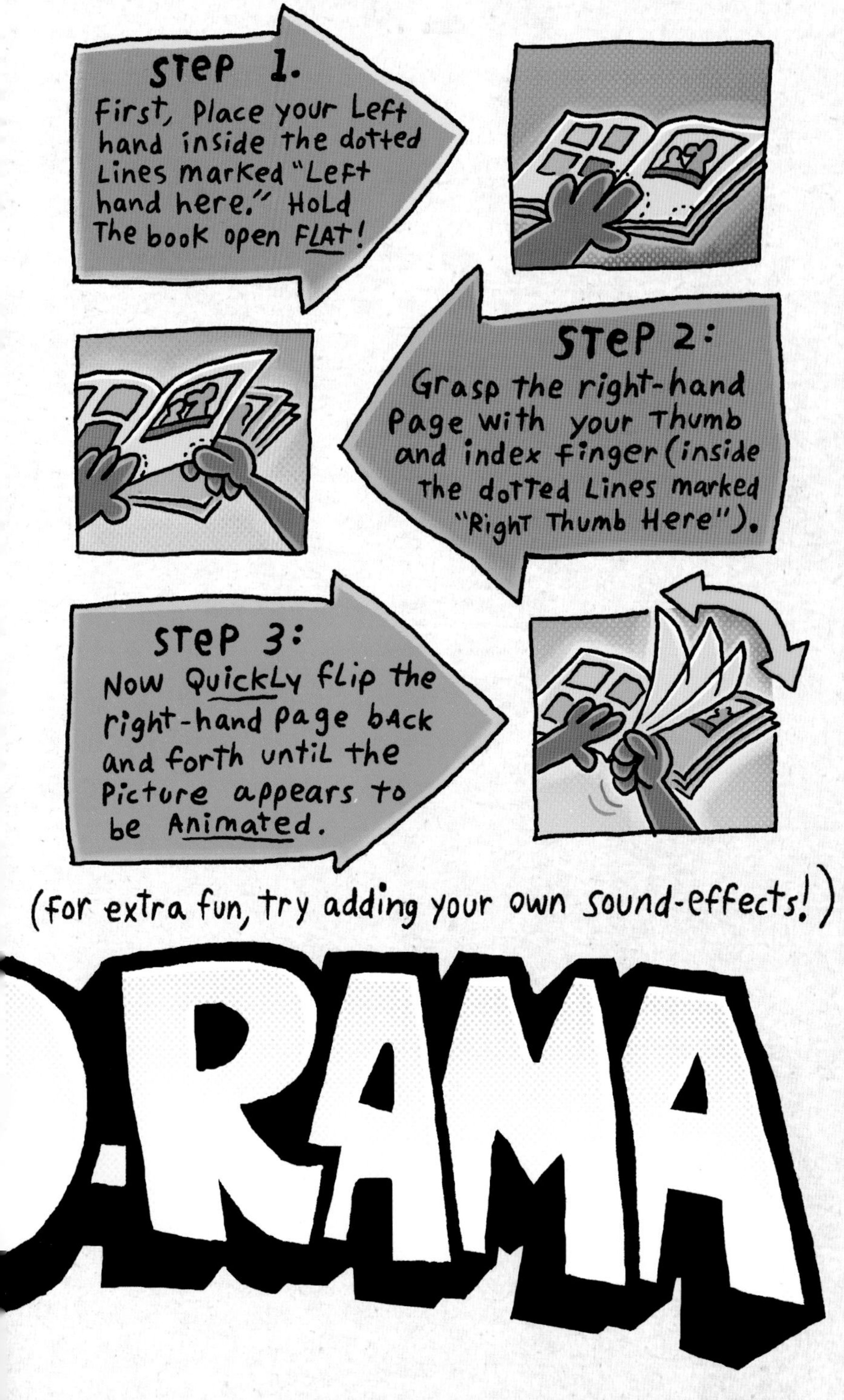
STEP 1.
First, Place your Left hand inside the dotted Lines marked "Left hand here." HoLd The book open FLAT!
STEP 2:
Grasp the right-hand Page with your Thumb and index finger (inside the dotted Lines marked "Right Thumb Here").
STEP 3:
Now QuickLy fLip the right-hand page back and forth until the Picture appears to be Animated.
(for extra fun, try adding your own sound-effects!)
RAMA

RemembeR,

While you are flipping, be sure you can see the image on page **23** **AND** the image on page **25**.

If you flip Quickly, the two pictures will Start to look Like **ONE** **ANIMATED** cartoon.

Don't forget to add your own Sound-effects!!!

Left hand here.

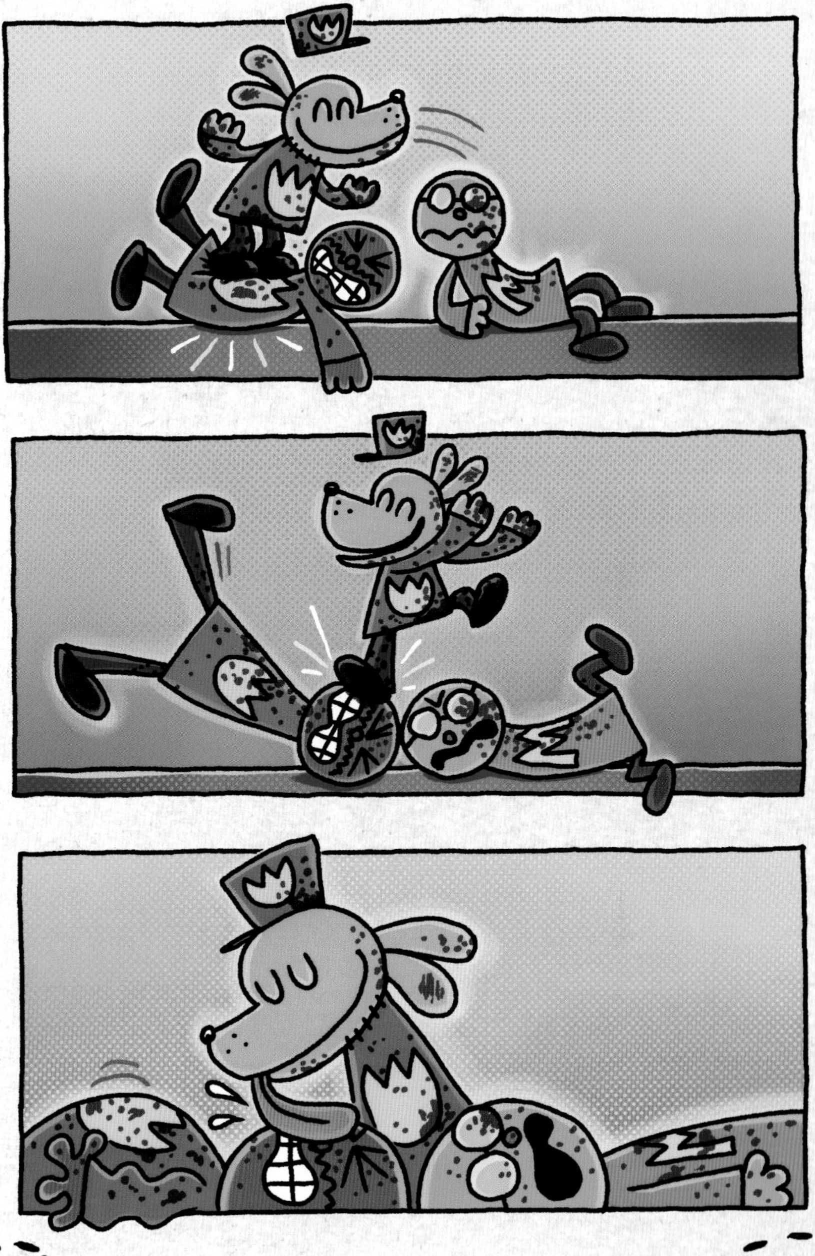

Right Thumb here.

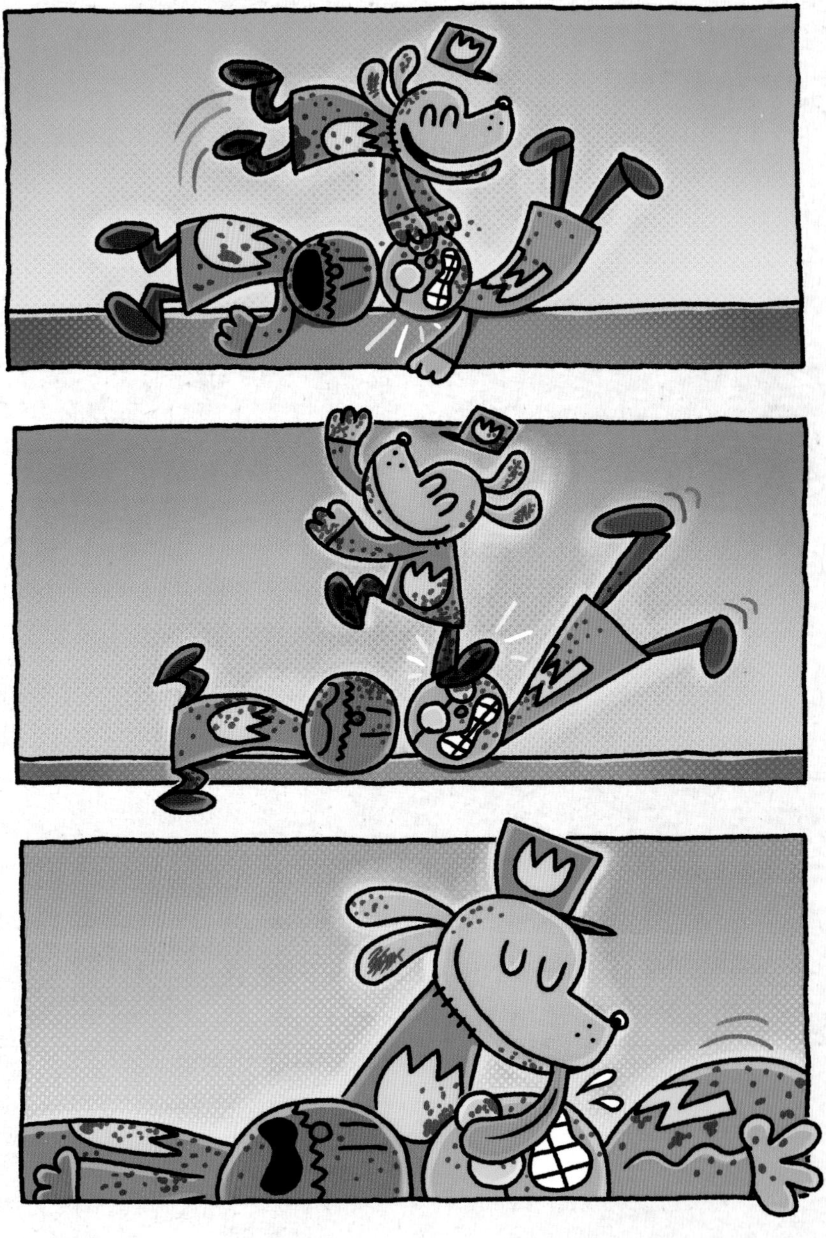

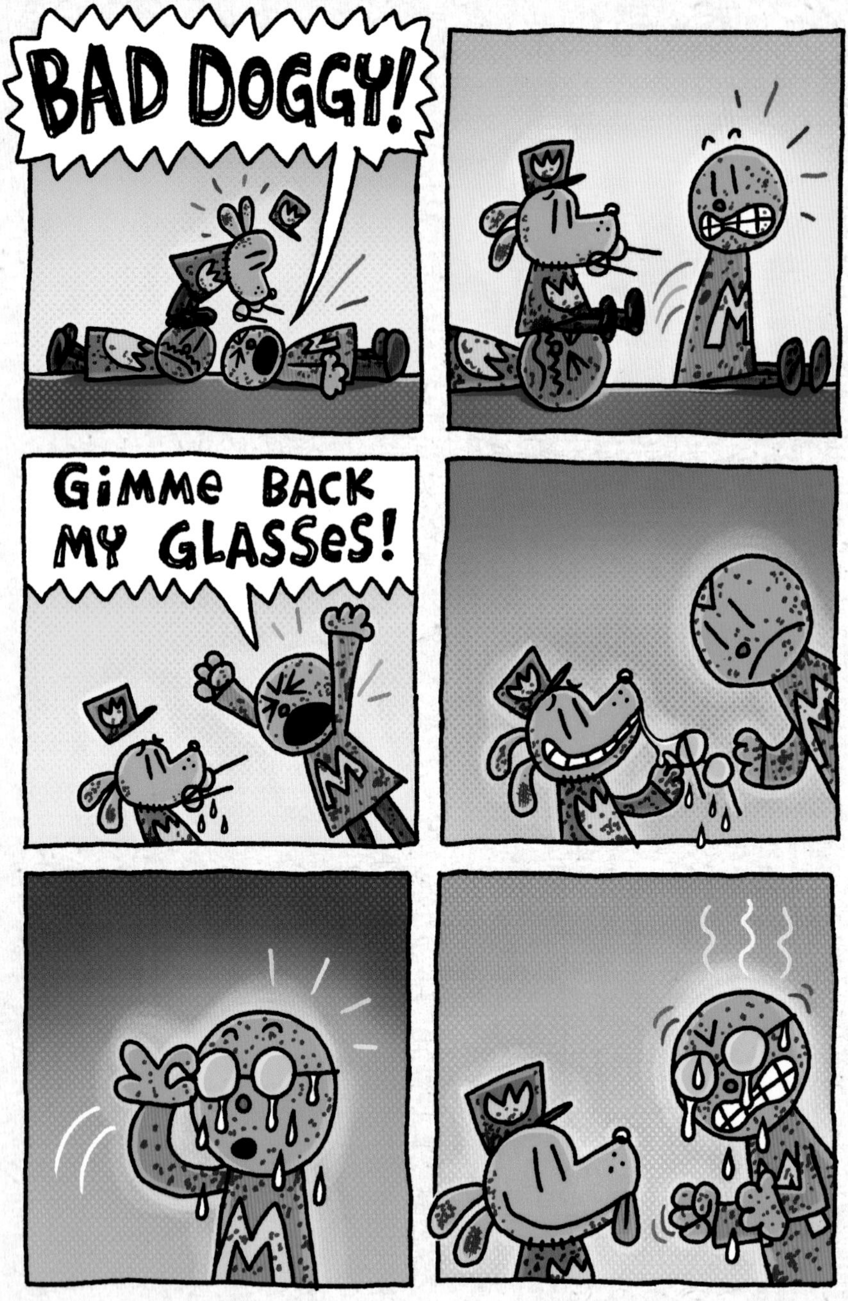
BAD DOGGY!
GIMME BACK MY GLASSES!

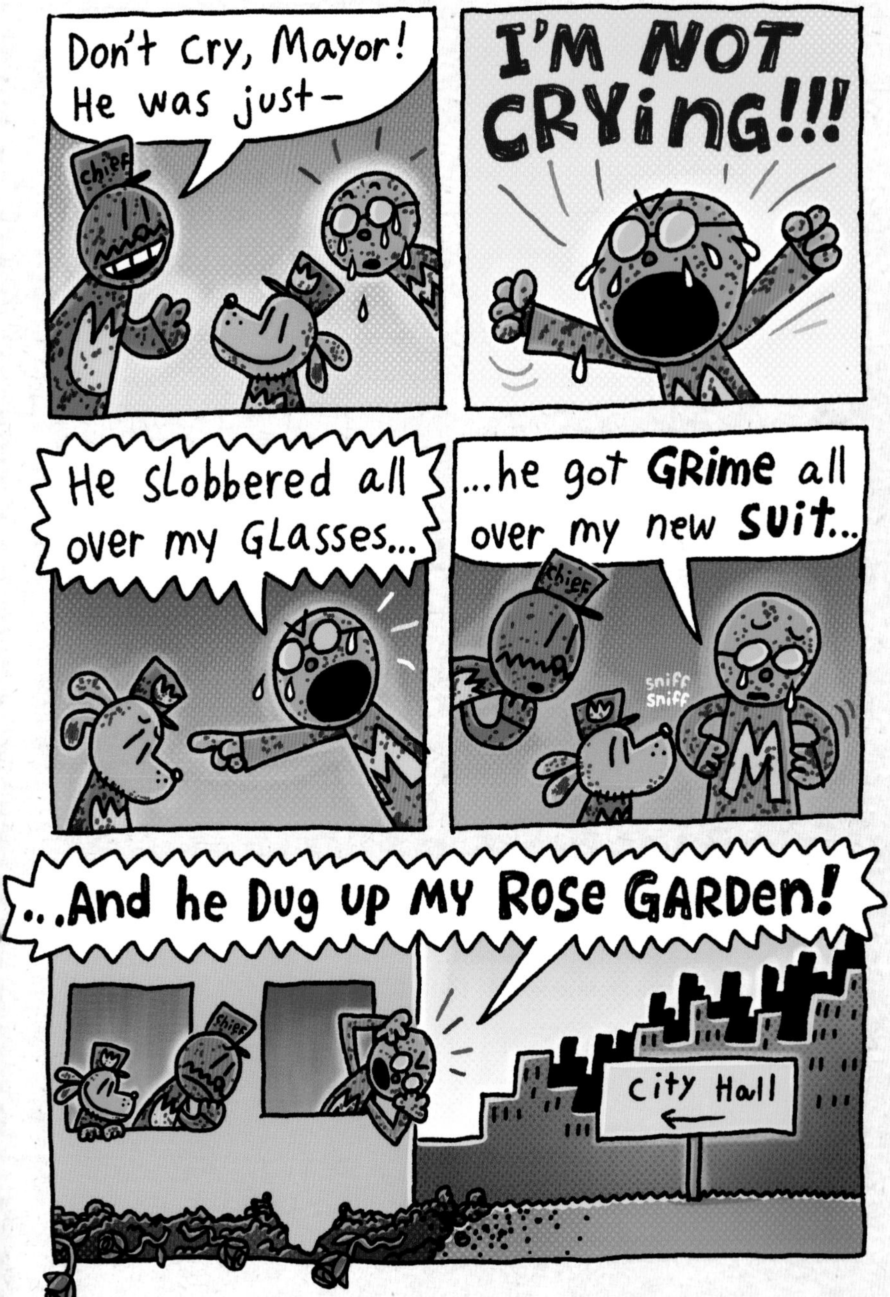
Don't cry, Mayor! He was just—
I'M NOT CRYING!!!
He slobbered all over my glasses...
...he got GRIME all over my new SUIT...
sniff sniff
...And he Dug up MY ROSE GARDEN!
City Hall

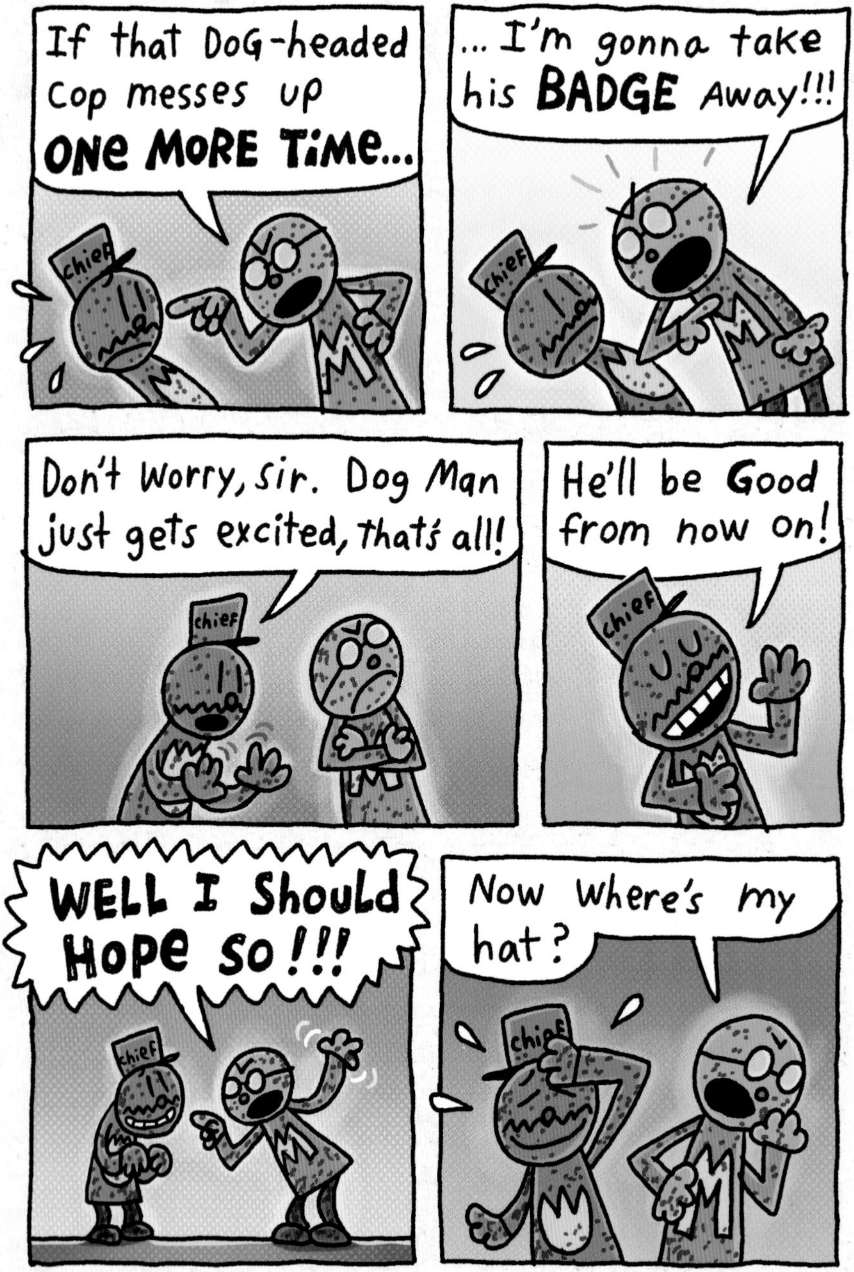
If that DoG-headed Cop messes up ONE MORE TiMe...
... I'm gonna take his BADGE Away!!!
Don't Worry, Sir. Dog Man just gets excited, that's all!
chief
He'll be Good from now on!
chief
WELL I Should HOPe so!!!
chief
Now Where's my hat?
chief

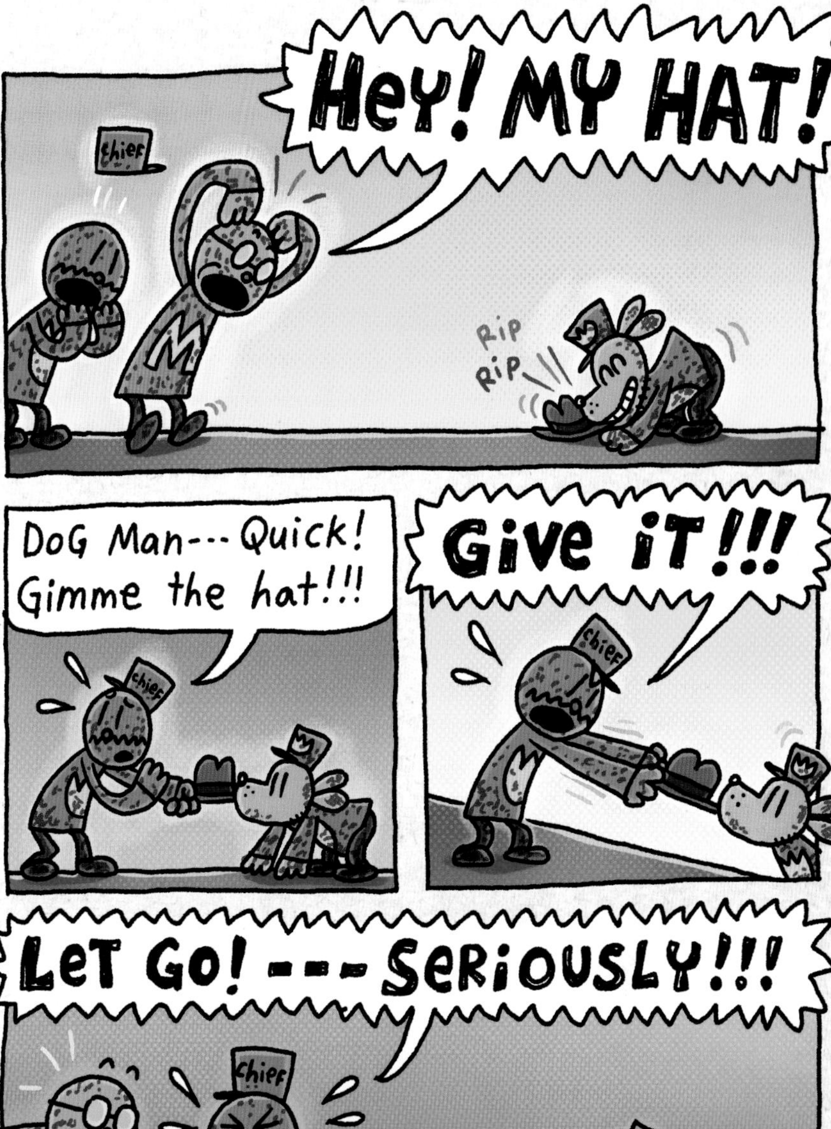
HEY! MY HAT!
chief
RIP
RIP
DOG Man--- Quick! Gimme the hat!!!
chief
GIVE IT!!!
chief
LET GO! --- SERIOUSLY!!!
chief

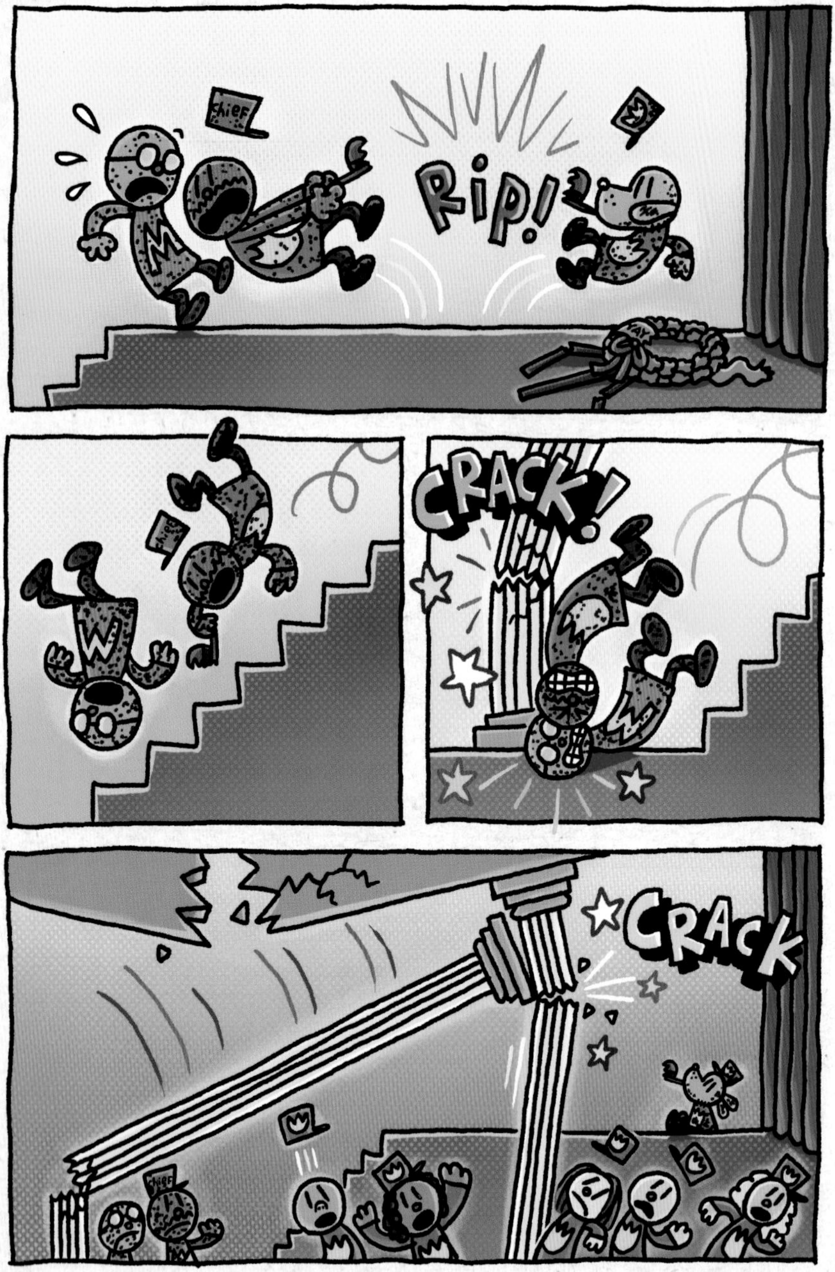
CHIEF
RIP!
CRACK!
CRACK

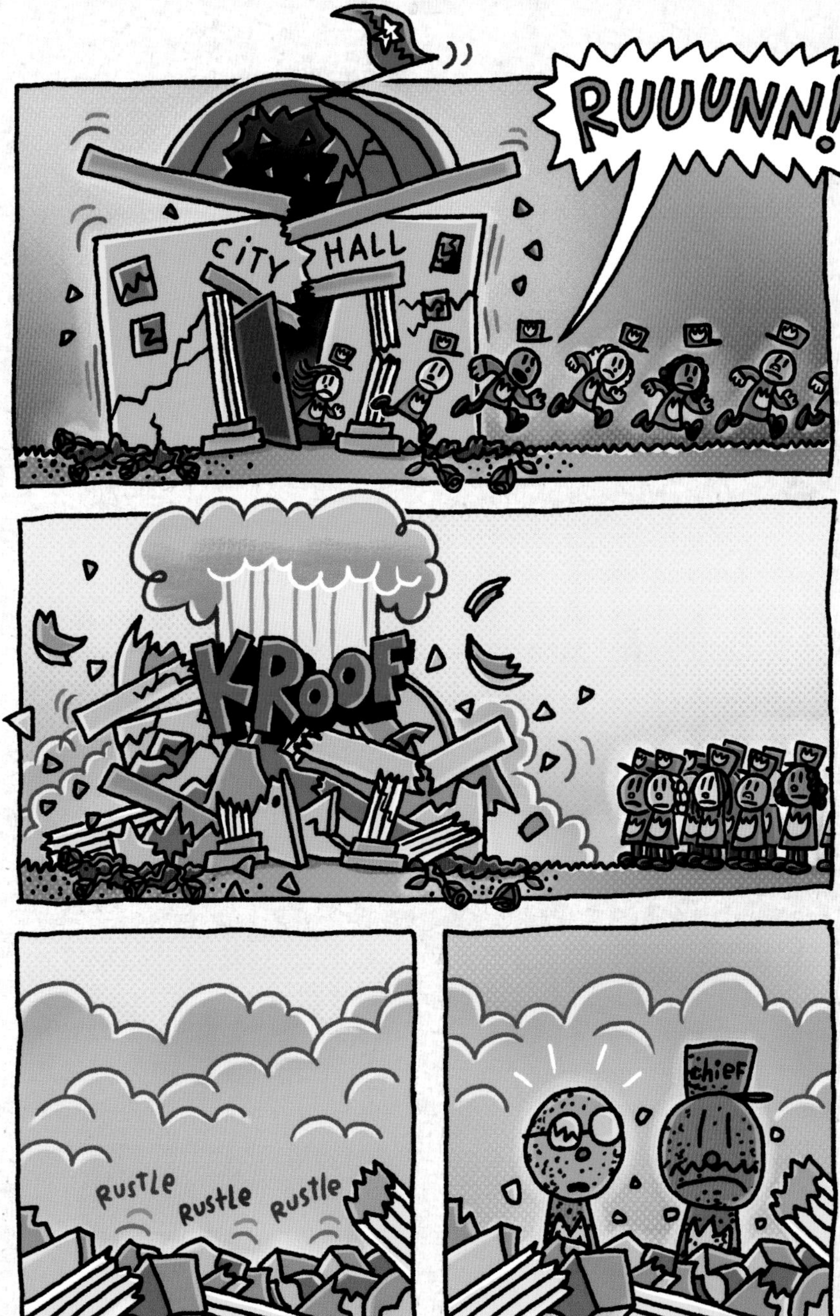
RUUUNN!
CITY HALL
KROOF
RUSTLE RUSTLE RUSTLE
CHIEF

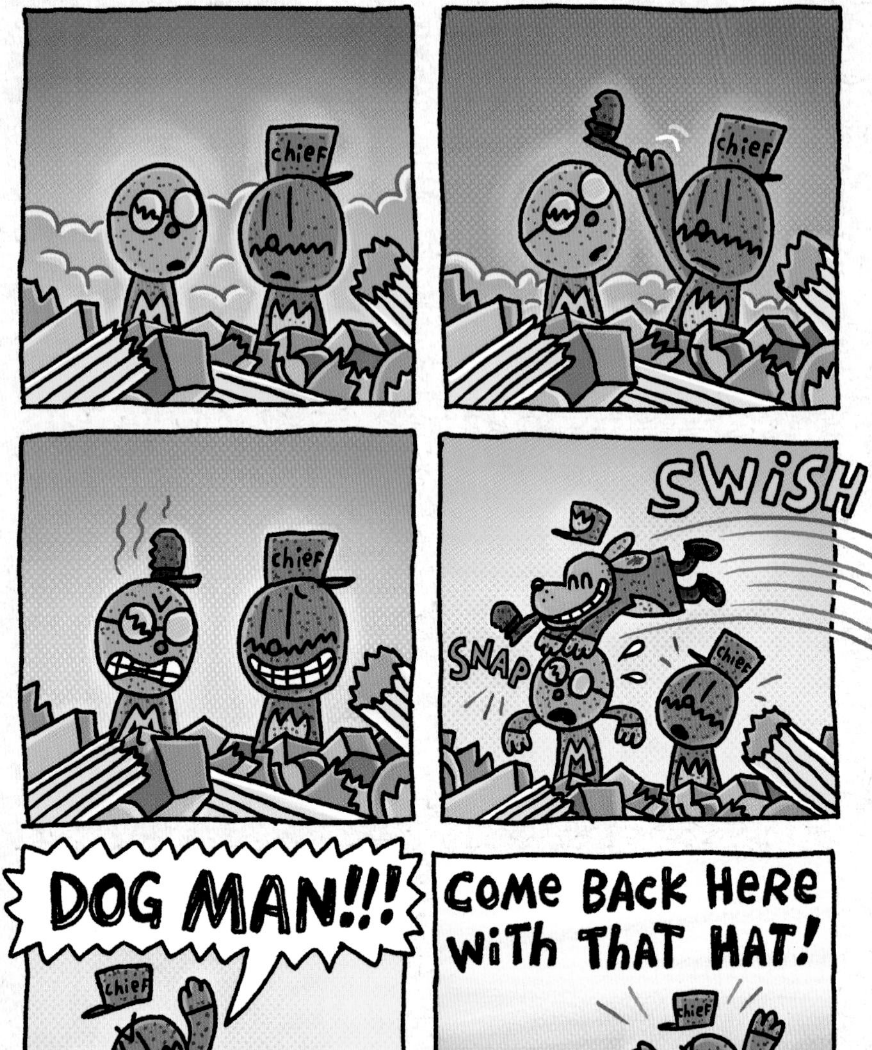
chief
chief
chief
SWISH
SNAP
chief
DOG MAN!!!
chief
Come Back Here With That HAT!
chief

CHAPTER 2

The Saddest CHAPTER Ever Written

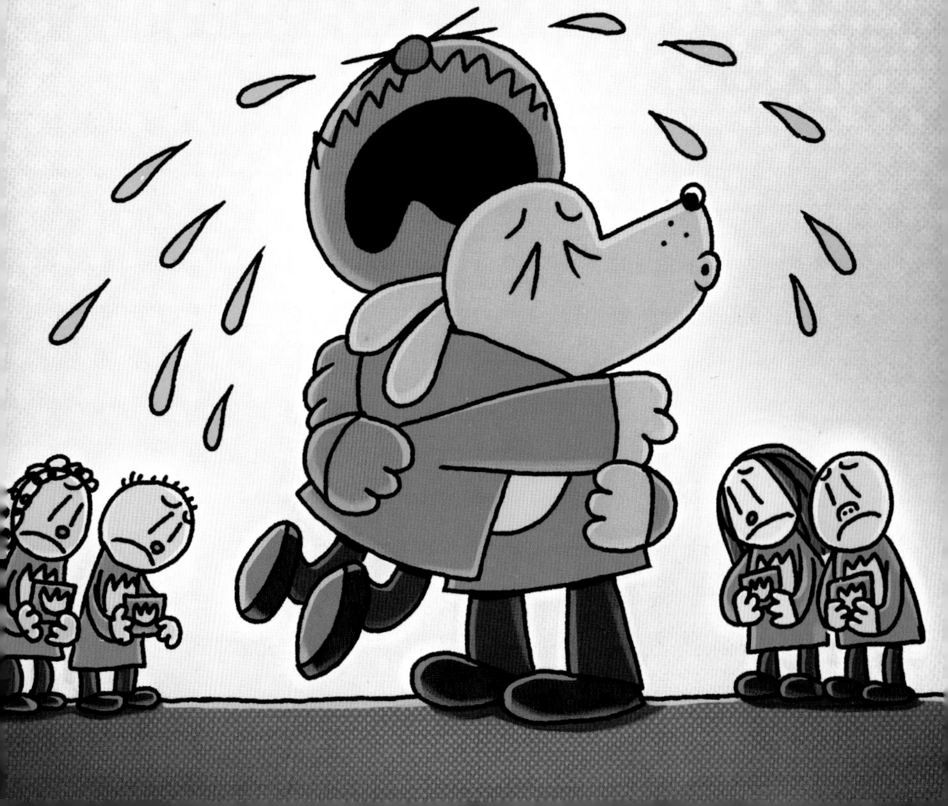

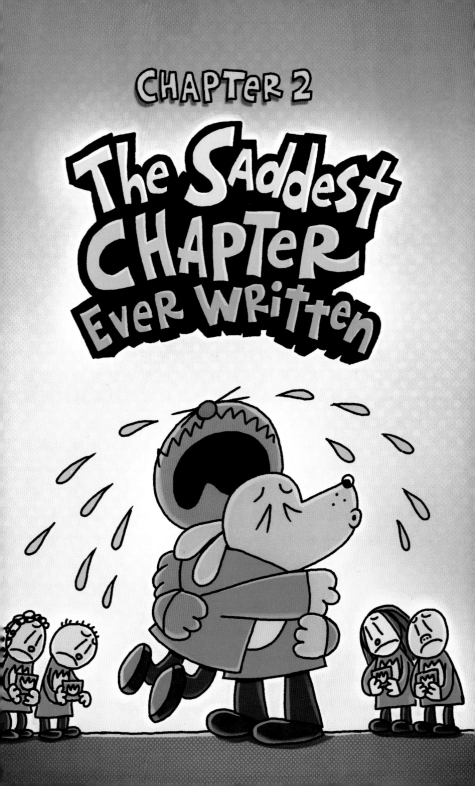

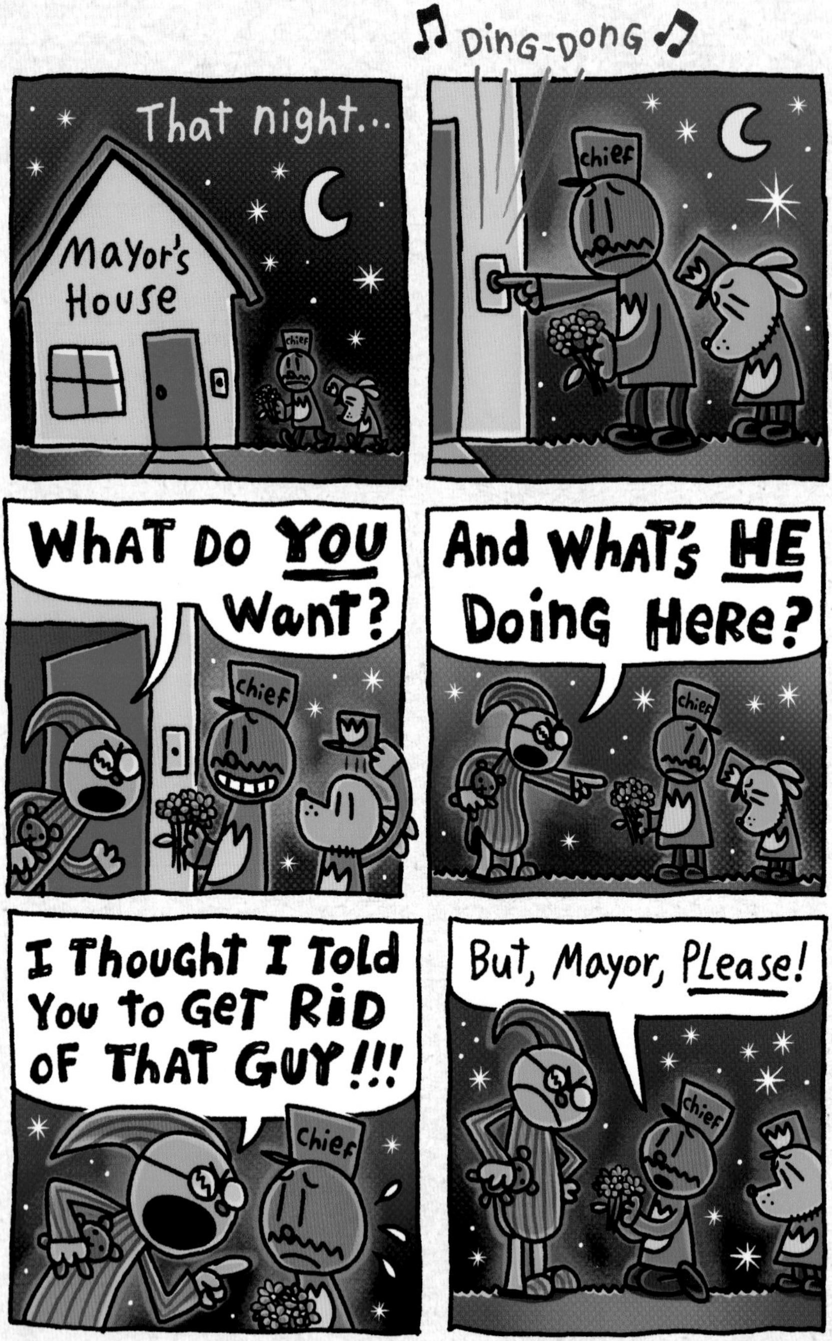
That night...
Mayor's House
chief
DING-DONG
chief
WHAT DO YOU Want?
chief
And WHAT'S HE Doing Here?
chief
I Thought I Told You to GET RID OF THAT GUY!!!
Chief
But, Mayor, PLease!
chief

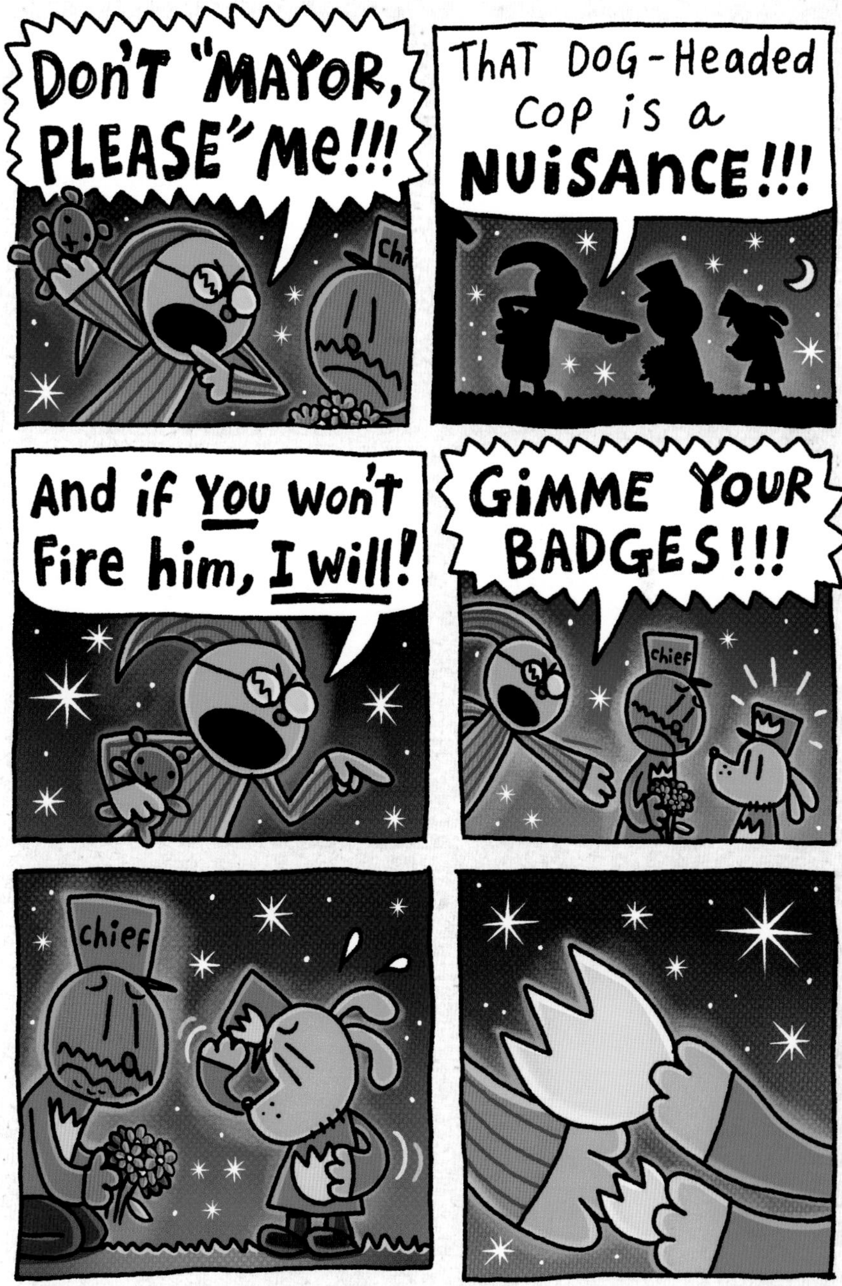
Don't "MAYOR, PLEASE" Me!!!
ThAT DOG-Headed Cop is a NUiSANCE!!!
And if YOU won't Fire him, I will!
GiMME YOUR BADGES!!!
chief
chief

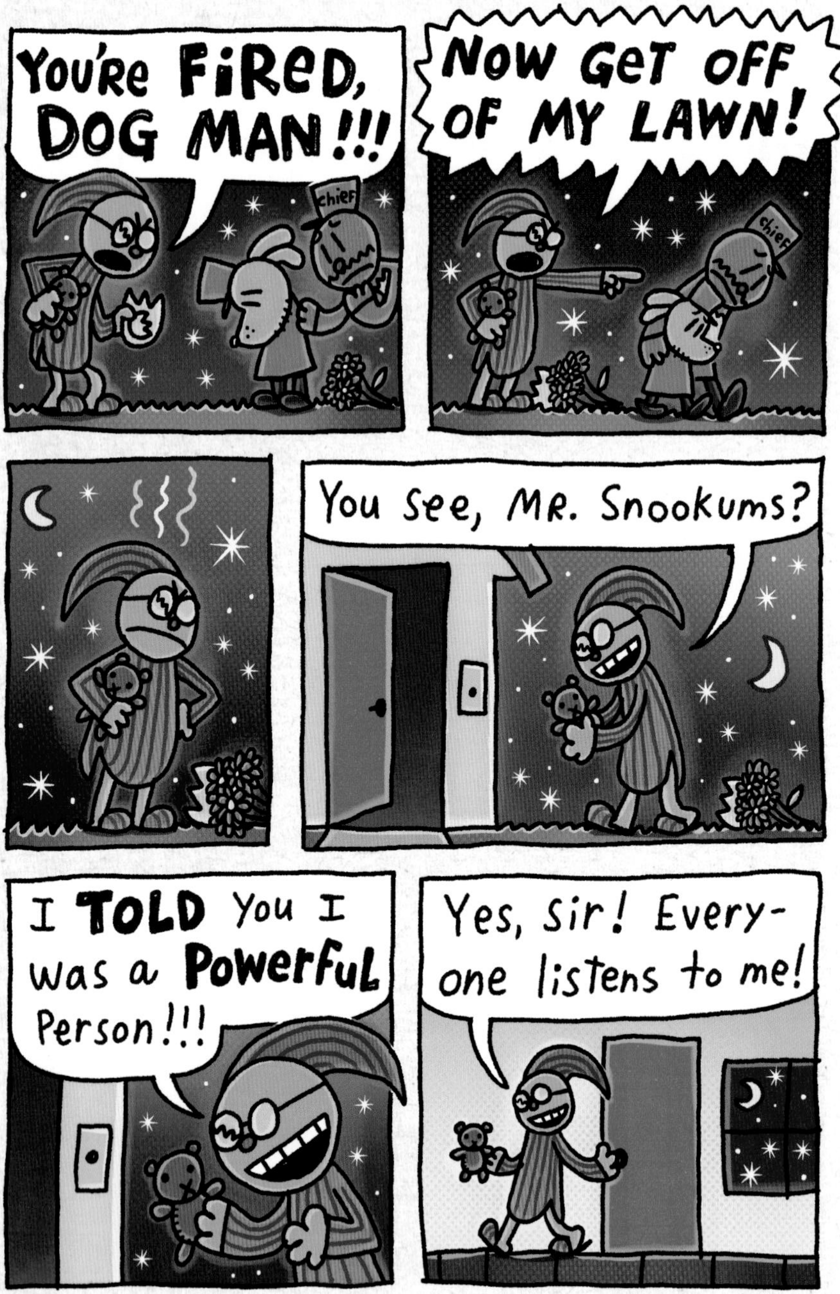
YOU'RE FIRED, DOG MAN!!!
NOW GET OFF OF MY LAWN!
chief
You see, Mr. Snookums?
I TOLD you I was a Powerful Person!!!
Yes, Sir! Every-one listens to me!

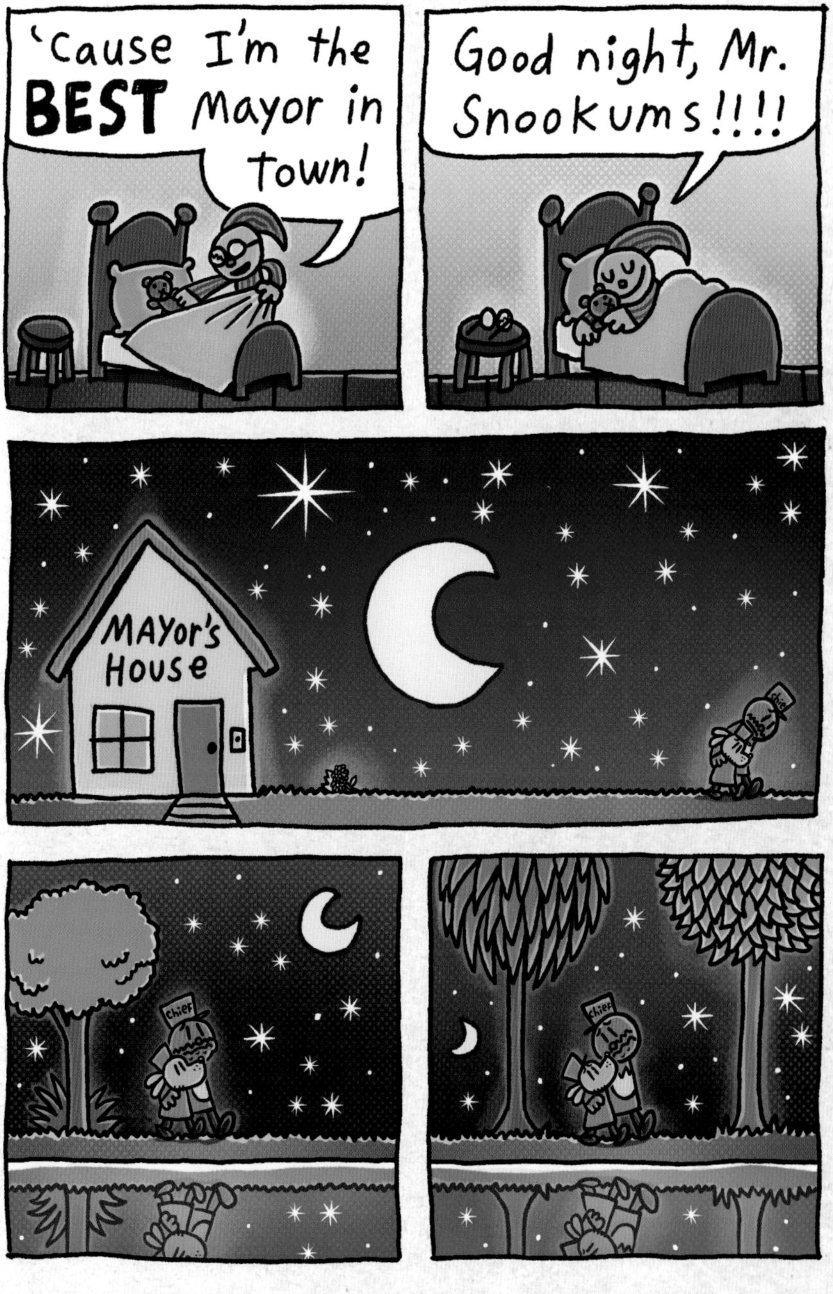
'Cause I'm the BEST Mayor in town!
Good night, Mr. Snookums!!!!
MAYor's House
Chief

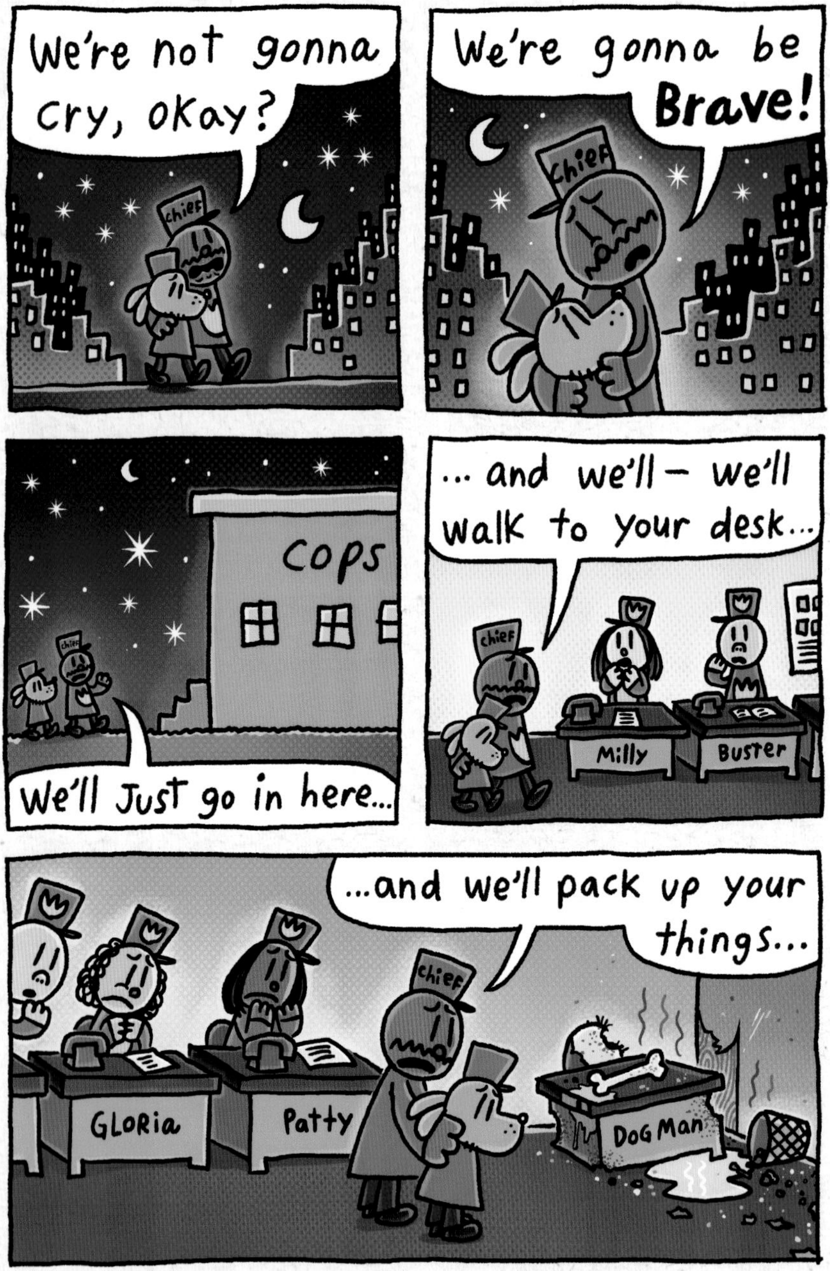

We're not gonna cry, OKay?
chief
We're gonna be Brave!
chief
COPS
chief
We'll Just go in here...
... and we'll— we'll walk to your desk...
chief
Milly
Buster
...and we'll pack up your things...
chief
GLORIA
Patty
DOG Man

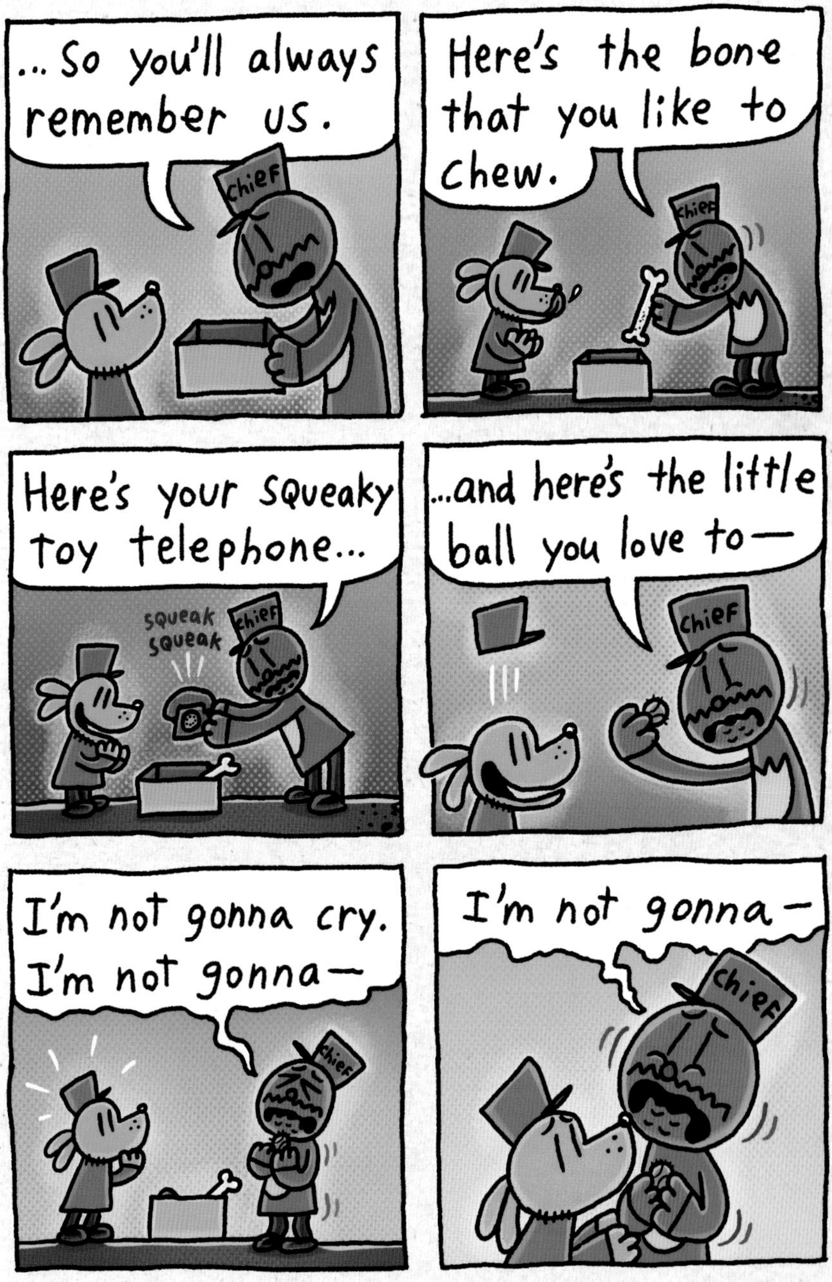
...So you'll always remember us.
chief
Here's the bone that you like to chew.
chief
Here's your squeaky toy telephone...
squeak squeak
chief
...and here's the little ball you love to—
chief
I'm not gonna cry. I'm not gonna—
chief
I'm not gonna—
chief

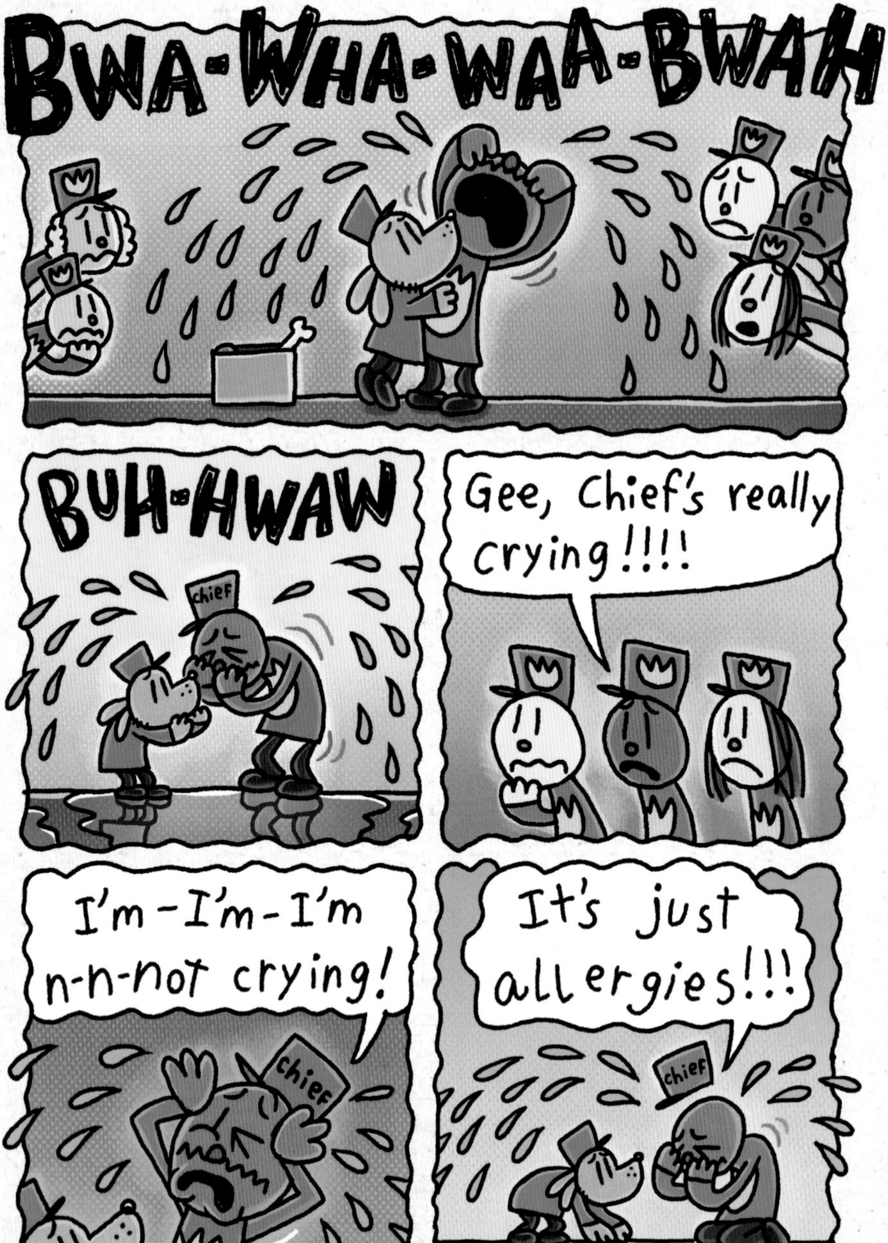

BWA-WHA-WAA-BWAH
BUH-HWAW
chief
Gee, Chief's really crying!!!!
I'm-I'm-I'm n-n-not crying!
chief
It's just allergies!!!
chief

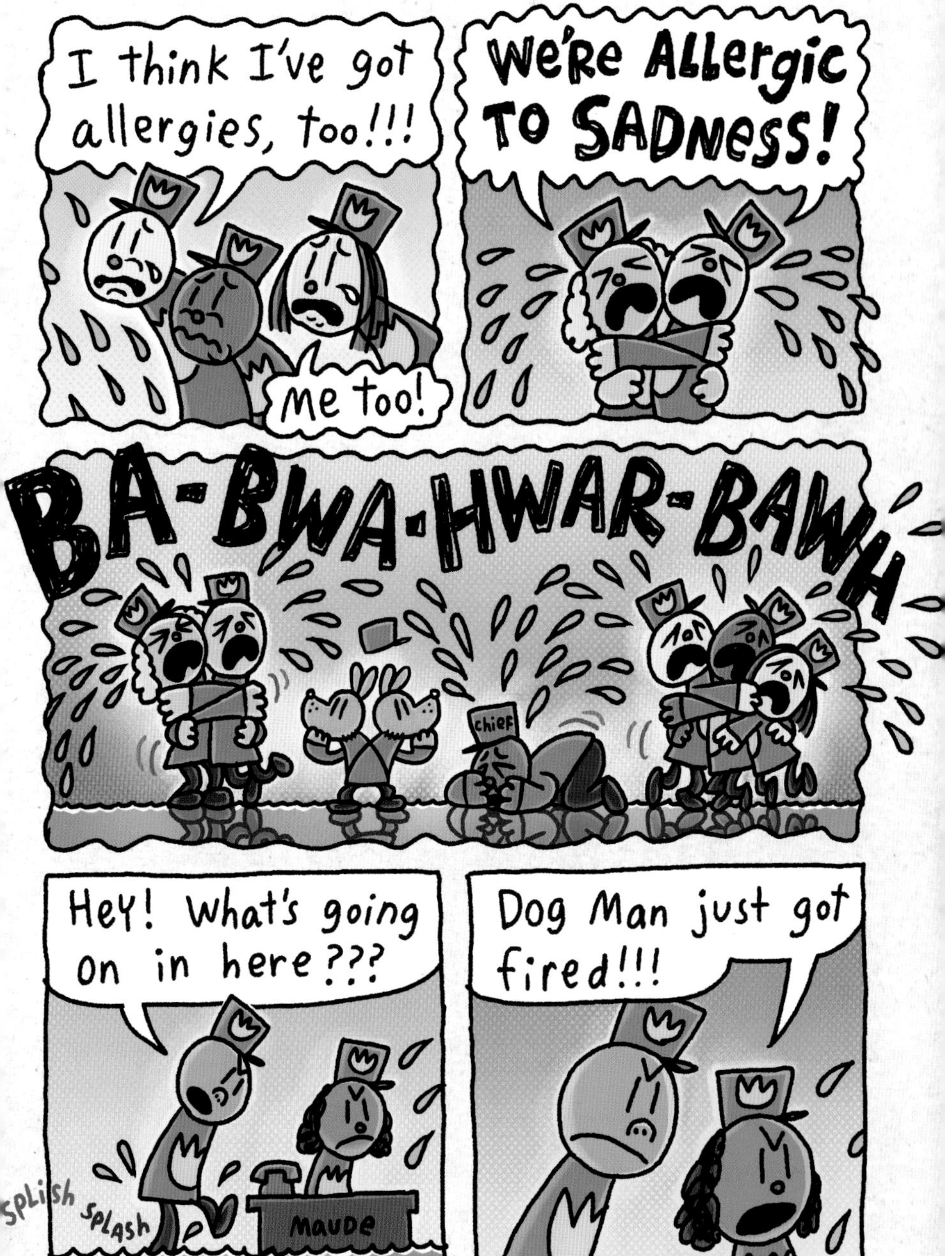

I think I've got allergies, too!!!
Me too!
We're Allergic TO SADNESS!
BA-BWA-HWAR-BAWH
CHIEF
Hey! What's going on in here???
SPLISH SPLASH
MAUDE
Dog Man just got fired!!!

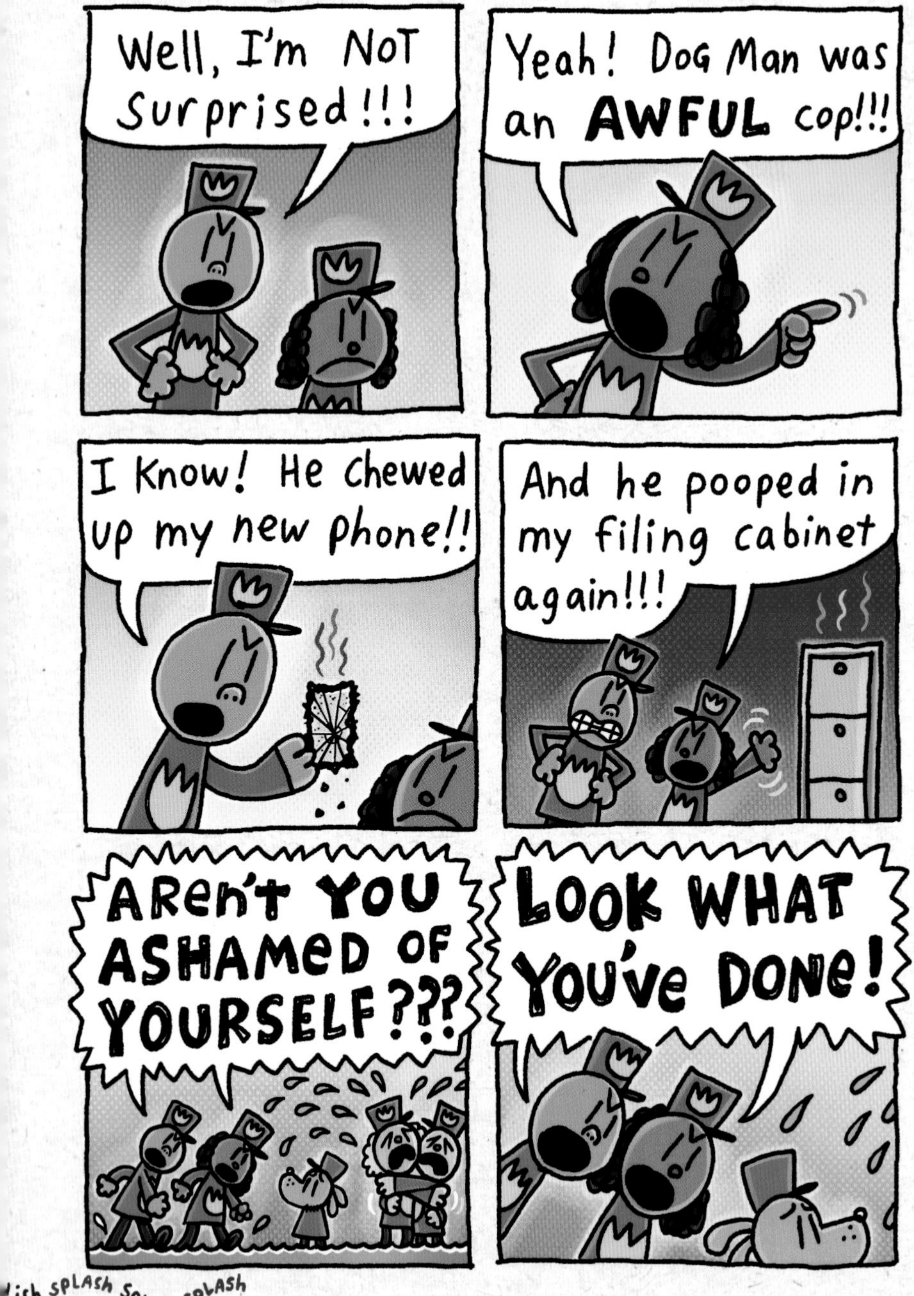

Well, I'm NOT Surprised!!!
Yeah! Dog Man was an AWFUL cop!!!
I Know! He chewed up my new phone!!
And he pooped in my filing cabinet again!!!
AREN'T YOU ASHAMED OF YOURSELF???
LOOK WHAT YOU'VE DONE!
lish SPLASH SPLISH SPLASH

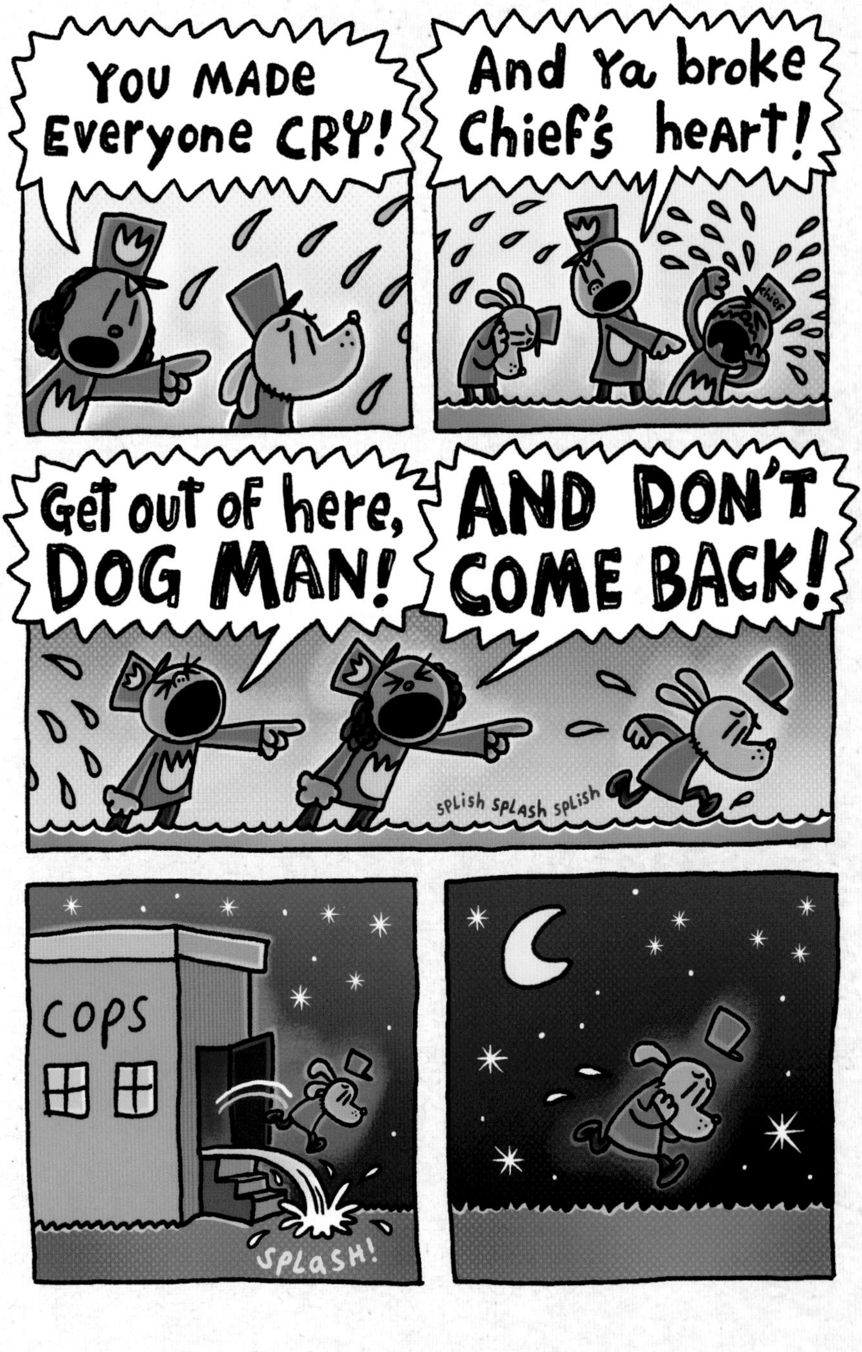
YOU MADE Everyone CRY!
And Ya broke Chief's heart!
Chief
Get out of here, DOG MAN!
AND DON'T COME BACK!
sPLish sPLAsh sPLish
COPS
SPLASH!

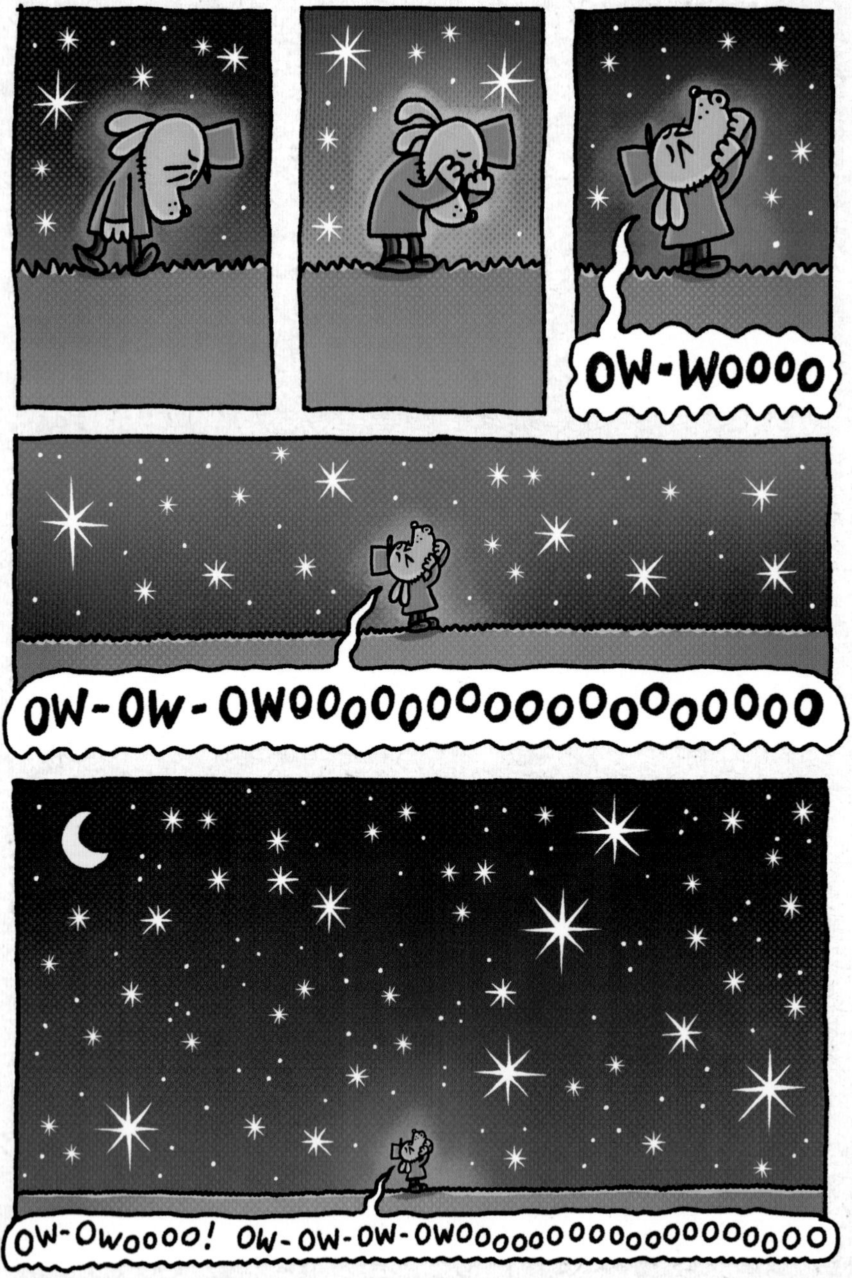
OW-WOOOO
OW-OW-OWOOOOOOOOOOOOOOOOOO
OW-OWOOOO! OW-OW-OW-OWOOOOOOOOOOOOOOOOOOOO

CHAPTER 3

The Chapter That's Totally Not as Sad as the Last One

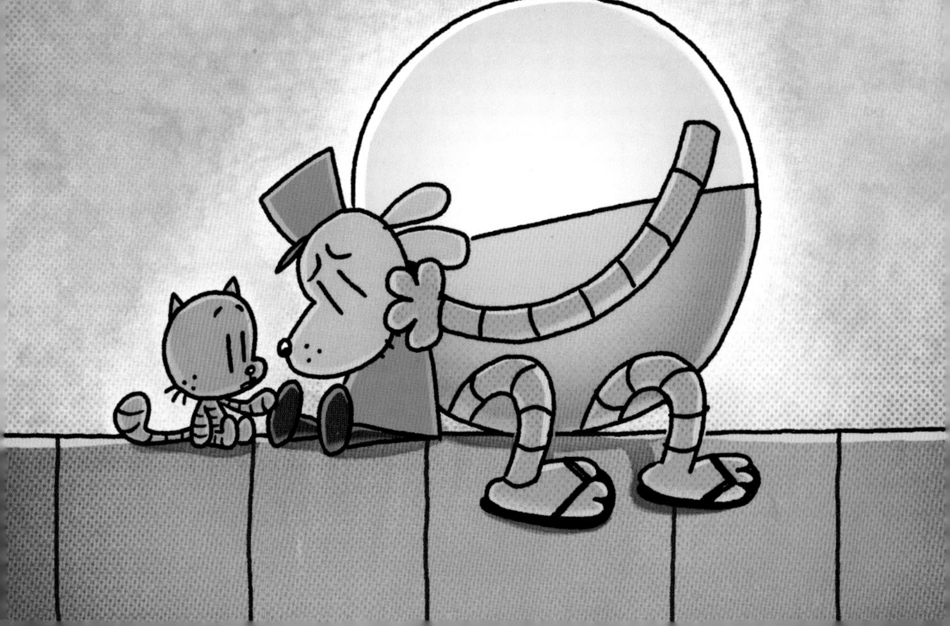

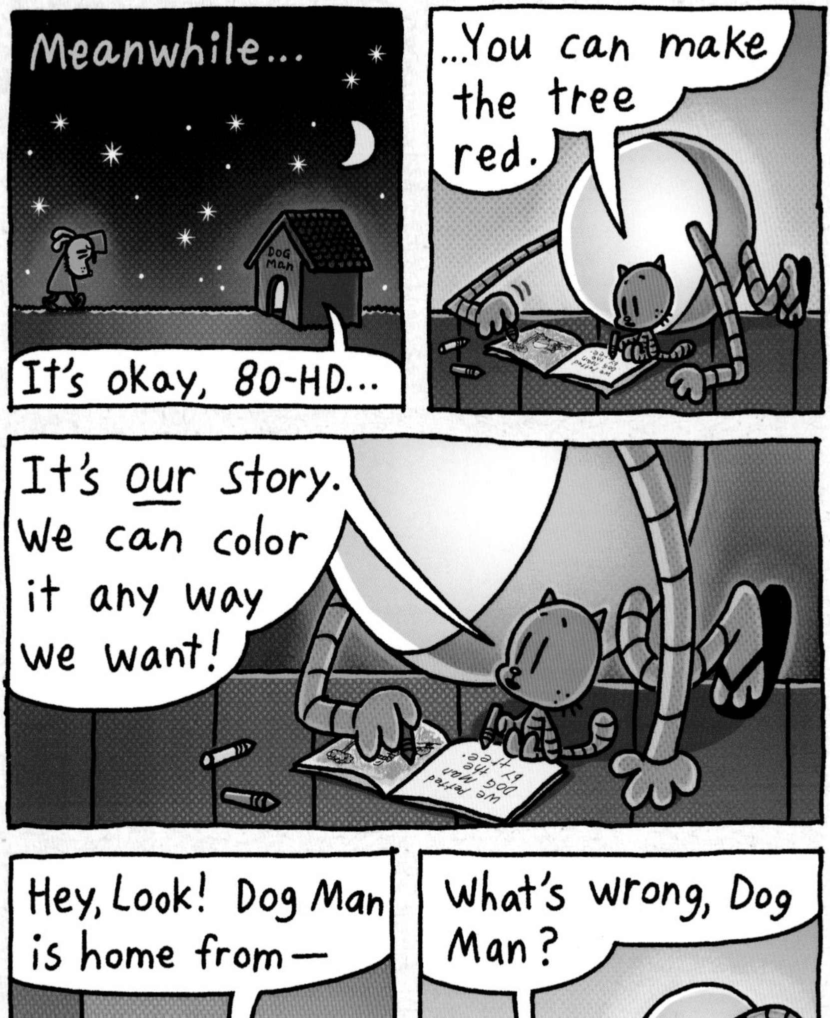
Meanwhile...
DOG Man
It's okay, 80-HD...
...You can make the tree red.
It's our story. We can color it any way we want!
We petted DOG Man by the tree.
Hey, Look! Dog Man is home from—
What's wrong, Dog Man?
FLIP FLOP FLIP FLOP FLIP

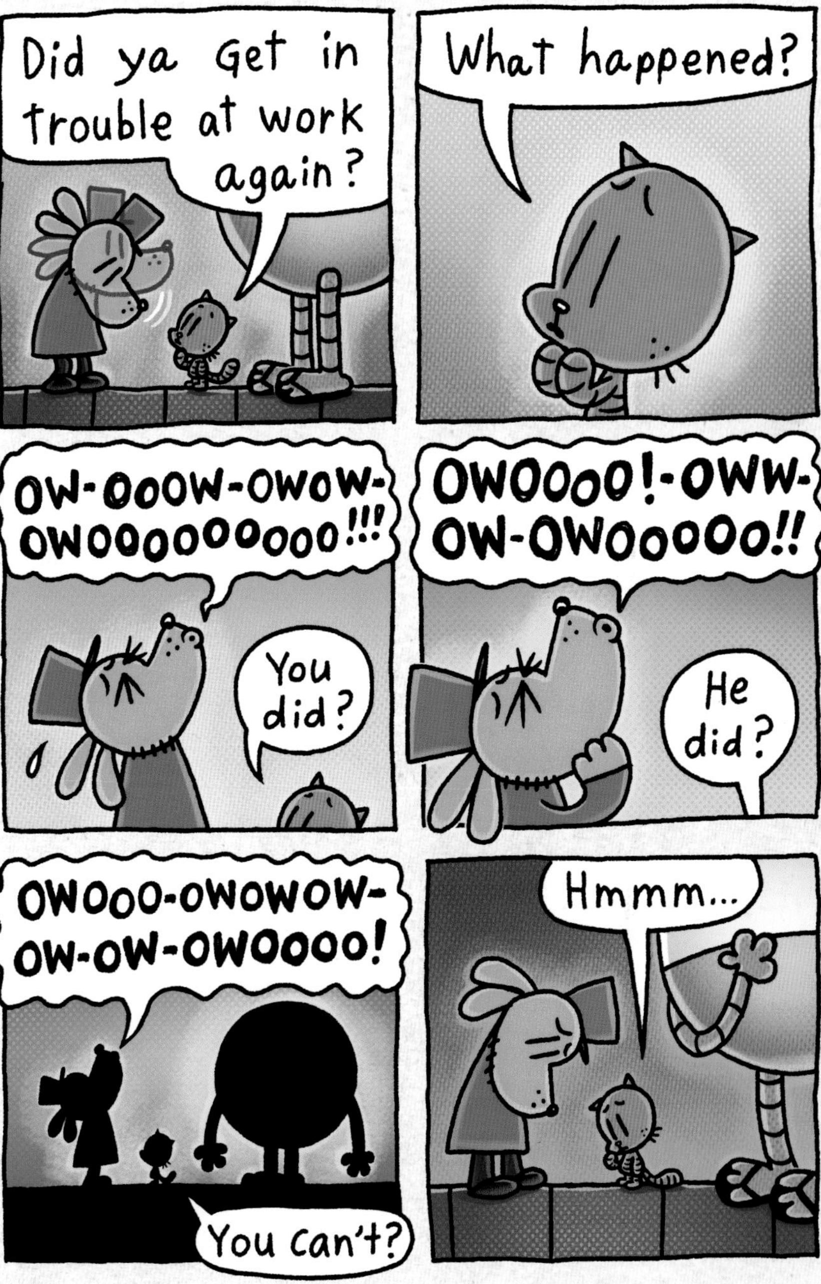
Did ya Get in trouble at work again?
What happened?
OW-OOOW-OWOW-OWOOOOOOOOO!!!
You did?
OWOOOO!-OWW-OW-OWOOOOO!!
He did?
OWOOO-OWOWOW-OW-OW-OWOOOO!
You can't?
Hmmm...

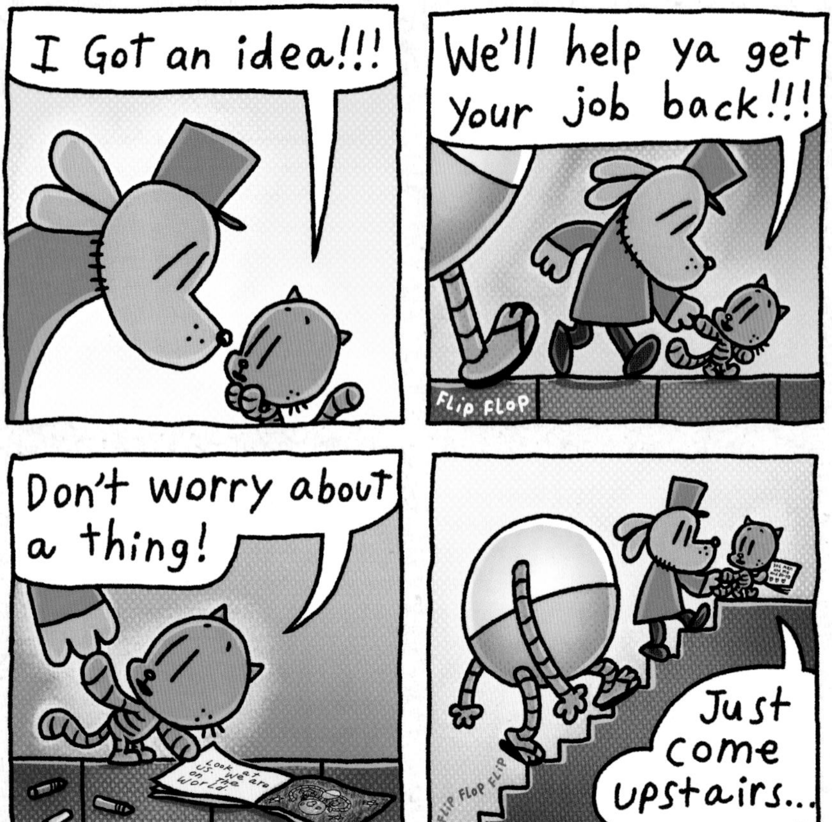
I Got an idea!!!
We'll help ya get your job back!!!
FLIP FLOP
Don't worry about a thing!
Look at us. We are on the world.
Just come upstairs...
FLIP FLOP FLIP
...and lie down on your bed...
...and I'll read you a bedtime story!
Dog Man and me and 80-HD

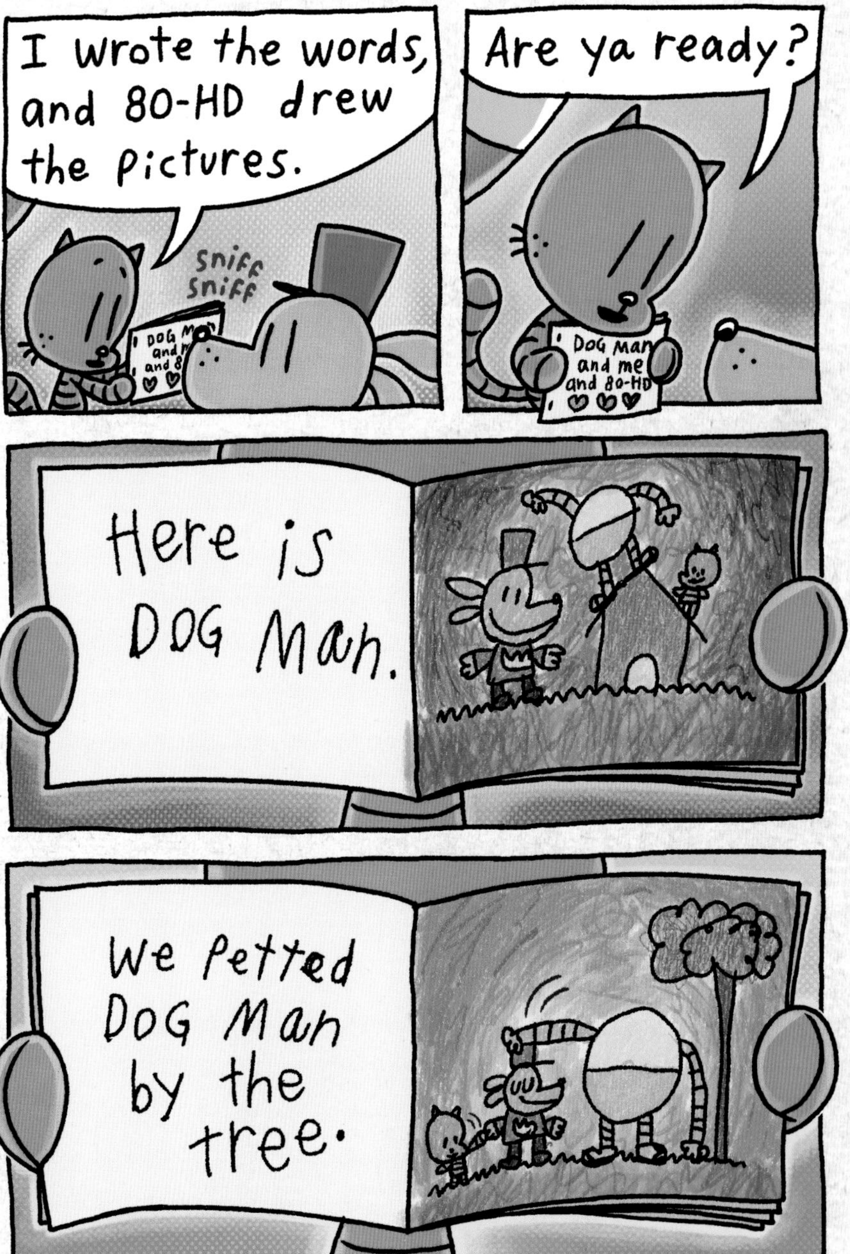
I wrote the words, and 80-HD drew the pictures.
Sniff Sniff
Are ya ready?
Dog Man and me and 80-HD
Here is DOG Man.
We petted DOG Man by the tree.

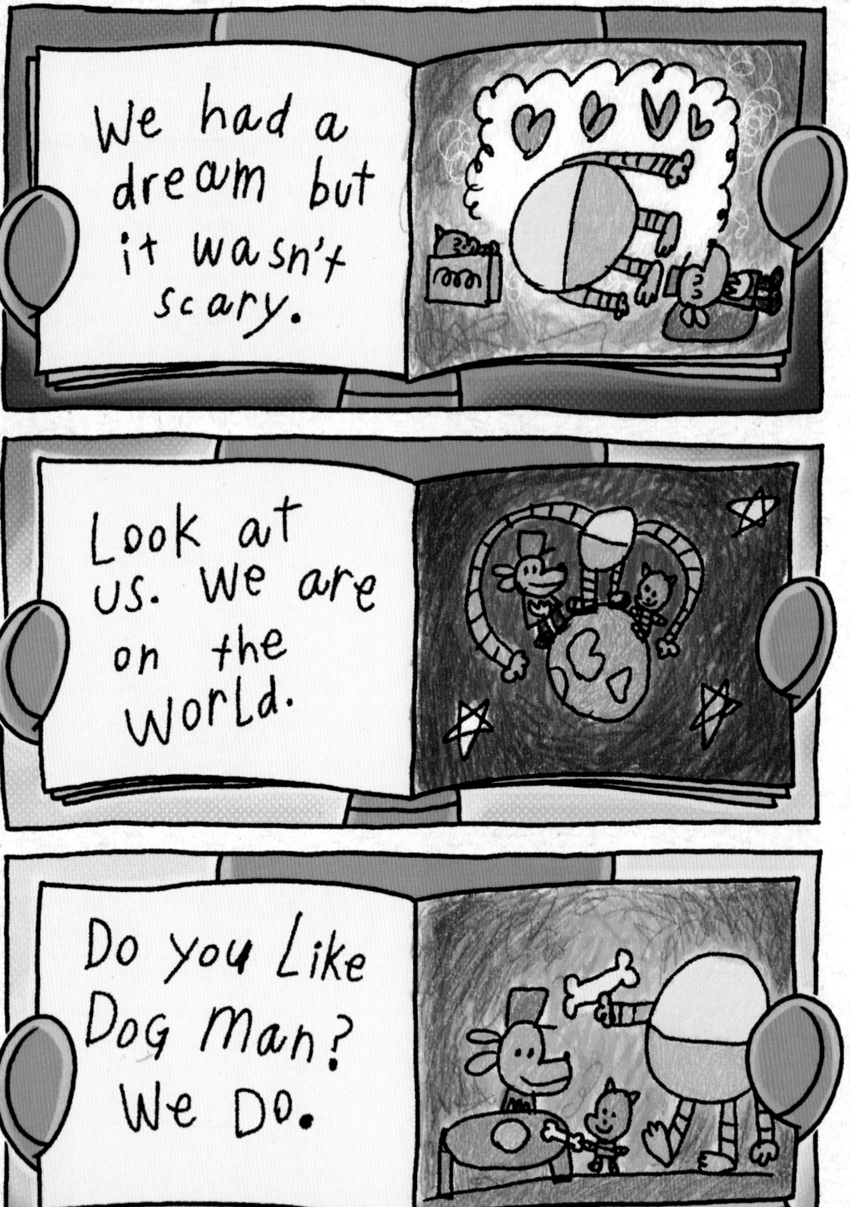
We had a dream but it wasn't scary.
Look at us. We are on the world.
Do you Like Dog Man? We Do.

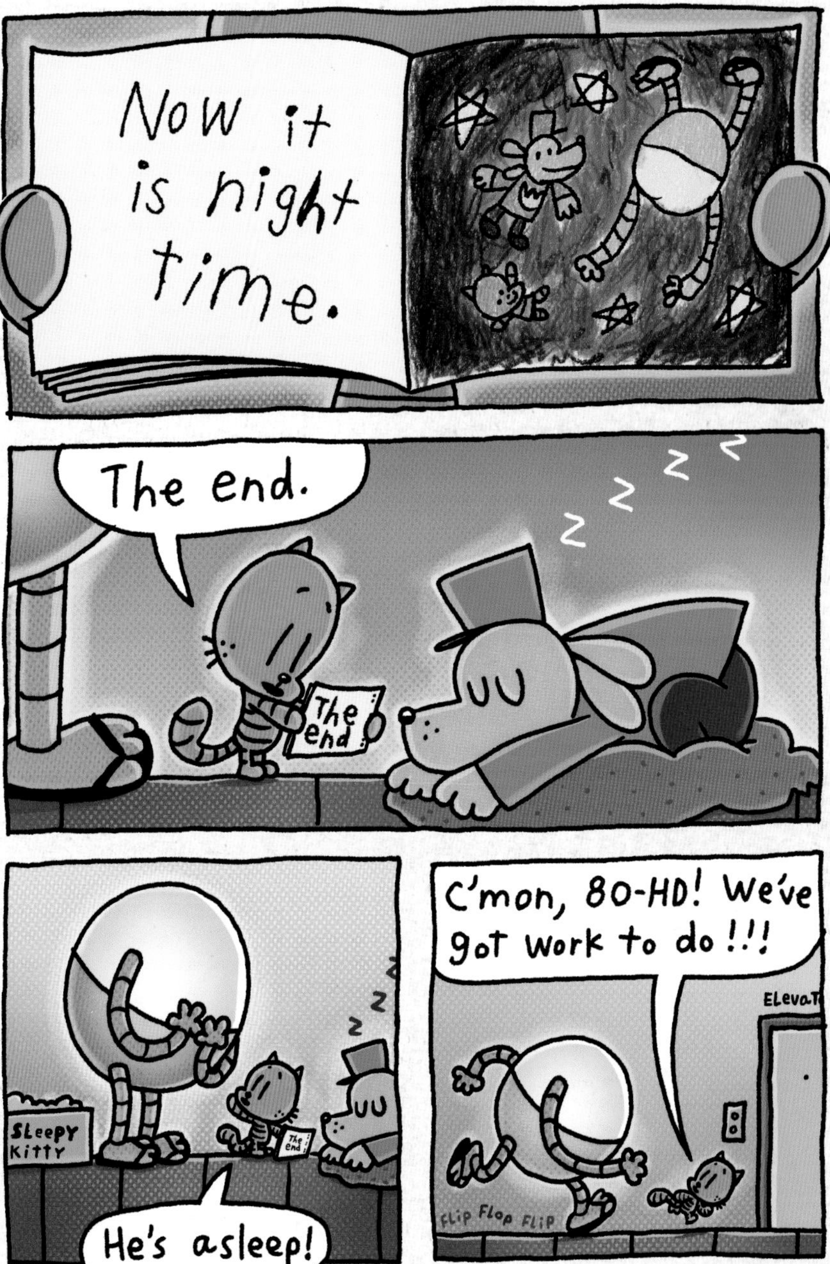
Now it is night time.
The end.
The end
SLEEPY KITTY
The end
He's asleep!
C'mon, 80-HD! We've got work to do!!!
FLIP FLOP FLIP

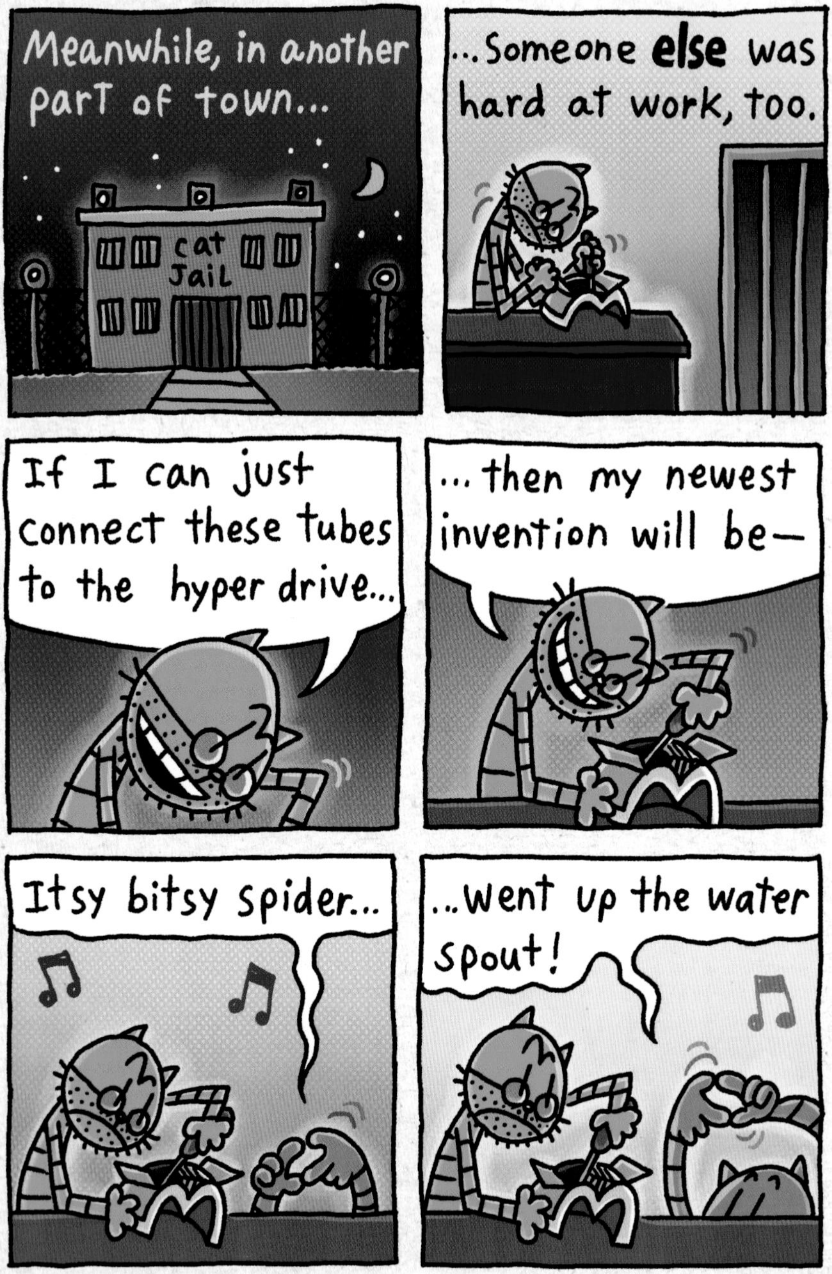
Meanwhile, in another part of town...
CAT JAIL
...Someone else was hard at work, too.
If I can just connect these tubes to the hyper drive...
...then my newest invention will be—
Itsy bitsy spider...
...went up the water spout!

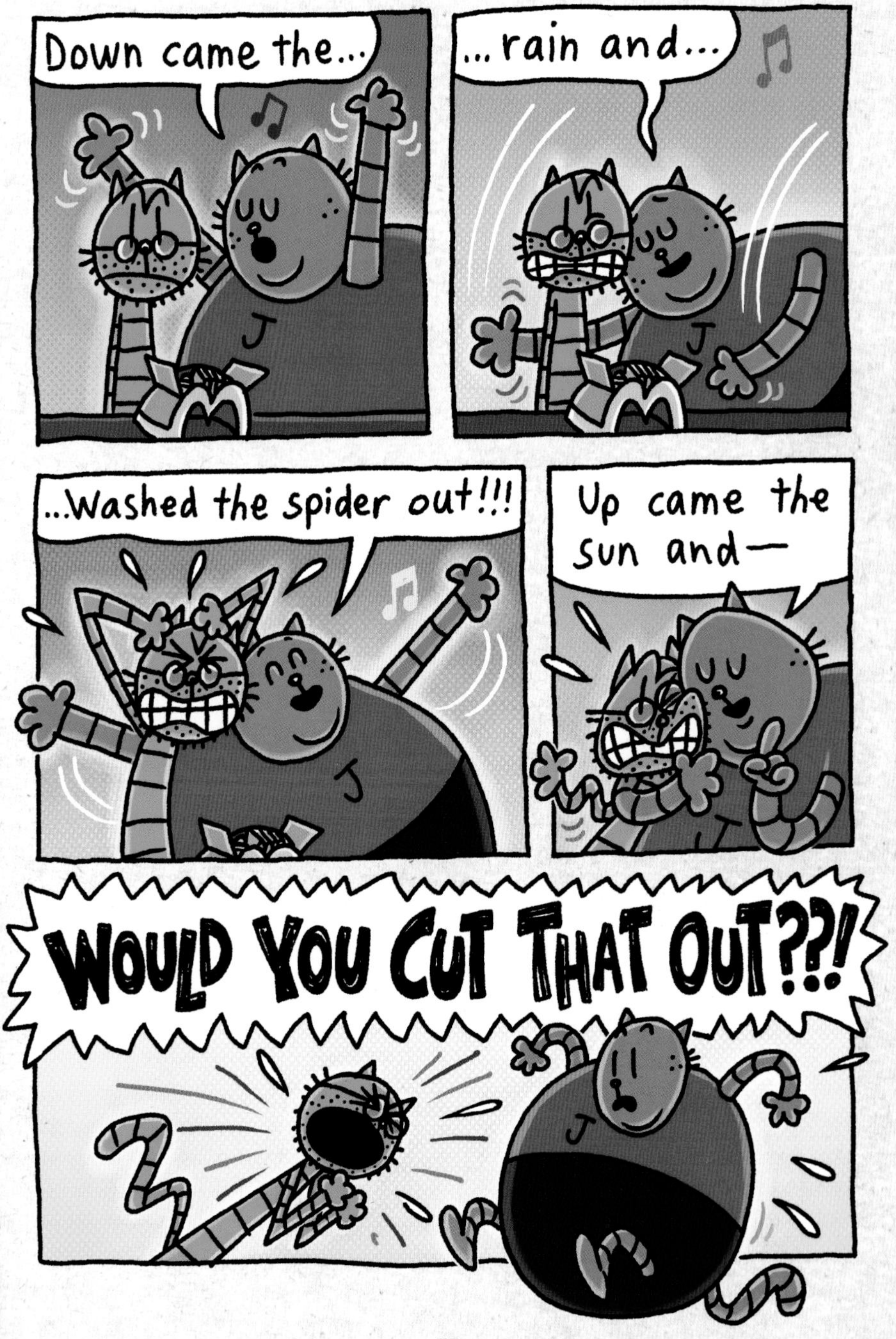
Down came the...
...rain and...
...Washed the spider out!!!
Up came the sun and—
WOULD YOU CUT THAT OUT??!

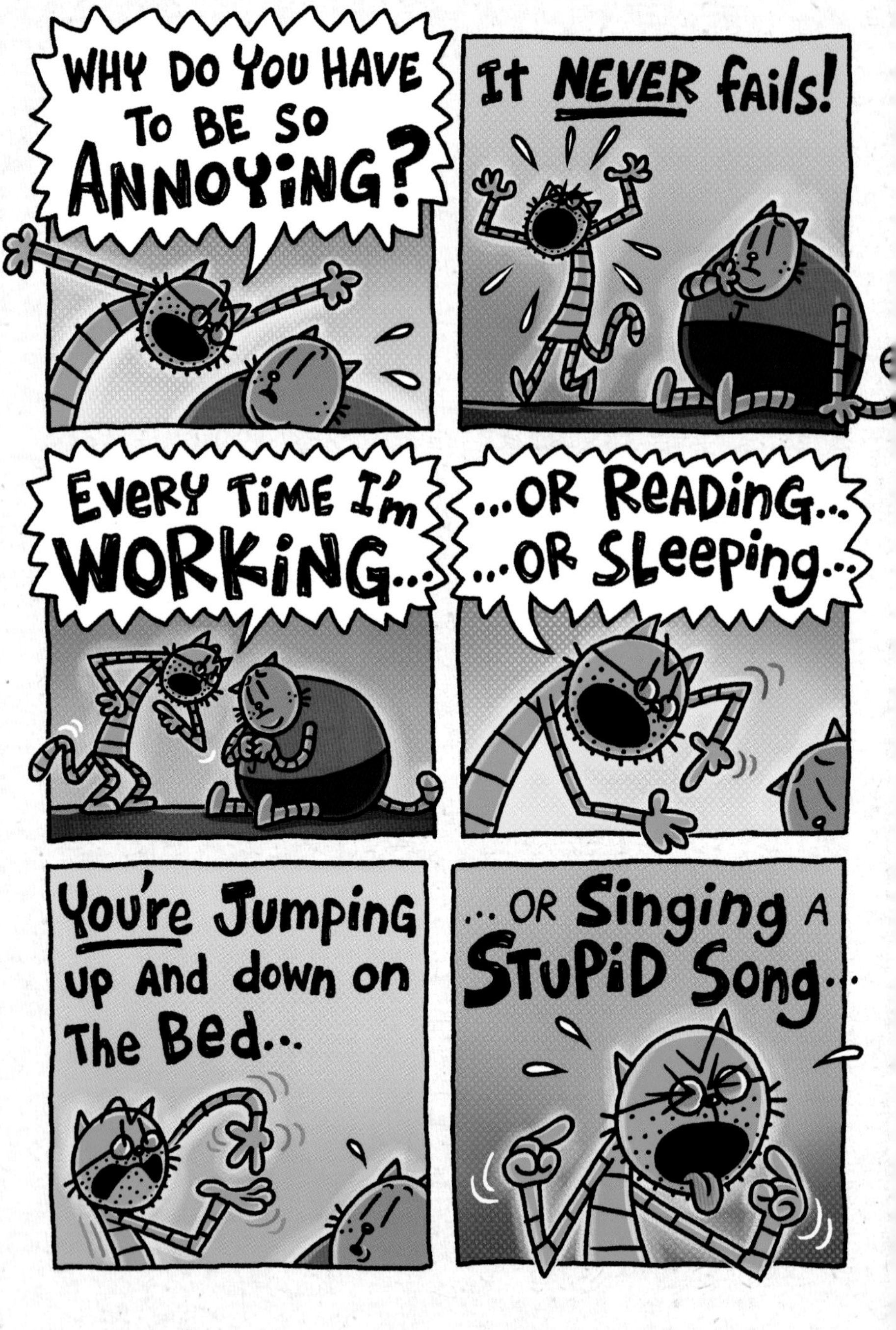
WHY DO YOU HAVE TO BE SO ANNOYING?
It NEVER fails!
EVERY TIME I'M WORKING...
...OR READING...
...OR SLEEPING...
YOU'RE JUMPING UP AND DOWN ON THE BED...
... OR SINGING A STUPID SONG...

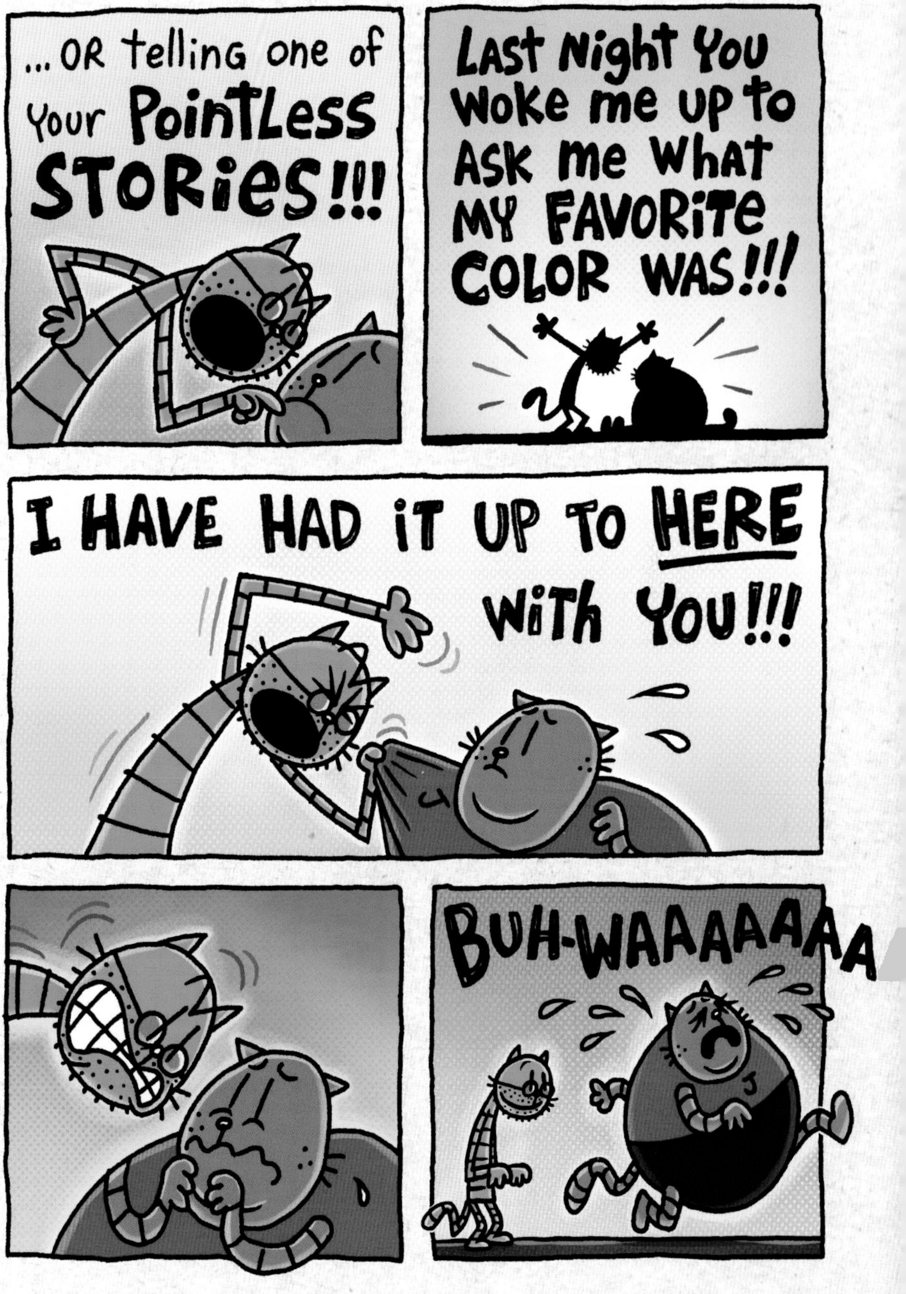
...OR telling one of your POINTLESS STORIES!!!
LAST NIGHT YOU WOKE ME UP TO ASK ME WHAT MY FAVORITE COLOR WAS!!!
I HAVE HAD IT UP TO HERE WITH YOU!!!
BUH-WAAAAAAA

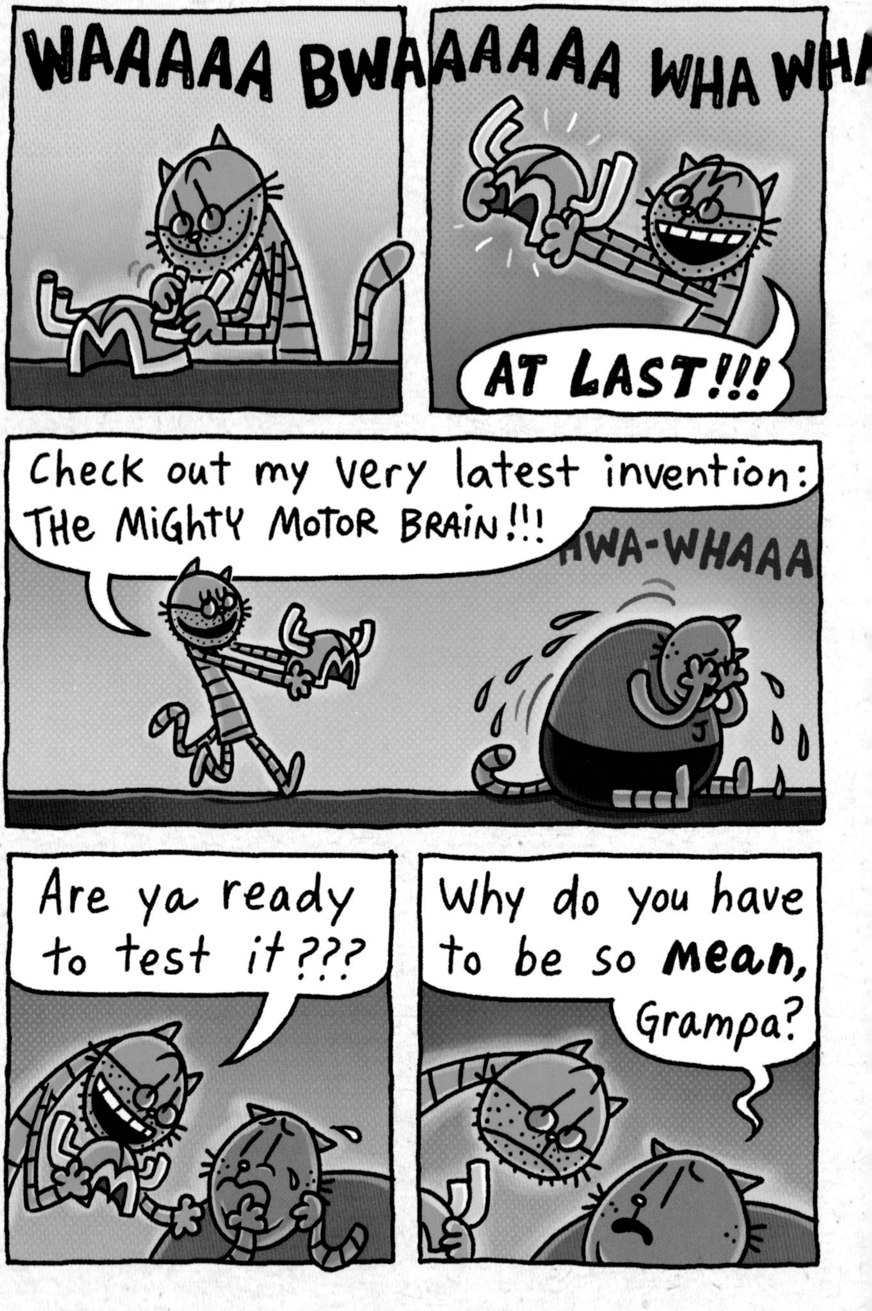
WAAAAA BWAAAAAA WHA WHA
AT LAST!!!
Check out my very latest invention: THE MIGHTY MOTOR BRAIN!!!
HWA-WHAAA
Are ya ready to test it???
Why do you have to be so **mean,** Grampa?

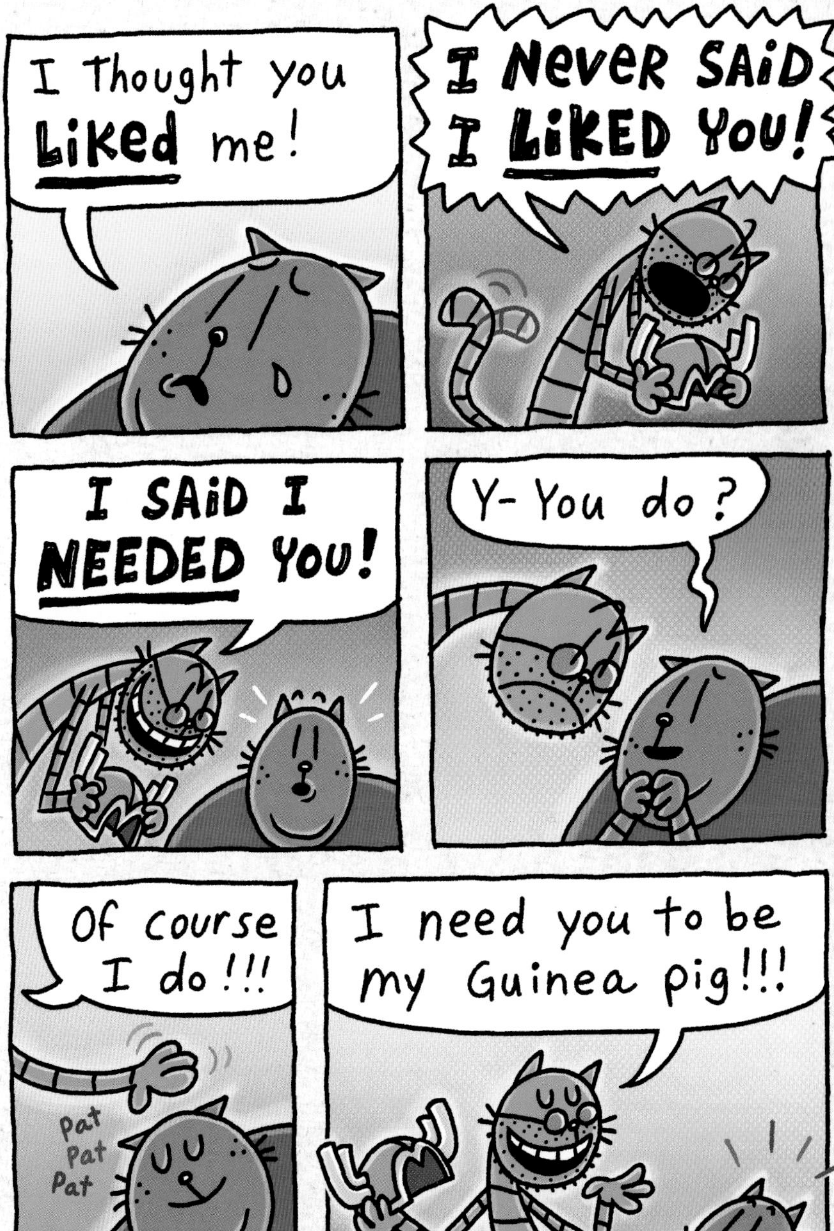
I Thought you **Liked** me!
I NEVER SAID I **LIKED** YOU!
I SAID I **NEEDED** YOU!
Y-You do?
Of course I do!!!
Pat Pat Pat
I need you to be my Guinea pig!!!

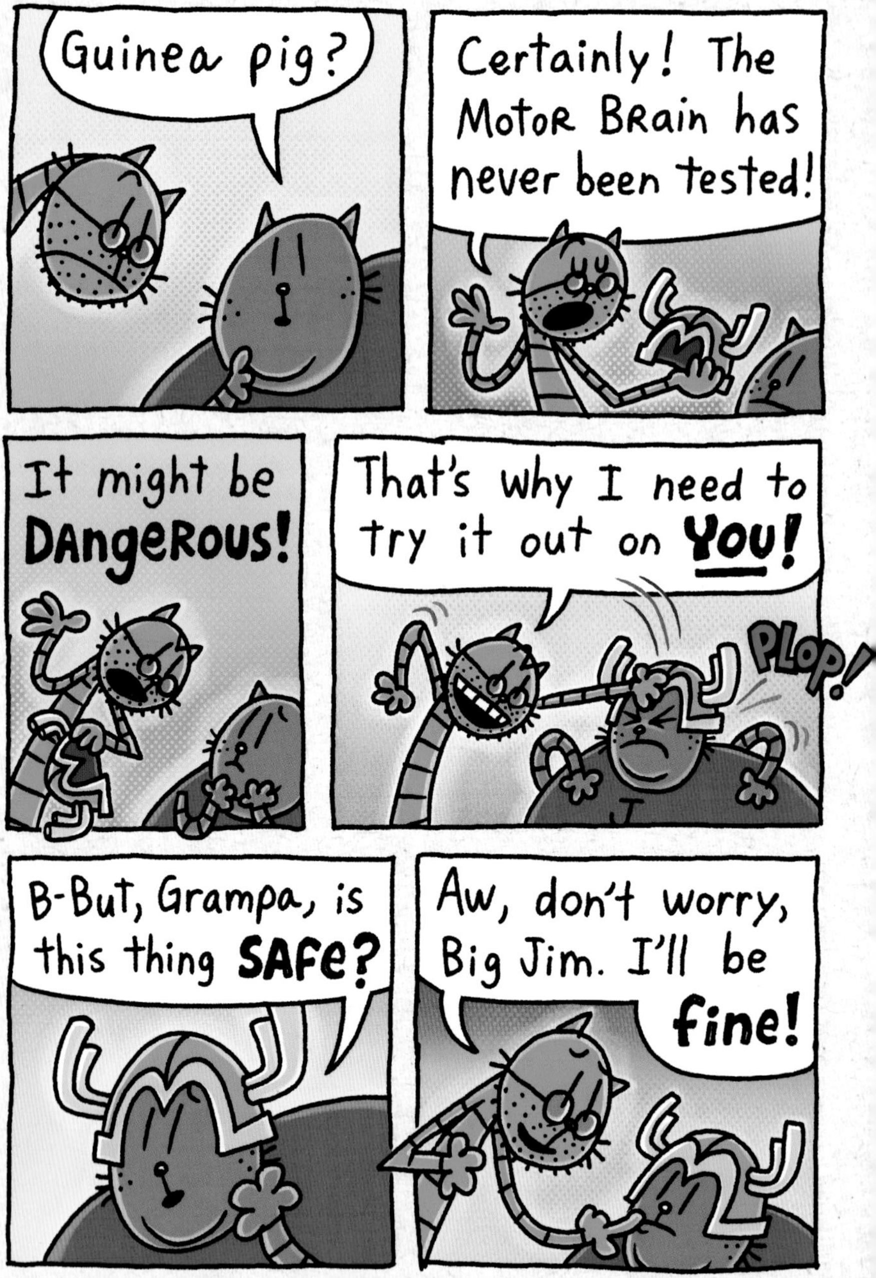
Guinea pig?
Certainly! The Motor Brain has never been tested!
It might be DANGEROUS!
That's why I need to try it out on YOU!
PLOP!
B-But, Grampa, is this thing SAFE?
Aw, don't worry, Big Jim. I'll be fine!

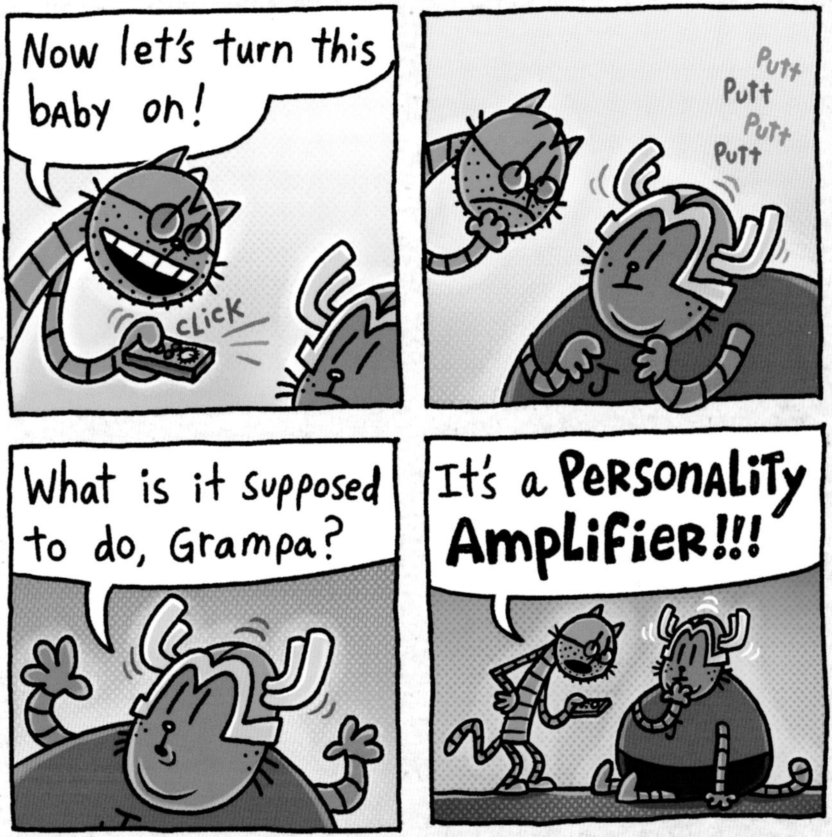
Now let's turn this baby on!
CLICK
PUTT
PUTT
PUTT
PUTT
What is it supposed to do, Grampa?
It's a PERSONALITY AMPLIFIER!!!
It takes your own innermost psyche...
...And MULTIPLIES it EXPONENTIALLY!

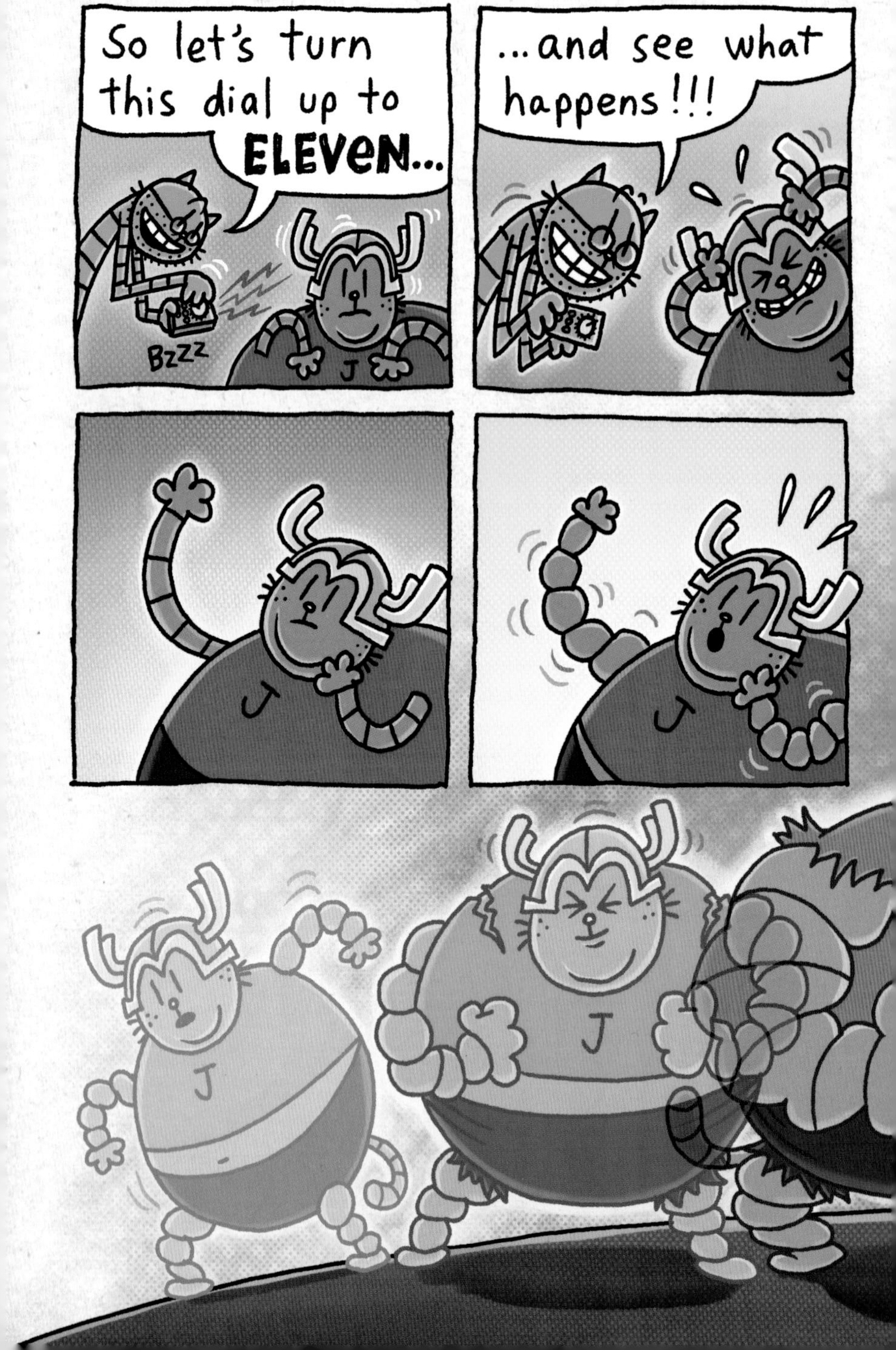
So let's turn this dial up to ELEVEN...
BZZZ
...and see what happens!!!

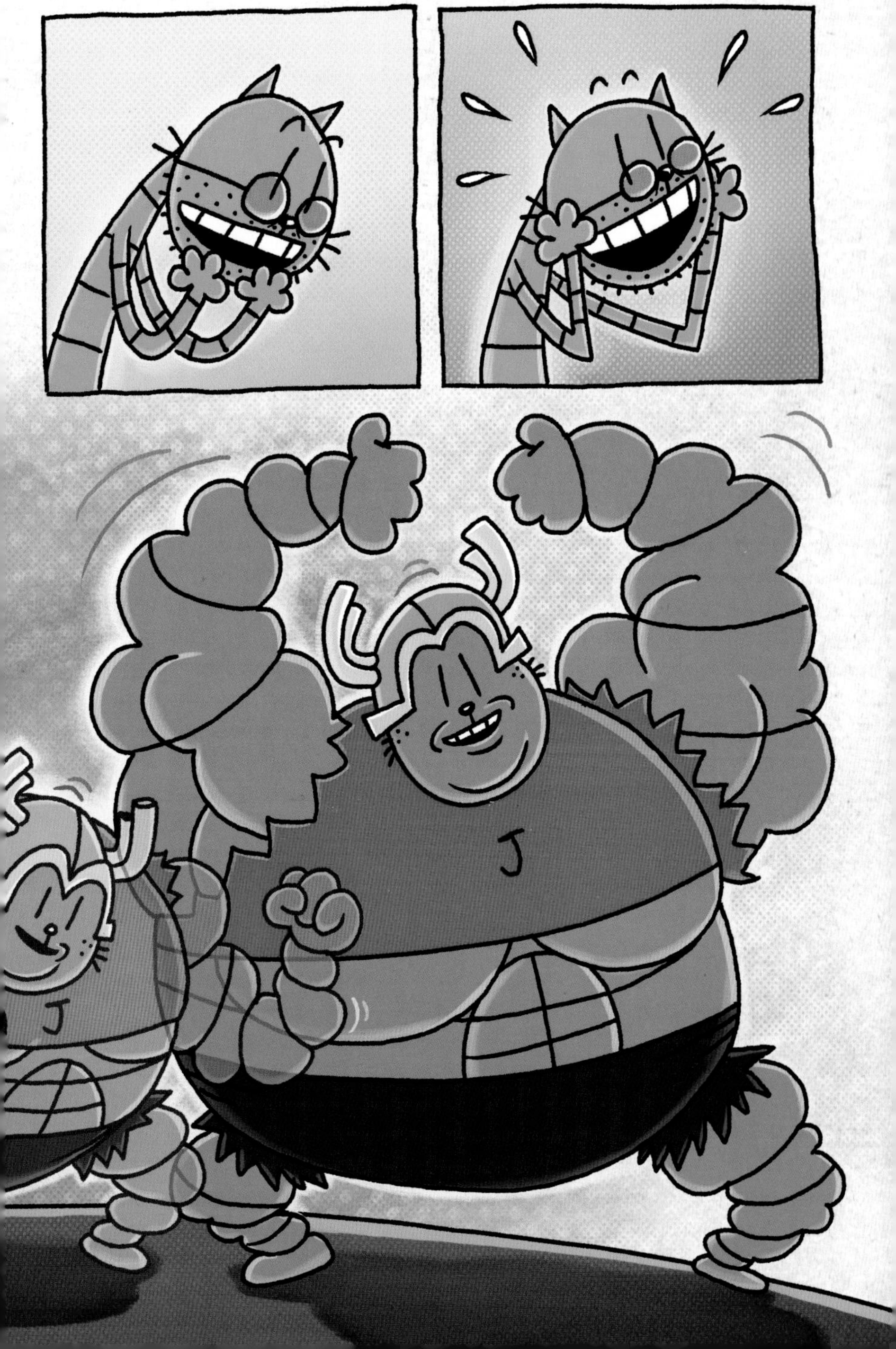

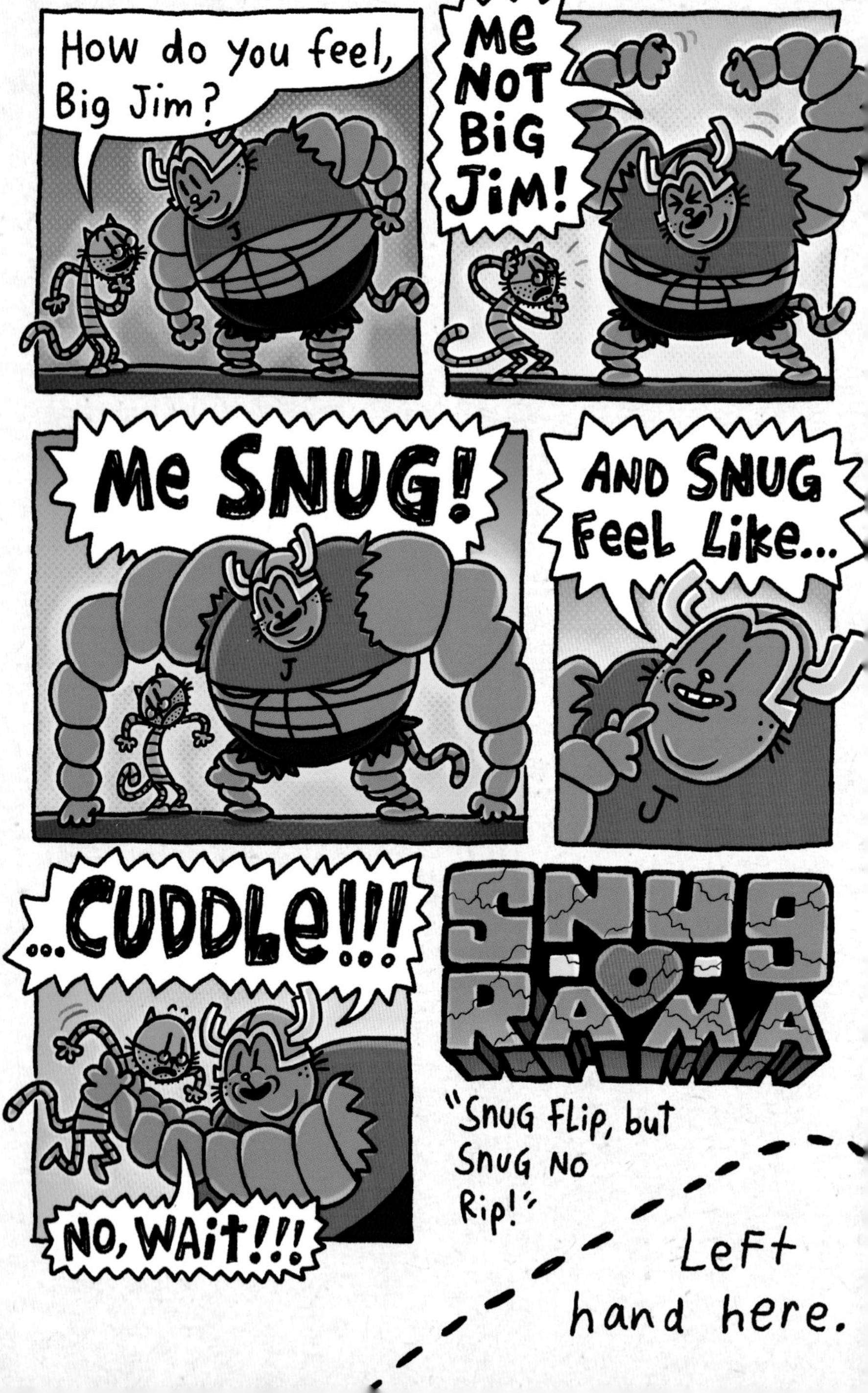
How do you feel, Big Jim?
Me NOT BIG JIM!
Me SNUG!
AND SNUG Feel Like...
...CUDDLE!!!
NO, WAIT!!!
SNUG-O-RAMA
"SNUG FLip, but SNUG NO Rip!"
Left hand here.

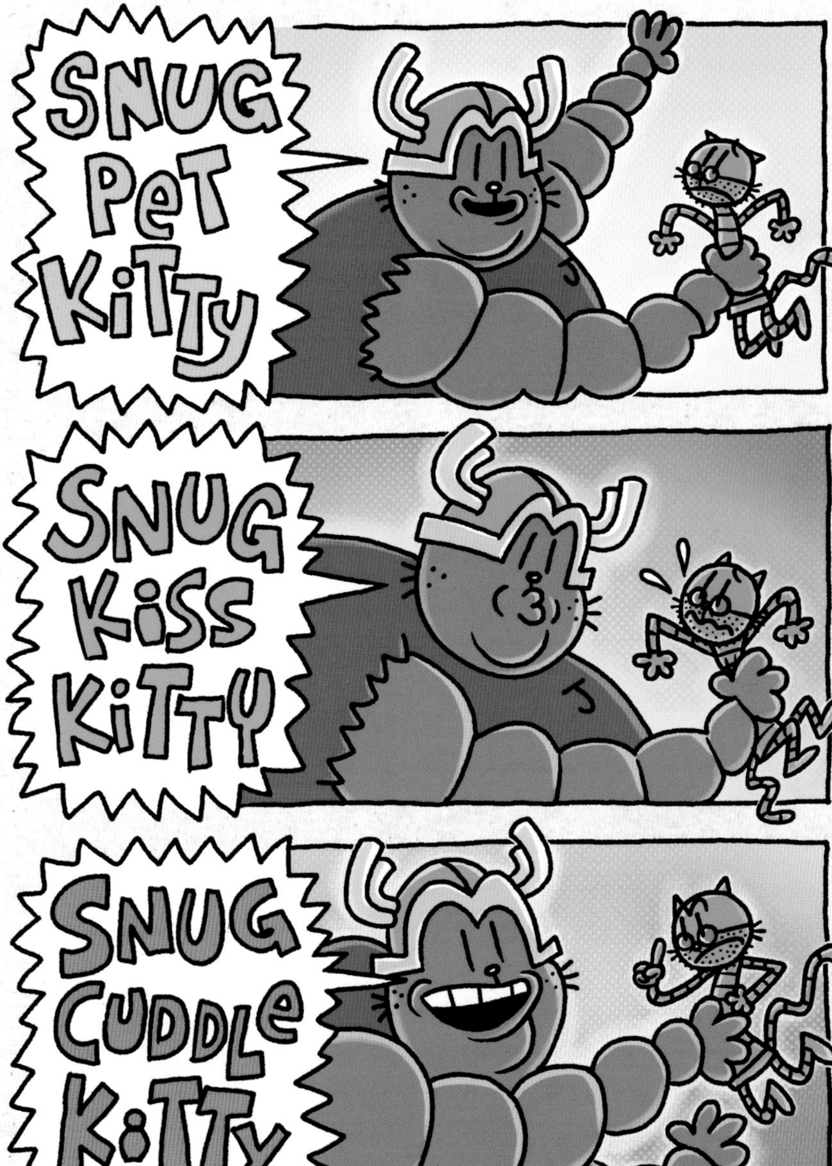
SNUG PET KITTY
SNUG KISS KITTY
SNUG CUDDLE KITTY

Right Thumb here.

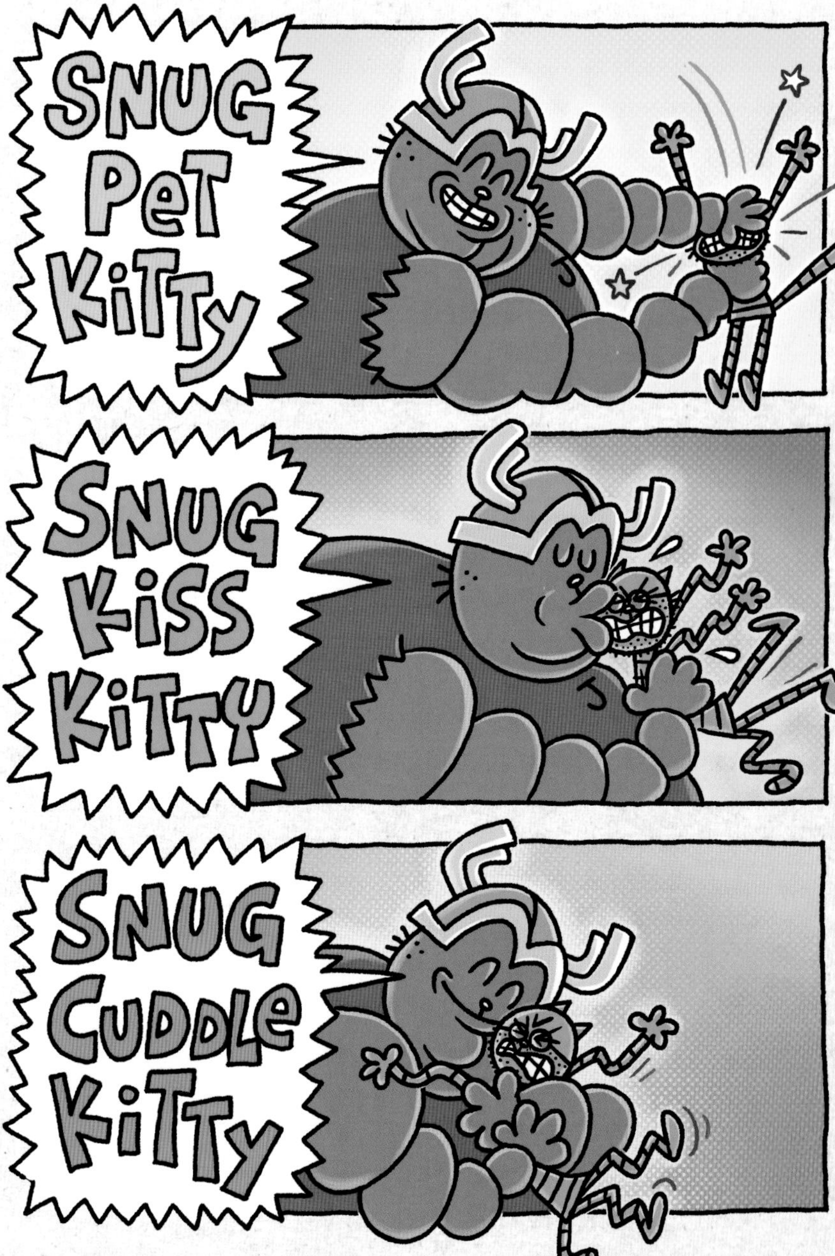
SNUG PET KITTY
SNUG KISS KITTY
SNUG CUDDLE KITTY

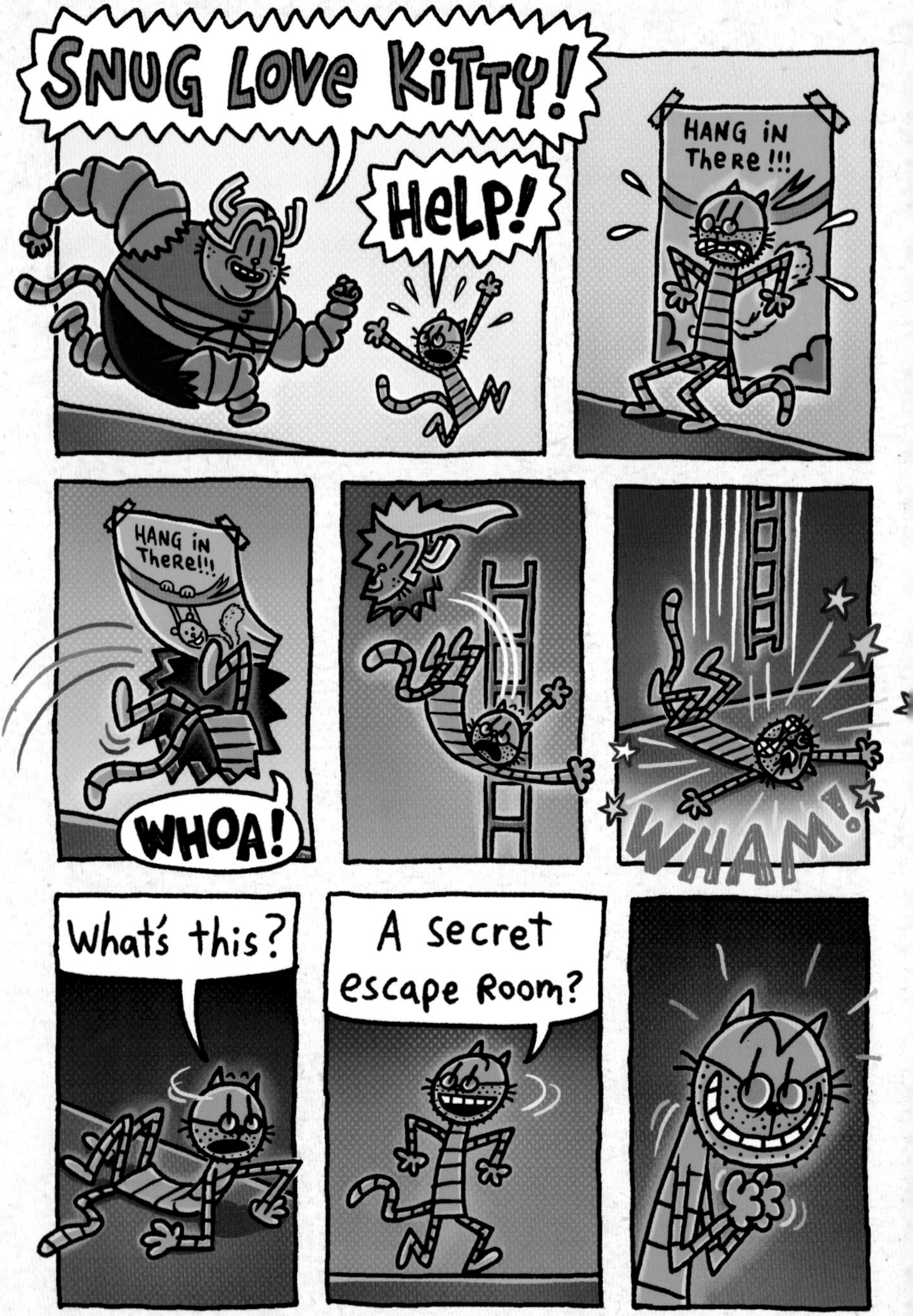
SNUG LOVE KITTY!
HELP!
HANG IN There!!!
HANG IN There!!!
WHOA!
WHAM!
What's this?
A secret escape Room?

CHAPTER 4

The Dog in The Hat

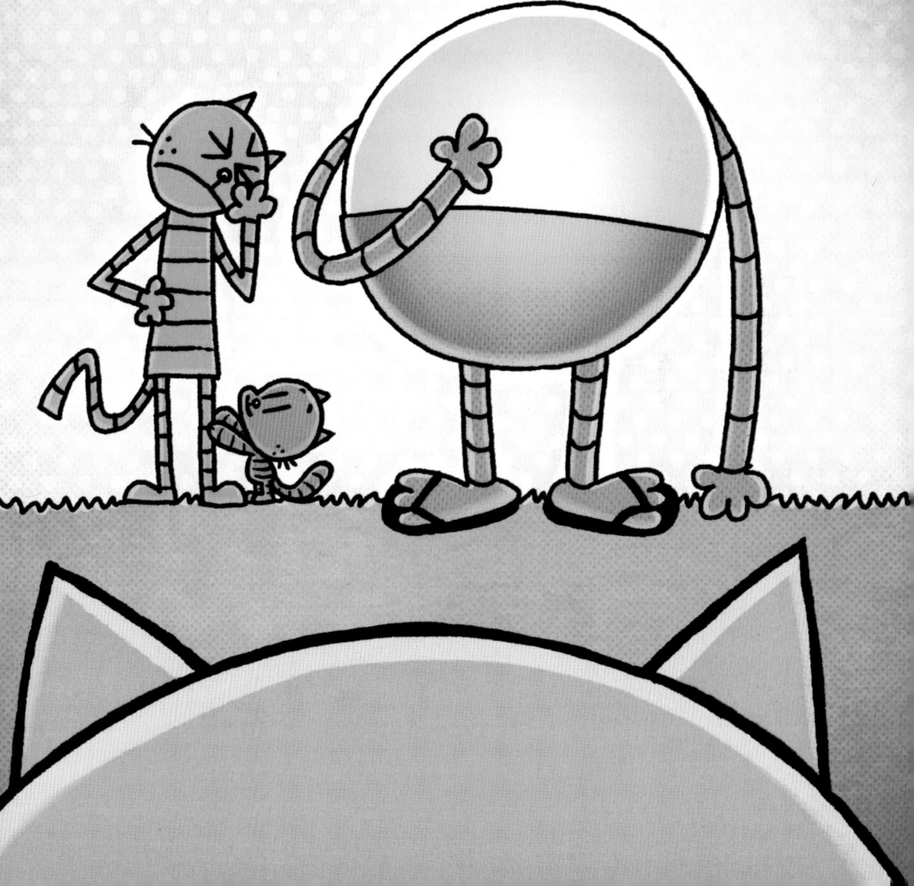

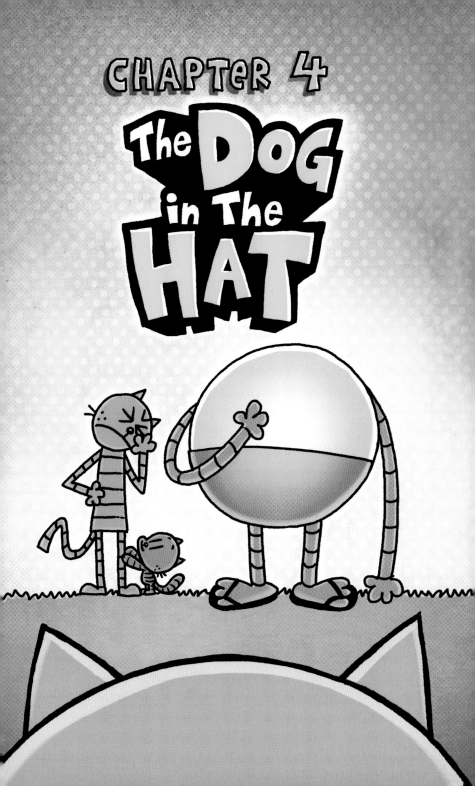

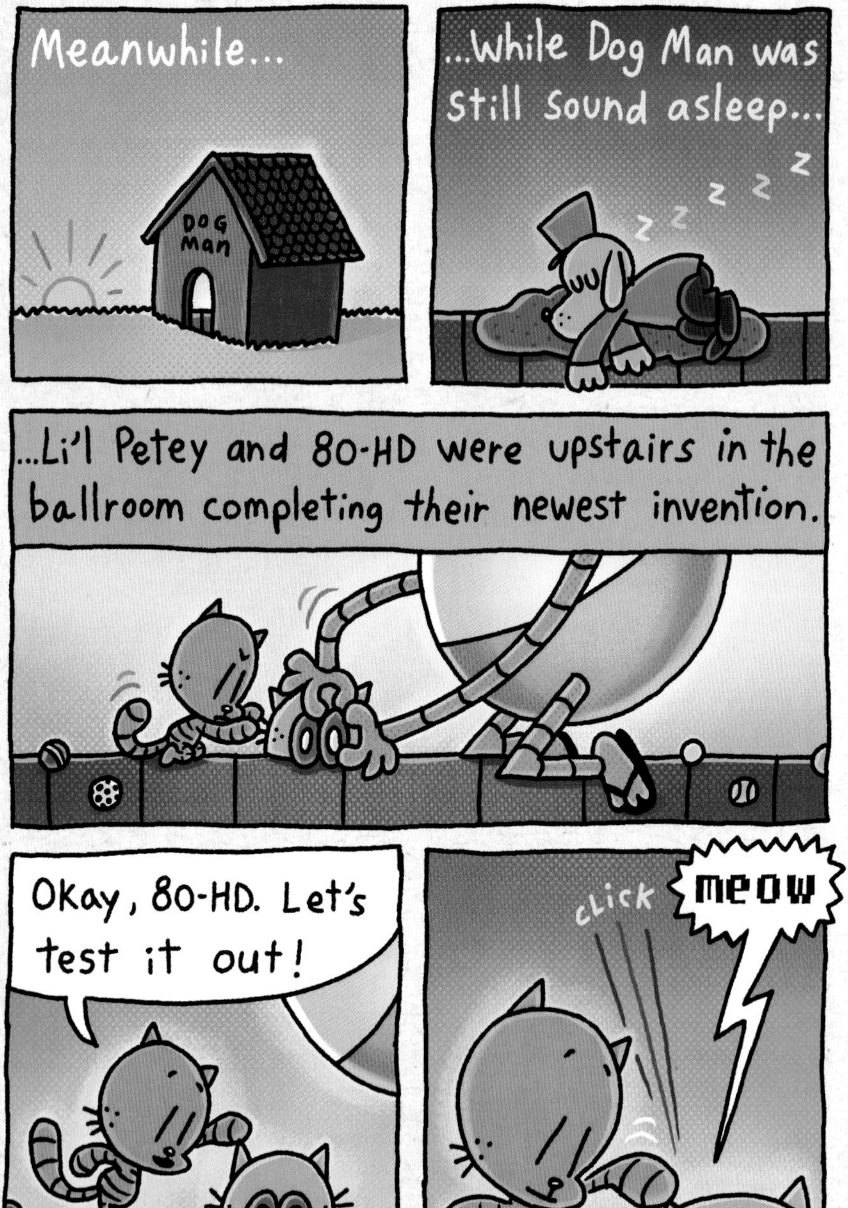

Meanwhile...
...While Dog Man was still sound asleep...
DOG Man
Z Z Z Z Z
...Li'l Petey and 80-HD were upstairs in the ballroom completing their newest invention.
Okay, 80-HD. Let's test it out!
CLICK
meow

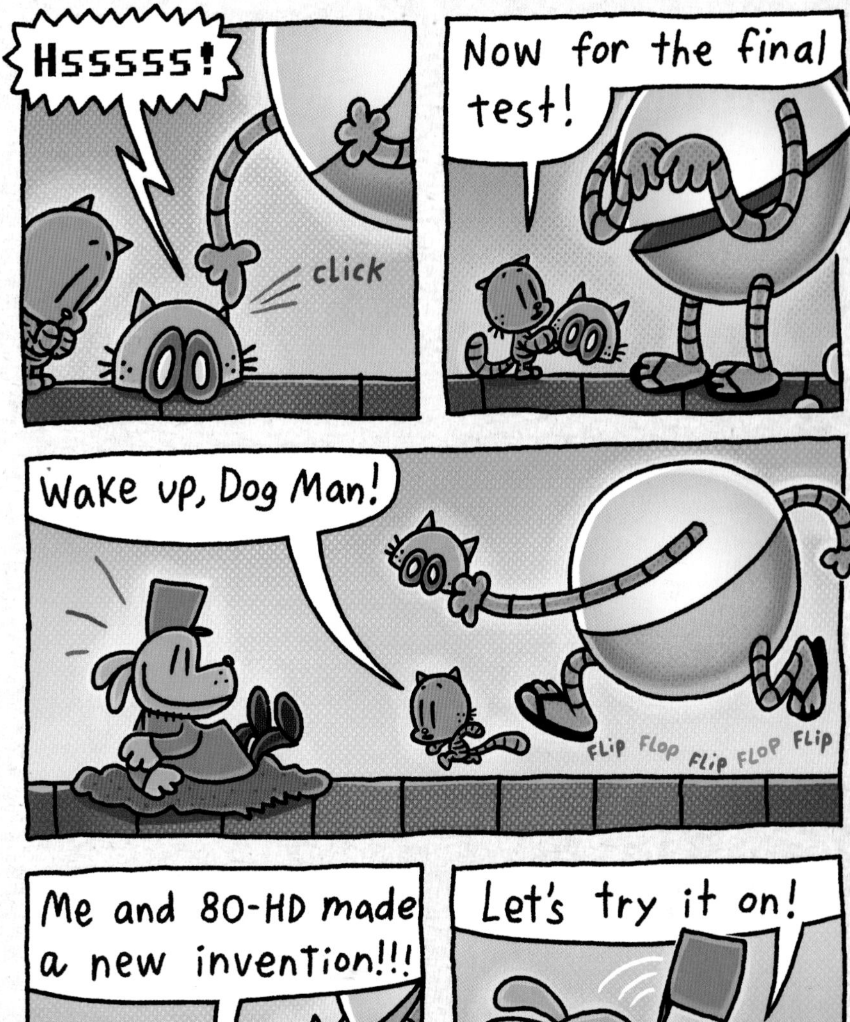
Hsssss!
click
Now for the final test!
Wake up, Dog Man!
FLIP FLOP FLIP FLOP FLIP
Me and 80-HD made a new invention!!!
Let's try it on!

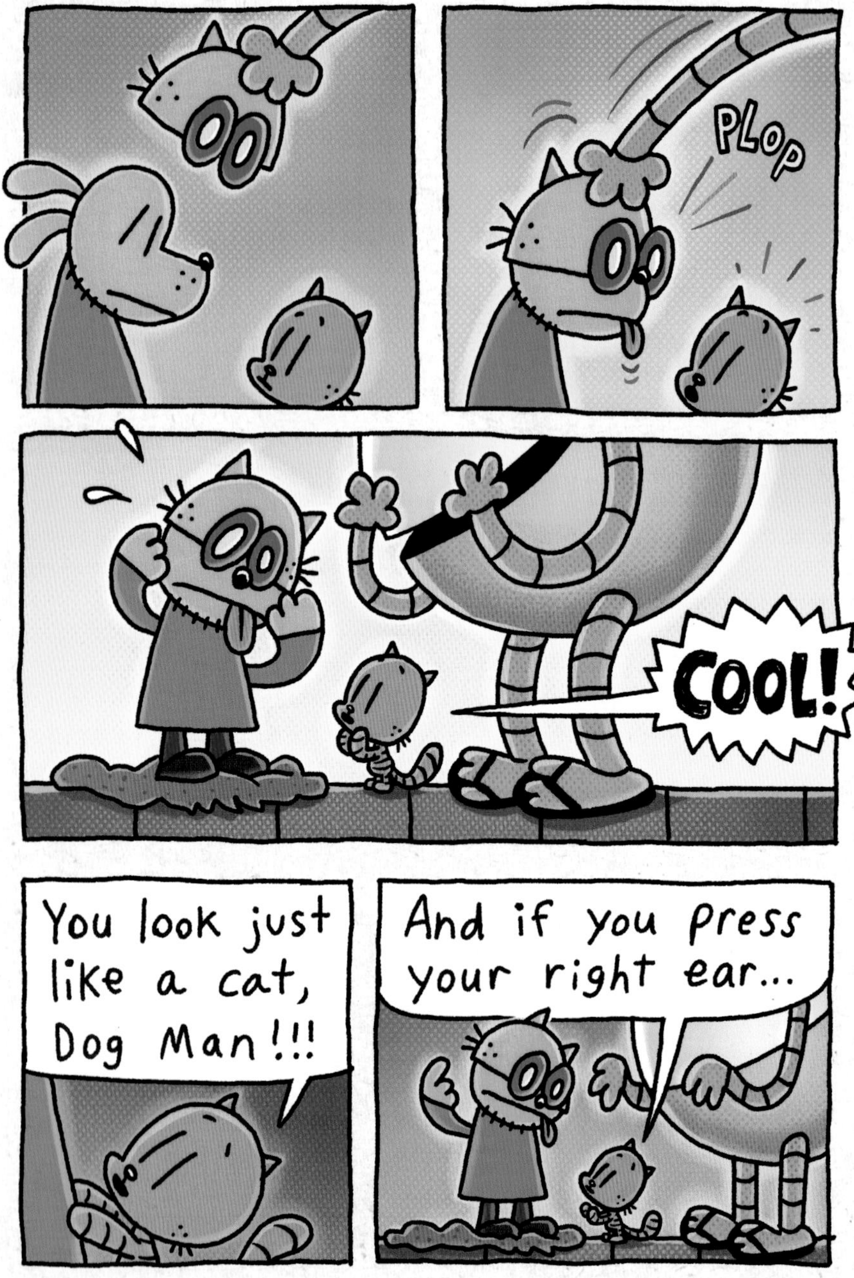
PLOP
COOL!
You look just like a cat, Dog Man!!!
And if you press your right ear...

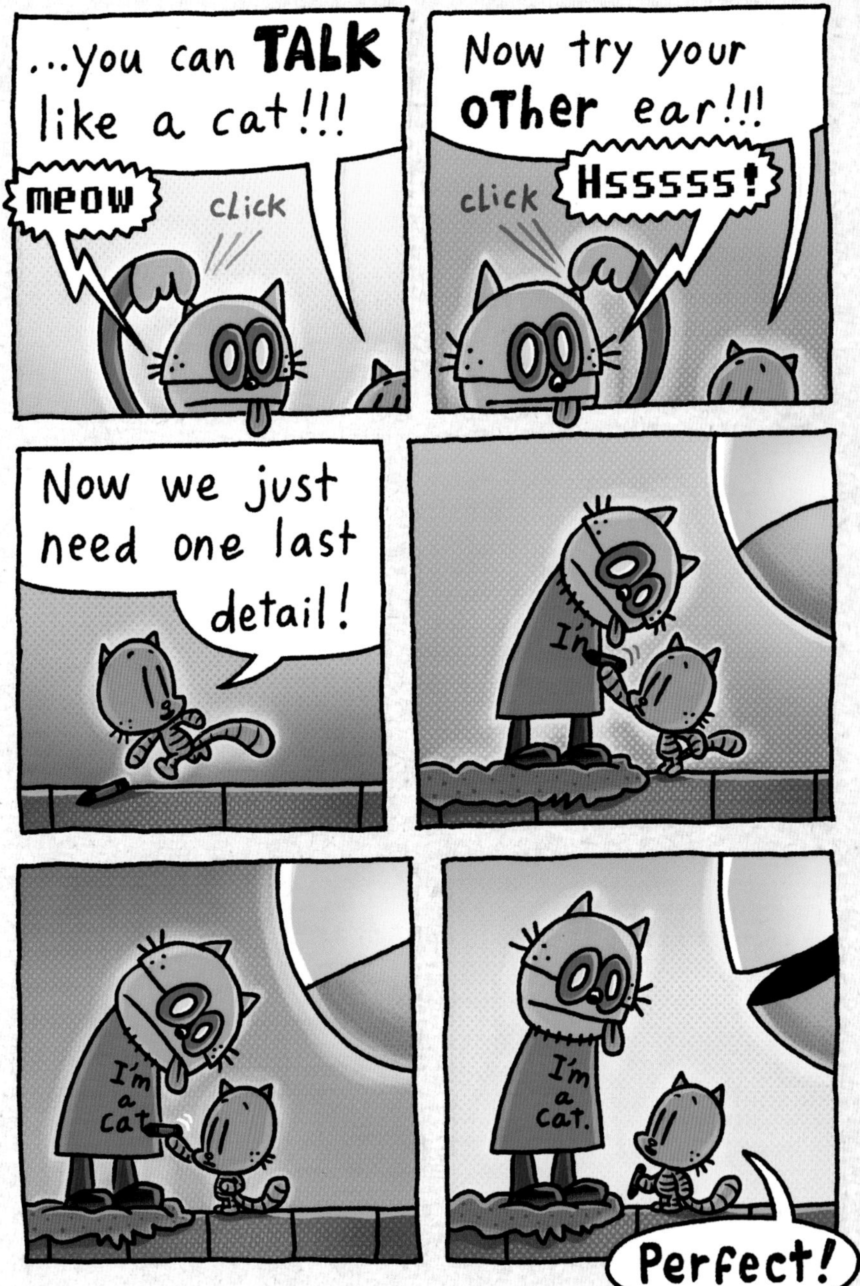
...you can TALK like a cat!!!
meow
click
Now try your OTher ear!!!
click
Hsssss!
Now we just need one last detail!
I'm
I'm a cat
I'm a cat.
Perfect!

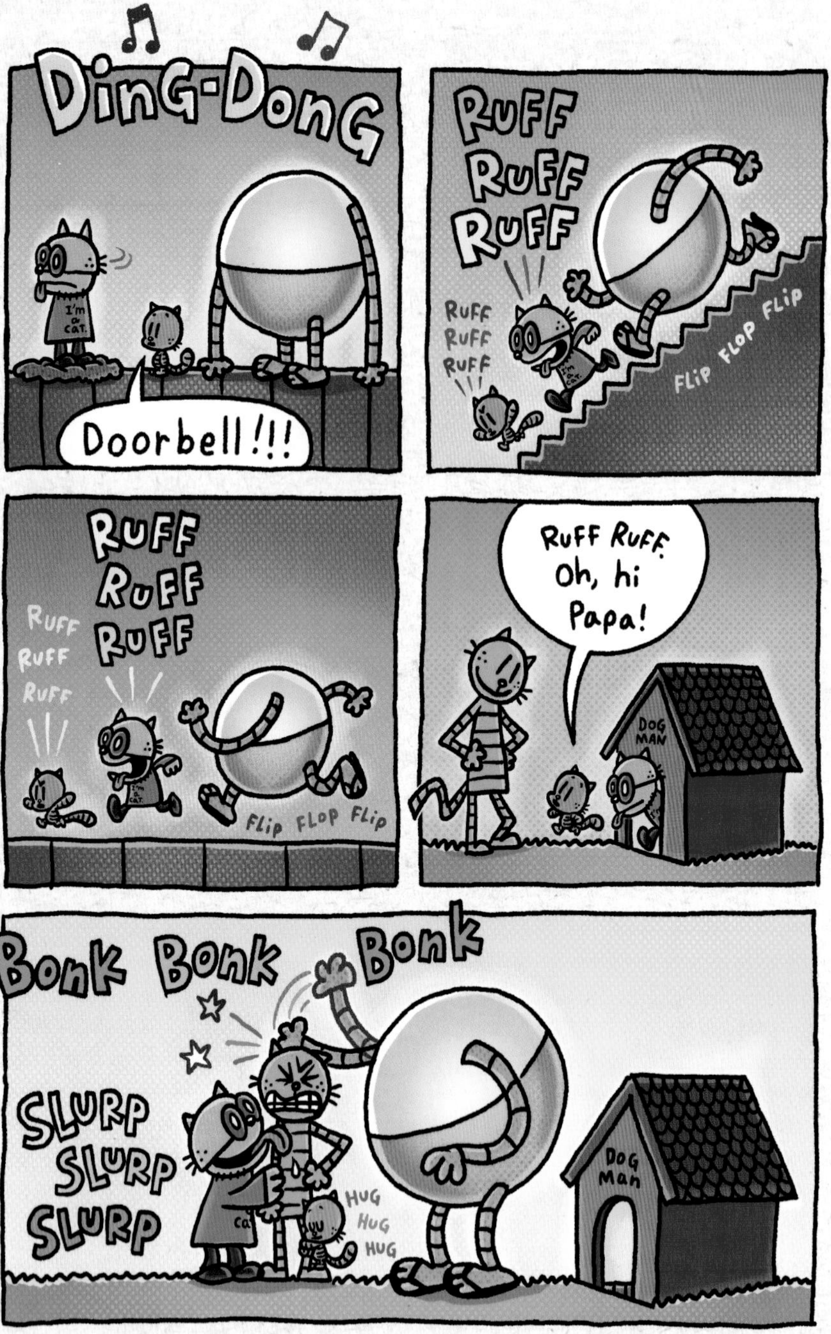

DING-DONG
I'm a CAT.
Doorbell!!!
RUFF RUFF RUFF
RUFF RUFF RUFF
FLIP FLOP FLIP
RUFF RUFF RUFF
RUFF RUFF RUFF
FLIP FLOP FLIP
RUFF RUFF. Oh, hi Papa!
DOG MAN
Bonk Bonk Bonk
SLURP SLURP SLURP
HUG HUG HUG
DOG MAN

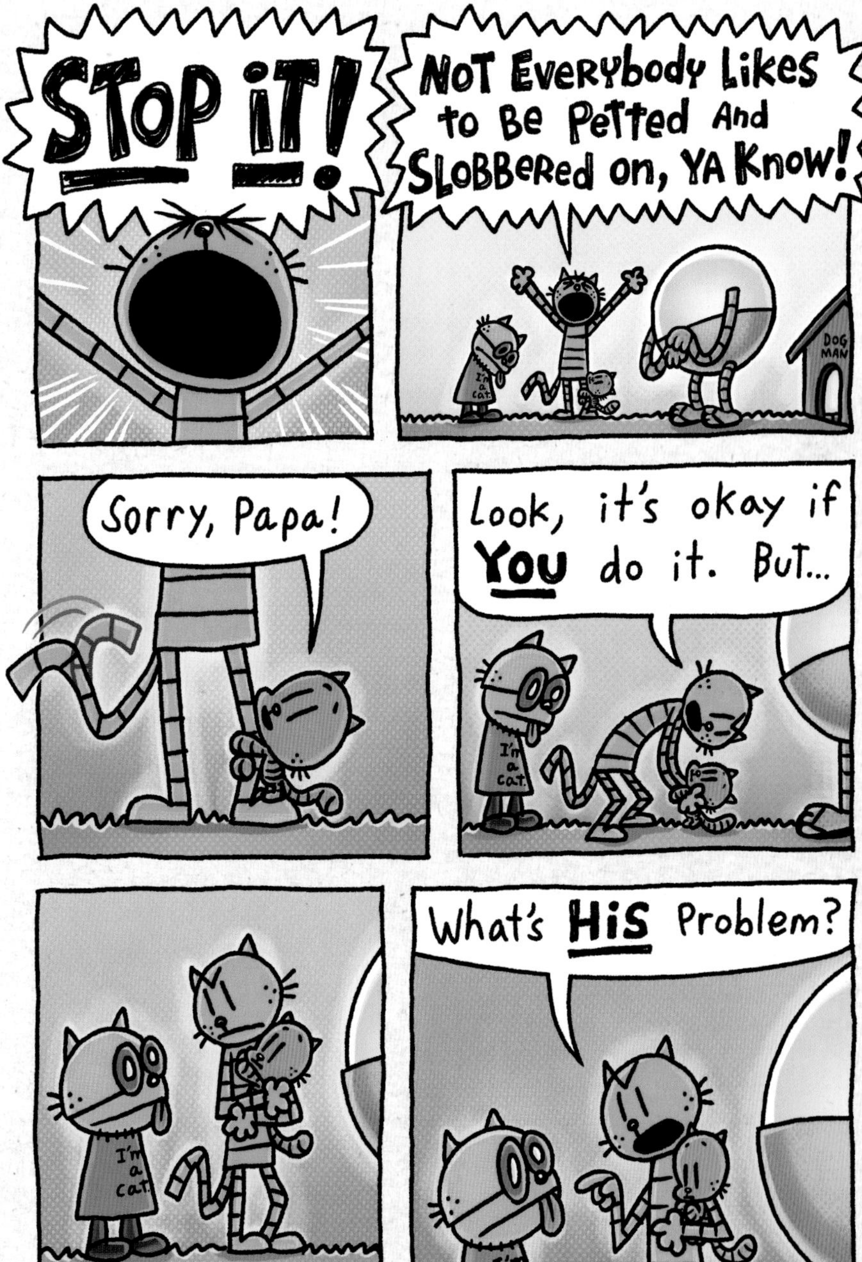
STOP IT!
NOT Everybody Likes to Be Petted And SLOBBERED on, YA Know!
DOG MAN
I'm a cat.
Sorry, Papa!
Look, it's okay if YOU do it. BUT...
I'm a cat.
I'm a cat.
What's HIS Problem?

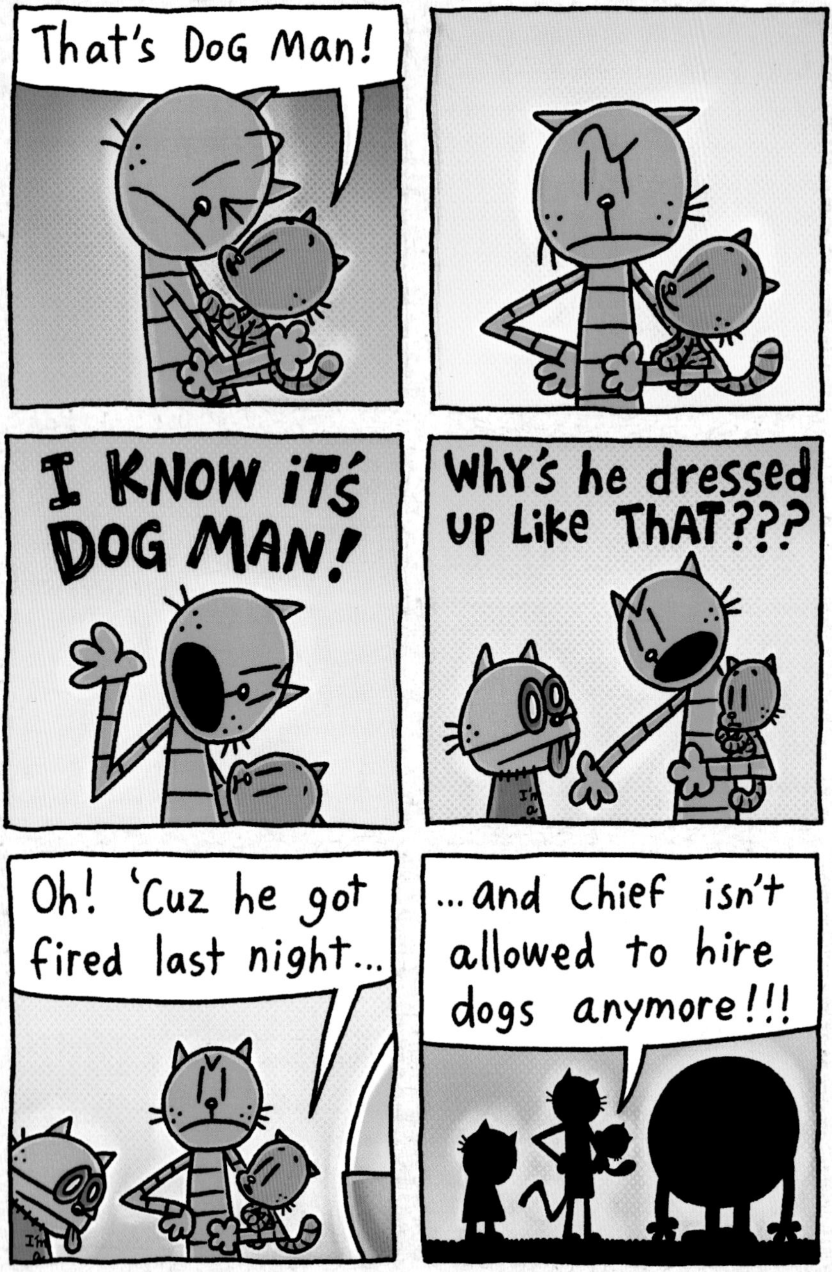
That's DoG Man!
I KNOW iT'S DOG MAN!
WhY's he dressed up Like ThAT???
Oh! 'Cuz he got fired last night...
...and Chief isn't allowed to hire dogs anymore!!!

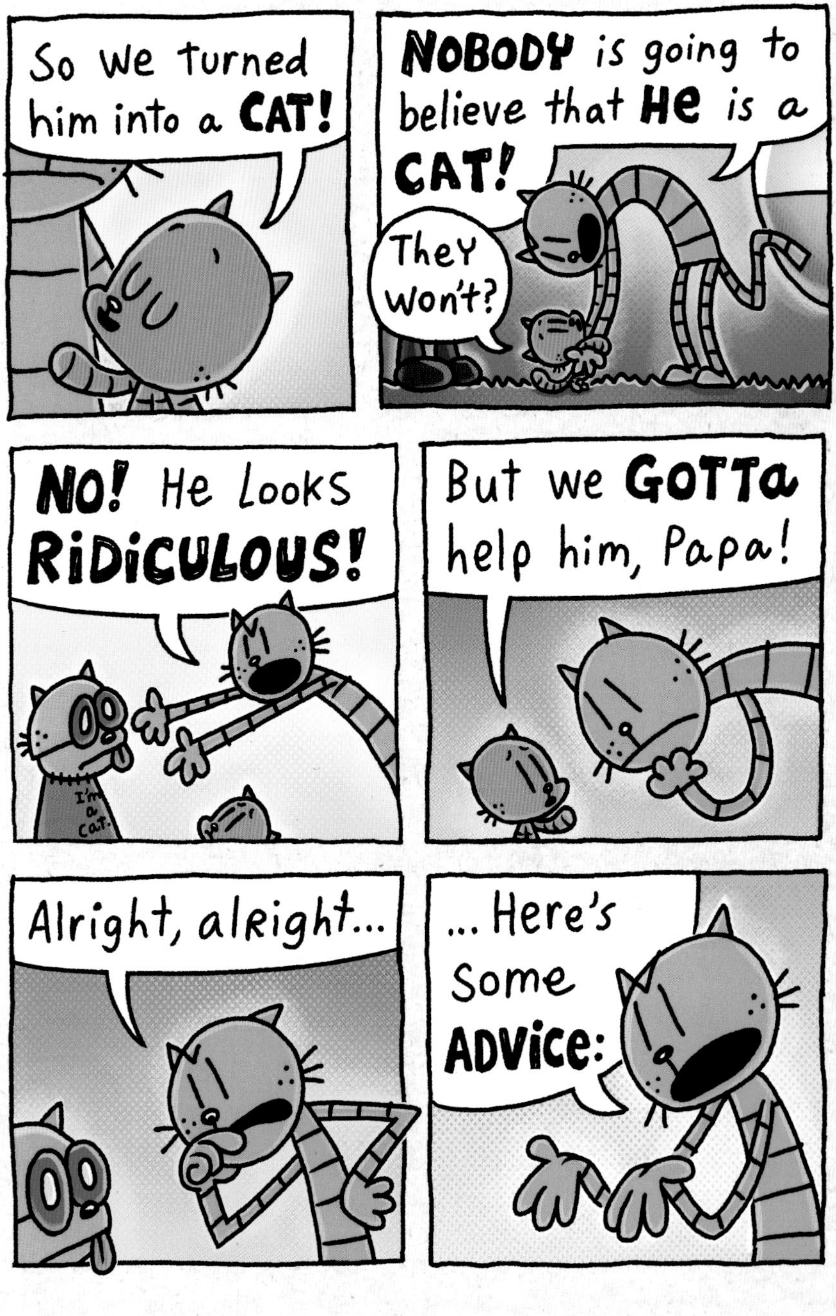
So we turned him into a CAT!
NOBODY is going to believe that HE is a CAT!
They won't?
NO! He looks RIDICULOUS!
I'm a cat.
But we GOTTA help him, Papa!
Alright, alright...
...Here's some ADVICE:

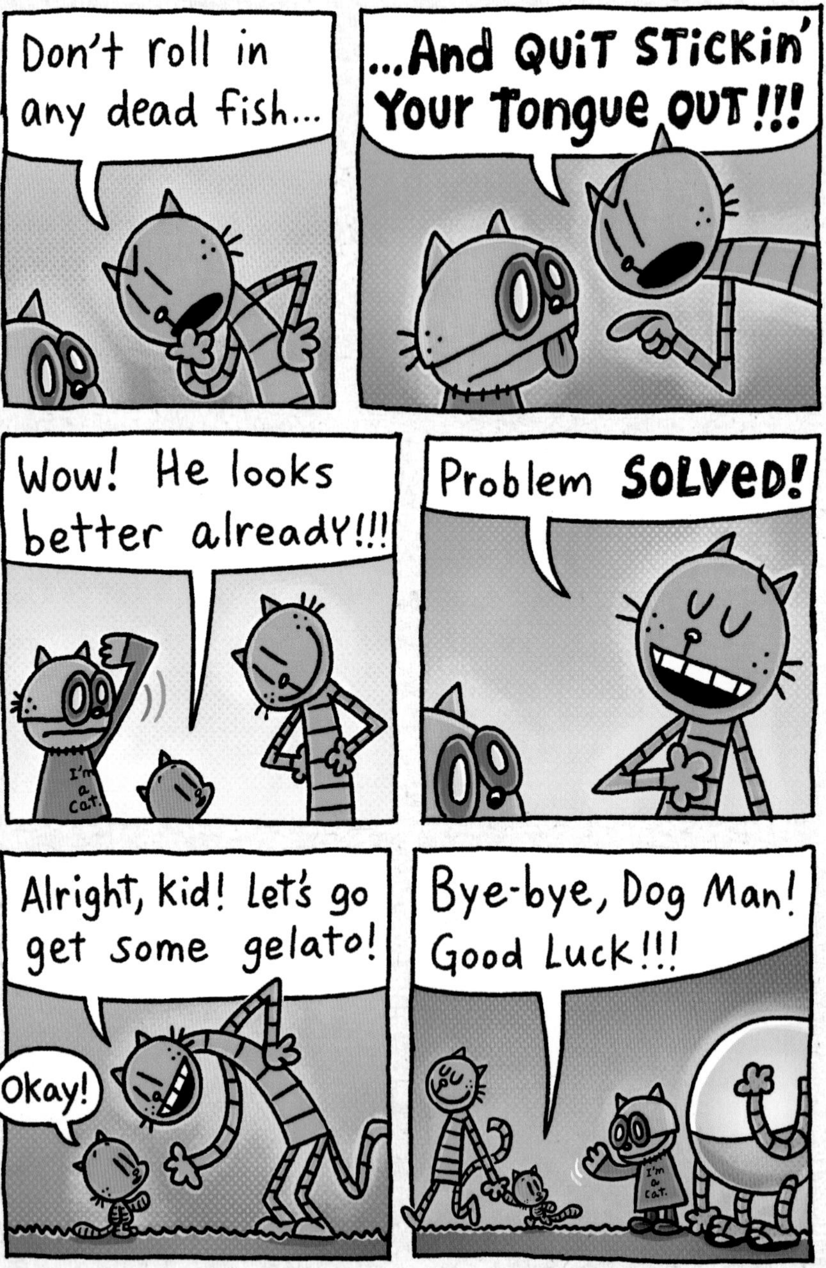

Don't roll in any dead fish...
...And QUIT STICKIN' YOUR TONGUE OUT!!!
Wow! He looks better already!!!
I'm a cat.
Problem SOLVED!
Alright, kid! Let's go get some gelato!
Okay!
Bye-bye, Dog Man! Good Luck!!!
I'm a cat.

CHAPTER 5

A Buncha Stuff That Happened Next

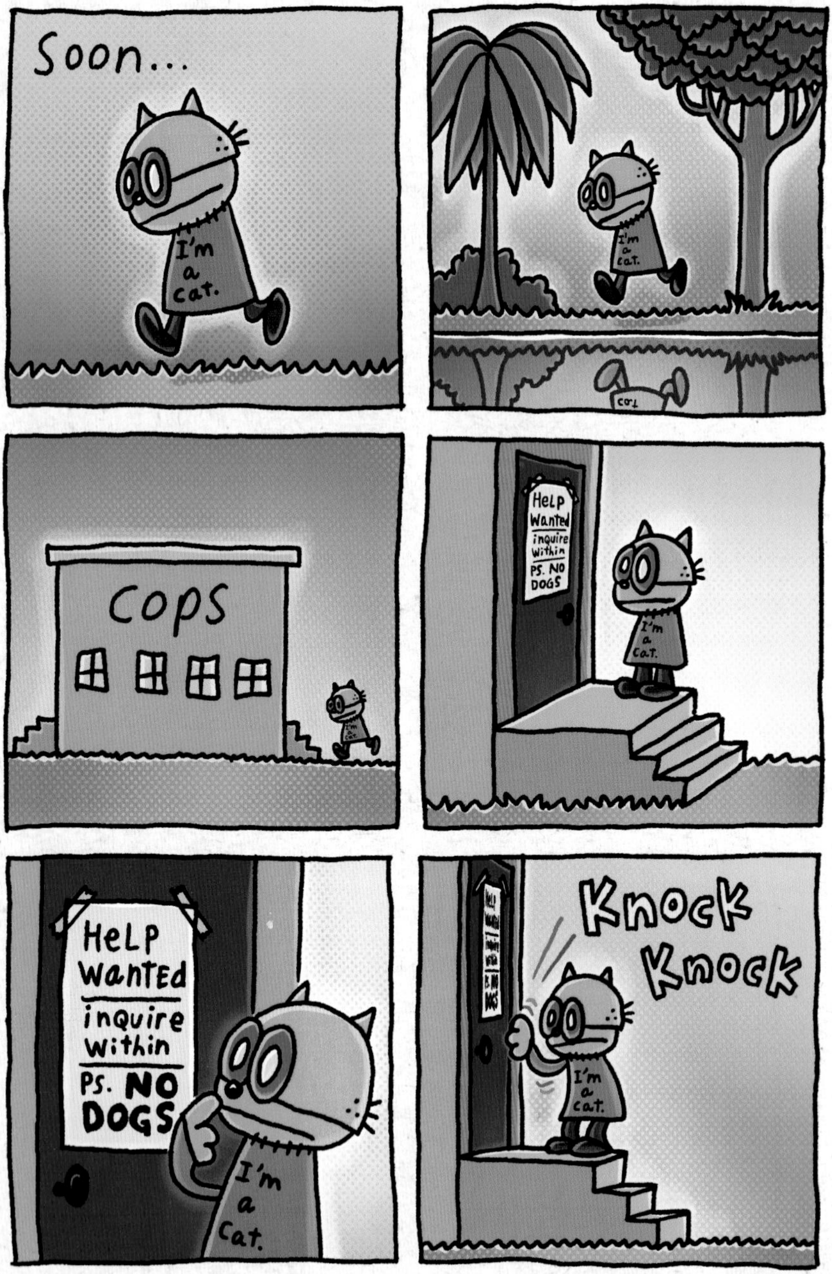
Soon...
I'm a cat.
I'm a cat.
cat
COPS
Help Wanted
inquire within
PS. NO DOGS
I'm a cat.
Help Wanted
inquire within
PS. NO DOGS
I'm a cat.
Knock Knock
I'm a cat.

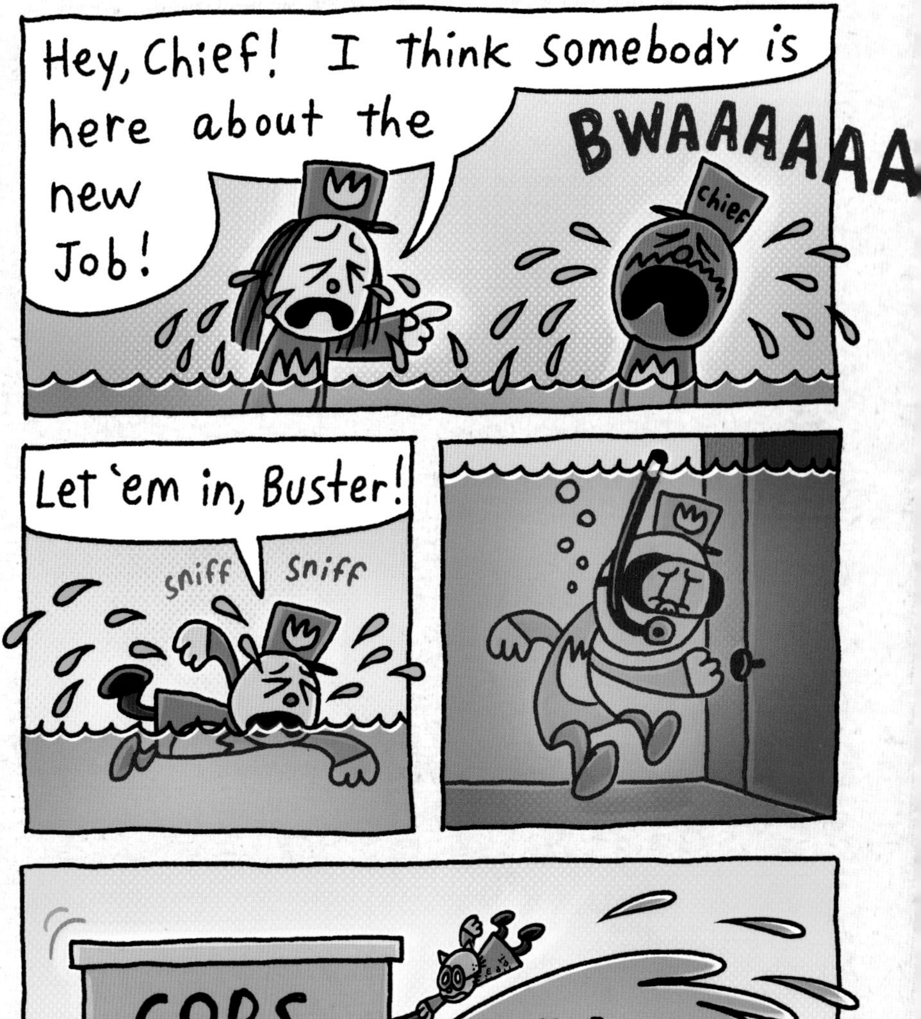

Hey, Chief! I think somebody is here about the new Job!
BWAAAAAA
Chief
Let 'em in, Buster!
sniff
sniff
COPS
SPLASH!!

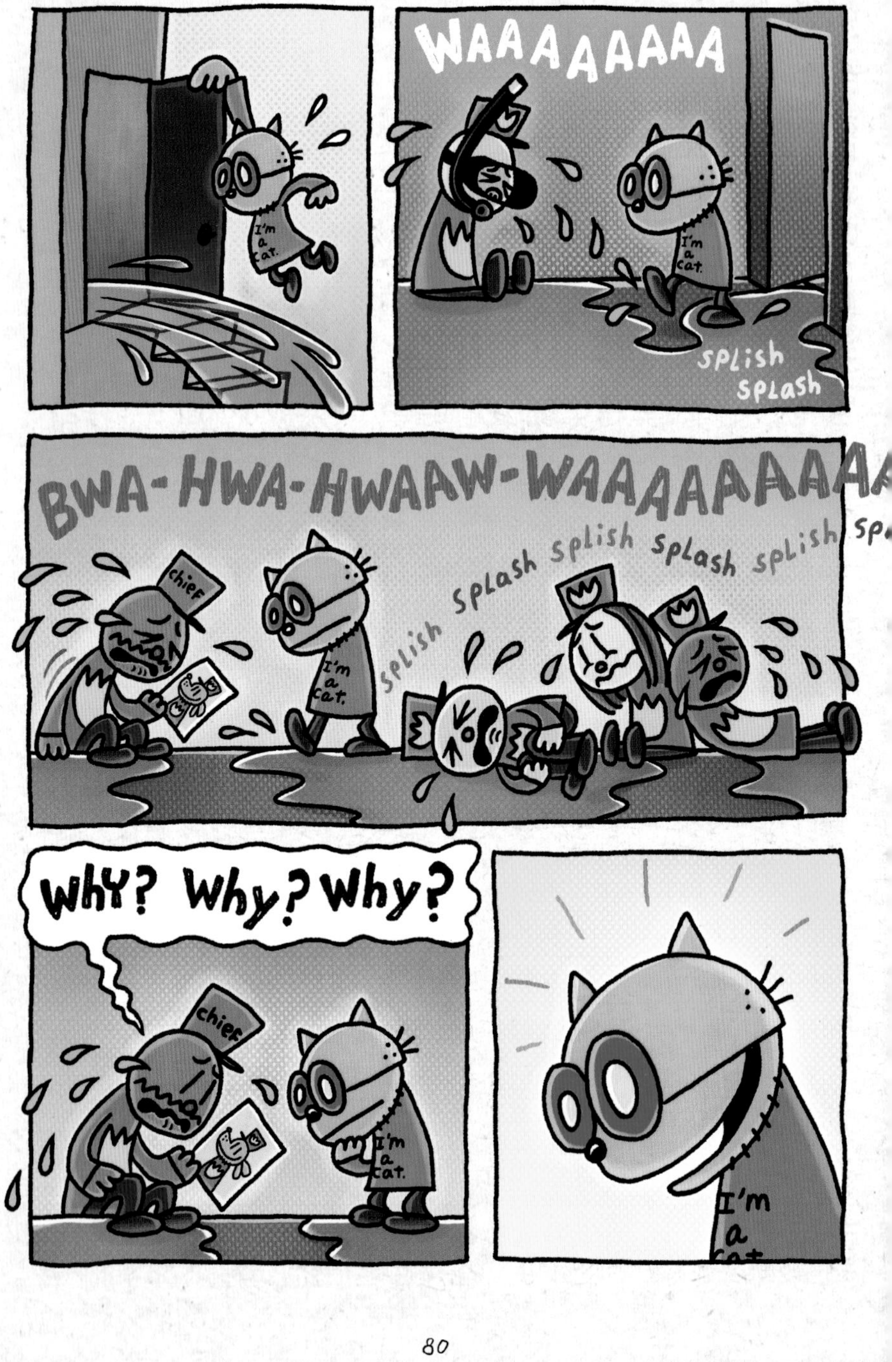
I'm a cat.
WAAAAAAAA
I'm a cat.
splish splash
BWA-HWA-HWAAW-WAAAAAAAA
chief
I'm a cat.
splish splash splish splash splish
WHY? Why? Why?
chief
I'm a cat.
I'm a

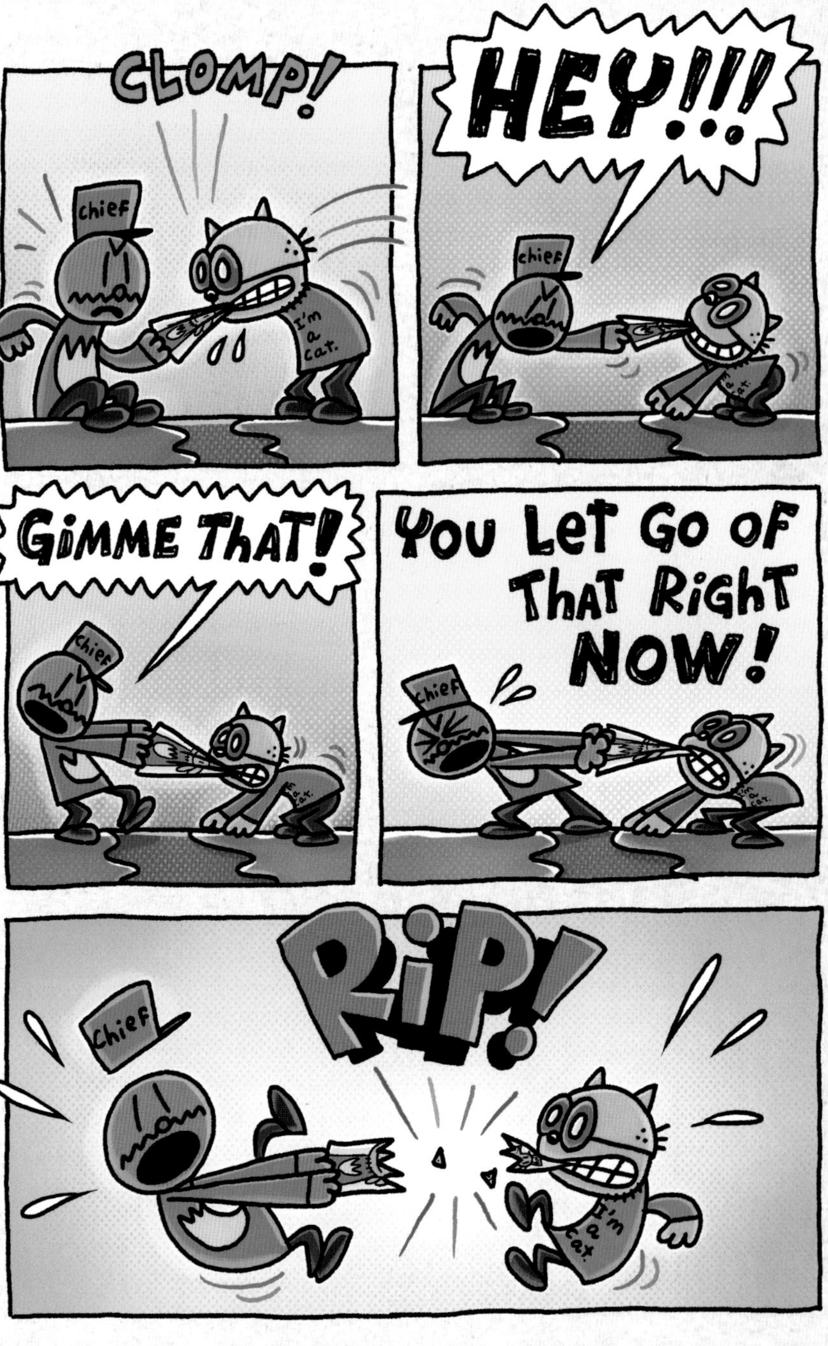
CLOMP!
chief
I'm a cat.
HEY!!!
GIMME THAT!
YOU LET GO OF THAT RIGHT NOW!
RIP!

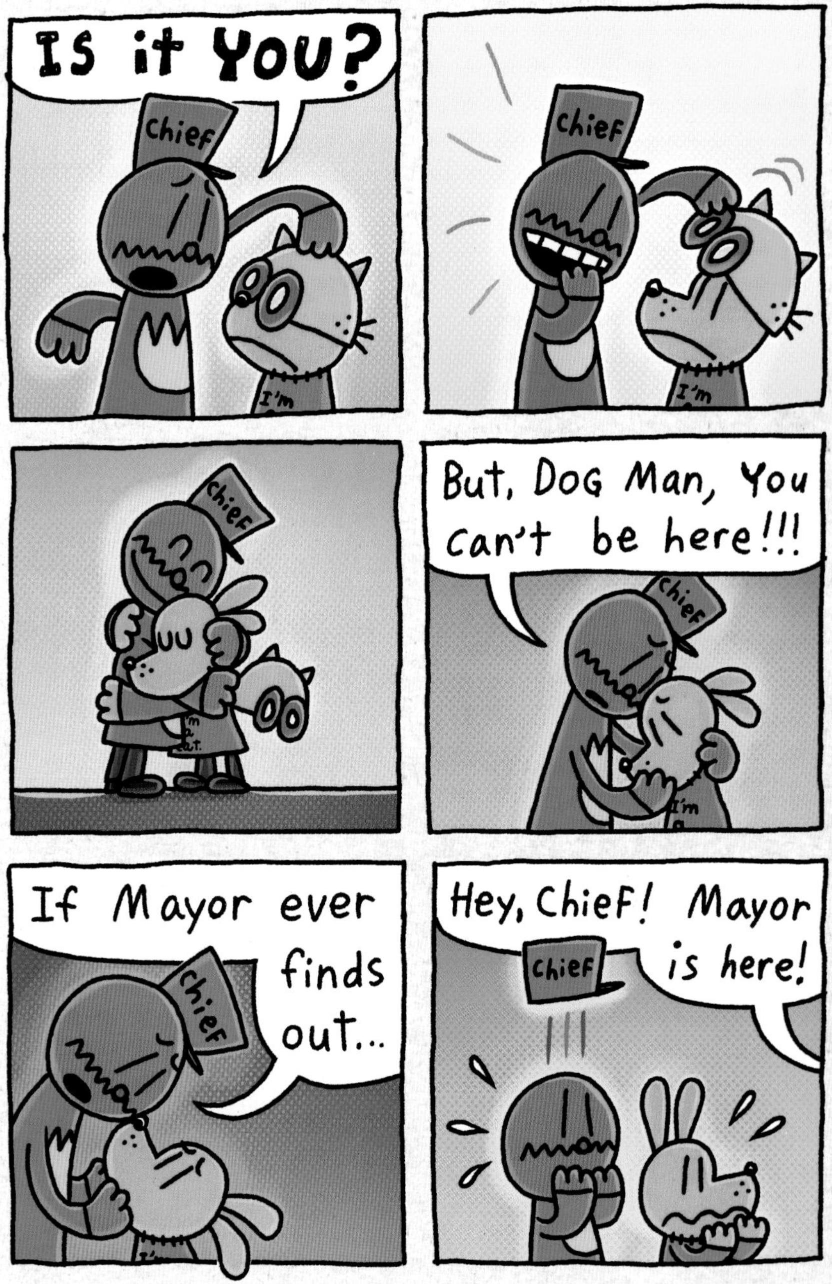
IS it YOU?
Chief
I'm
Chief
I'm
Chief
I'm a cat.
But, DOG Man, You can't be here!!!
Chief
I'm a
If Mayor ever finds out...
Chief
Hey, Chief! Mayor is here!
Chief

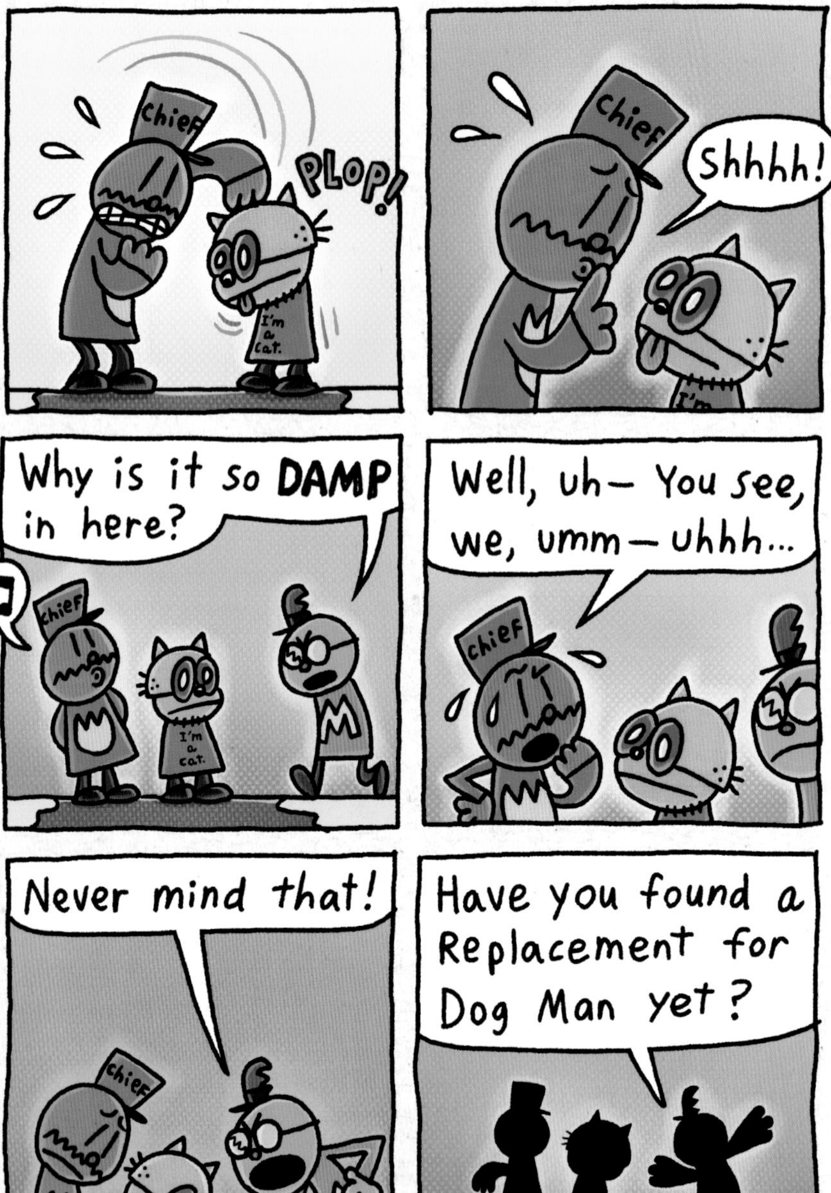
Chief
PLOP!
I'm a cat.
Chief
Shhhh!
Why is it so **DAMP** in here?
♫
Chief
I'm a cat.
Well, uh— You see, we, umm—uhhh...
Chief
Never mind that!
Chief
Have you found a Replacement for Dog Man yet?

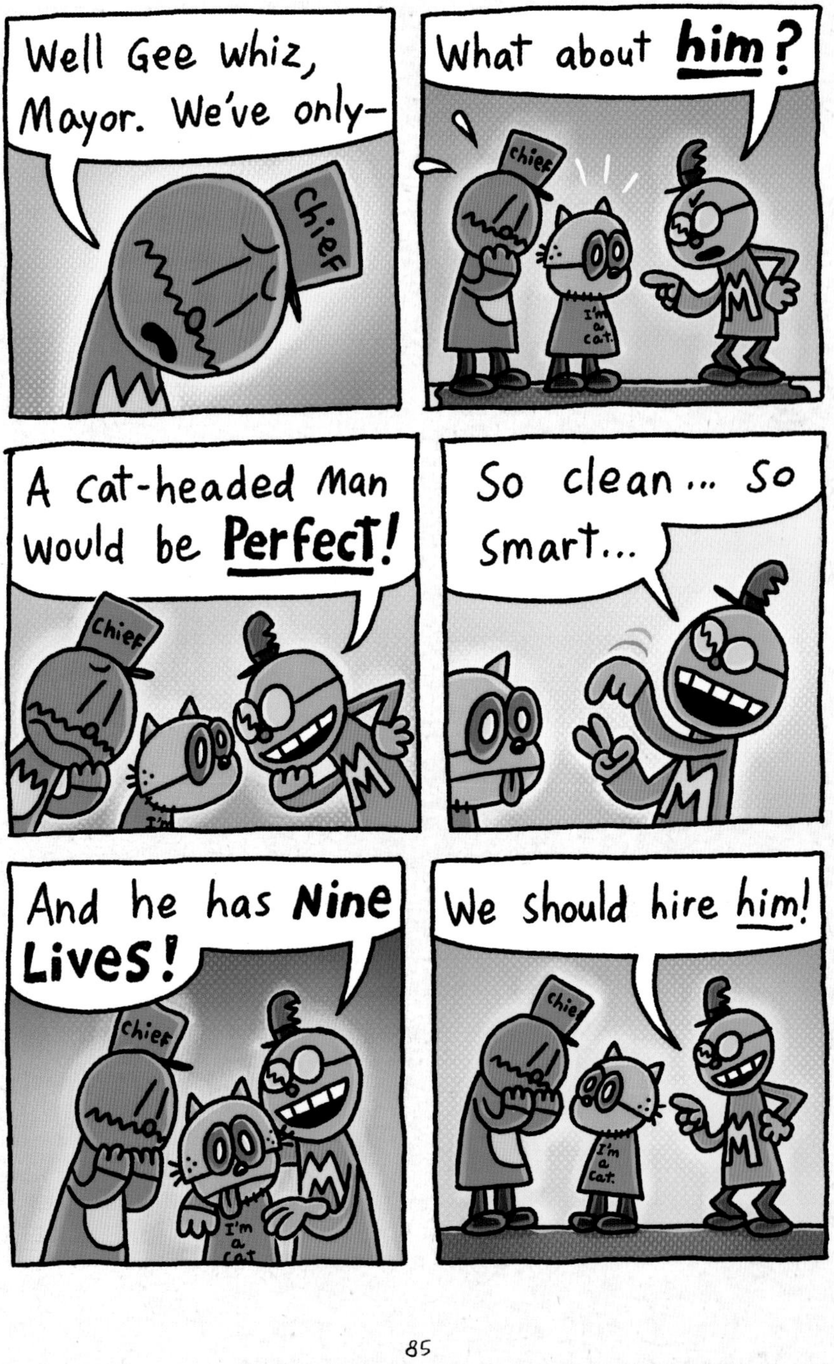
Well Gee whiz, Mayor. We've only—
chief
What about him?
chief
I'm a cat.
M
A cat-headed Man would be Perfect!
Chief
M
So clean... So Smart...
M
And he has Nine Lives!
Chief
M
We should hire him!
chief
I'm a cat.
M

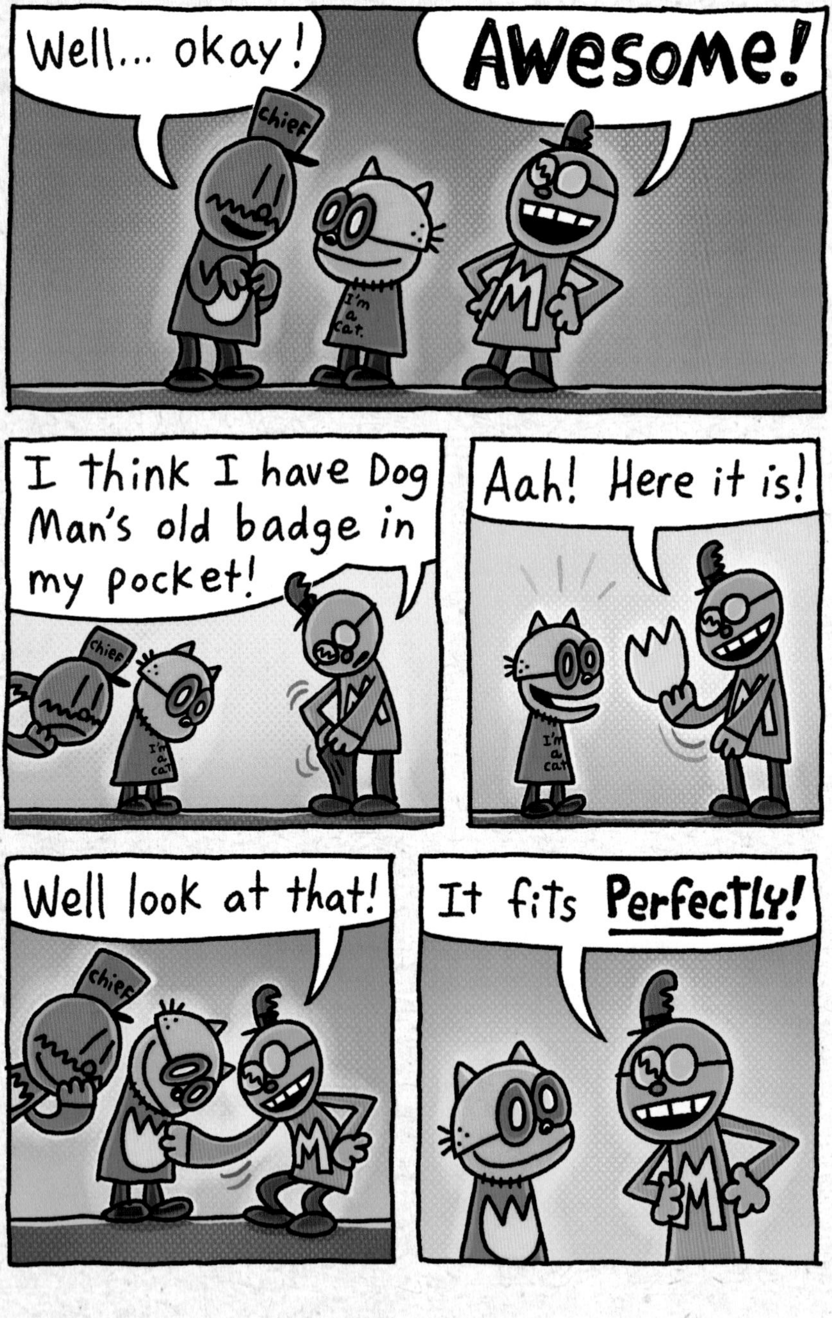
Well... okay!
AWESOME!
chief
I'm a cat.
I think I have Dog Man's old badge in my pocket!
Aah! Here it is!
Well look at that!
It fits PERFECTLY!

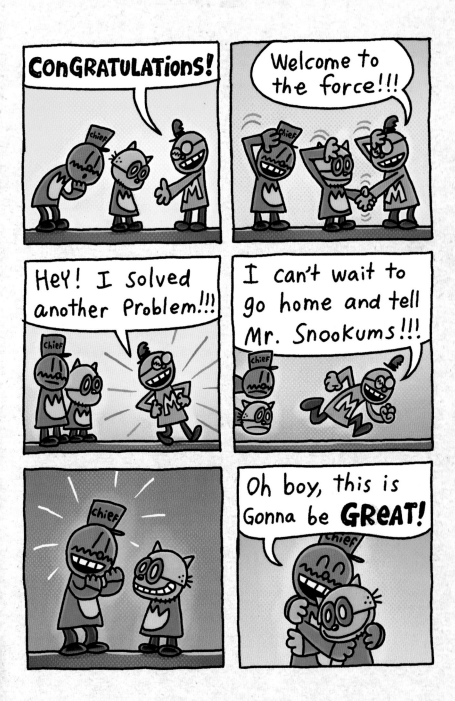

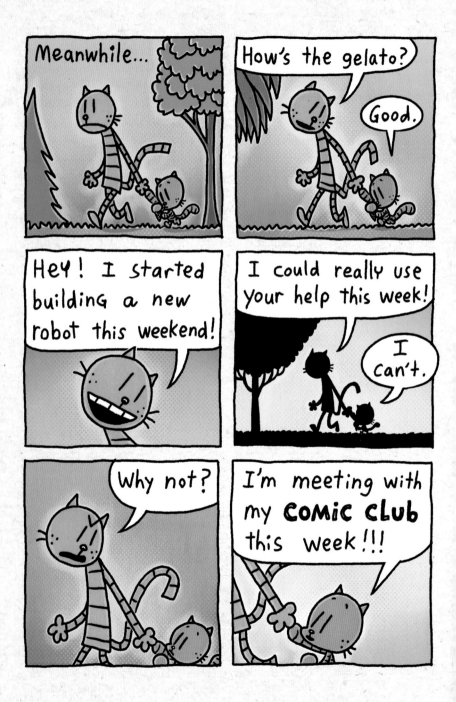

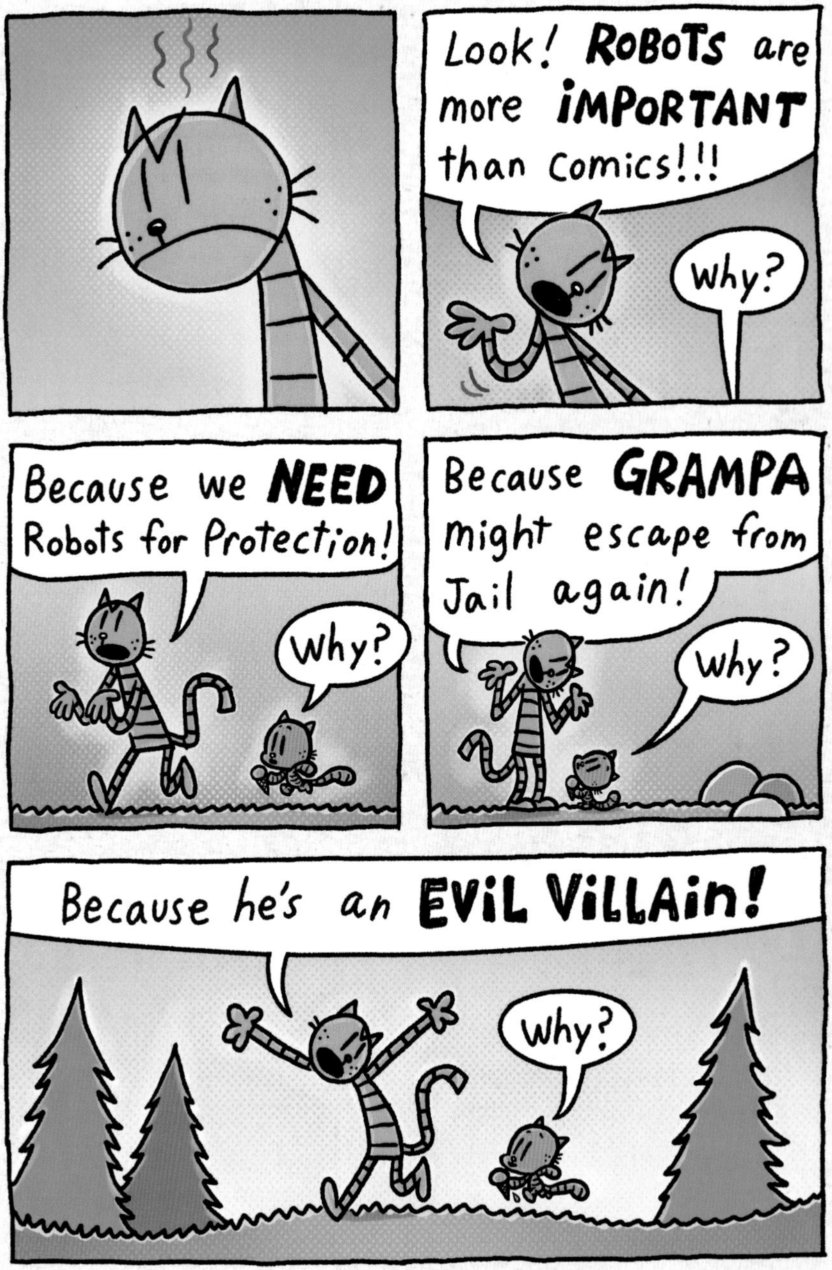
Look! ROBOTS are more IMPORTANT than comics!!!
Why?
Because we NEED Robots for Protection!
Why?
Because GRAMPA might escape from Jail again!
Why?
Because he's an EVIL VILLAIN!
Why?

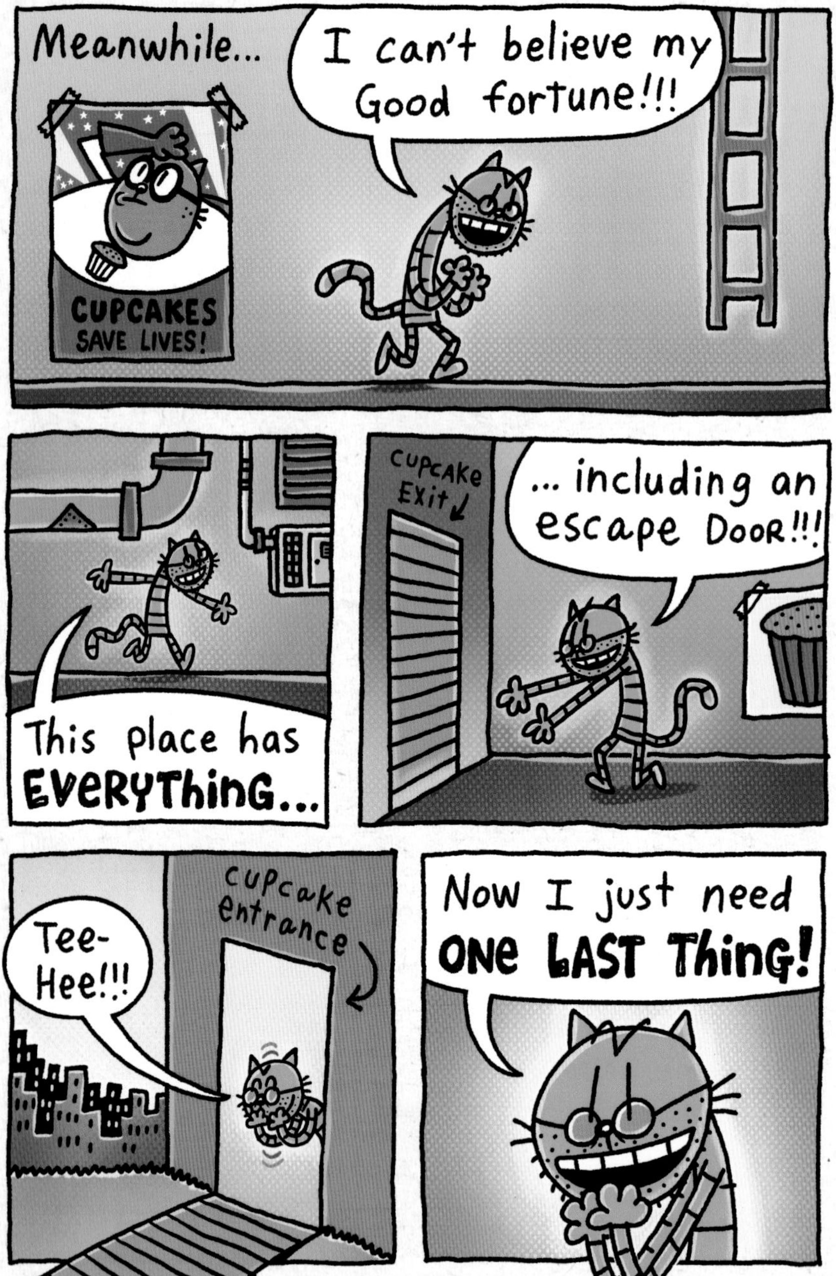
Meanwhile...
I can't believe my Good fortune!!!
CUPCAKES SAVE LIVES!
This place has EVERYThinG...
CUPCAKE EXIT
... including an escape DooR!!!
Tee-Hee!!!
cupcake entrance
Now I just need ONE LAST Thing!

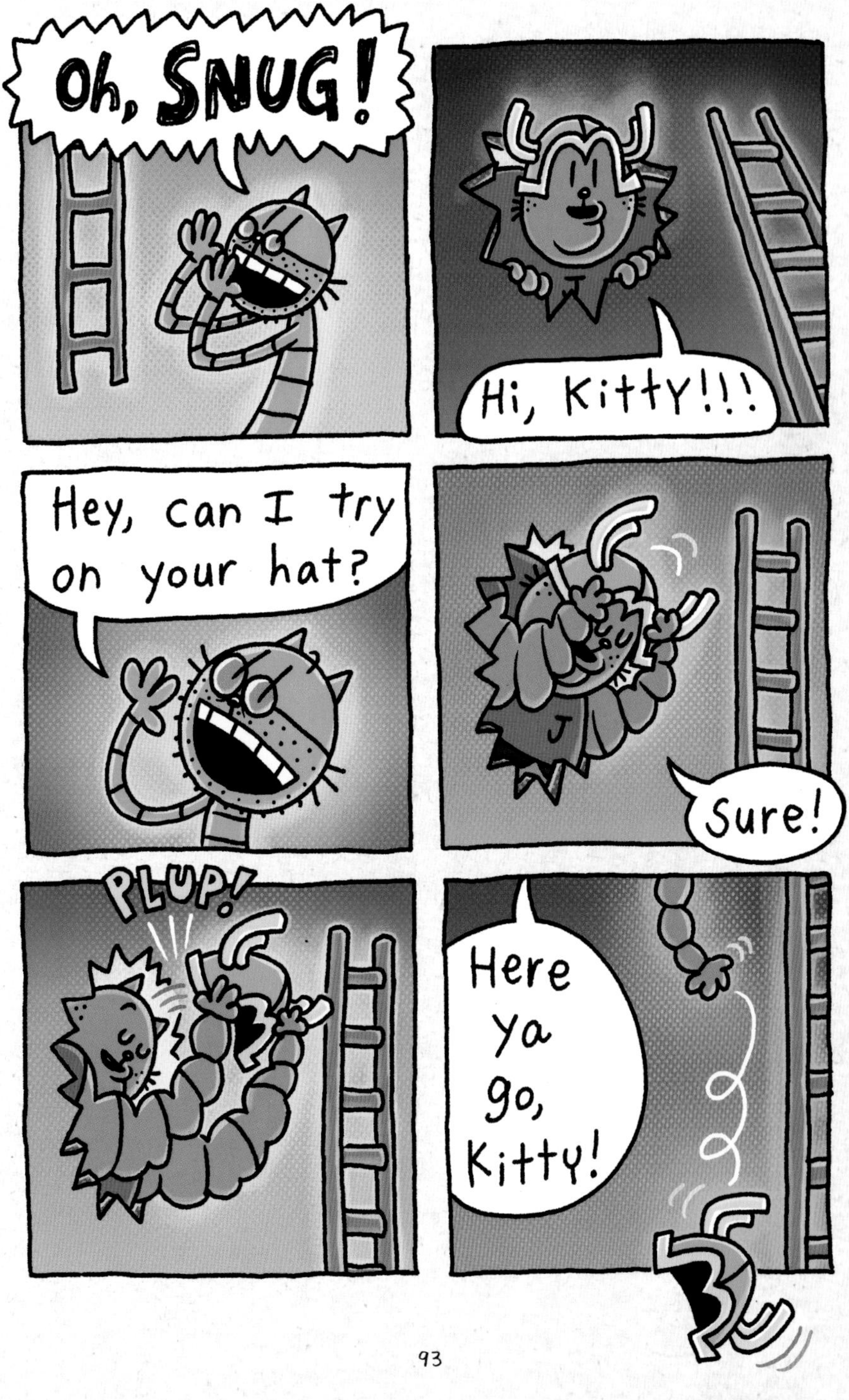
Oh, SNUG!
Hi, Kitty!!!
Hey, can I try on your hat?
Sure!
PLUP!
Here ya go, Kitty!

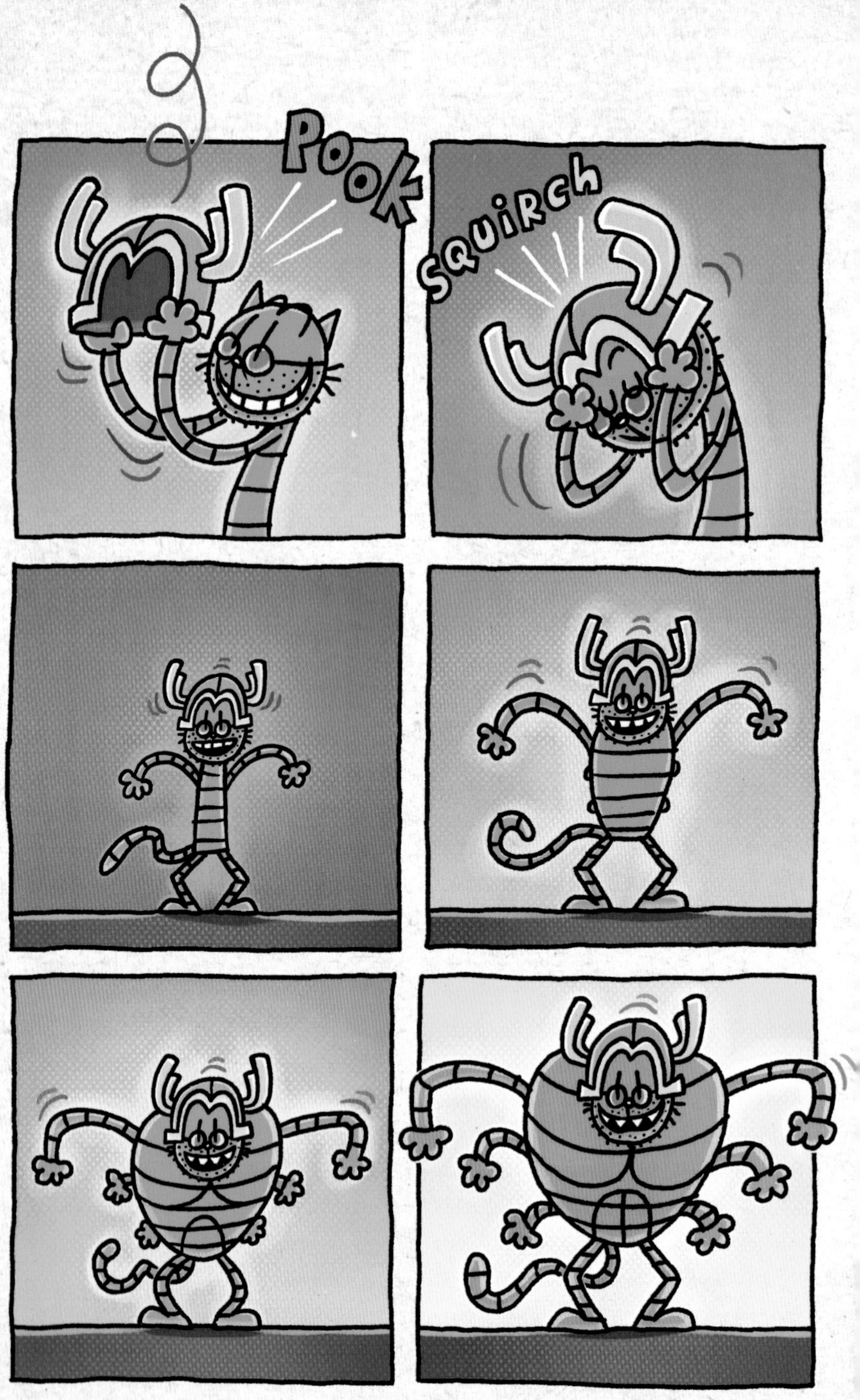
POOK
SQUIRCH

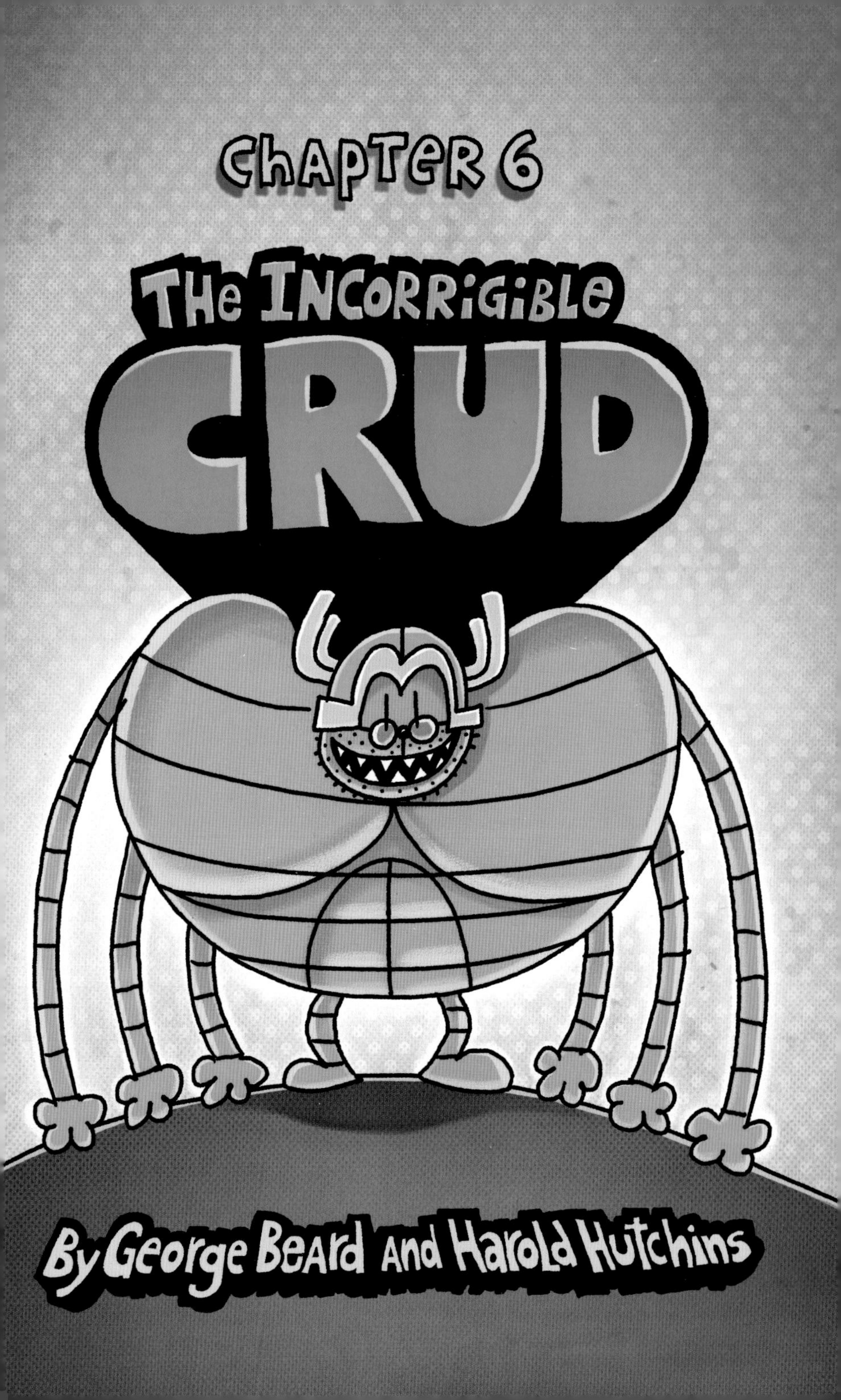
Chapter 6
The Incorrigible
CRUD
By George Beard and Harold Hutchins

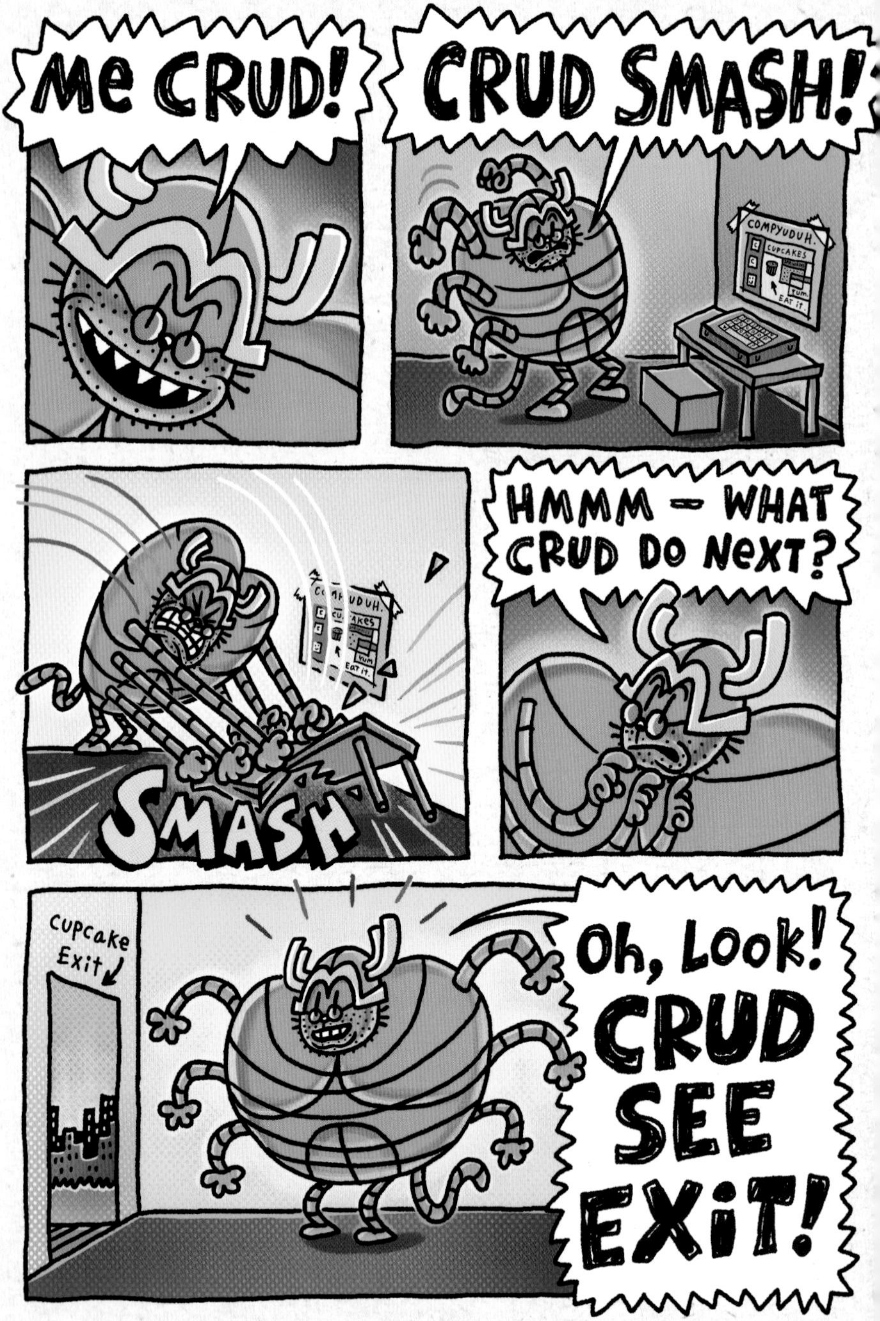
Me CRUD!
CRUD SMASH!
COMPYUDUH.
CUPCAKES
YUM.
EAT IT.
SMASH
HMMM — WHAT CRUD DO NeXT?
CUPCake Exit
Oh, Look! CRUD SEE EXiT!

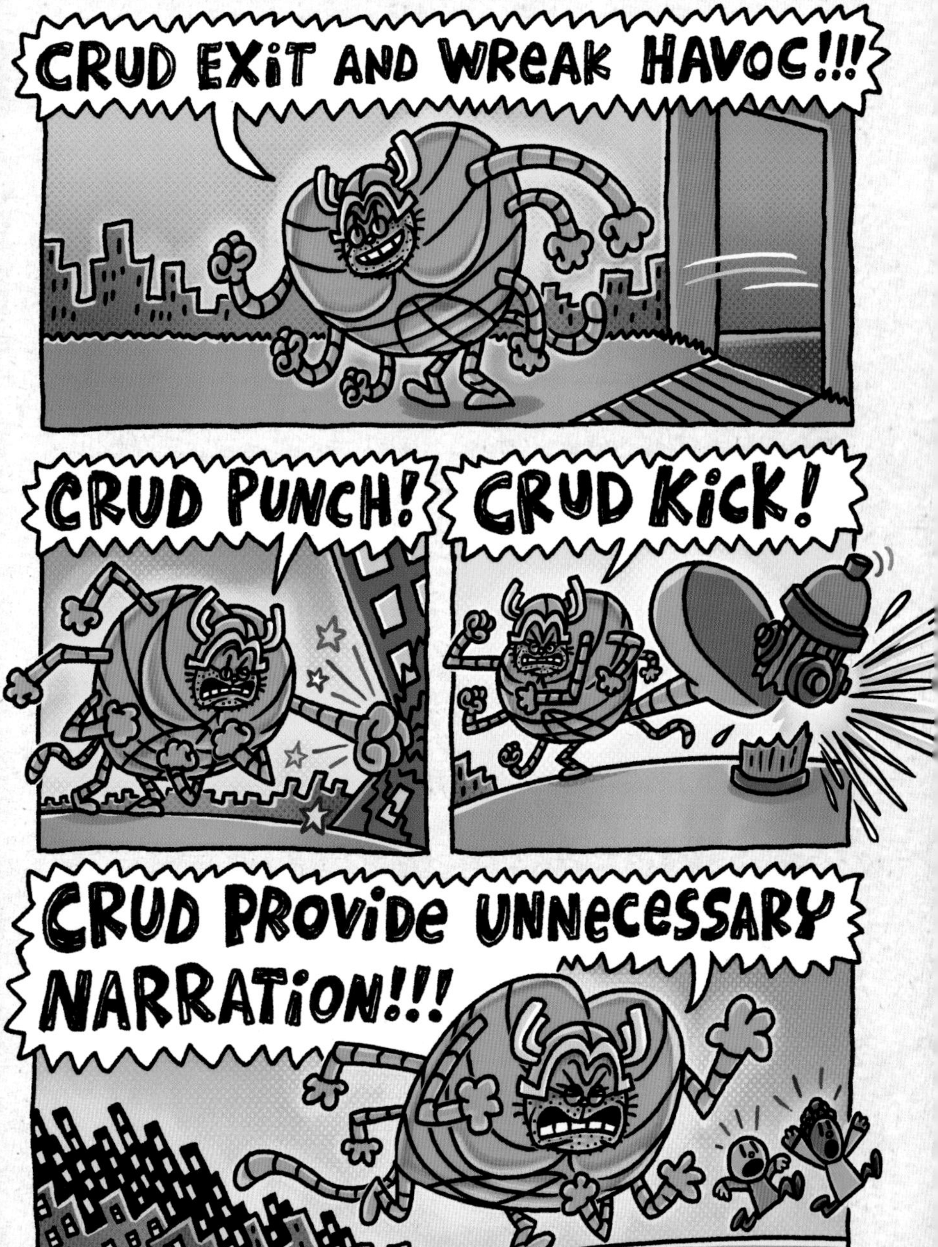
CRUD EXIT AND WREAK HAVOC!!!
CRUD PUNCH!
CRUD KICK!
CRUD PROVIDE UNNECESSARY NARRATION!!!

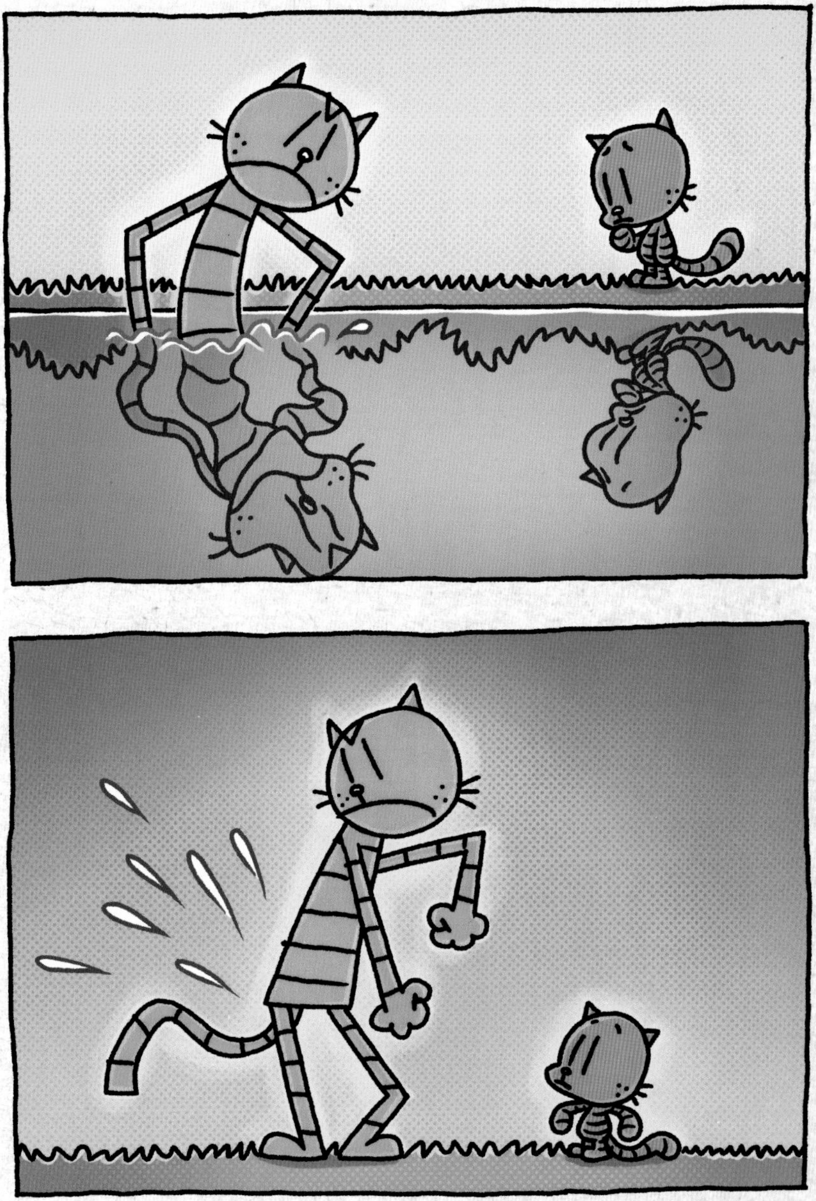

Right Thumb here.

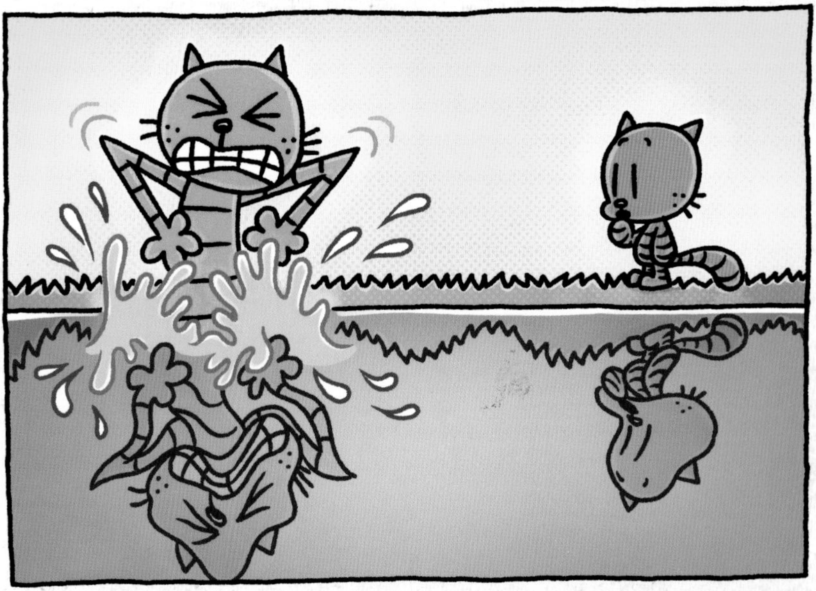

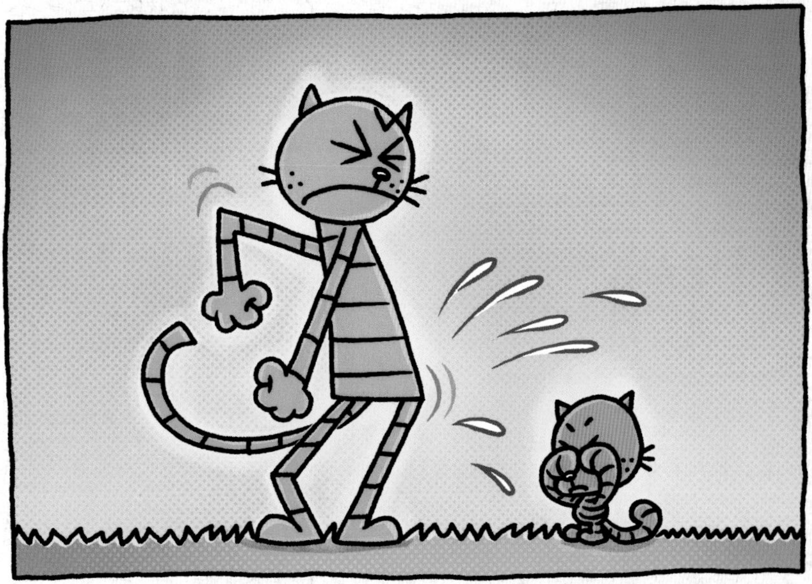

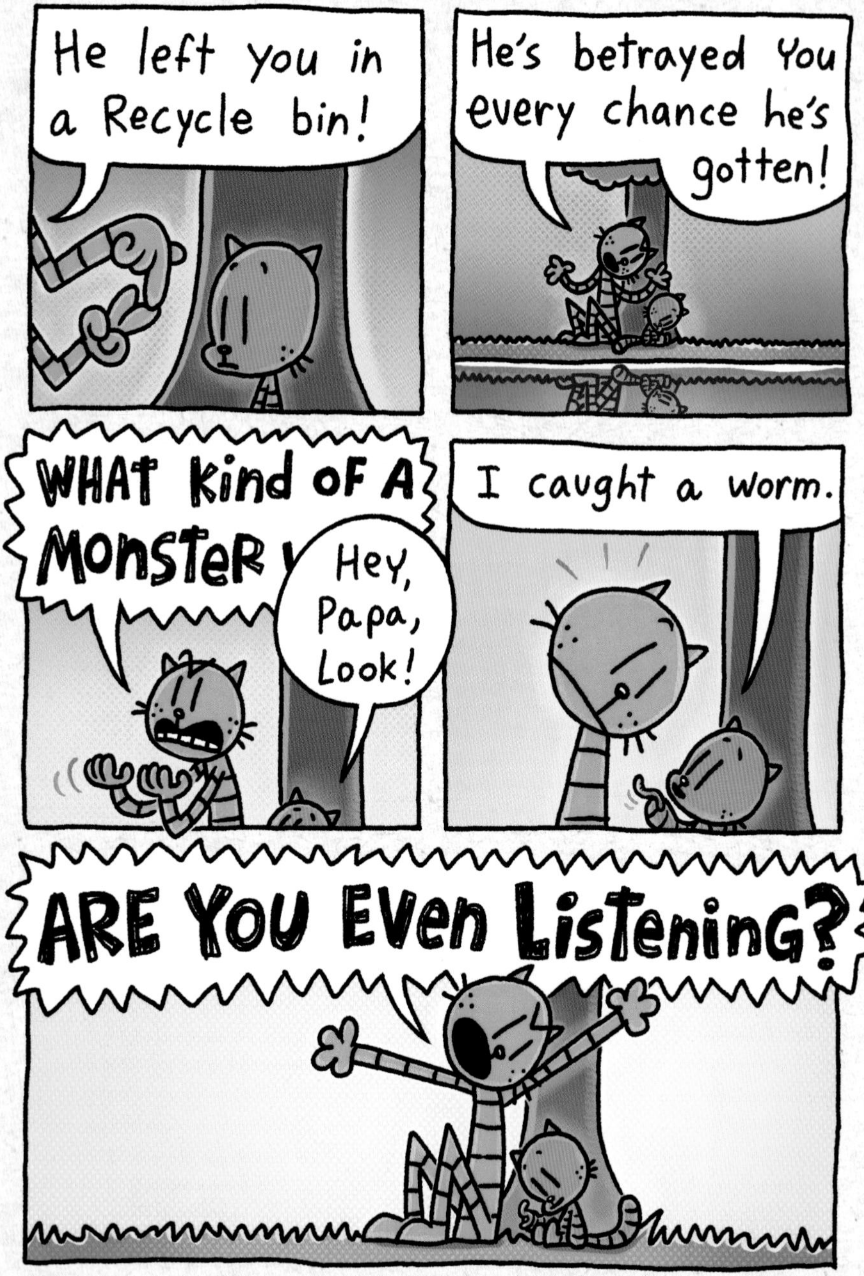
He left you in a Recycle bin!
He's betrayed You every chance he's gotten!
WHAT Kind OF A MONSTER
Hey, Papa, Look!
I caught a worm.
ARE YOU EVen LisTeninG?

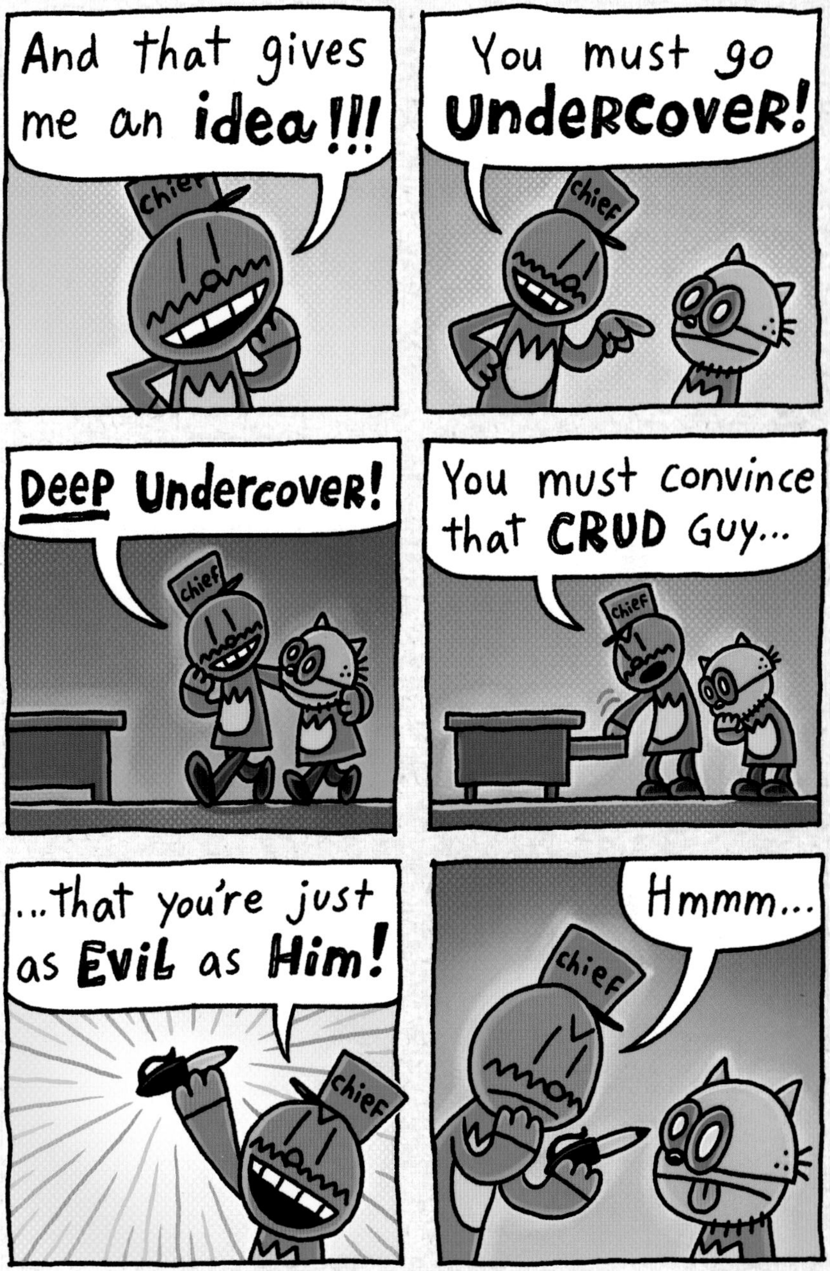

And that gives me an idea!!!
chief
You must go UNDERCOVER!
chief
DEEP Undercover!
chief
You must convince that CRUD Guy...
chief
...that you're just as EVIL as Him!
chief
Hmmm...
chief

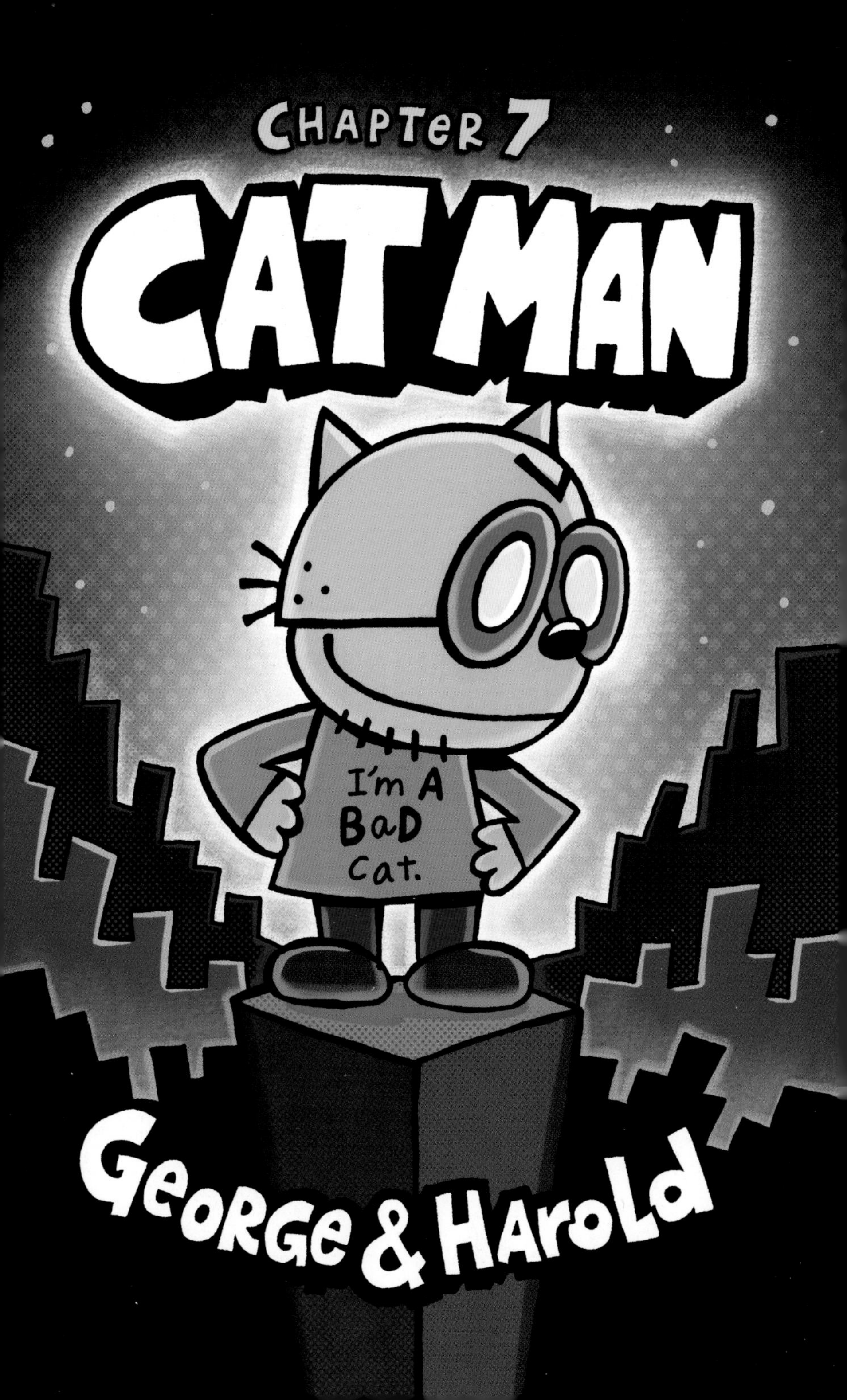
CHAPTER 7
CAT MAN
I'm A BaD cat.
George & Harold

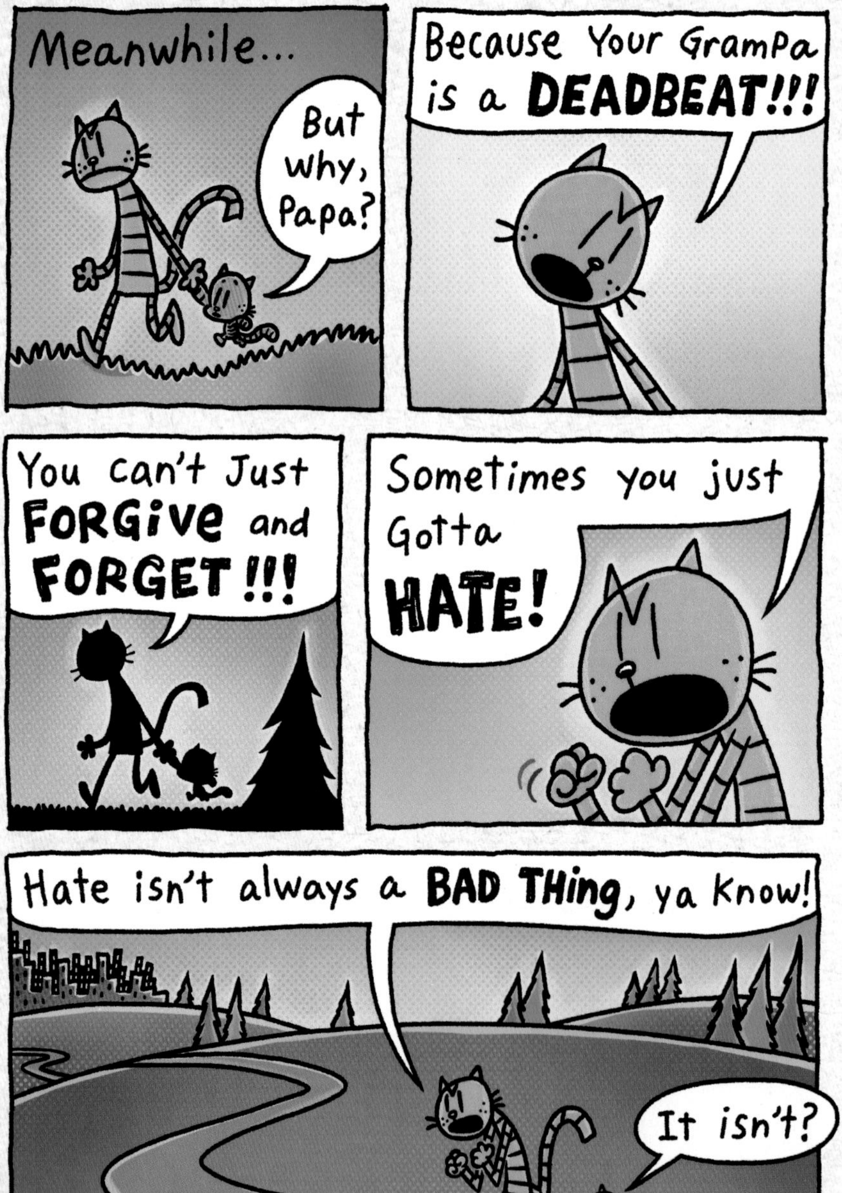
Meanwhile...
But why, Papa?
Because Your Grampa is a DEADBEAT!!!
You can't Just FORGiVe and FORGET!!!
Sometimes you just Gotta HATE!
Hate isn't always a BAD THiNg, ya Know!
It isn't?

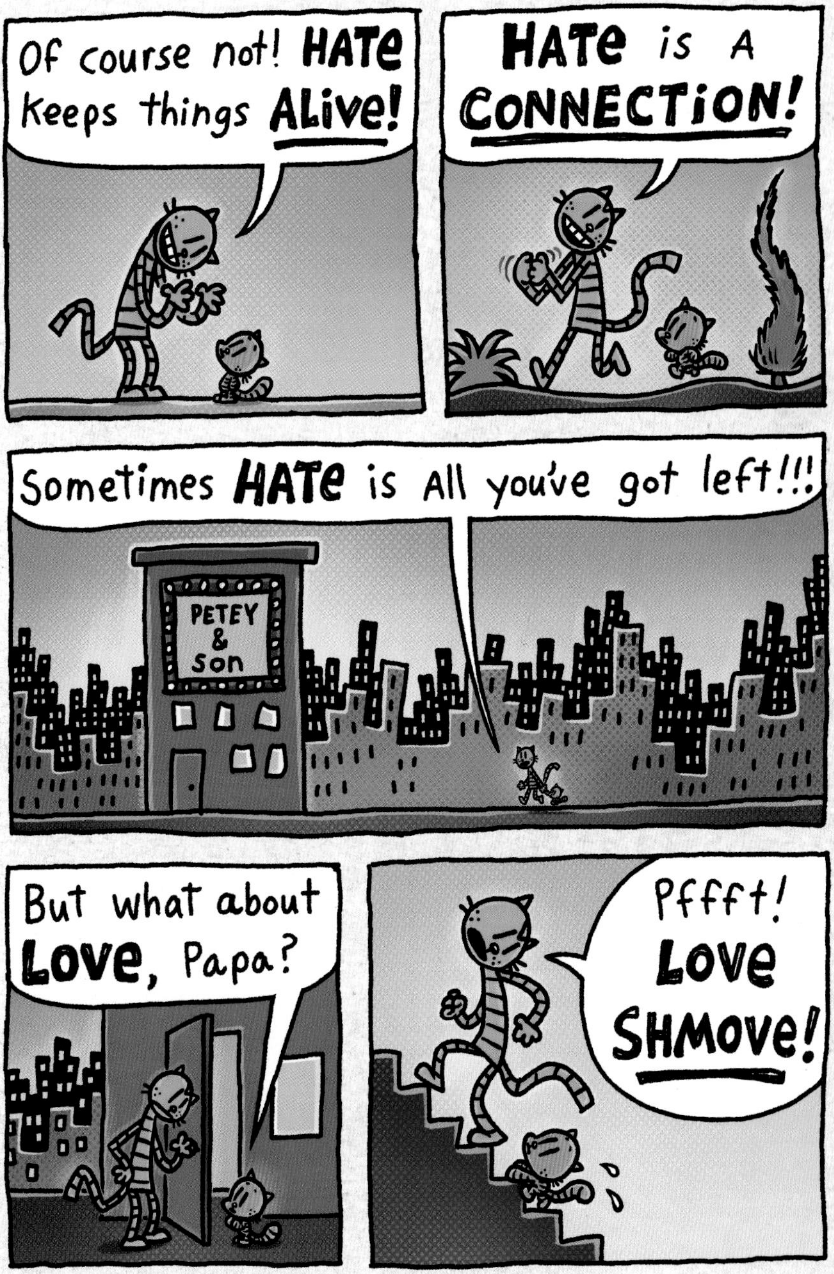
Of course not! HATE Keeps things ALive!
HATE is A CONNECTiON!
Sometimes HATE is All you've got left!!!
PETEY & Son
But what about Love, Papa?
Pffft! Love SHMOVe!

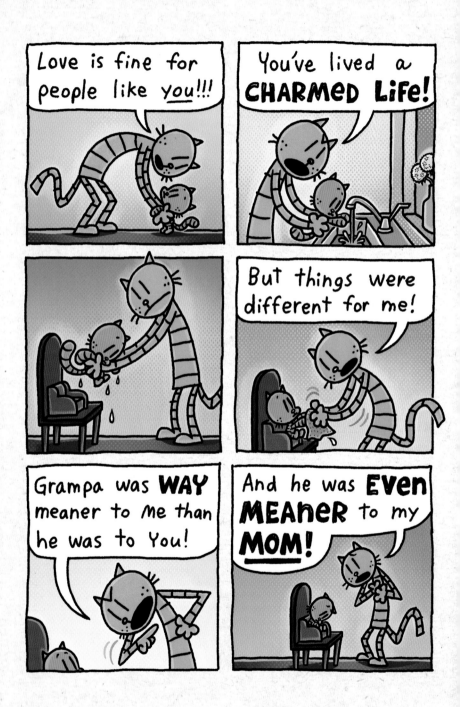

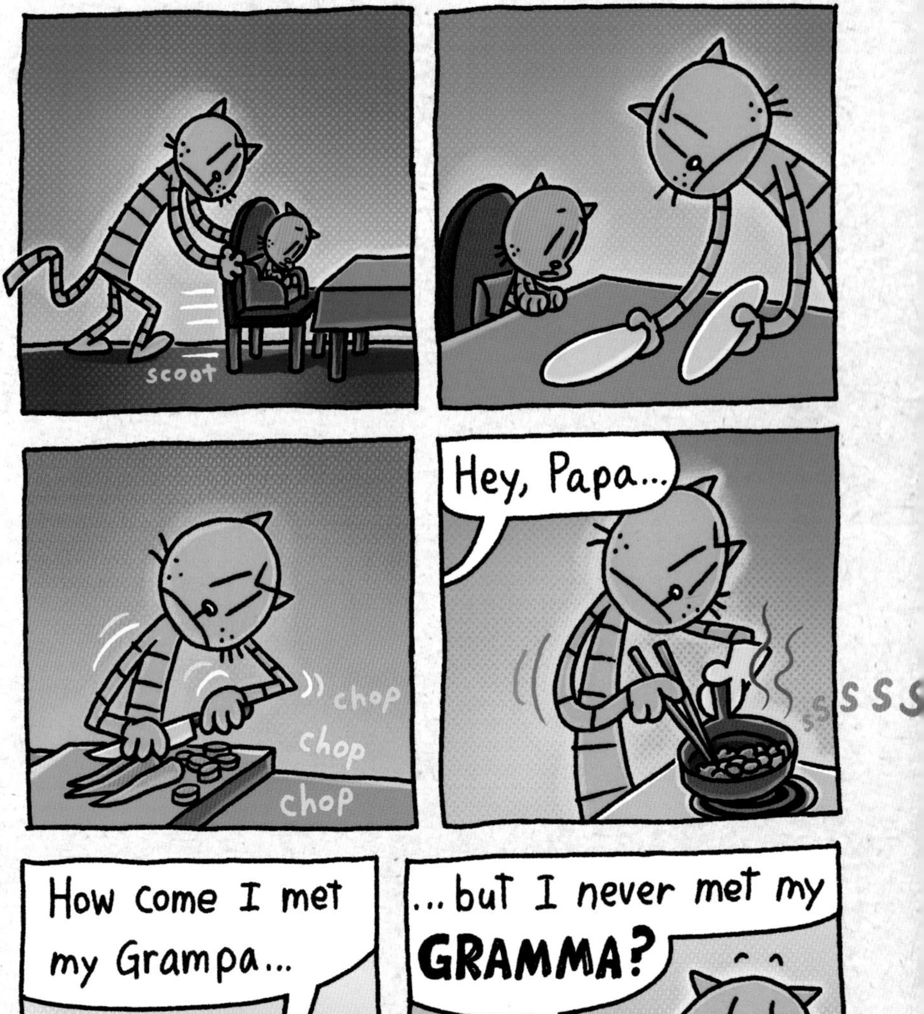
scoot
Hey, Papa...
chop
chop
chop
ssss
How come I met my Grampa...
...but I never met my GRAMMA?

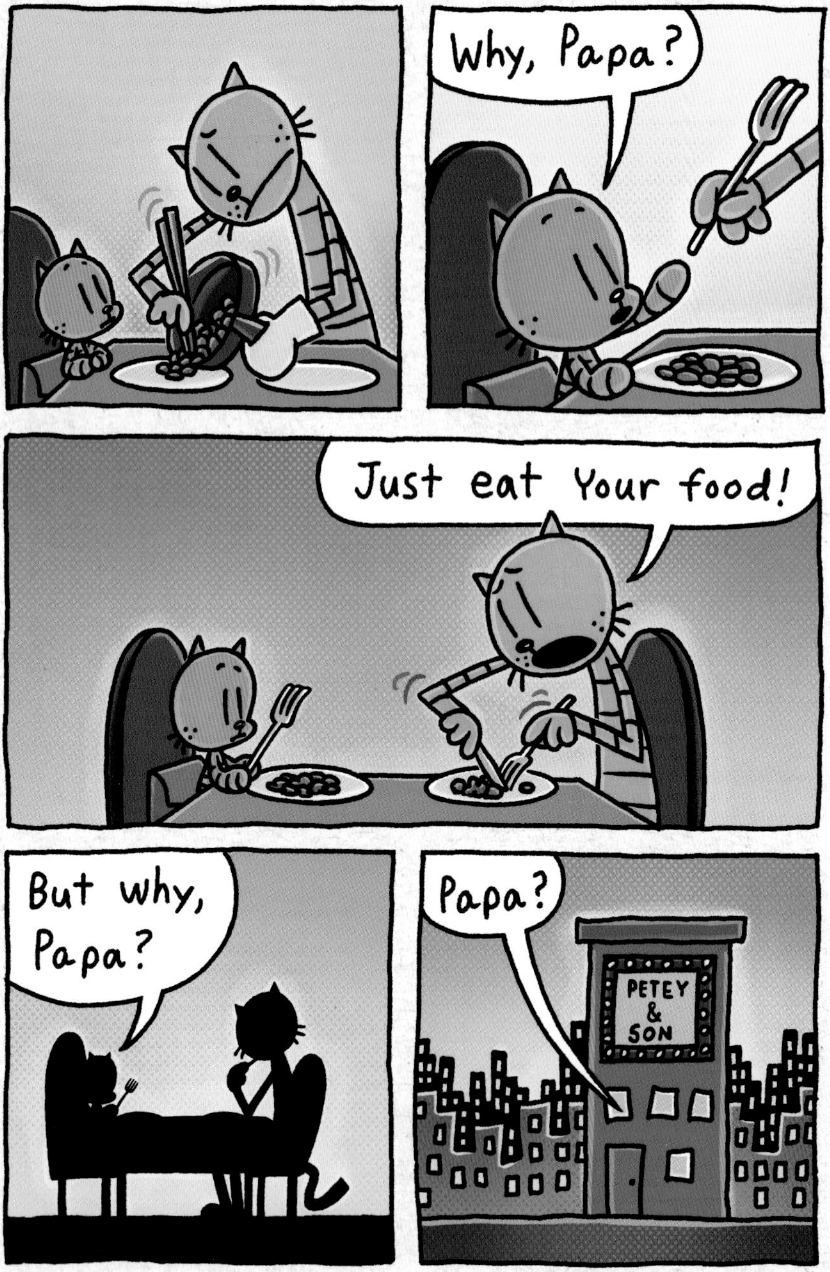
Why, Papa?
Just eat your food!
But why, Papa?
Papa?
PETEY & SON

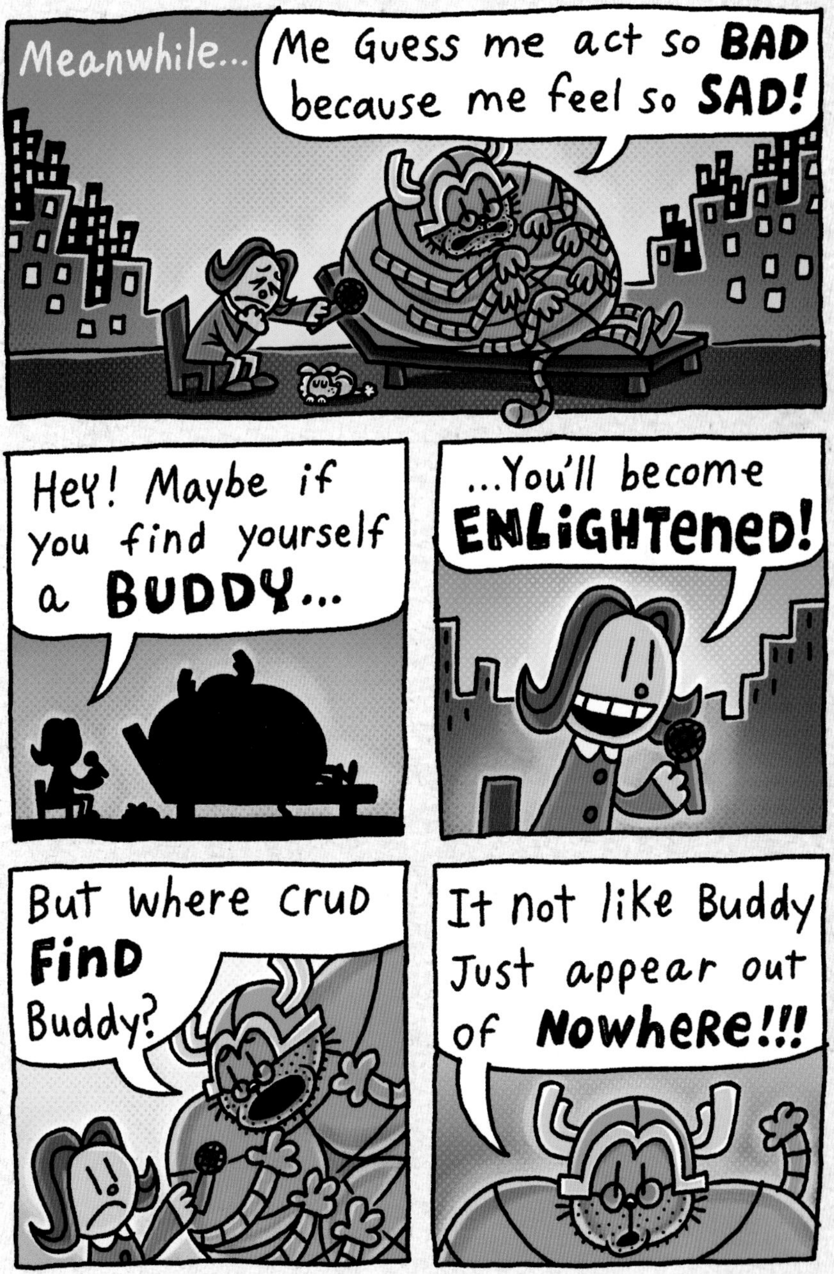
Meanwhile...
Me Guess me act so BAD because me feel so SAD!
Hey! Maybe if you find yourself a BUDDY...
...You'll become ENLIGHTENED!
But where CRUD FIND Buddy?
It not like Buddy Just appear out of NOWHERE!!!

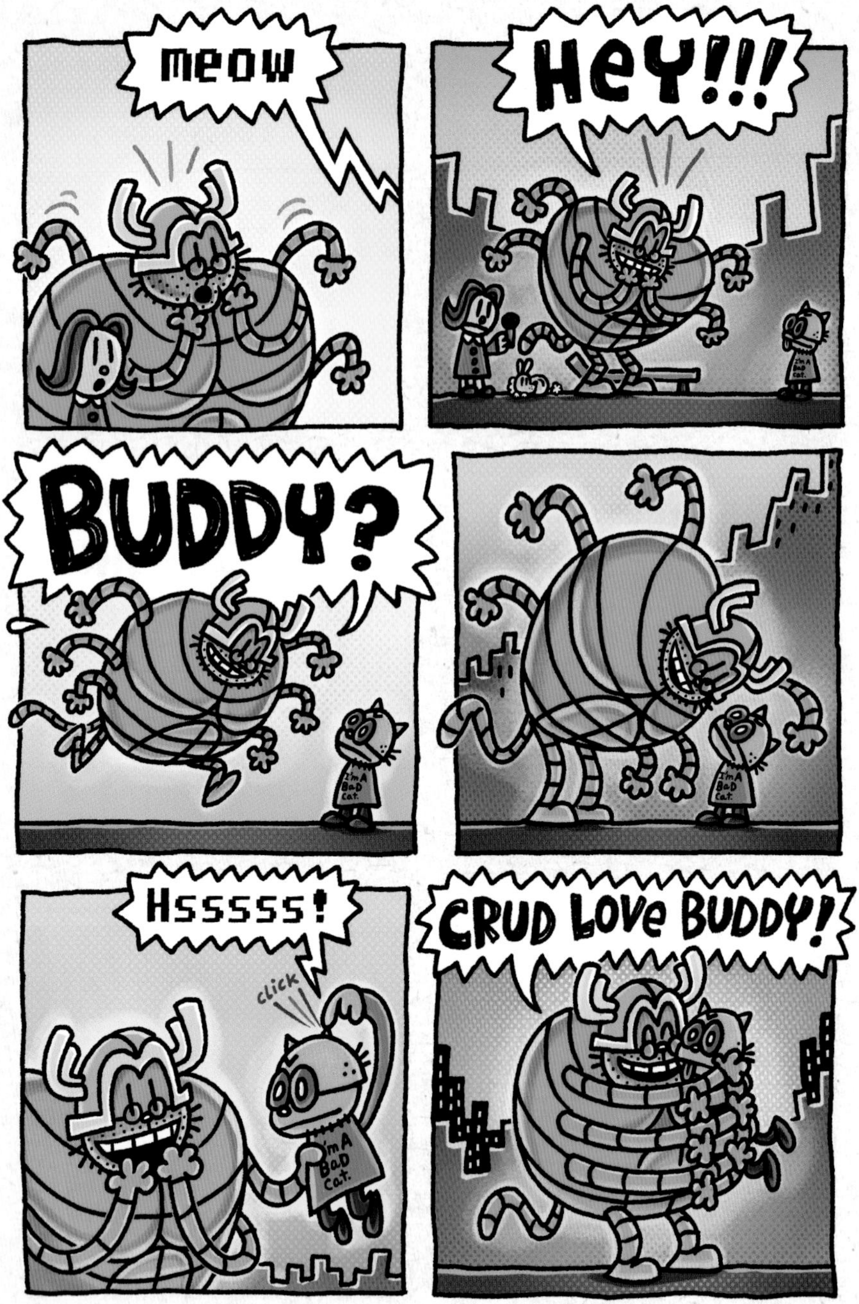
meow
HEY!!!
I'm A BaD cat.
BUDDY?
I'm A BaD cat.
I'm A BaD cat.
Hsssss!
click
I'm A BaD cat.
CRUD LOVE BUDDY!

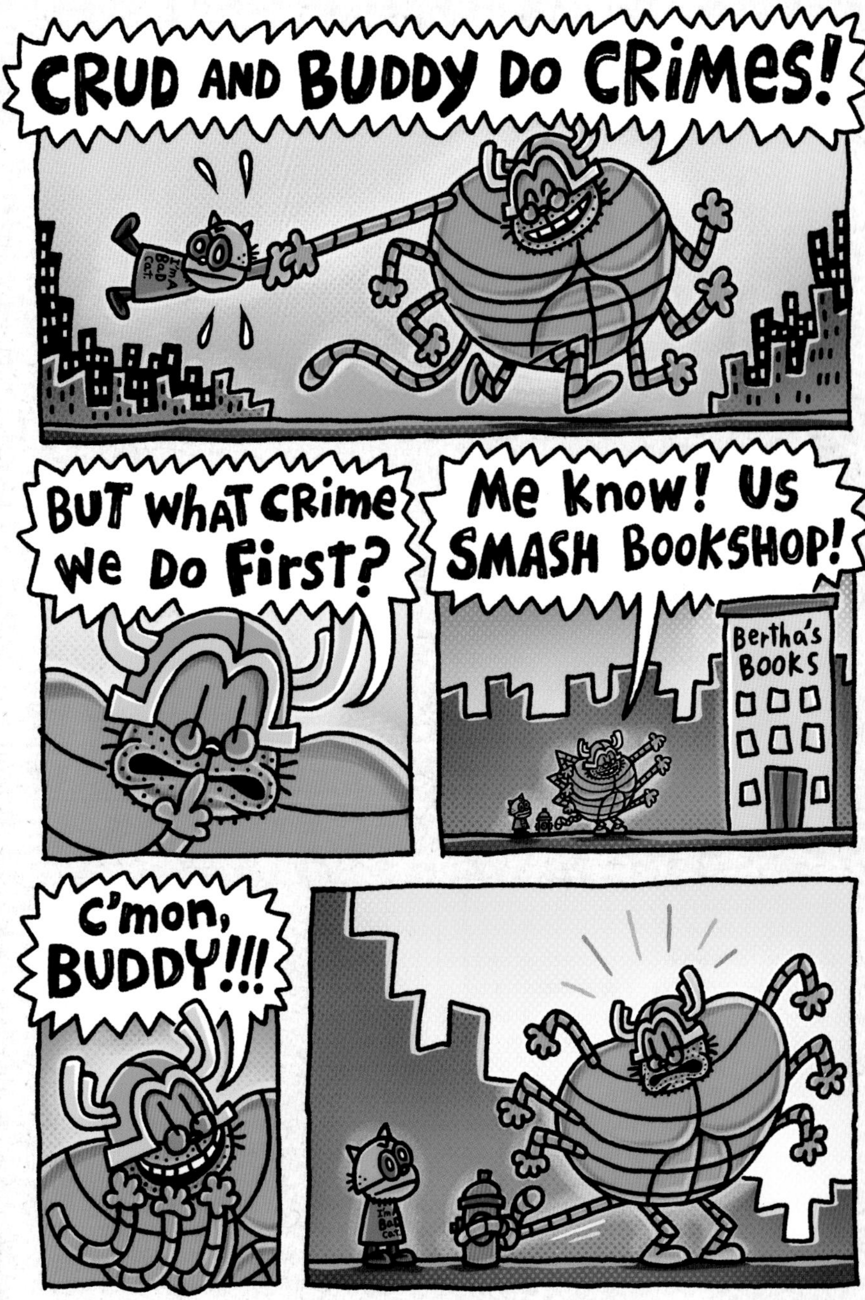
CRUD AND BUDDY DO CRIMES!
I'm A Bad Cat.
BUT WHAT CRIME WE DO FIRST?
Me Know! US SMASH BOOKSHOP!
Bertha's BOOKS
C'mon, BUDDY!!!
I'm A Bad Cat.

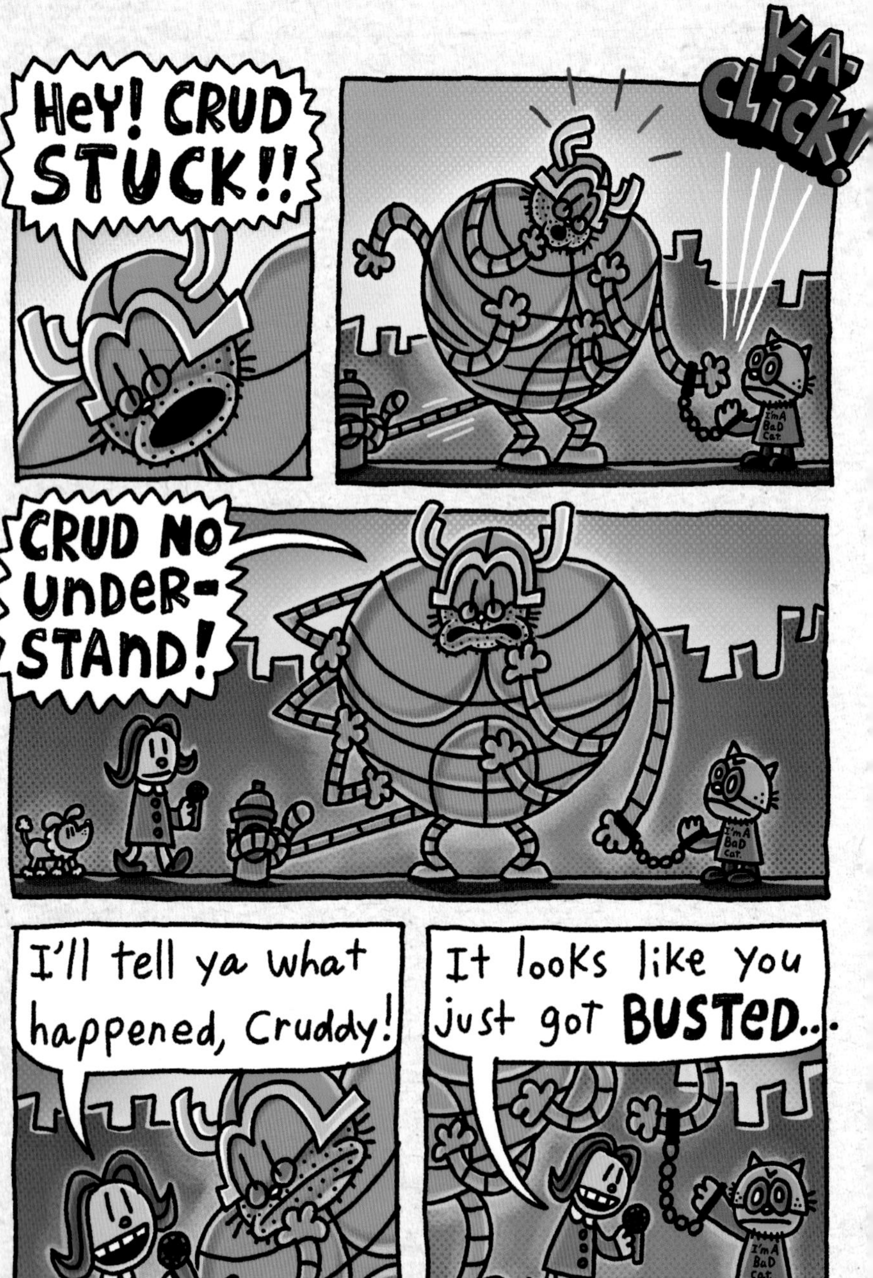
HEY! CRUD STUCK!!
KA-CLICK!
CRUD NO UNDER-STAND!
I'M A BAD CAT.
I'll tell ya what happened, Cruddy!
It looks like you just got BUSTED...

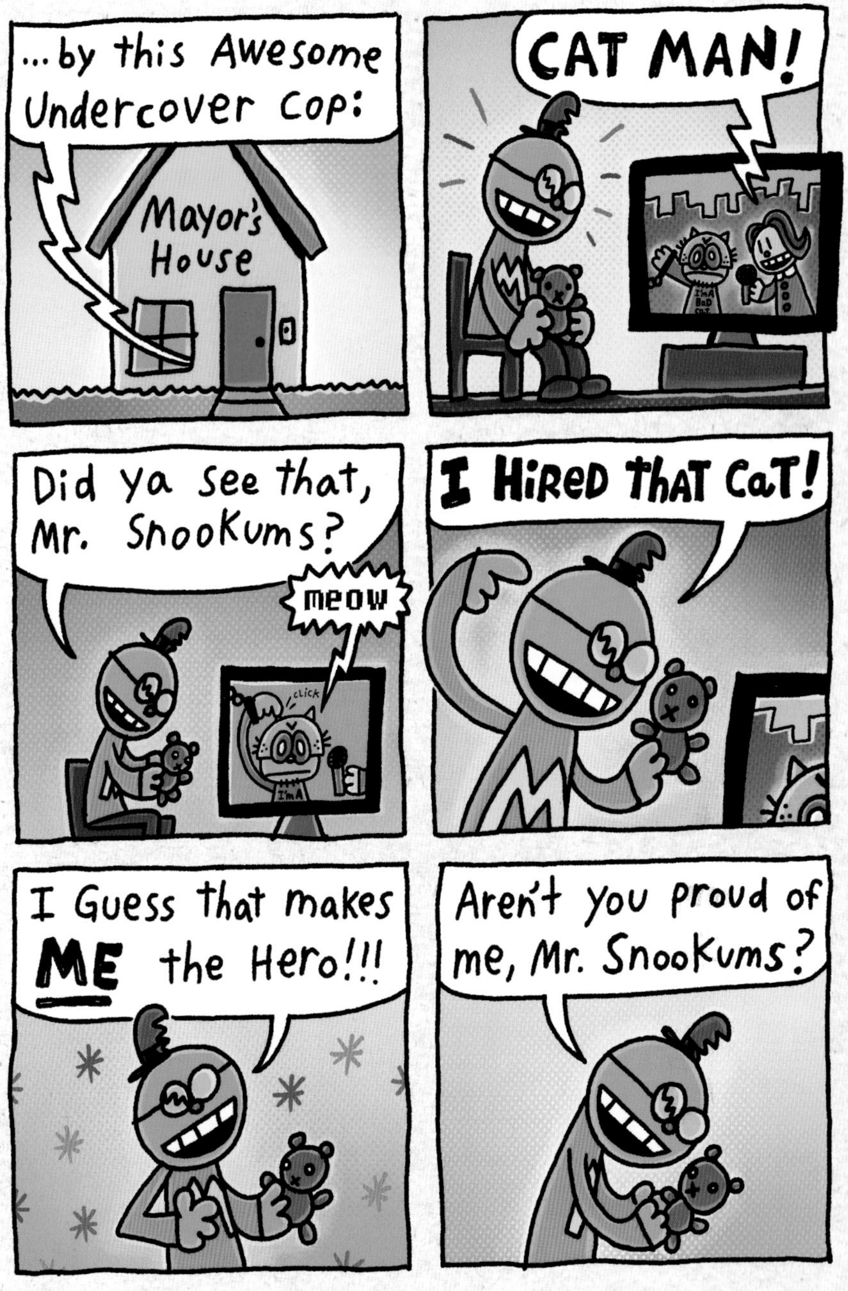
...by this Awesome Undercover Cop:
Mayor's House
CAT MAN!
I'M A BAD CAT
Did ya see that, Mr. Snookums?
meow
CLICK
I'M A
I HIRED THAT CAT!
I Guess that makes ME the Hero!!!
Aren't you proud of me, Mr. Snookums?

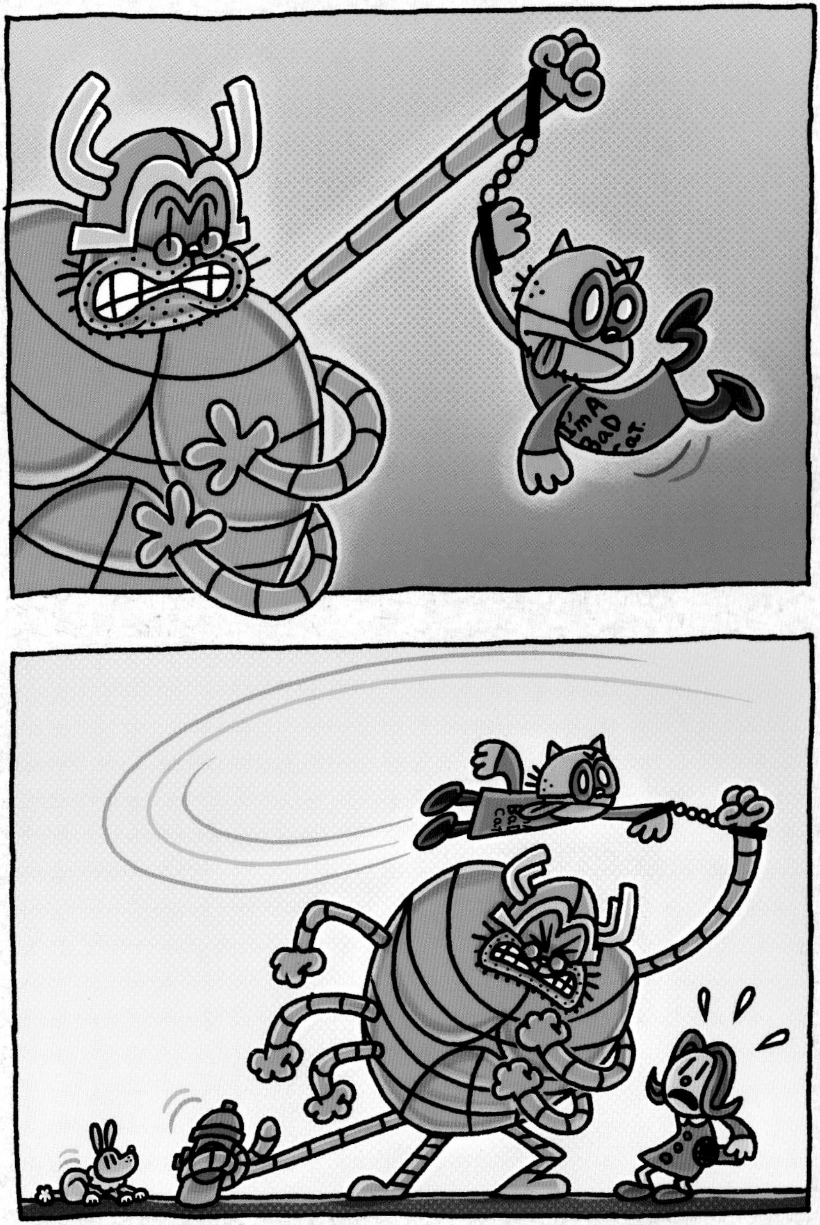
I'm A BAD cat.

Right Thumb here.

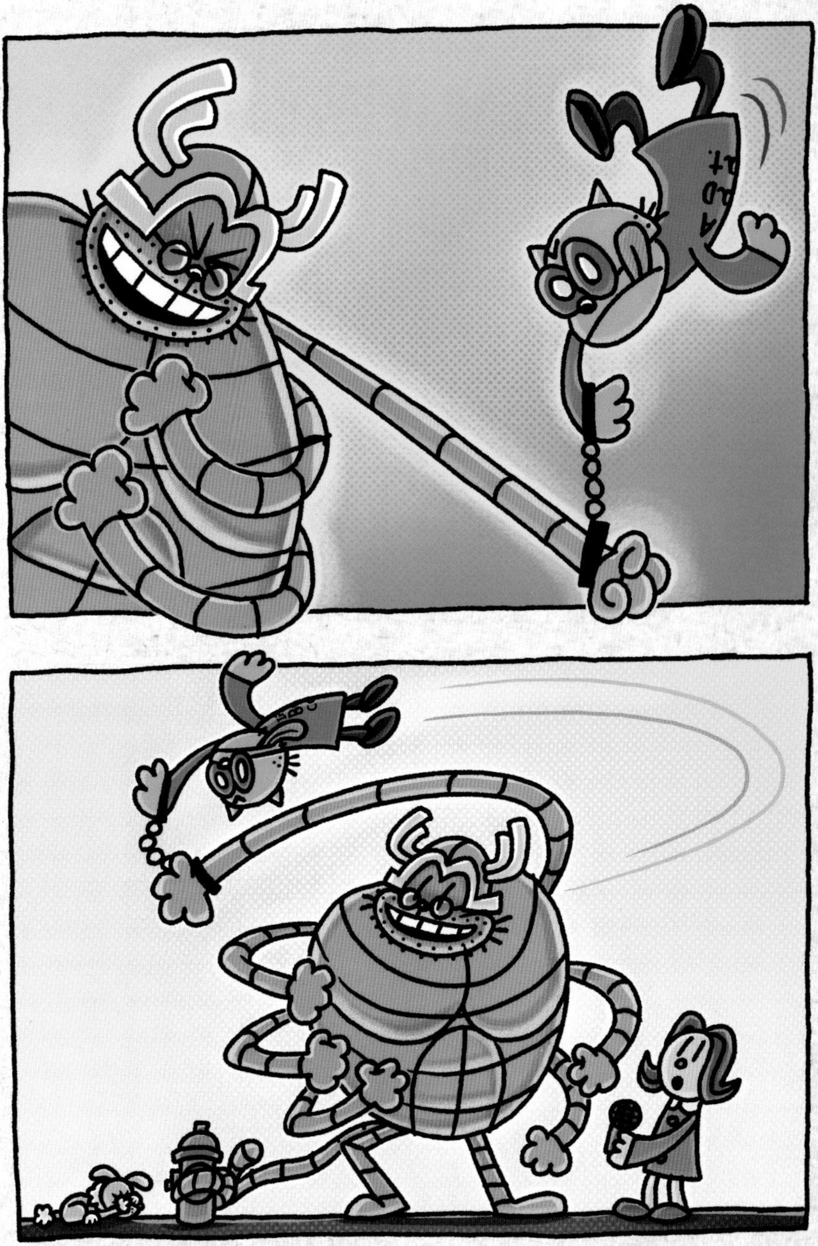

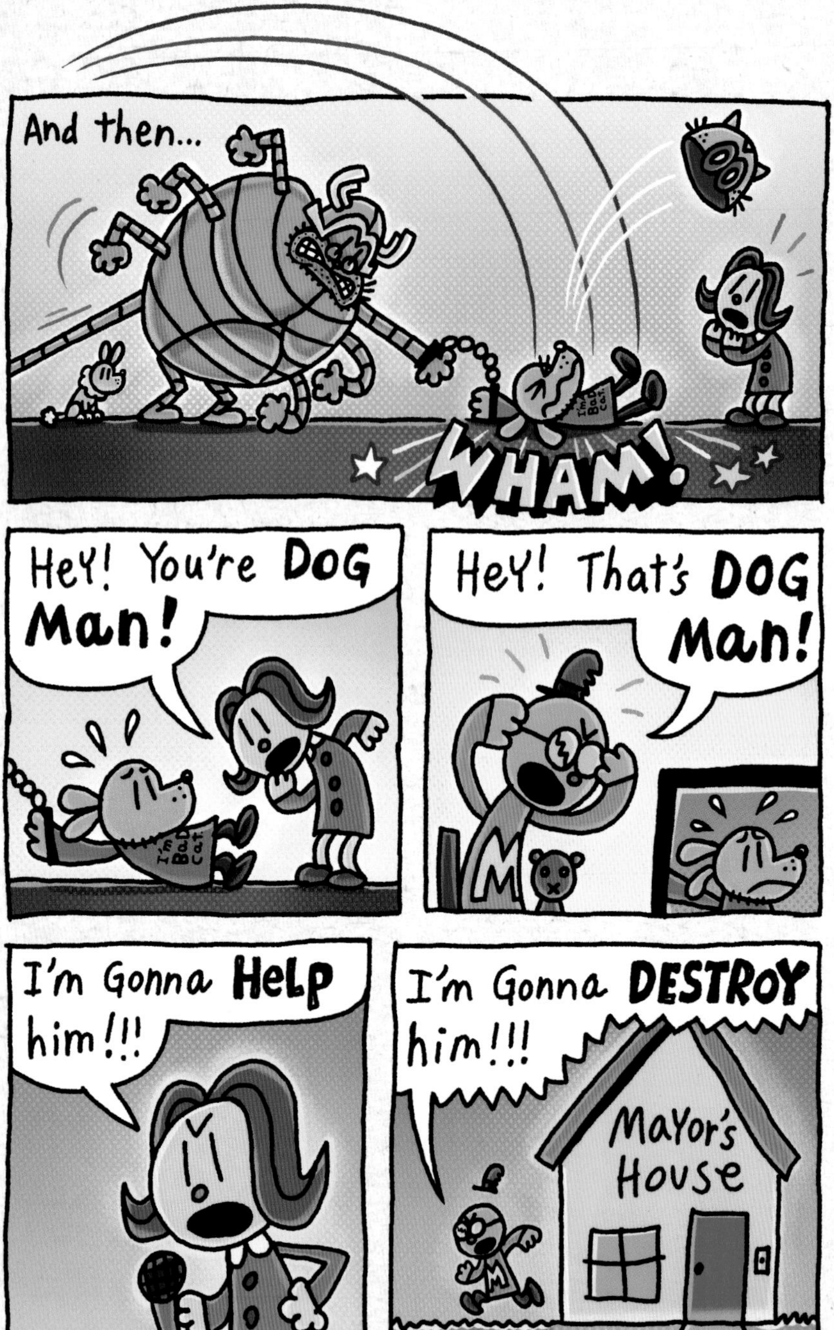
And then...
WHAM!
Hey! You're DOG Man!
Hey! That's DOG Man!
I'm Gonna HELP him!!!
I'm Gonna DESTROY him!!!
Mayor's House

CHAPTER 8

BIG FIGHT

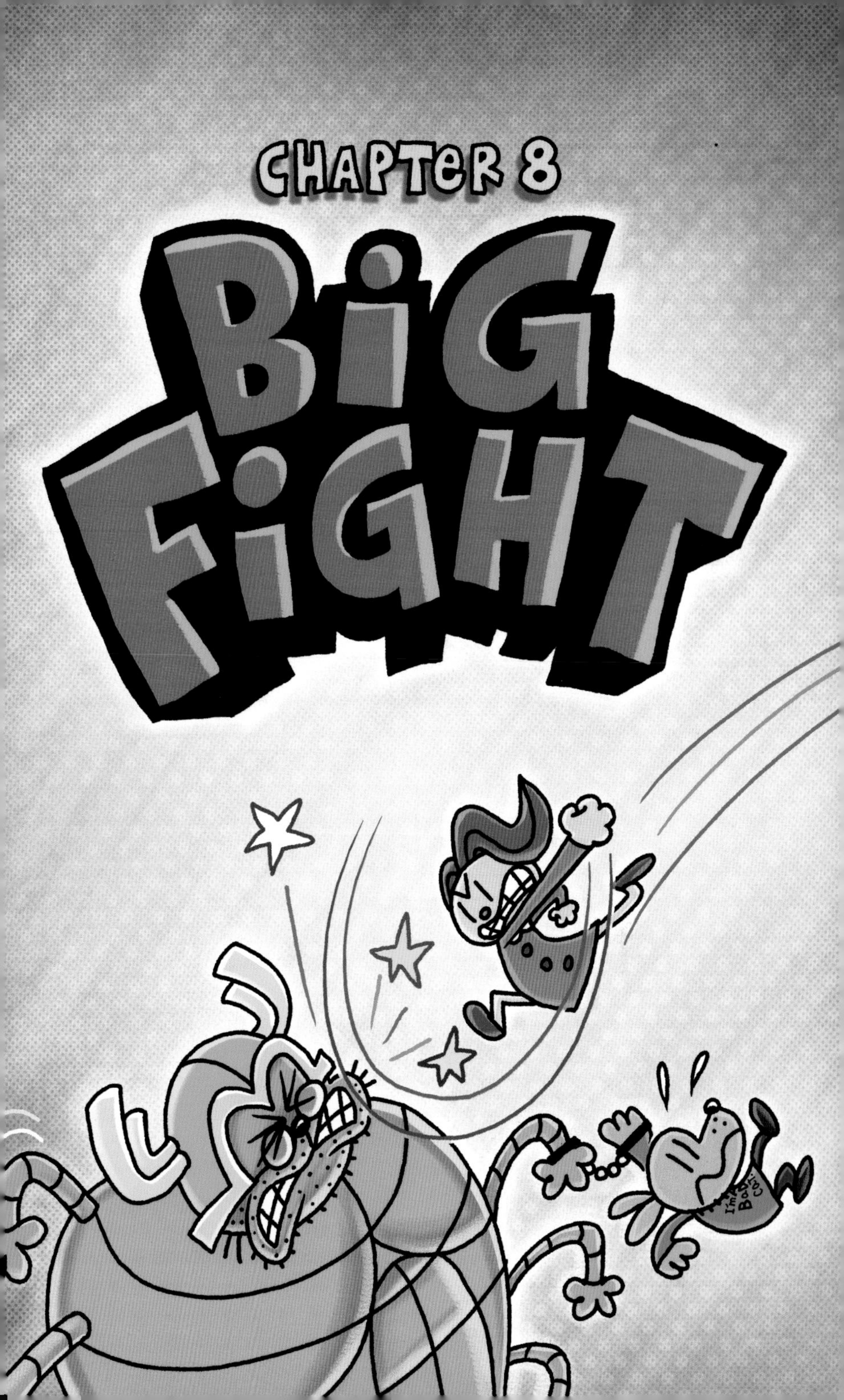

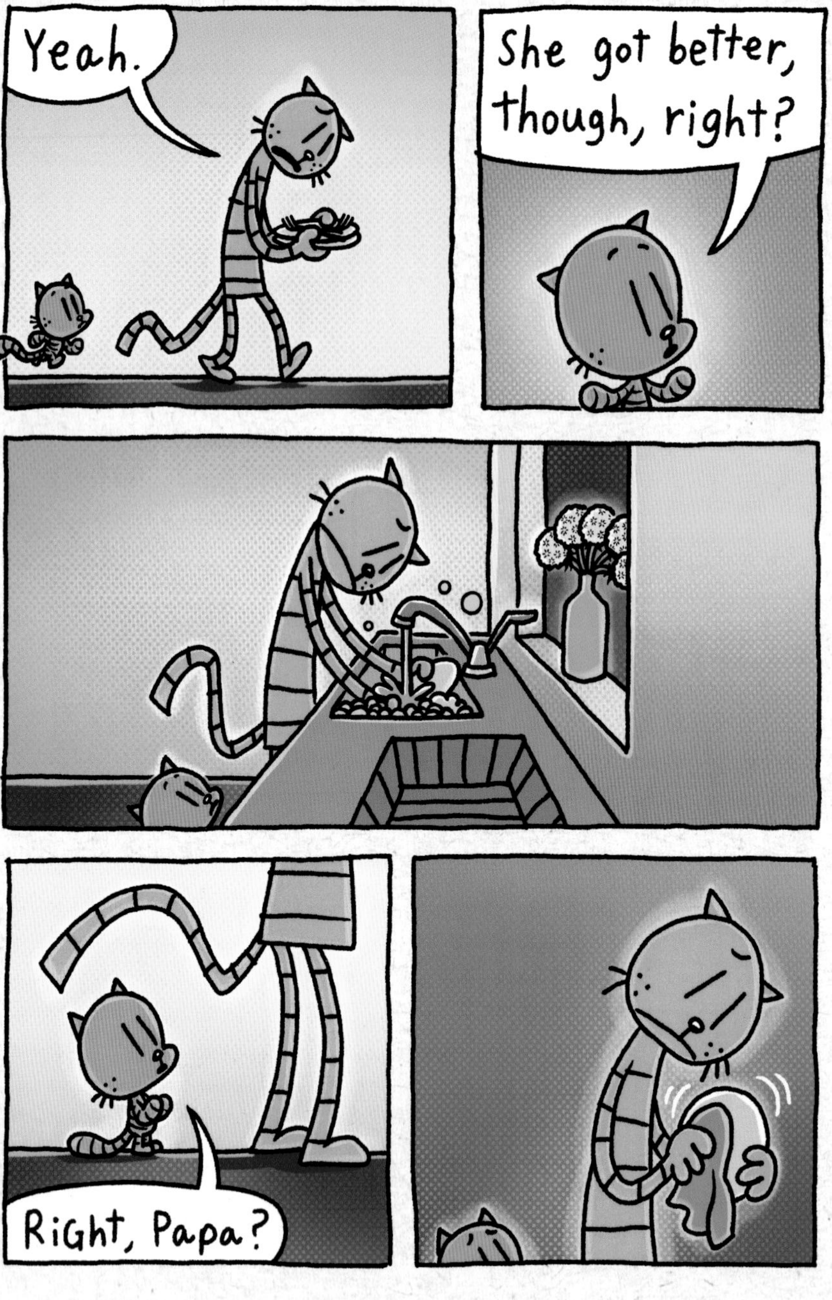
Yeah.
She got better, though, right?
Right, Papa?

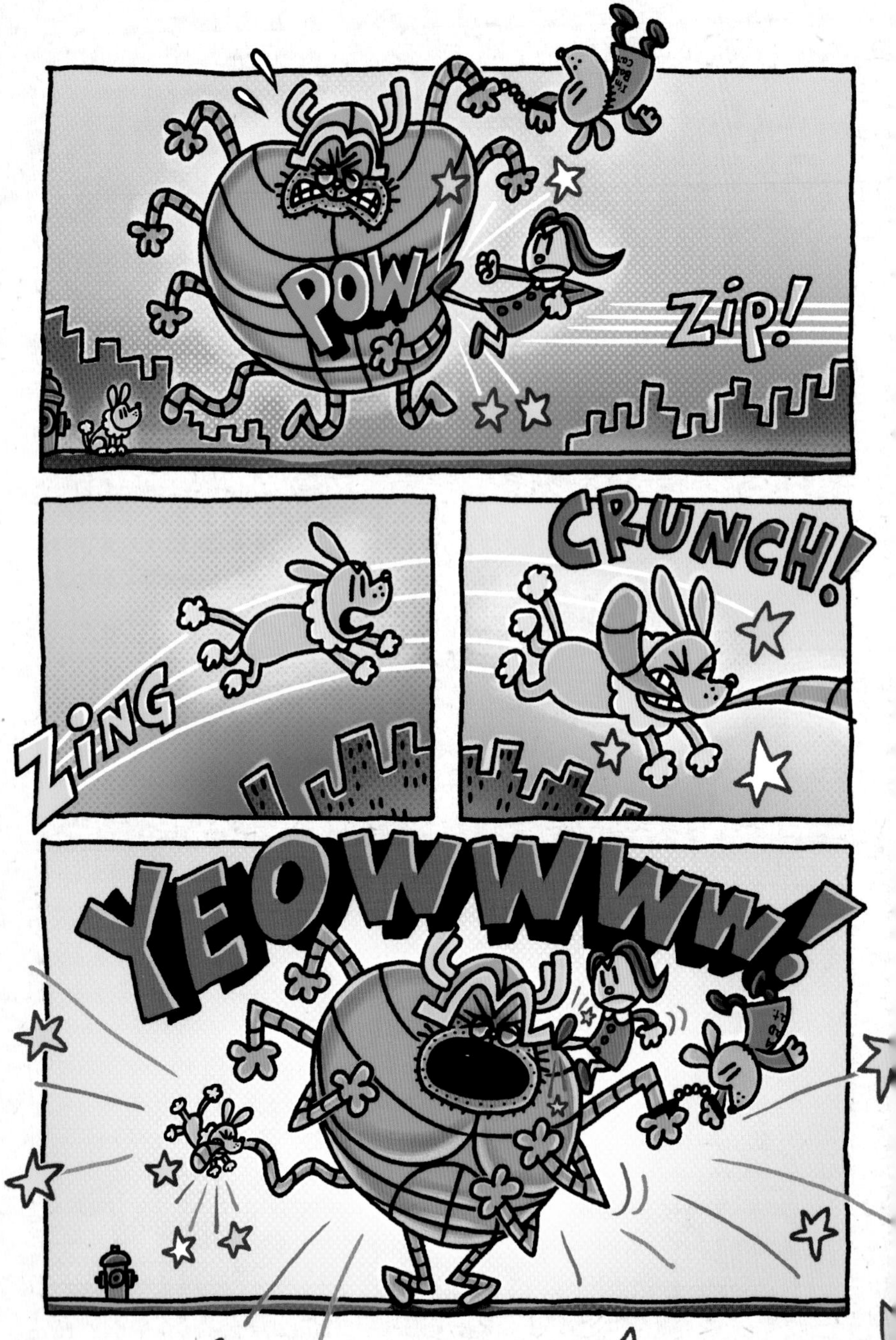
POW
ZIP!
ZING
CRUNCH!
YEOWWWW!

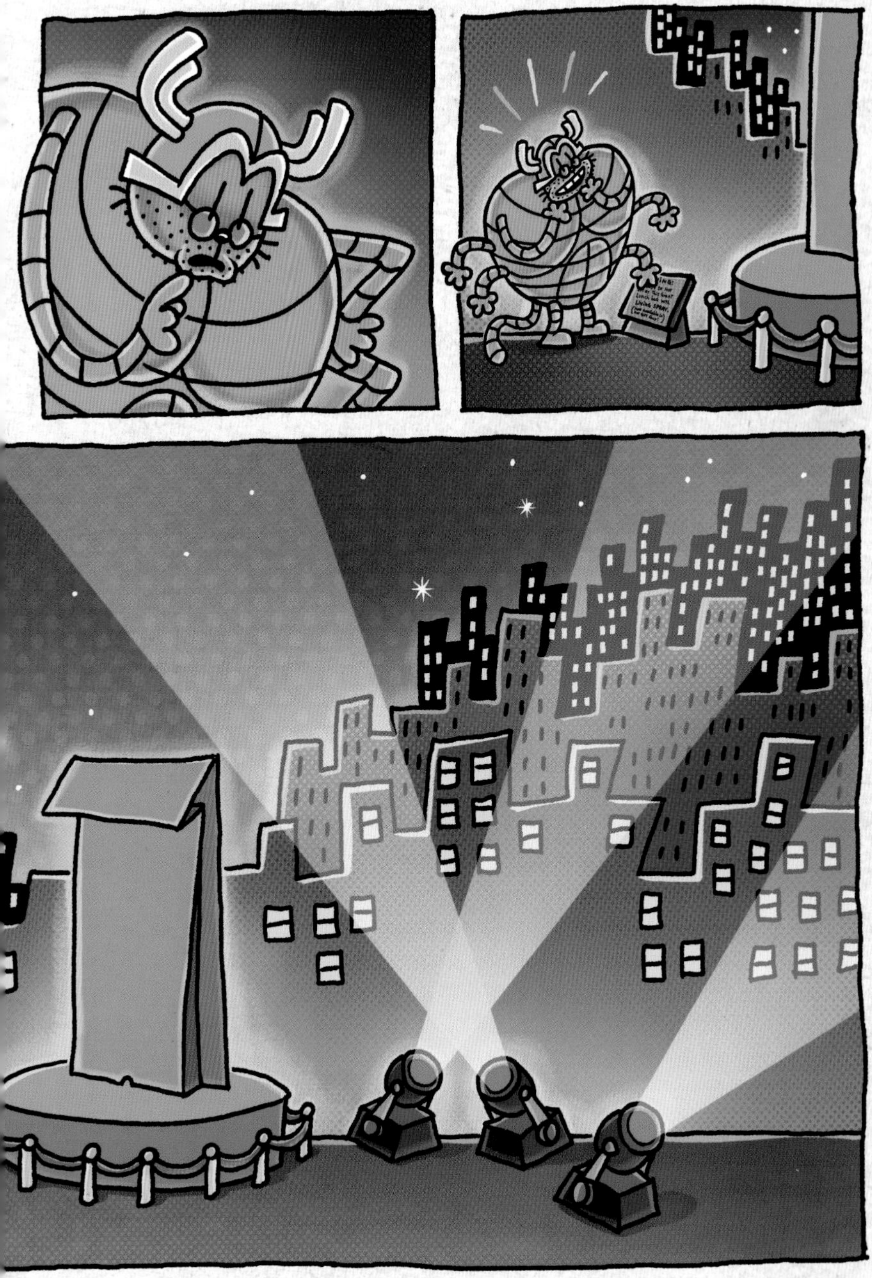
Lunch bag with
LIVING SPRAY.

Chapter 9

The Lunch Bag of Motor Brain

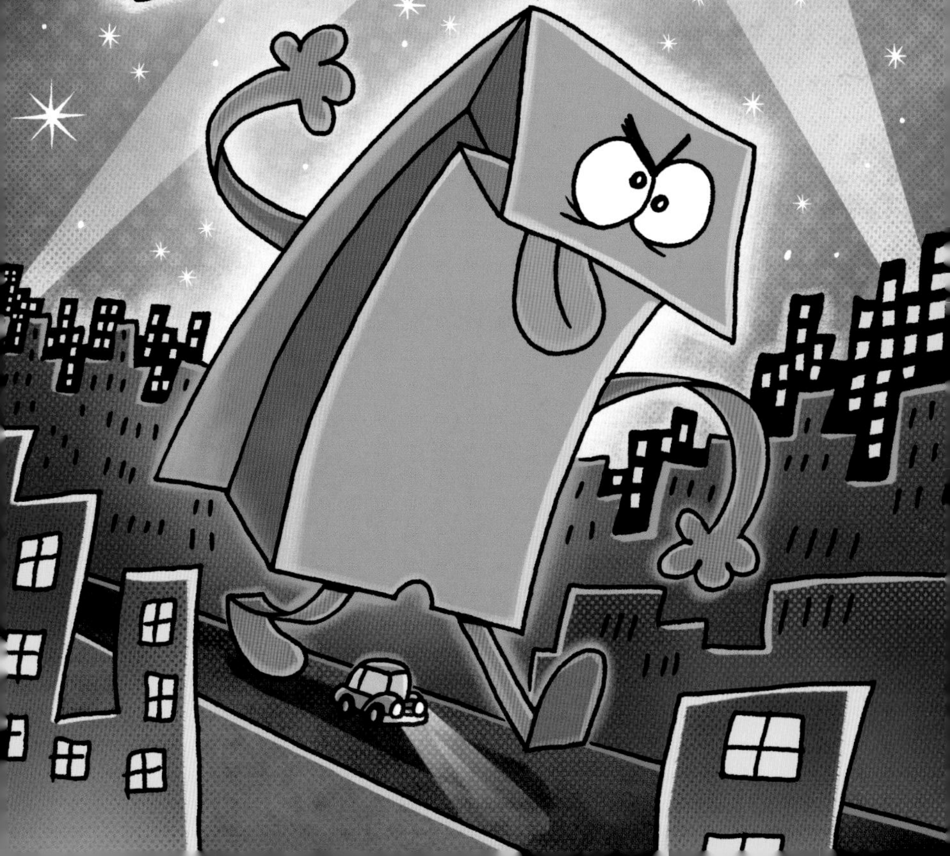

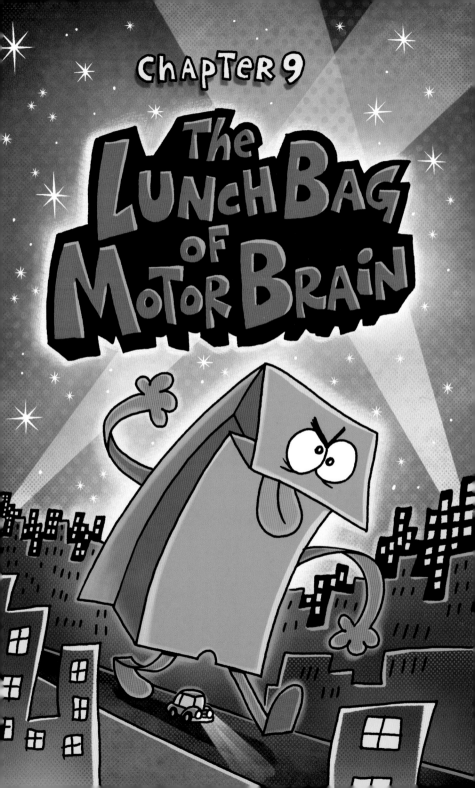

Left hand here.

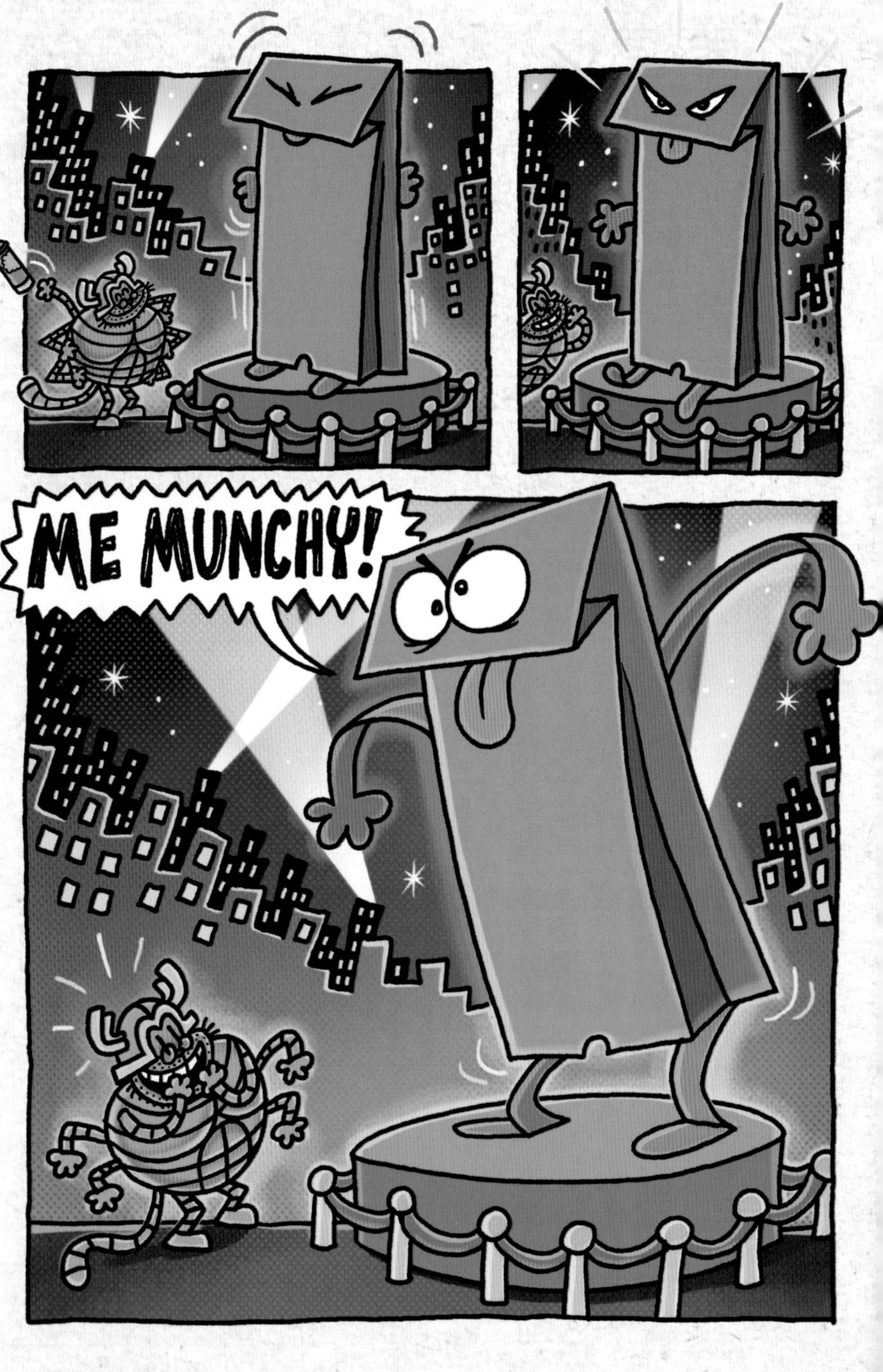
ME MUNCHY!

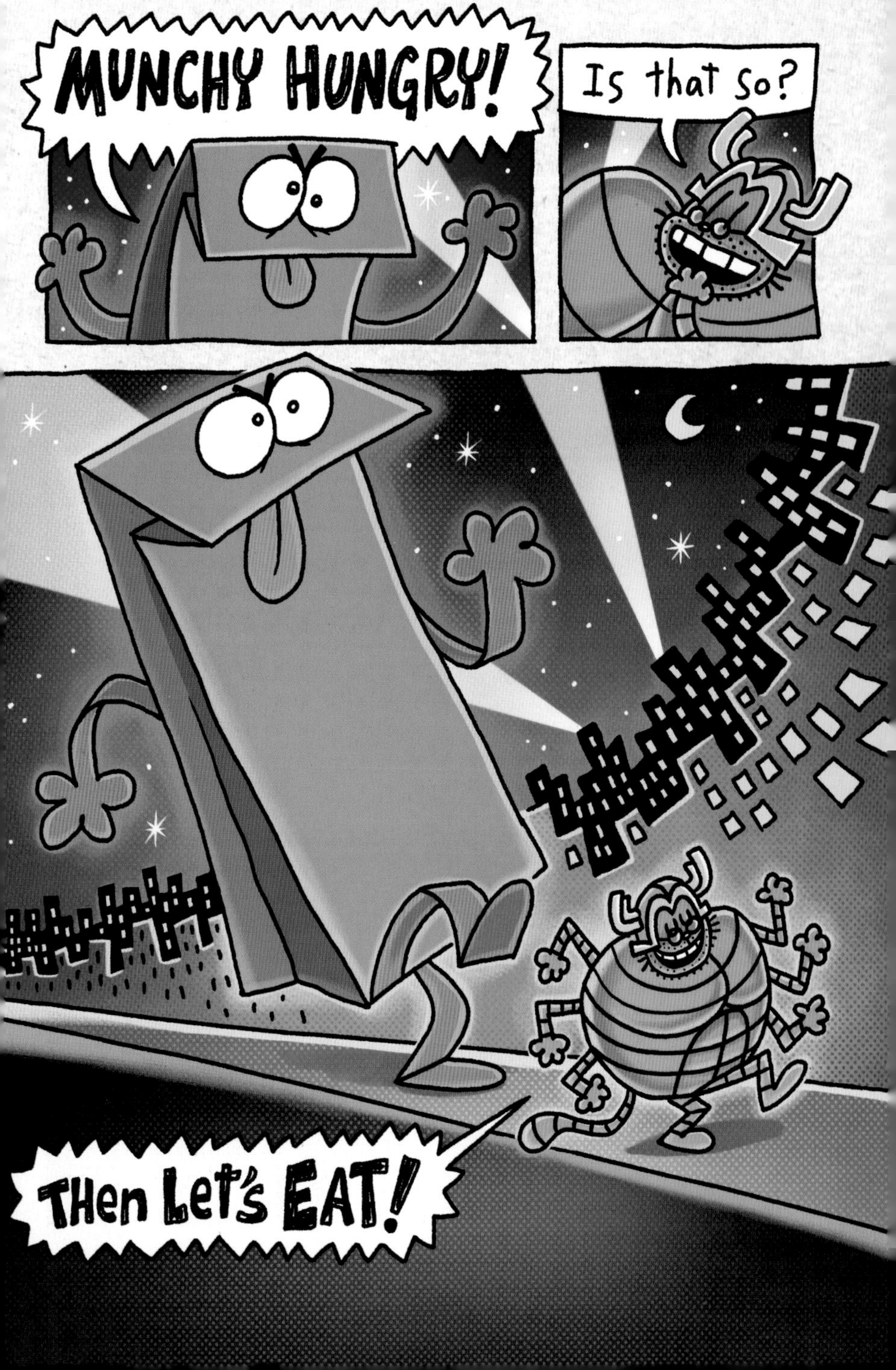
MUNCHY HUNGRY!
Is that so?
Then Let's EAT!

149

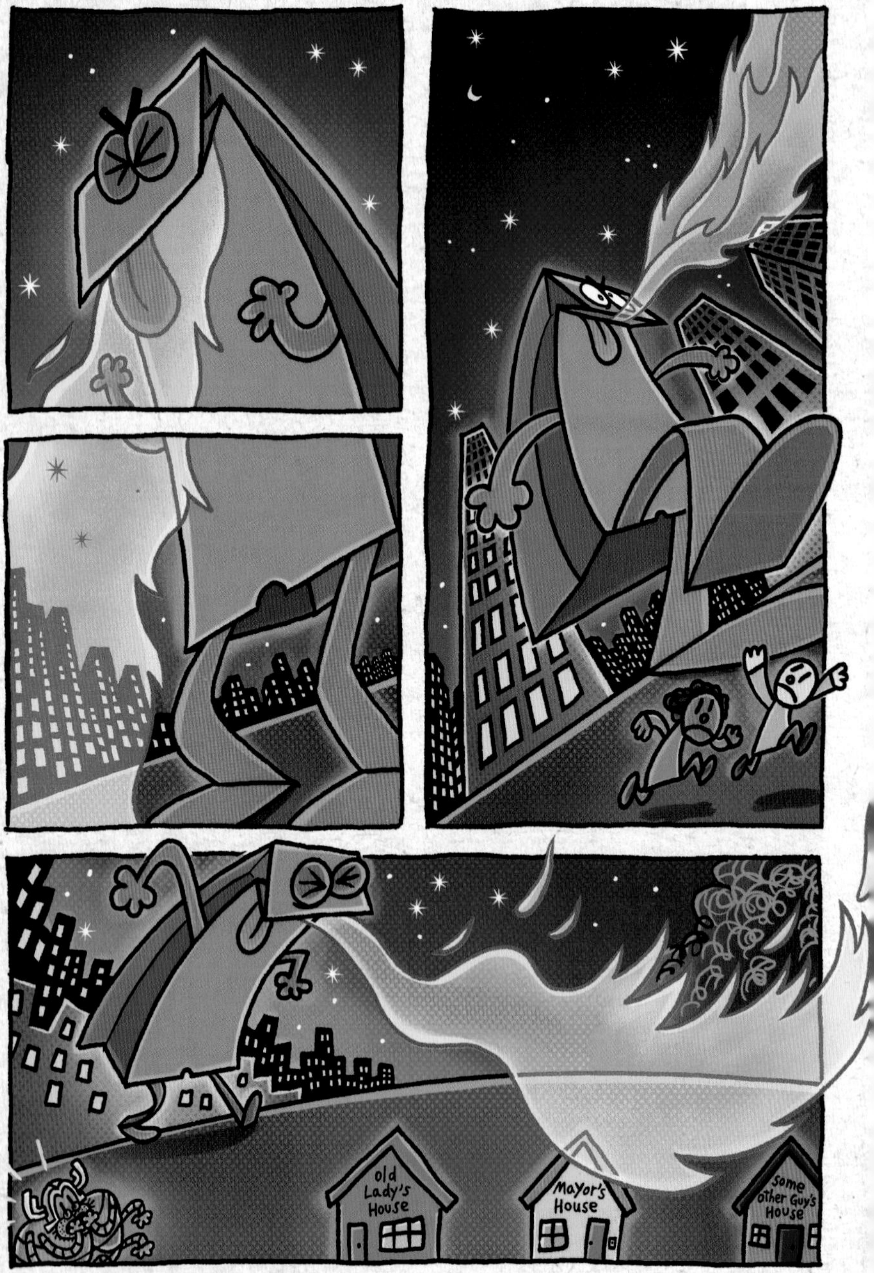
Old Lady's House
Mayor's House
Some other Guy's House

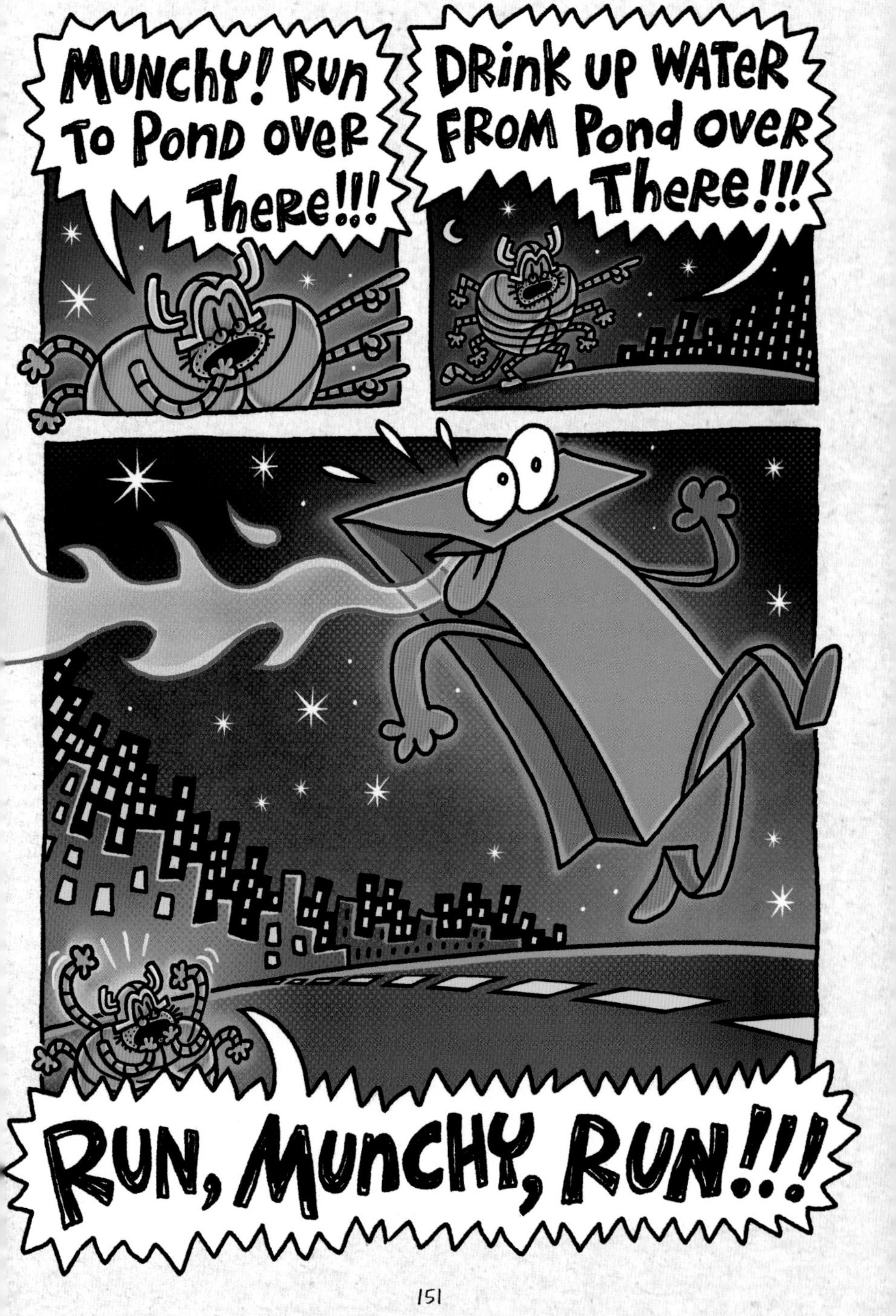
MUNCHY! RUN TO POND OVER THERE!!!
DRINK UP WATER FROM POND OVER THERE!!!
RUN, MUNCHY, RUN!!!

153

CHAPTER 10

80-HD POWER

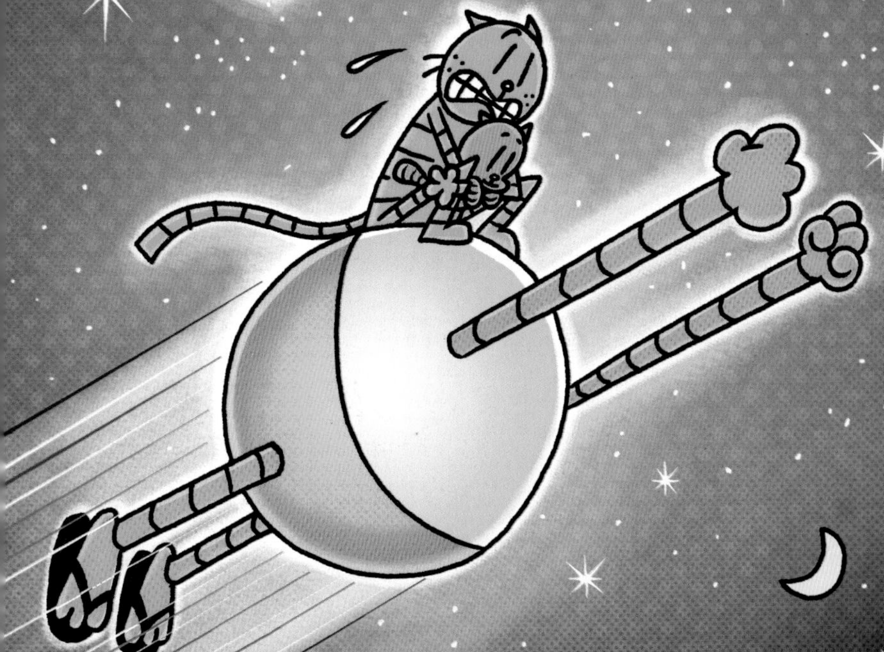

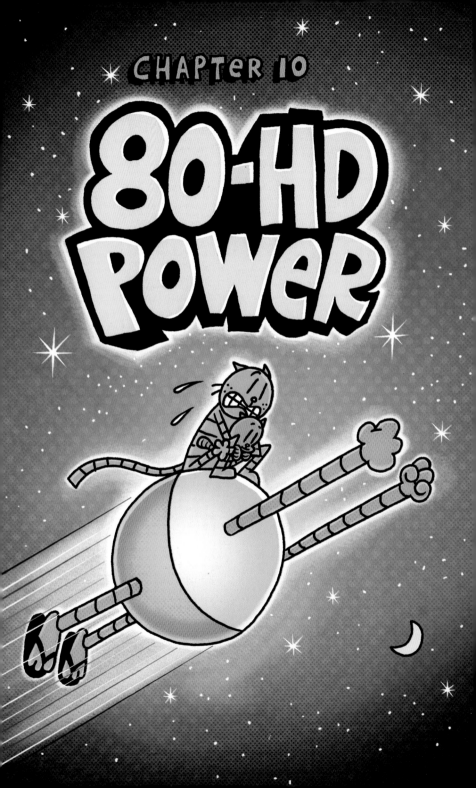

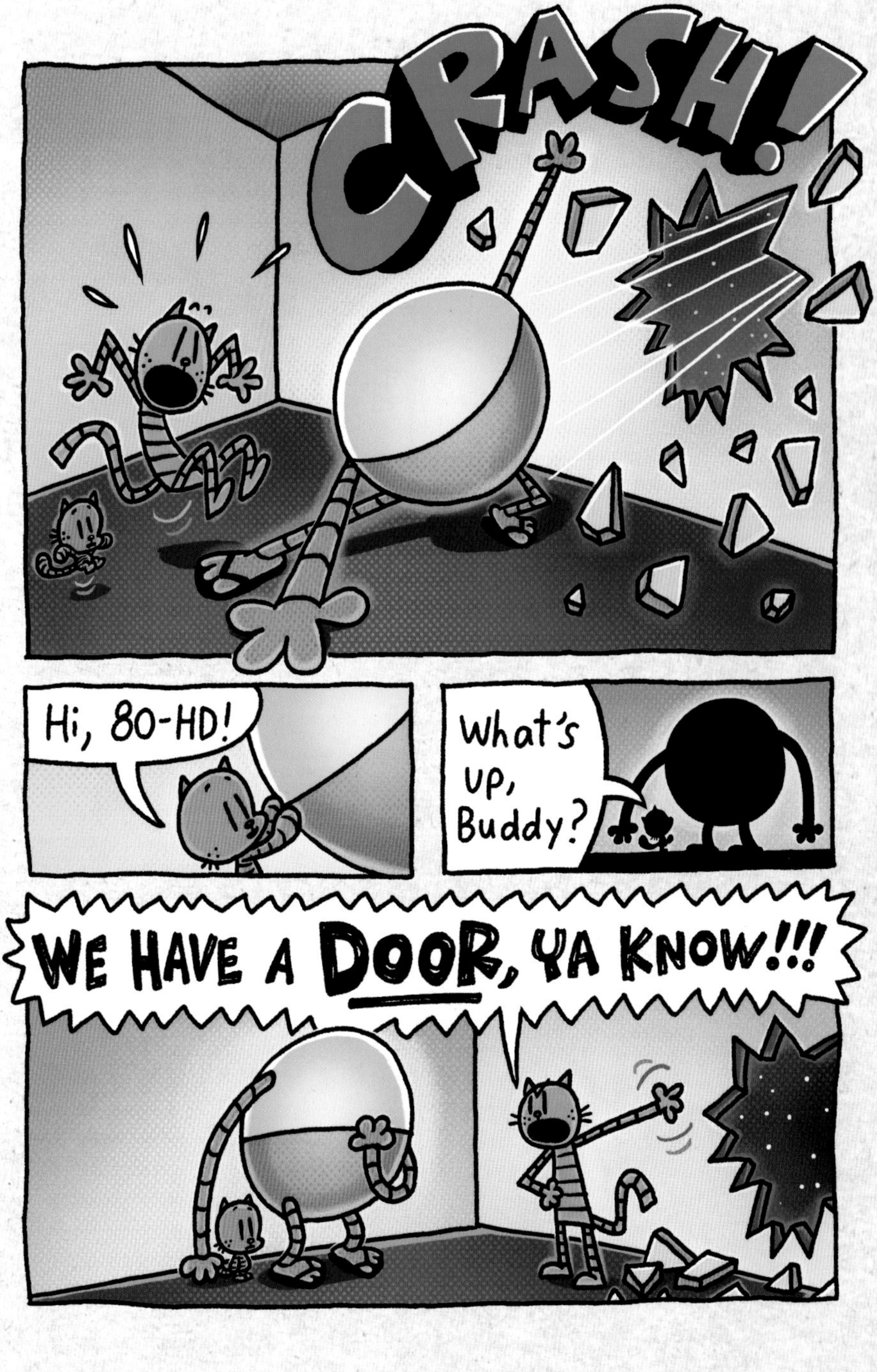
CRASH!
Hi, 80-HD!
What's up, Buddy?
WE HAVE A DOOR, YA KNOW!!!

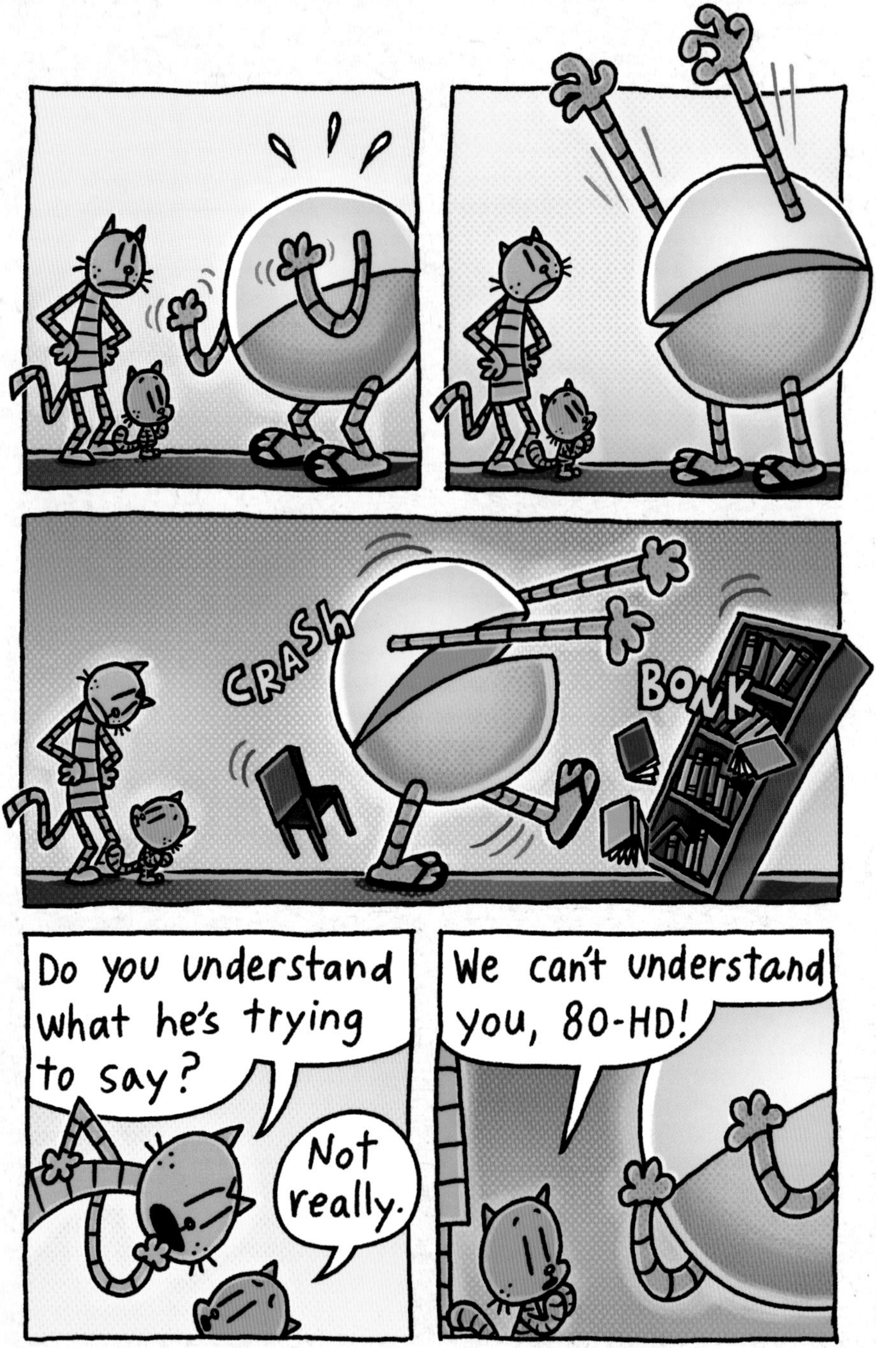
CRASh
BONK
Do you understand what he's trying to say?
Not really.
We can't understand you, 80-HD!

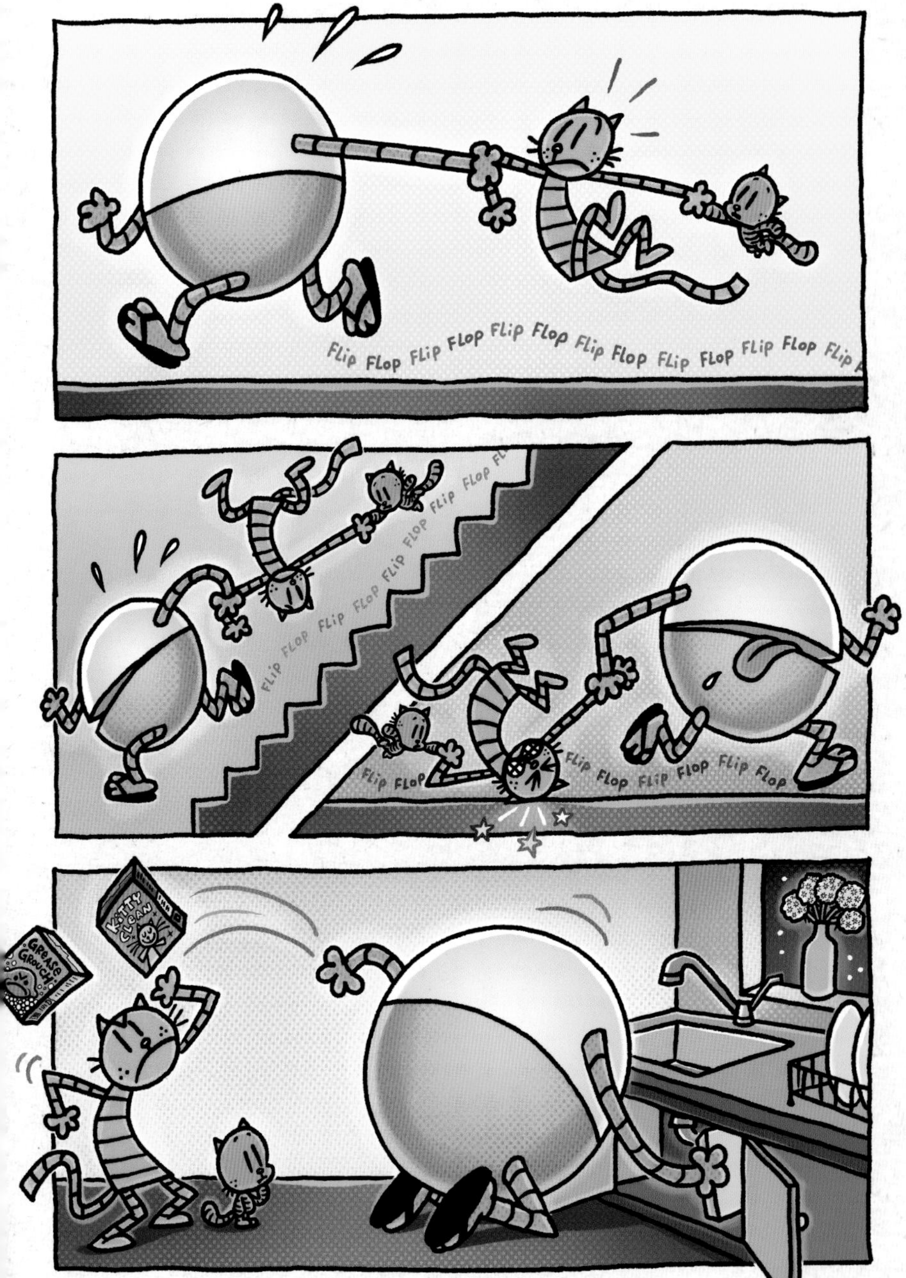

FLip FLop FLip FLop FLip FLop FLip FLop FLip FLop FLip FLop FLip
FLip FLOP FLip FLOP FLip FLOP FLip FLOP FLip FLOP FLip FLOP
FLip FLOP
FLip FLOP FLIP FLOP FLip FLOP
GREASE GROUCH
KITTY CLEAN

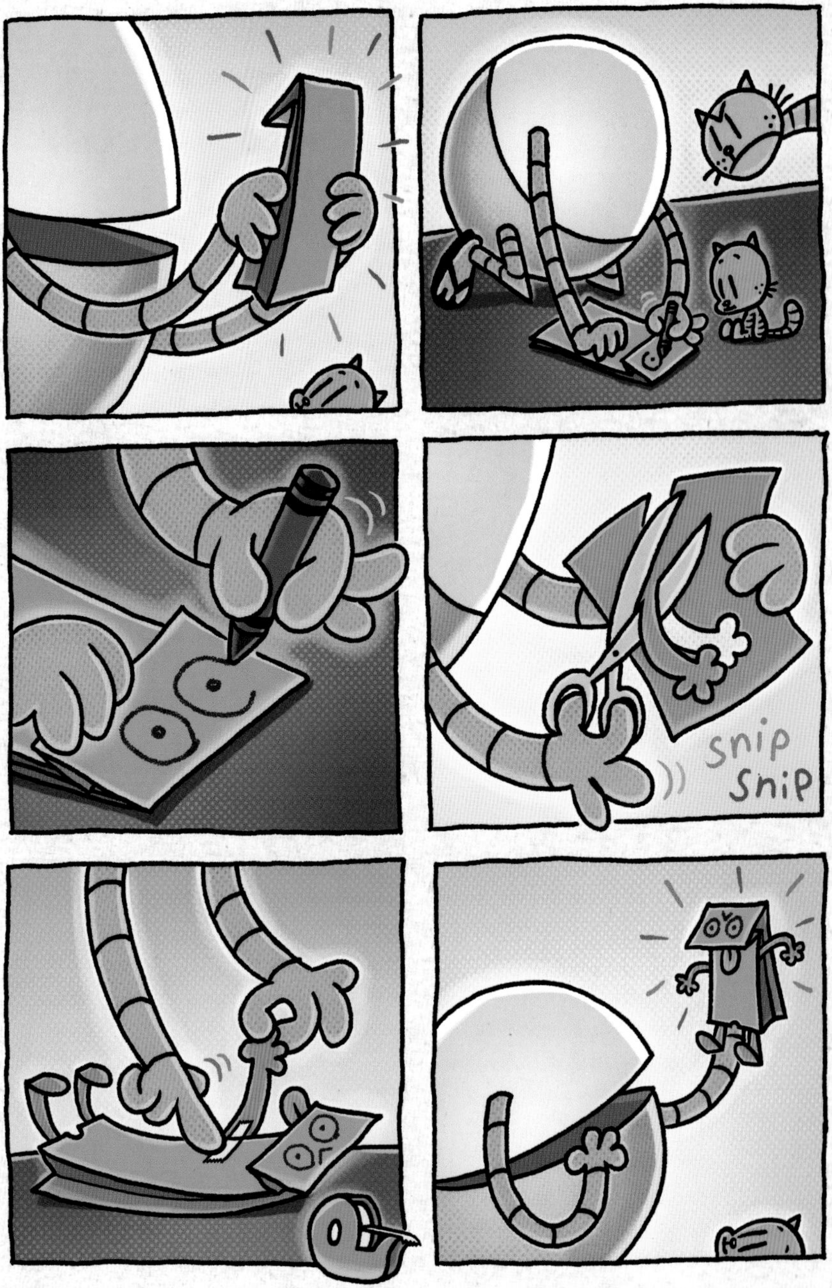
snip
snip

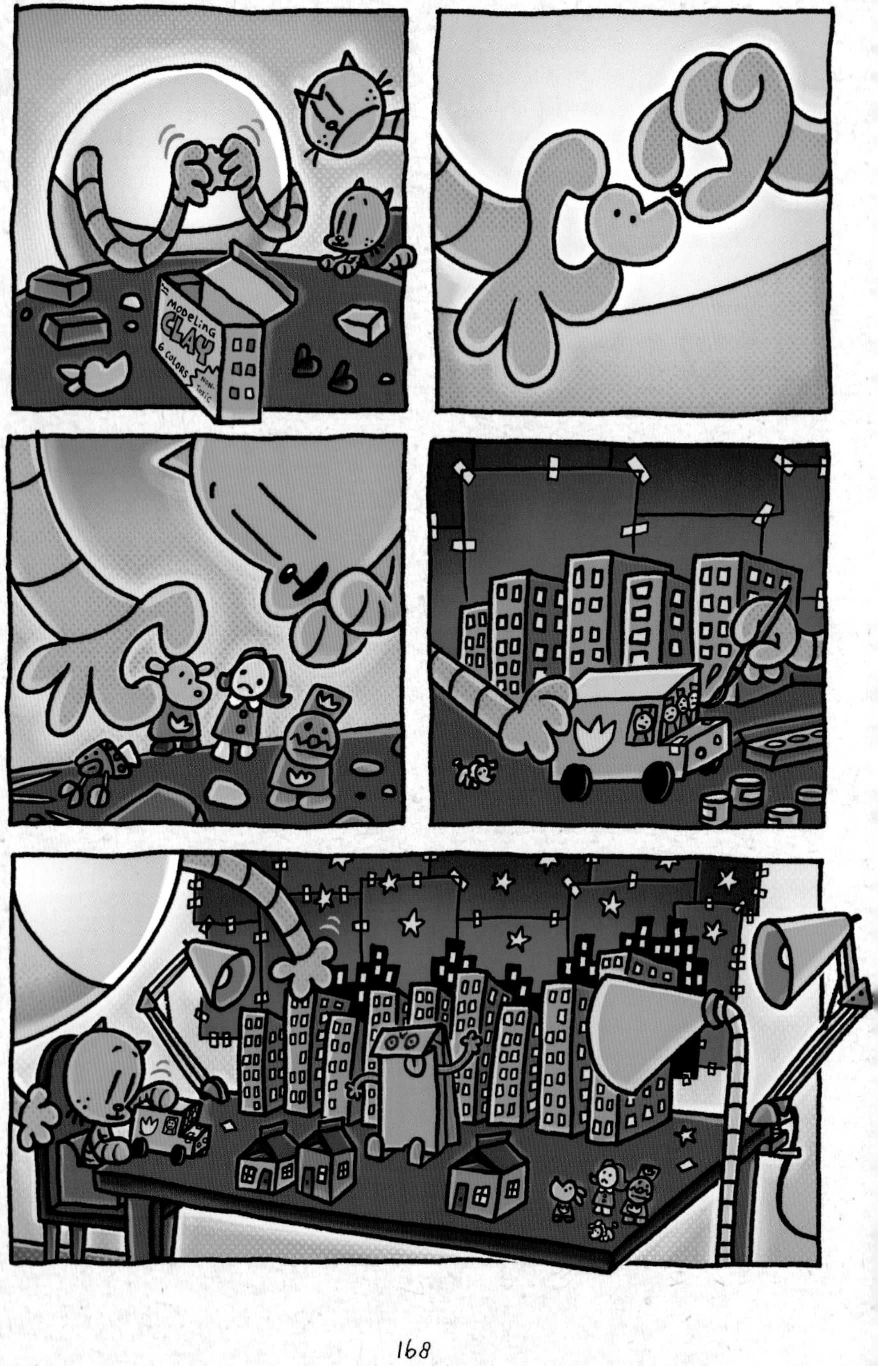
MODELING
CLAY
6 COLORS
NON-TOXIC

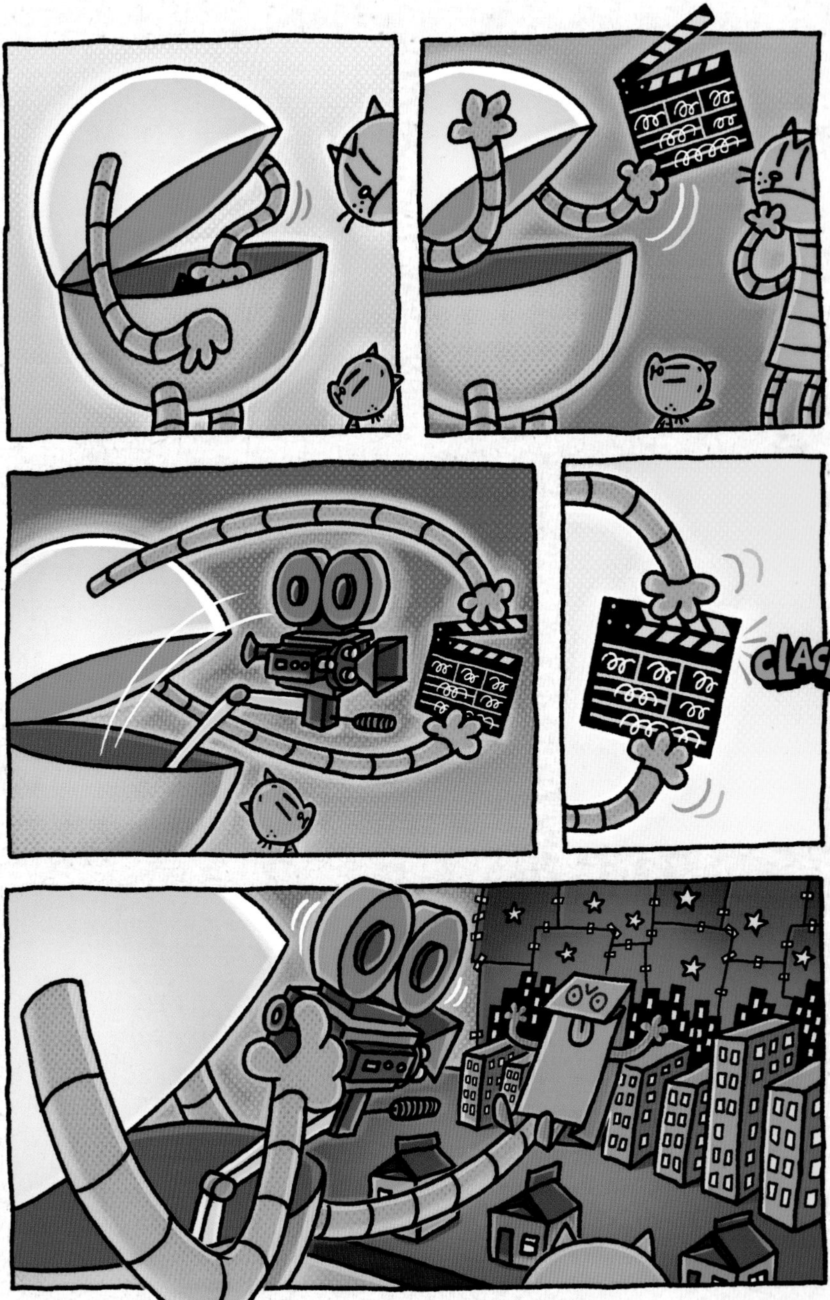
CLACK!

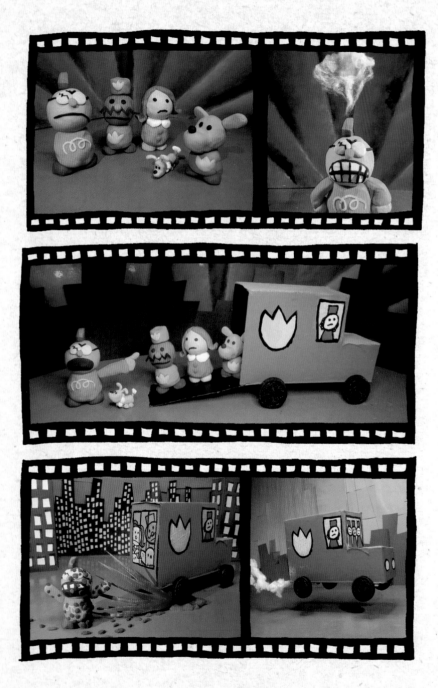

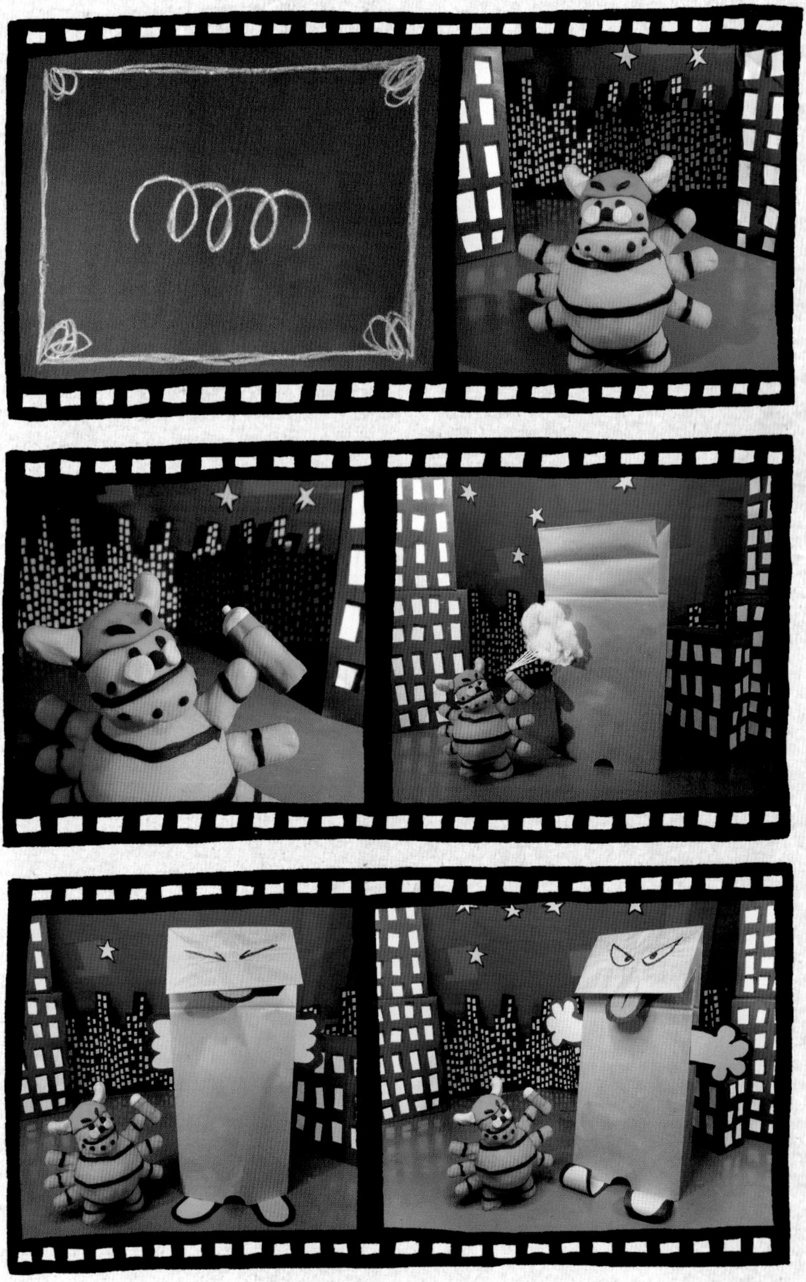

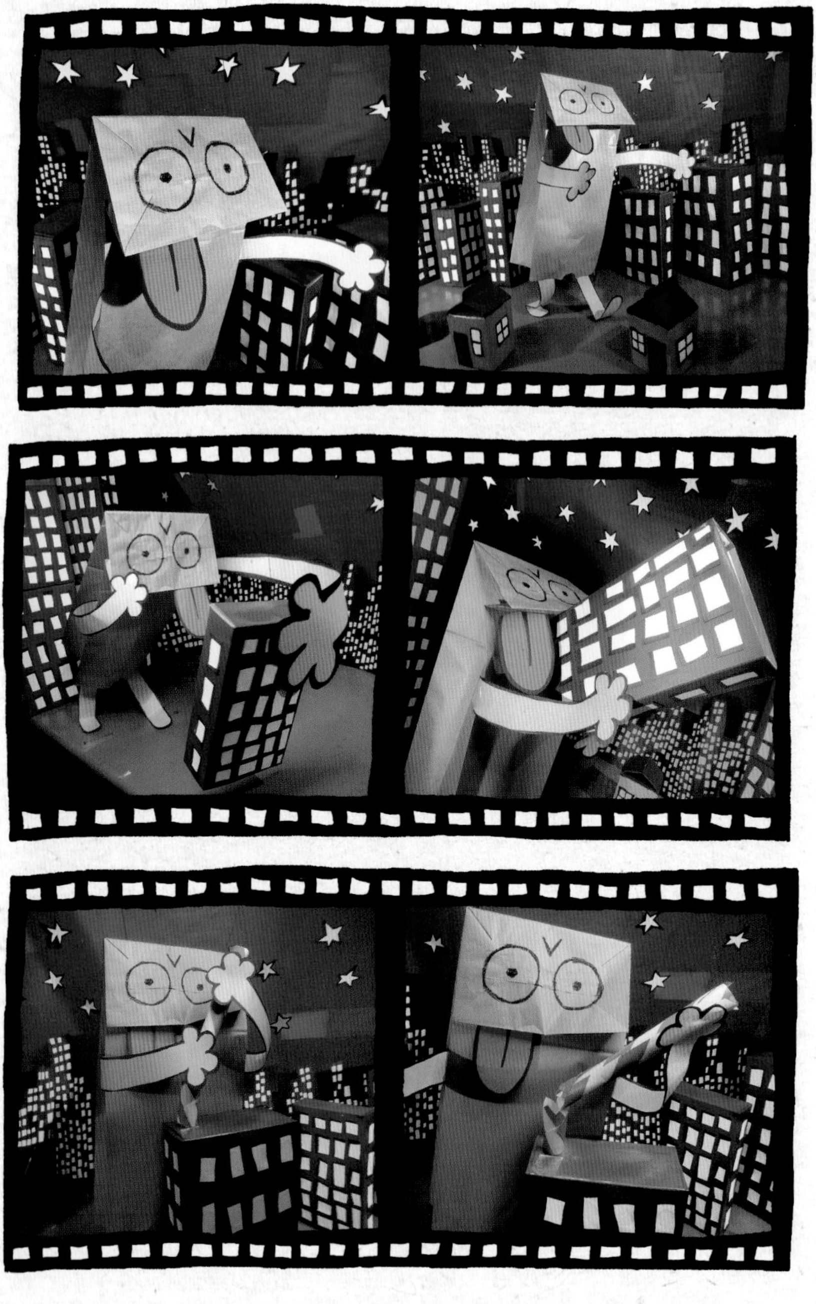

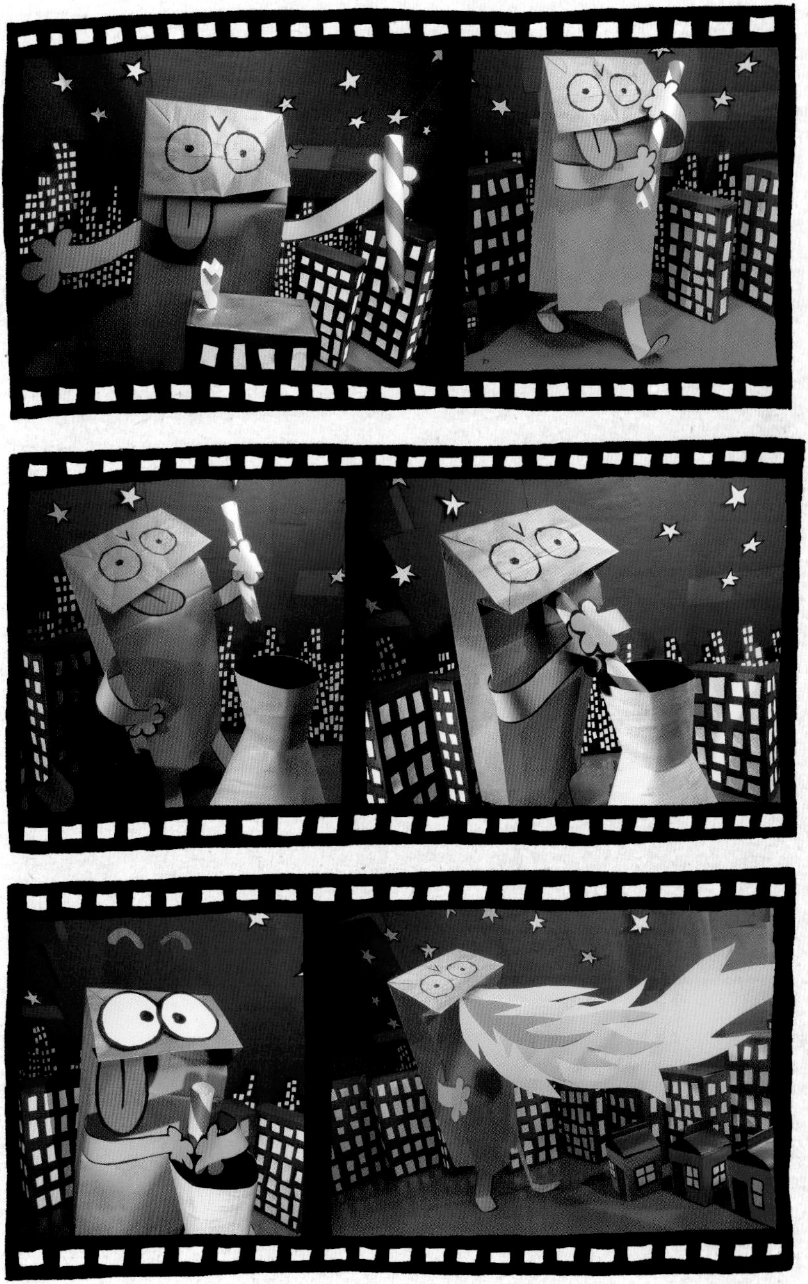

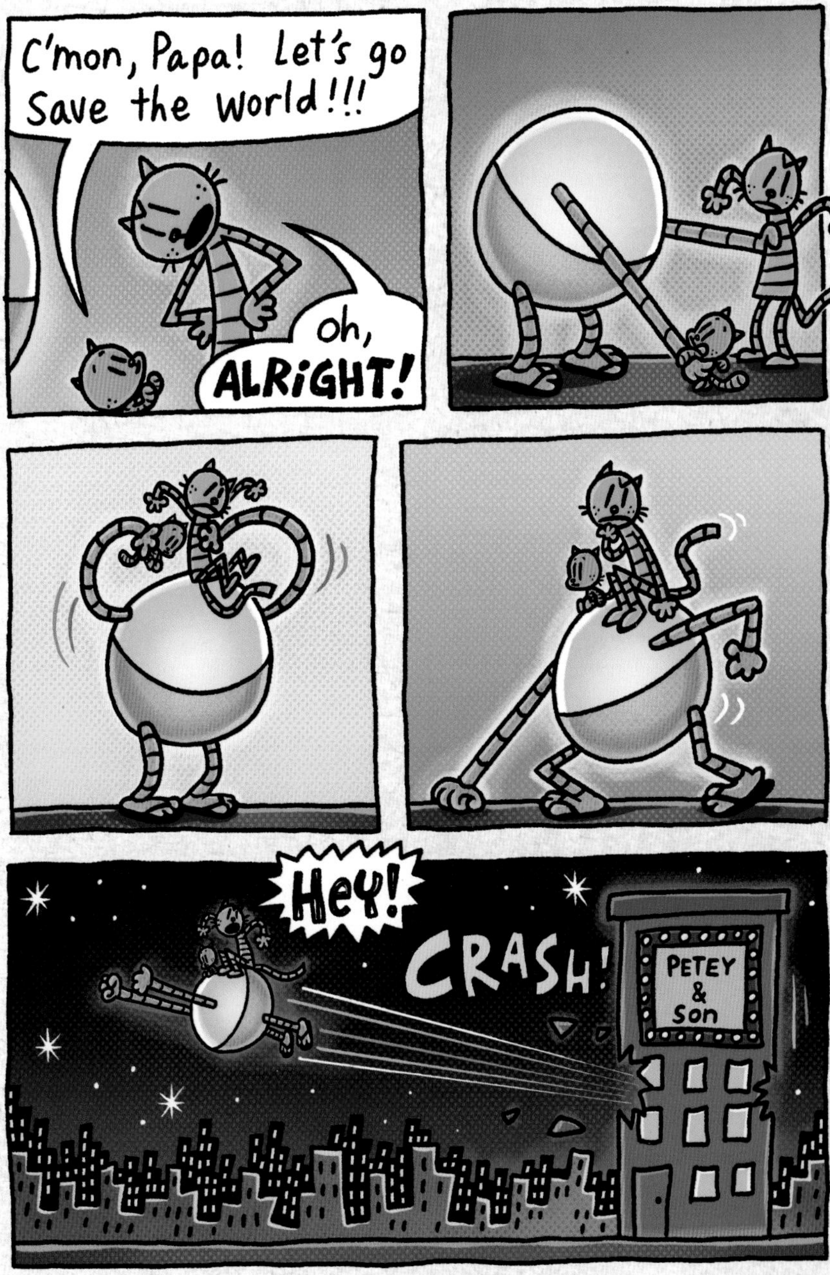
C'mon, Papa! Let's go Save the World!!!
oh, ALRIGHT!
Hey!
CRASH!
PETEY & Son

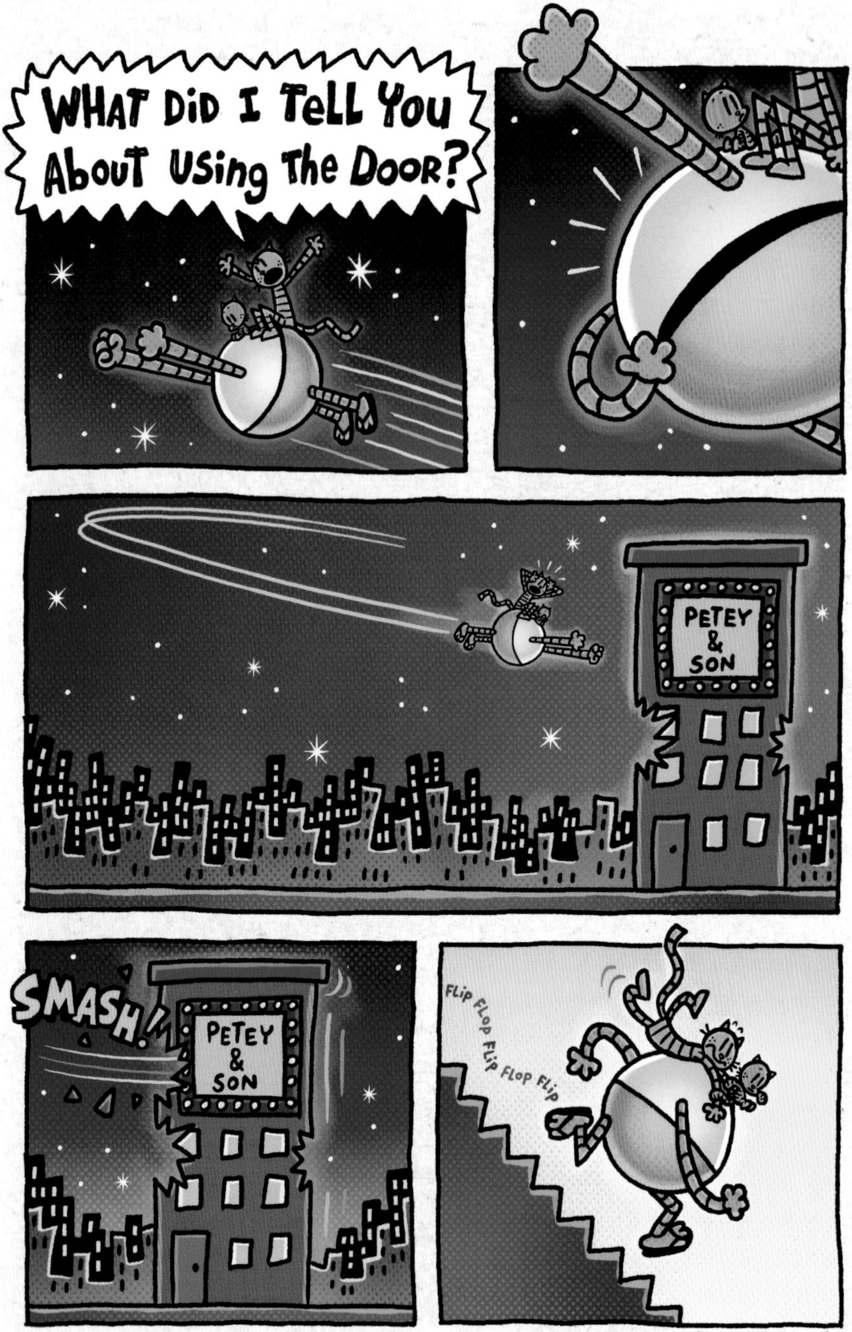
WHAT DID I TeLL You About USing The Door?
PETEY & SON
PETEY & SON
SMASH!
PETEY & SON
FLip FLop FLip FLop FLip

CHAPTER 11

Love vs. Hate: Who Will Win?

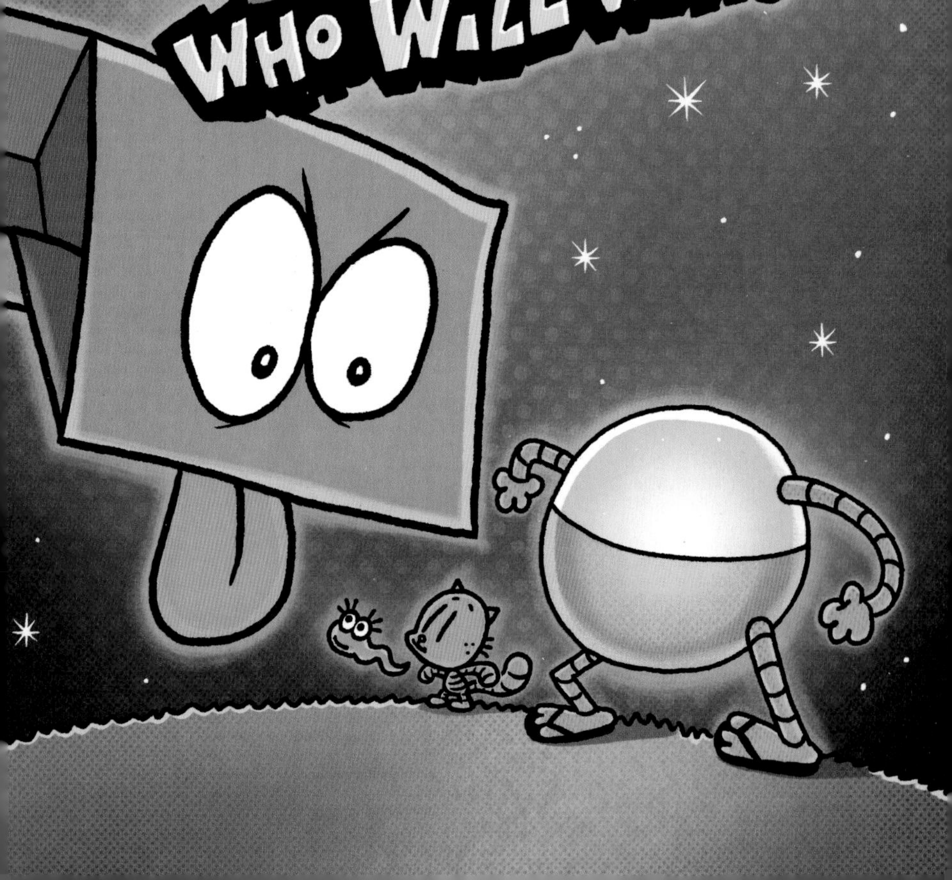

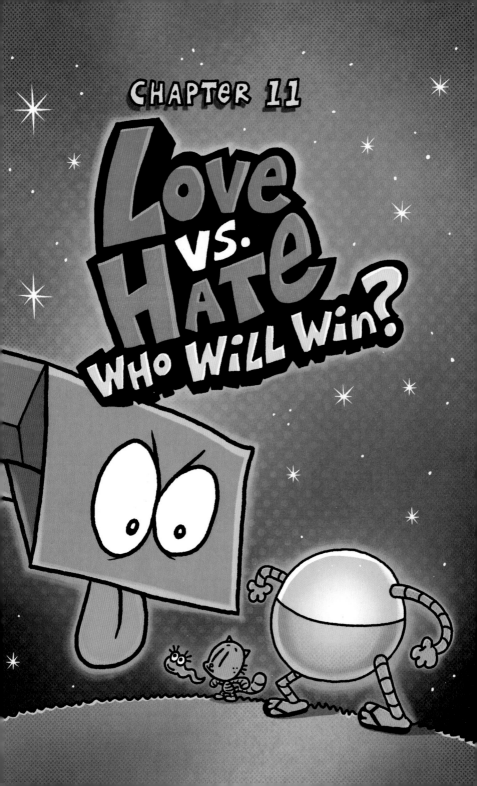

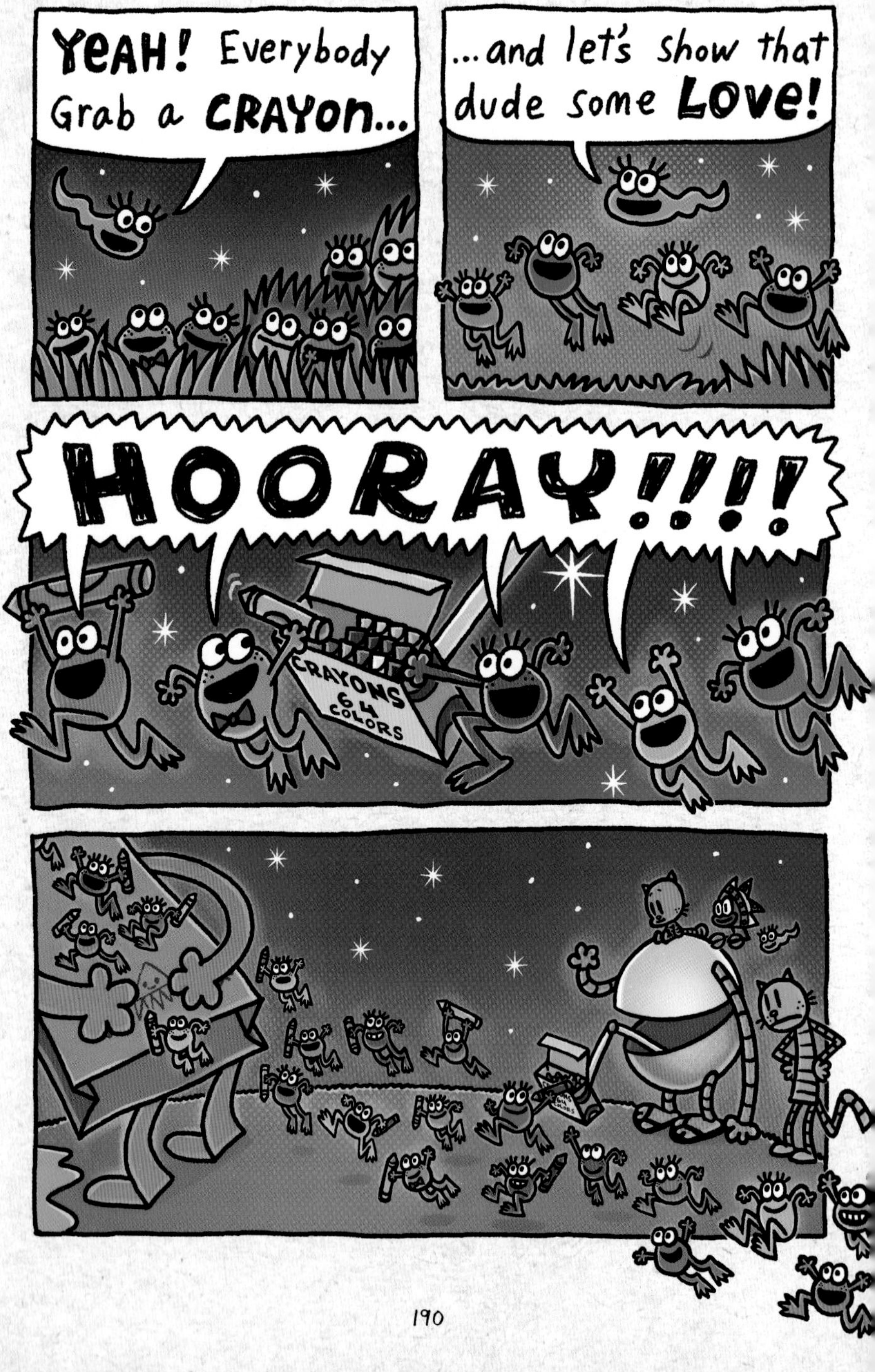
YEAH! Everybody Grab a CRAYON...
...and let's show that dude some LOVE!
HOORAY!!!!
CRAYONS 64 COLORS

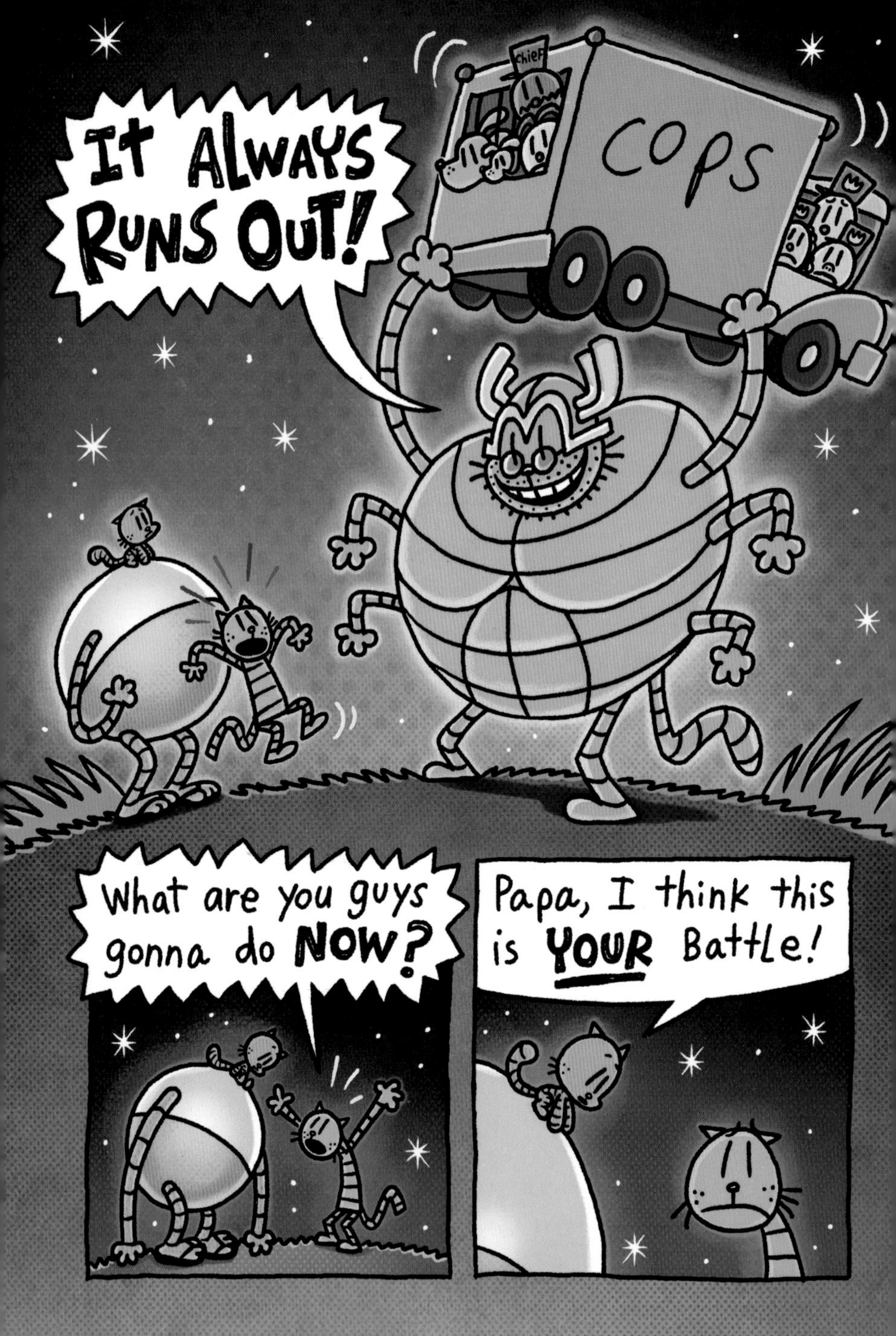
It ALWAYS RUNS OUT!
COPS
CHIEF
What are you guys gonna do NOW?
Papa, I think this is YOUR Battle!

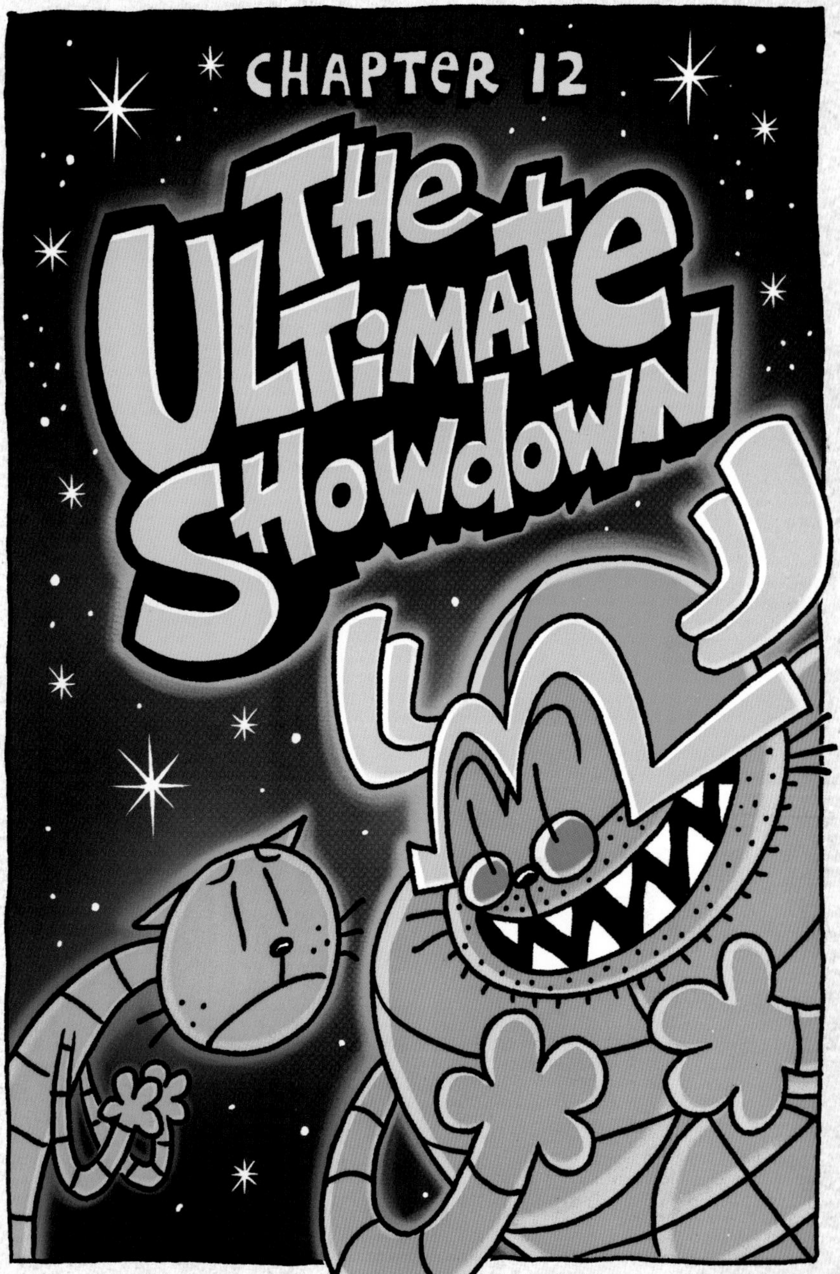
CHAPTER 12
THE ULTIMATE SHOWDOWN

197

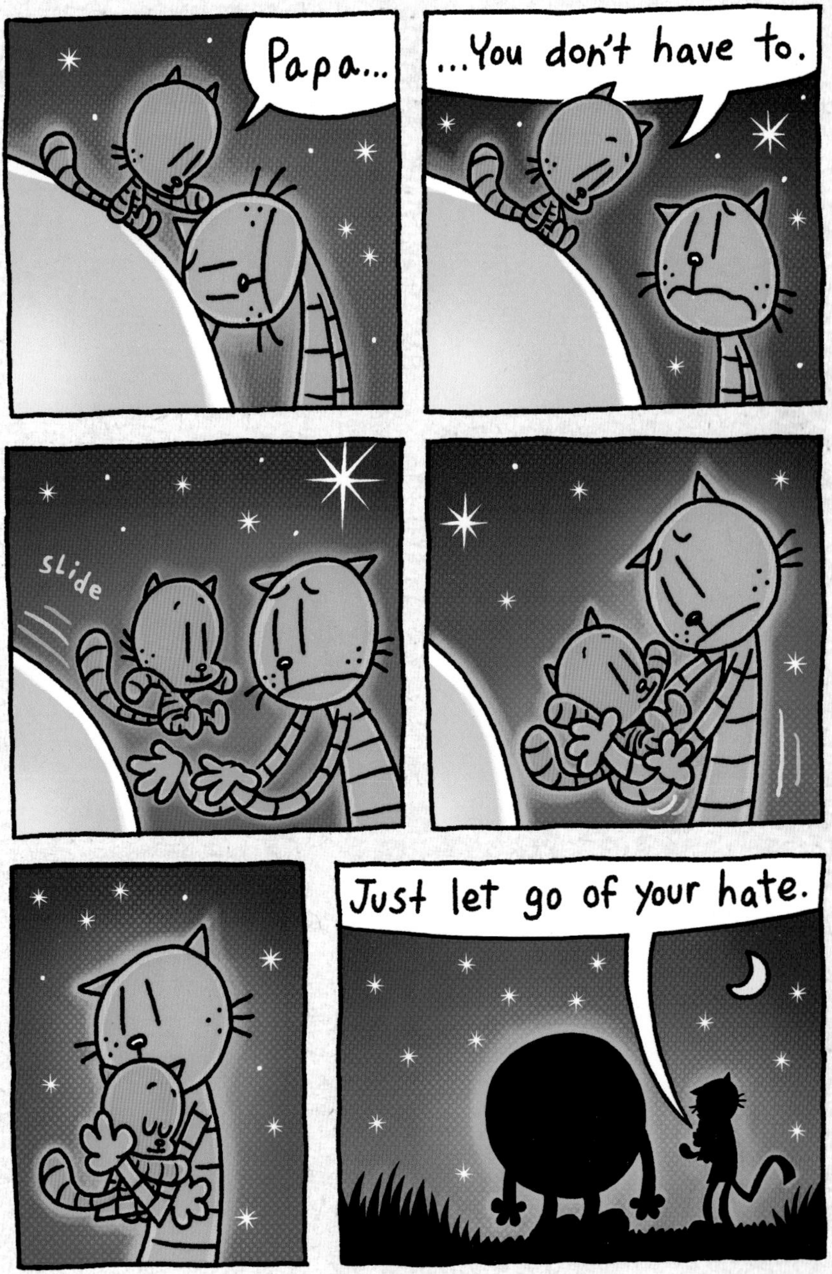
Papa...
...You don't have to.
slide
Just let go of your hate.

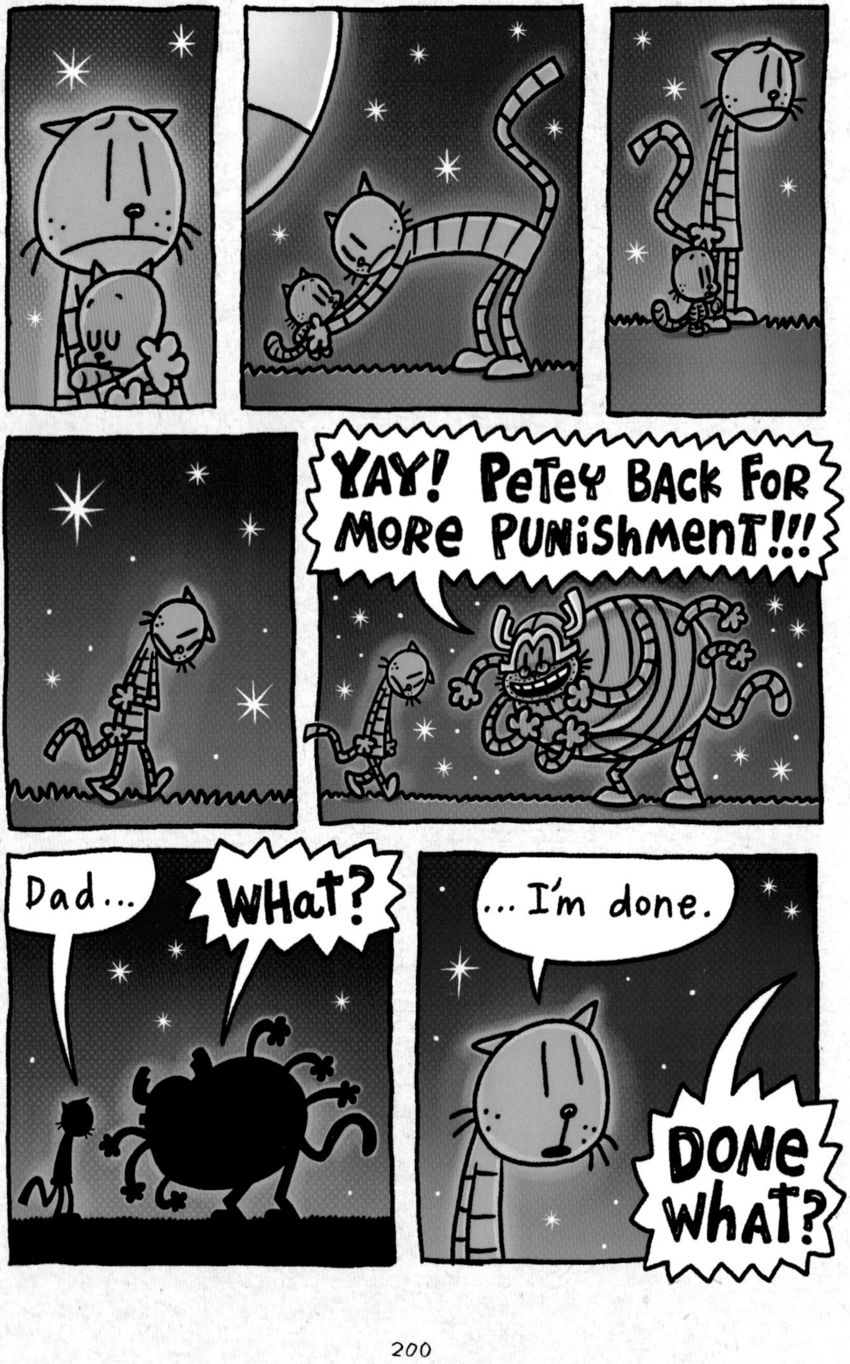
YAY! PETEY BACK FOR MORE PUNISHMENT!!!
Dad...
WHAT?
... I'm done.
DONE WHAT?

CHAPTER 13

Three Endings

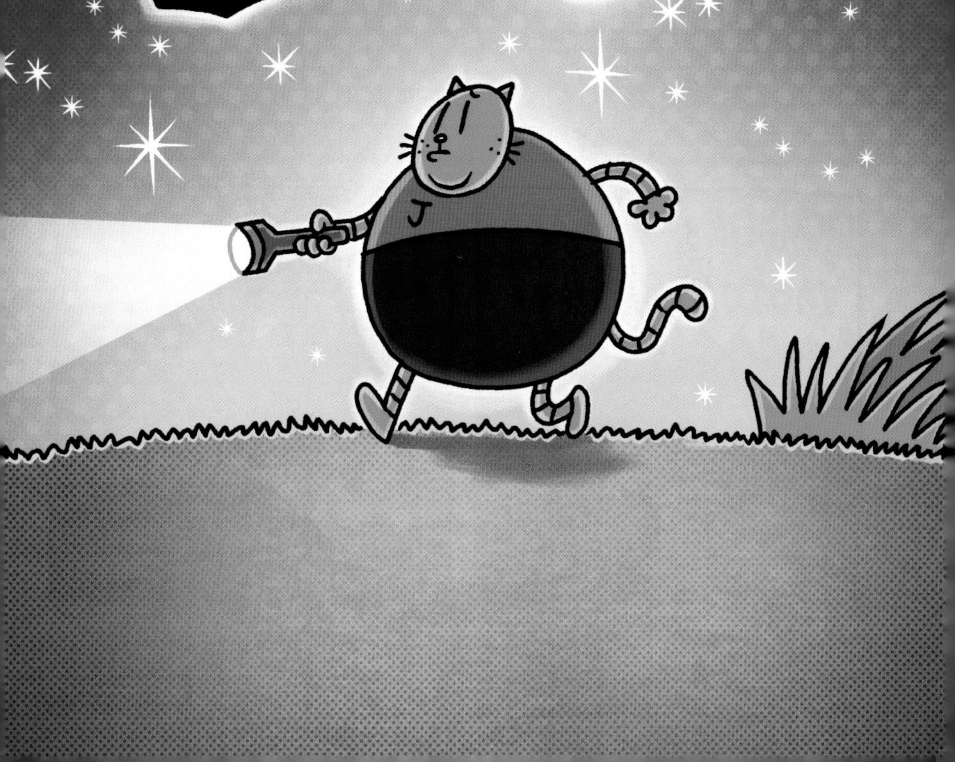

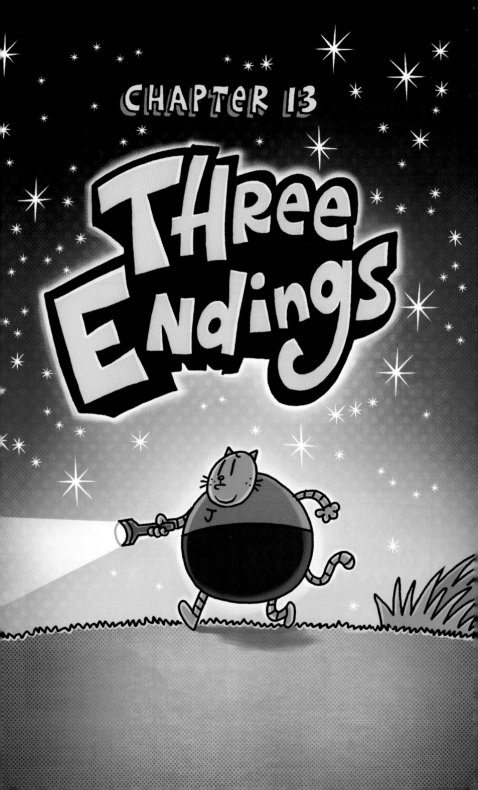

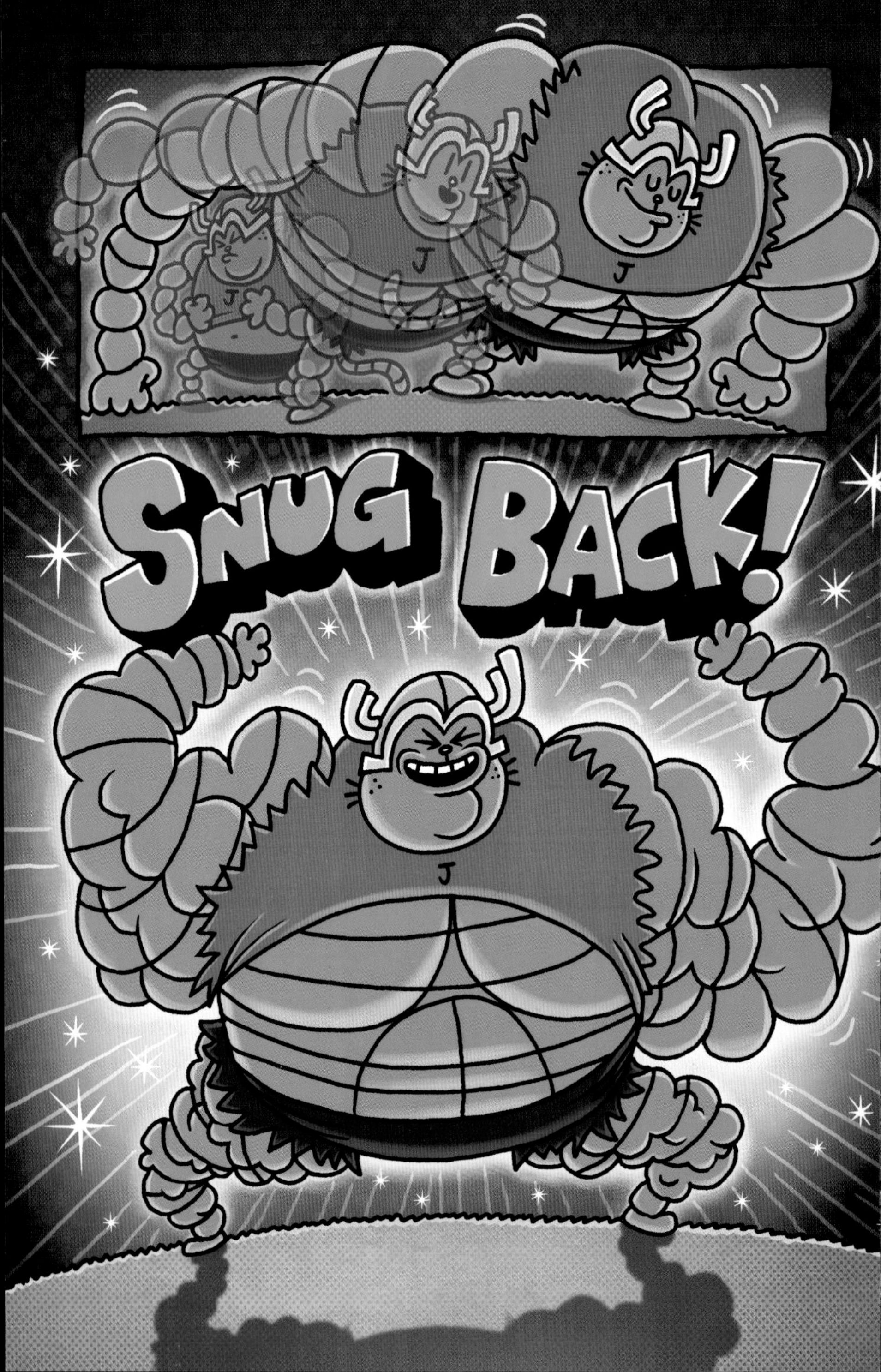
SNUG BACK!

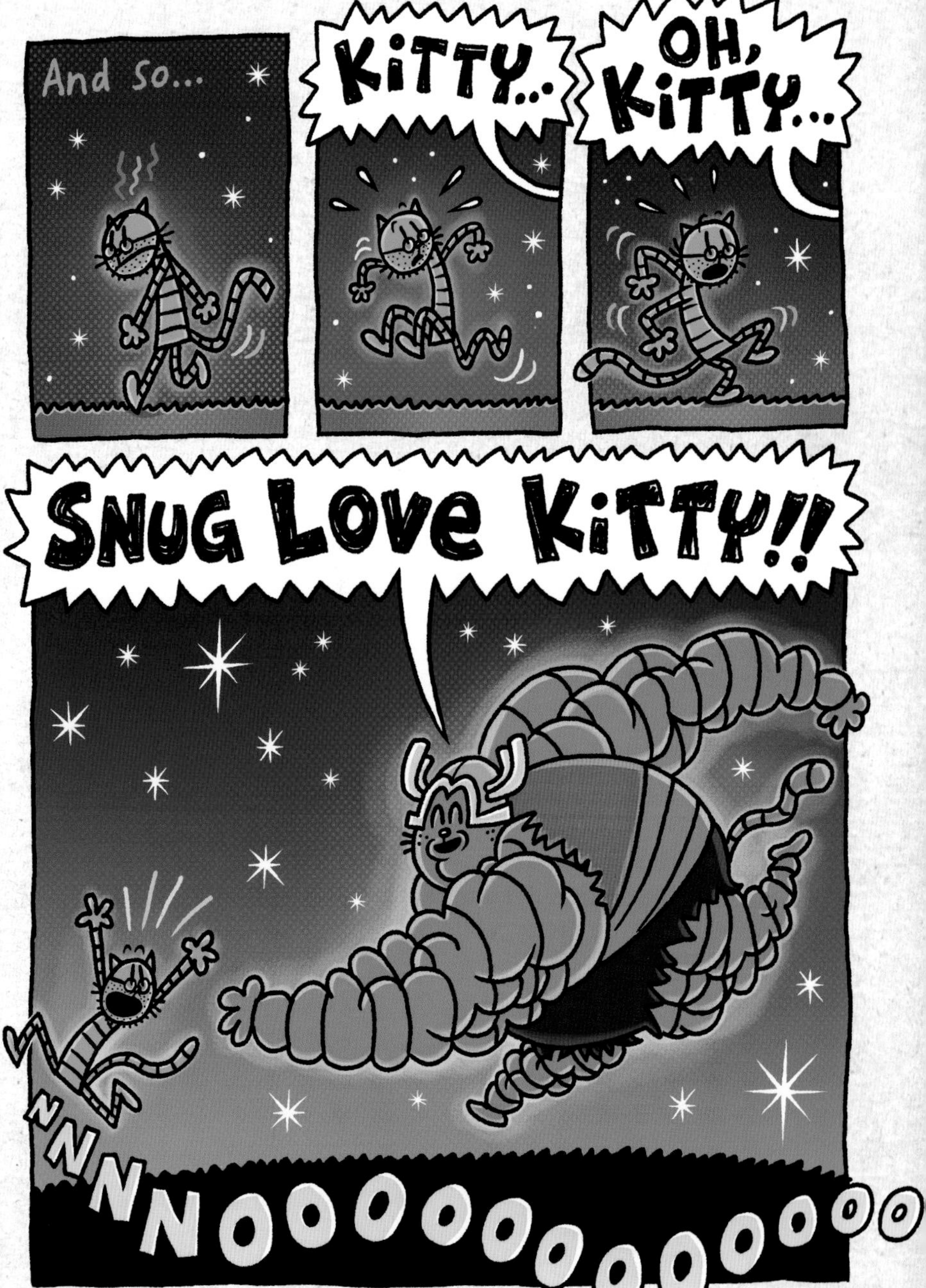
And so...
KITTY...
OH, KITTY...
SNUG LOVE KITTY!!
NNNNOOOOOOOOOOOOOOO

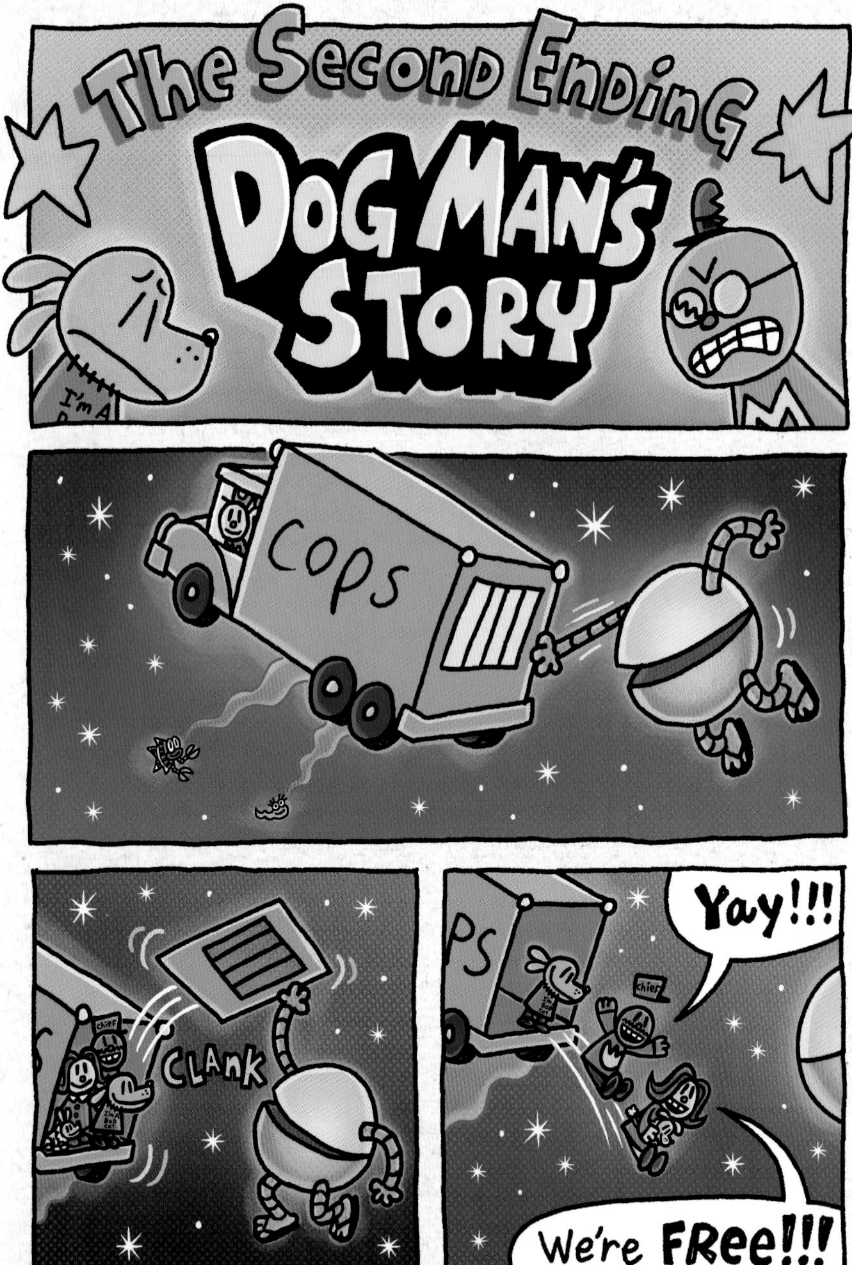
The Second Ending
Dog Man's Story
Cops
CLANK
Yay!!!
We're FREE!!!

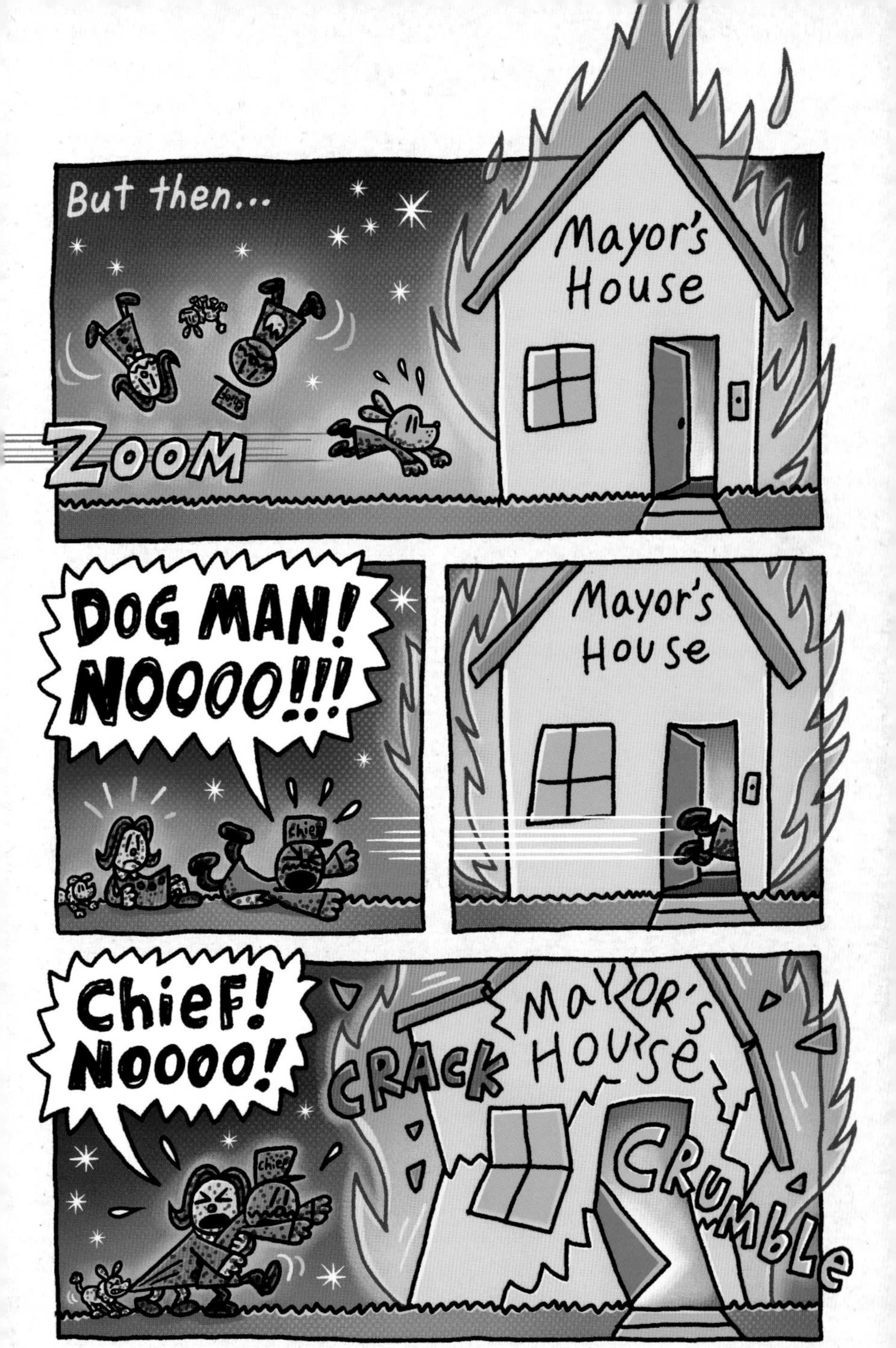
But then...
Mayor's House
ZOOM
DOG MAN! NOOOO!!!
Chief
Mayor's House
Chief! NOOOO!
Chief
MAYOR'S HOUSE
CRACK
CRUMBLE

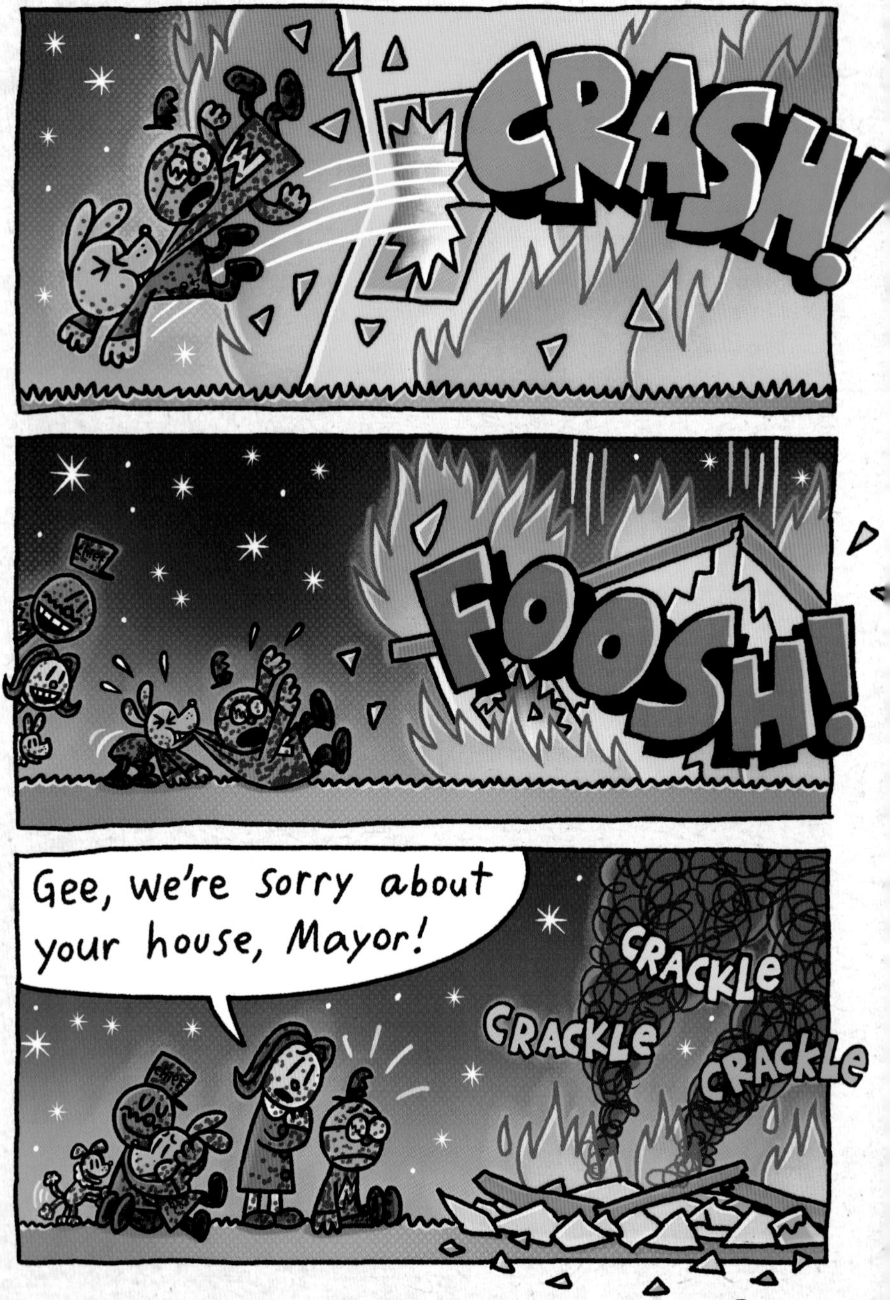
CRASH!
FOOSH!
Gee, we're sorry about your house, Mayor!
CRACKLE
CRACKLE
CRACKLE

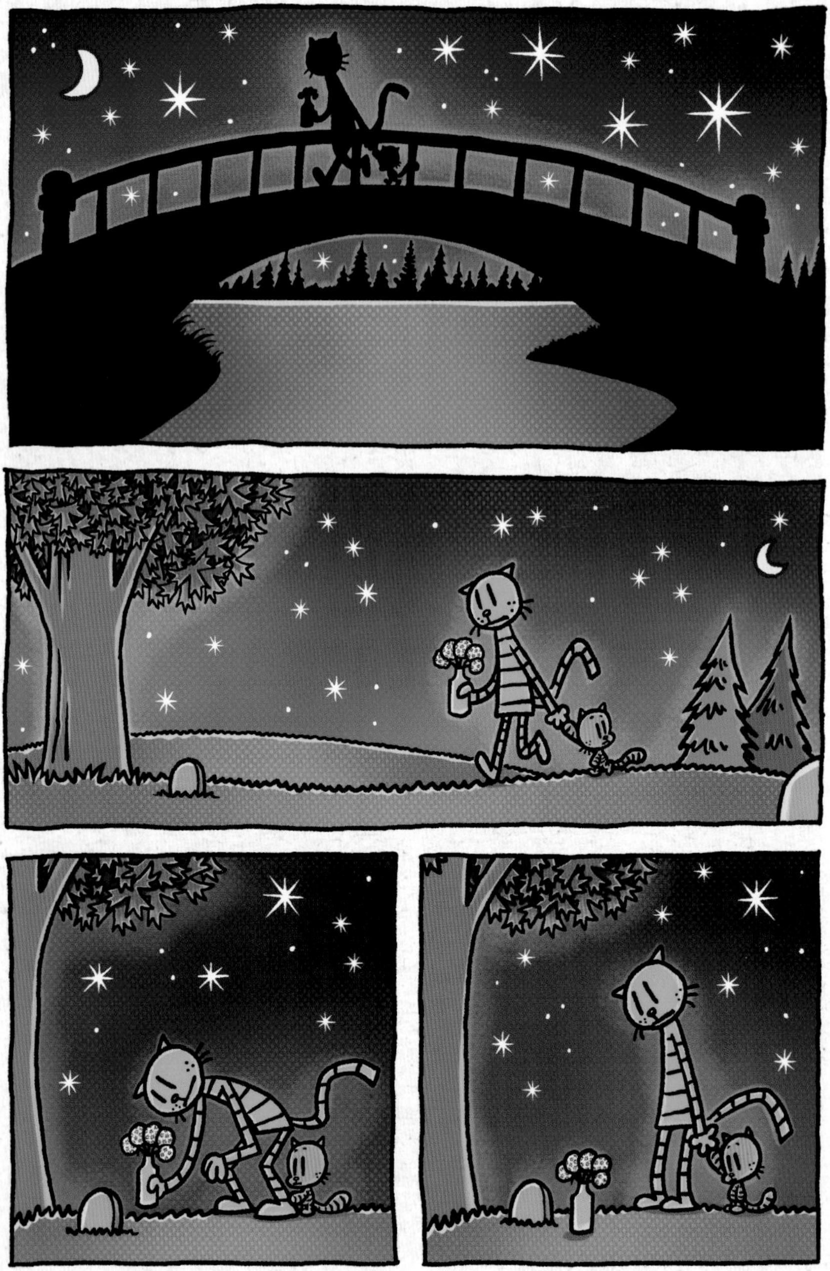

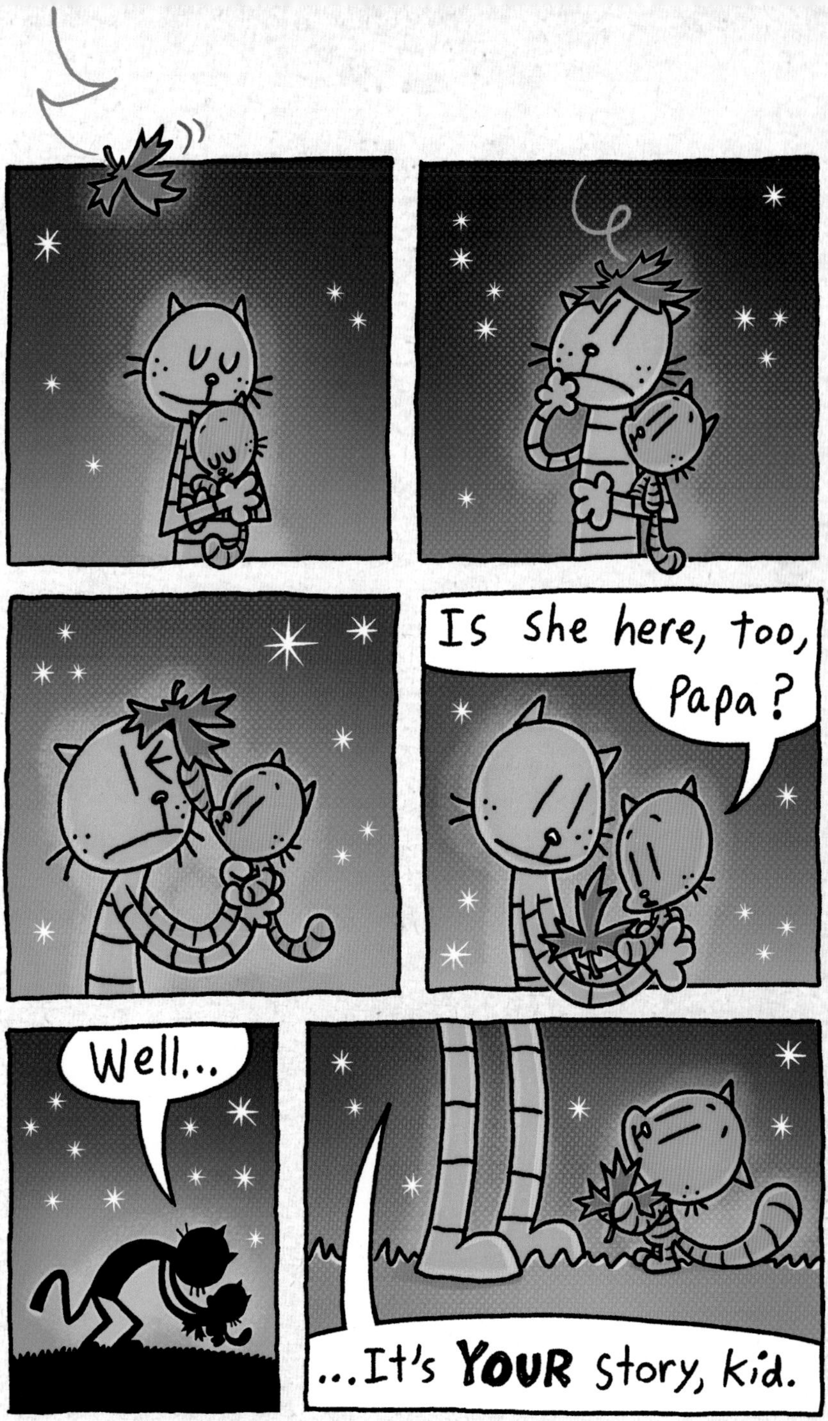
Is she here, too, Papa?
Well...
...It's YOUR story, kid.

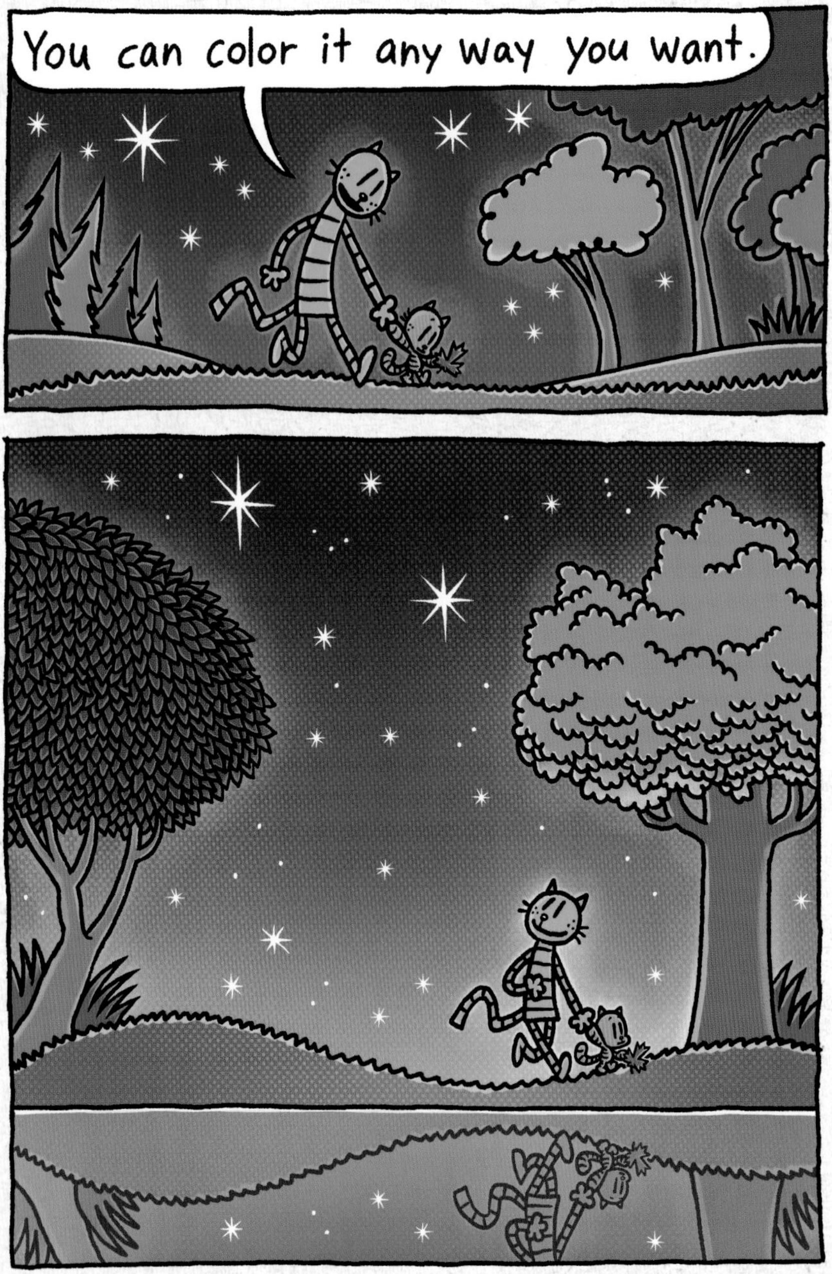
You can color it any way you want.

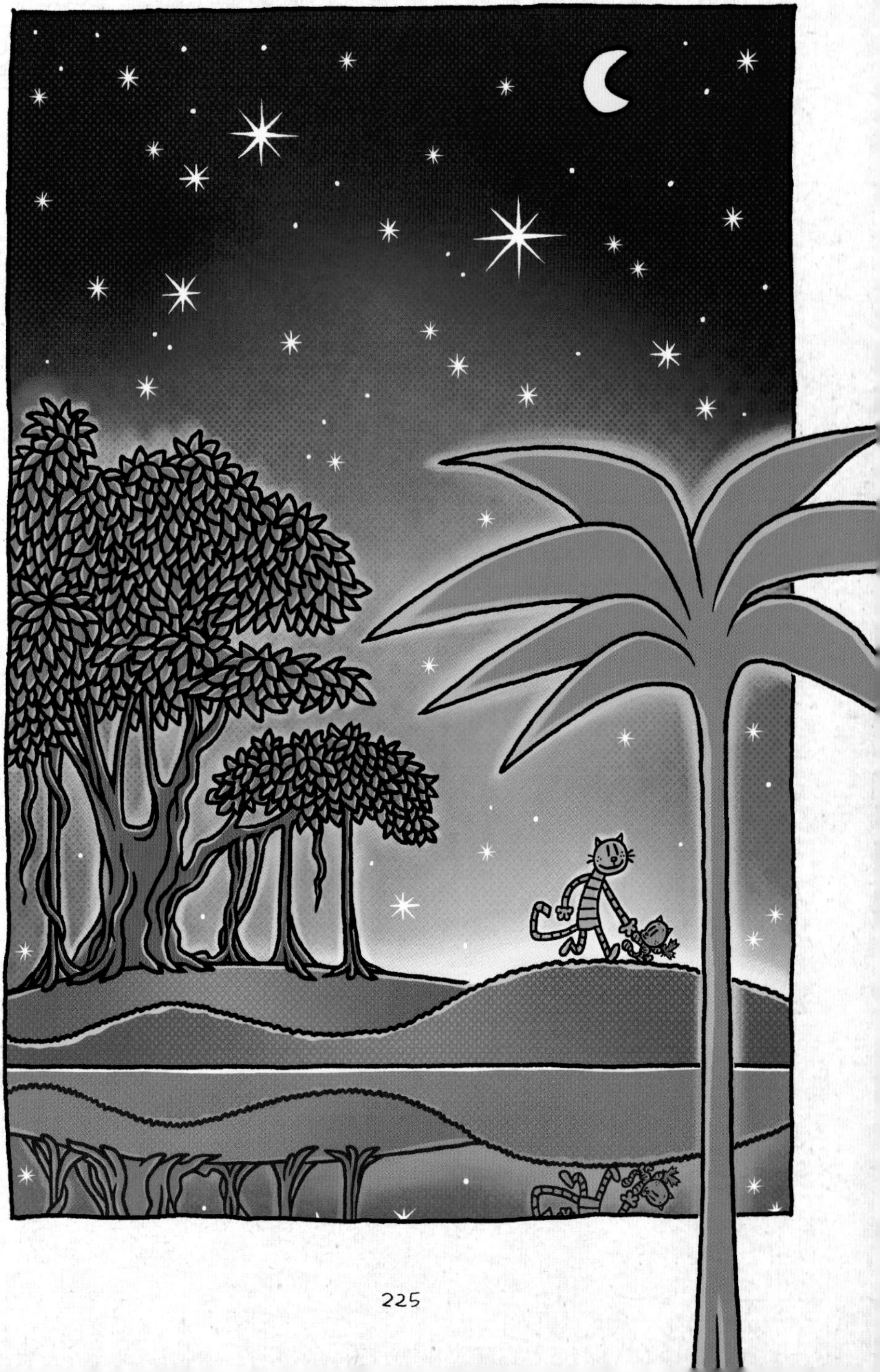

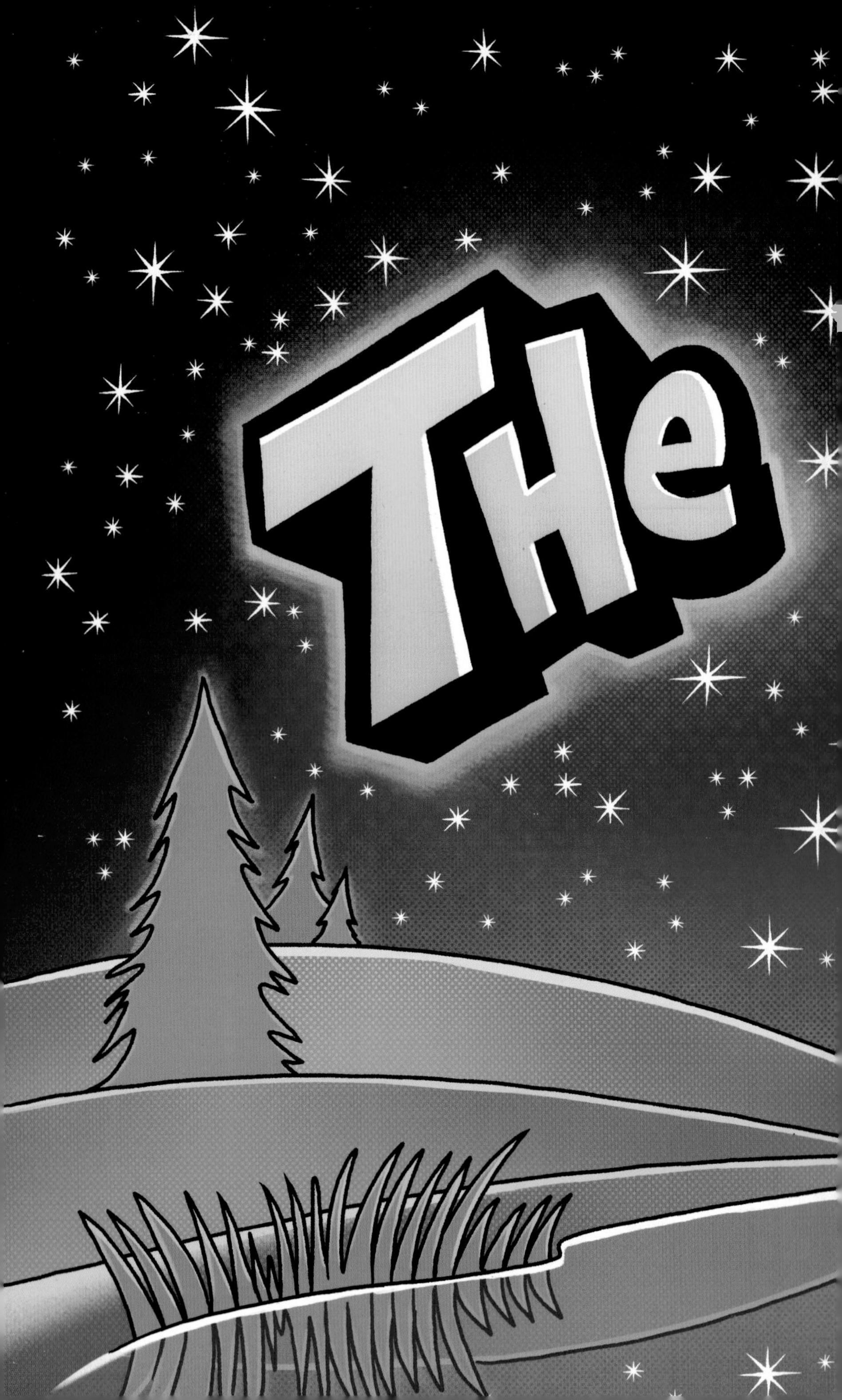
THe

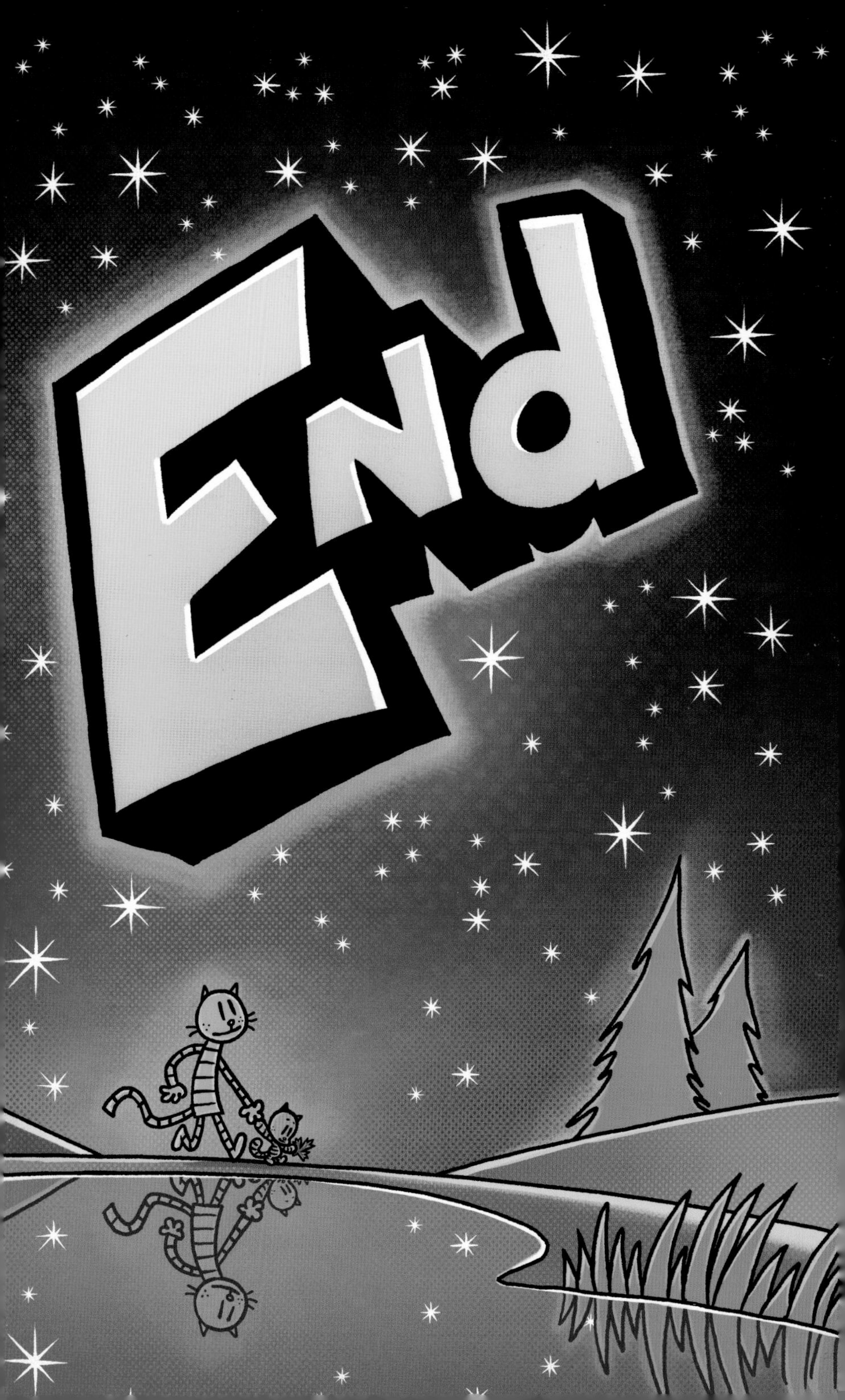
End

NOTES

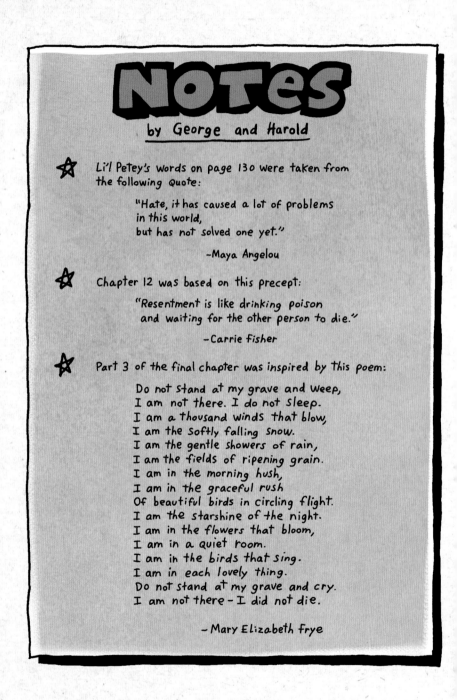

by George and Harold

★ Li'l Petey's words on page 130 were taken from the following quote:

> "Hate, it has caused a lot of problems
> in this world,
> but has not solved one yet."
>
> —Maya Angelou

★ Chapter 12 was based on this precept:

> "Resentment is like drinking poison
> and waiting for the other person to die."
>
> —Carrie Fisher

★ Part 3 of the final chapter was inspired by this poem:

> Do not stand at my grave and weep,
> I am not there. I do not sleep.
> I am a thousand winds that blow,
> I am the softly falling snow.
> I am the gentle showers of rain,
> I am the fields of ripening grain.
> I am in the morning hush,
> I am in the graceful rush
> Of beautiful birds in circling flight.
> I am the starshine of the night.
> I am in the flowers that bloom,
> I am in a quiet room.
> I am in the birds that sing.
> I am in each lovely thing.
> Do not stand at my grave and cry.
> I am not there — I did not die.
>
> — Mary Elizabeth Frye

HOW 2 DRAW Melvin The FROG

in 17 Ridiculously easy steps!

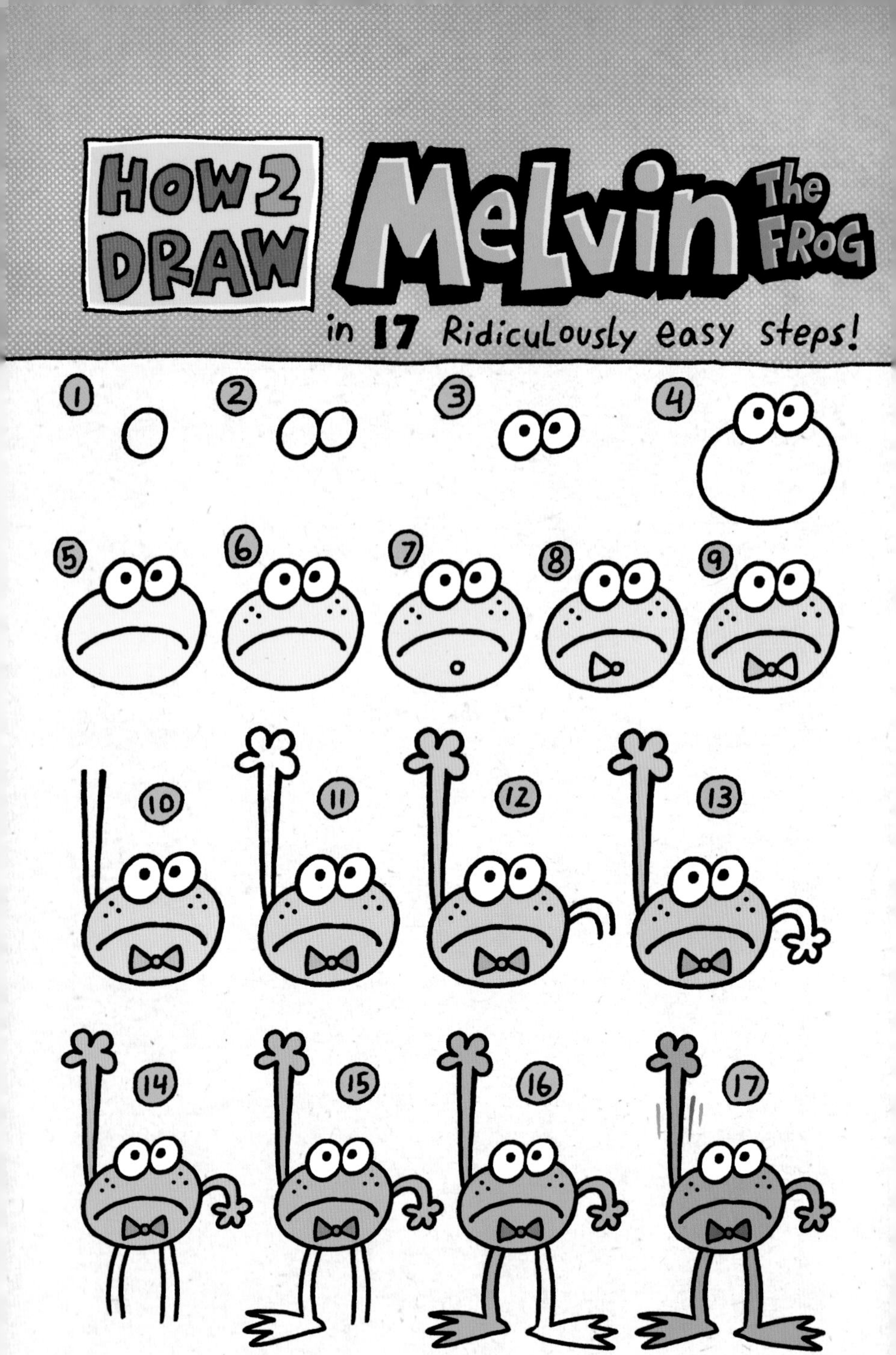

1
2
3
4
5
6
7
8
9
10
11
12
13
14
15
16
17

HOW 2 MAKE MUNCHY The Lunch BAG

in 4 Ridiculously easy steps!

Step 1:

Get Supplies:

- ★ Lunch bag
- ★ Pencil
- ★ Tape
- ★ Construction paper ★ Scissors
- ★ Crayons / markers / Colored Pencils

STEP 2:

Draw and cut out the arms, Legs, eyes + tongue.

FREE Printable/Colorable template available at: Scholastic.com/catkidcomicclub

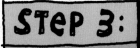

STEP 3:

Assemble as shown using tape or glue or paste.

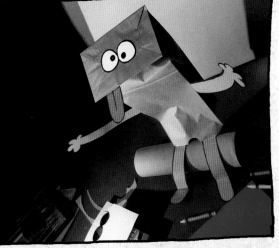

STEP 4:

Take away his evil powers by filling him up with all the people and things you **Love!** Use pencils, crayons, paint, or whatever!!!

SKATE
COMIX
Bling
Mom Dad Great-Granny

WRITE... DRAW... Be CREATIVE!

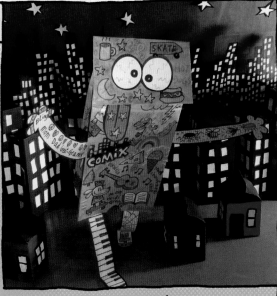

How 2 Draw The Insuppressible Snug

in **34** Ridiculously easy Steps!

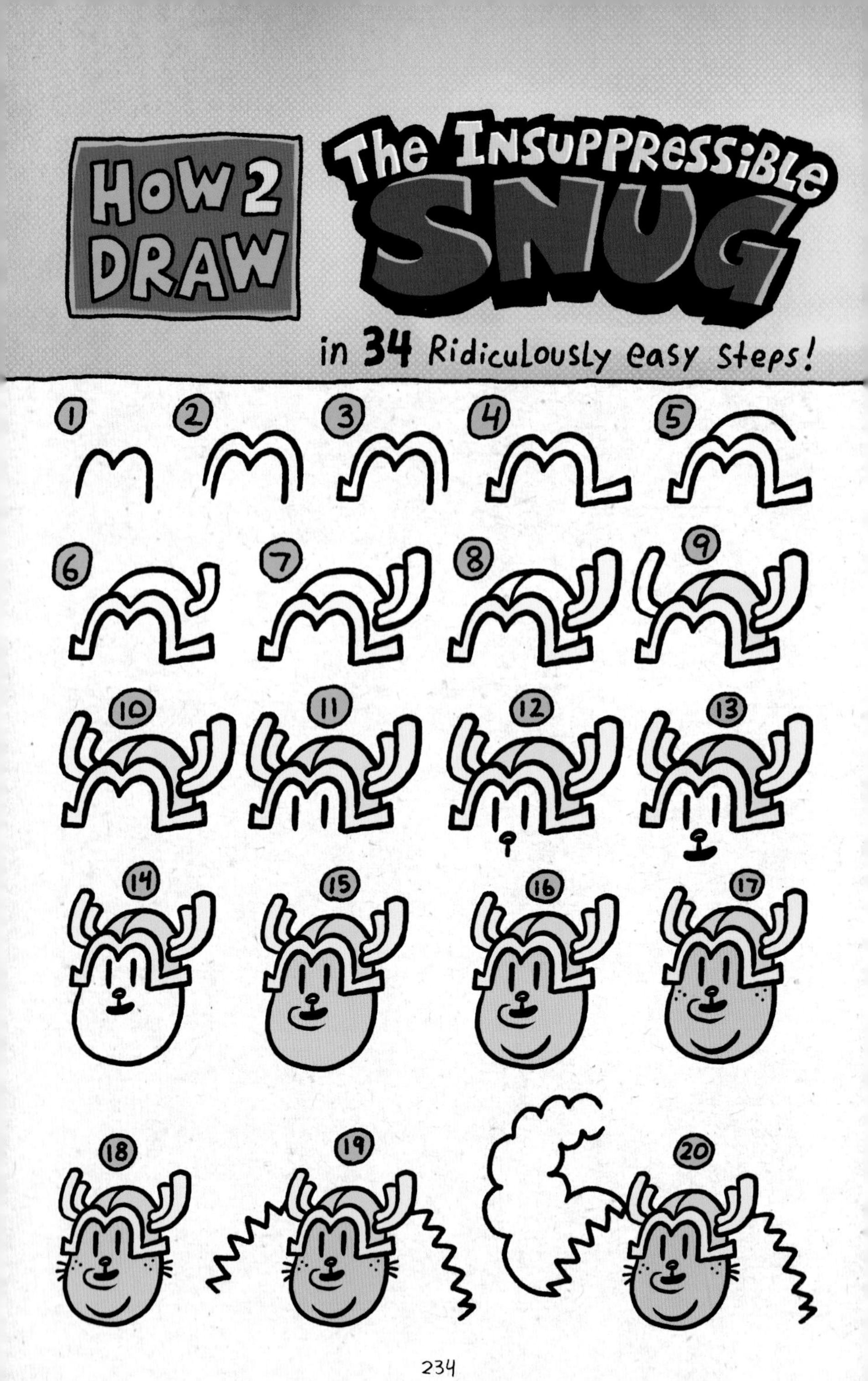
1
2
3
4
5
6
7
8
9
10
11
12
13
14
15
16
17
18
19
20

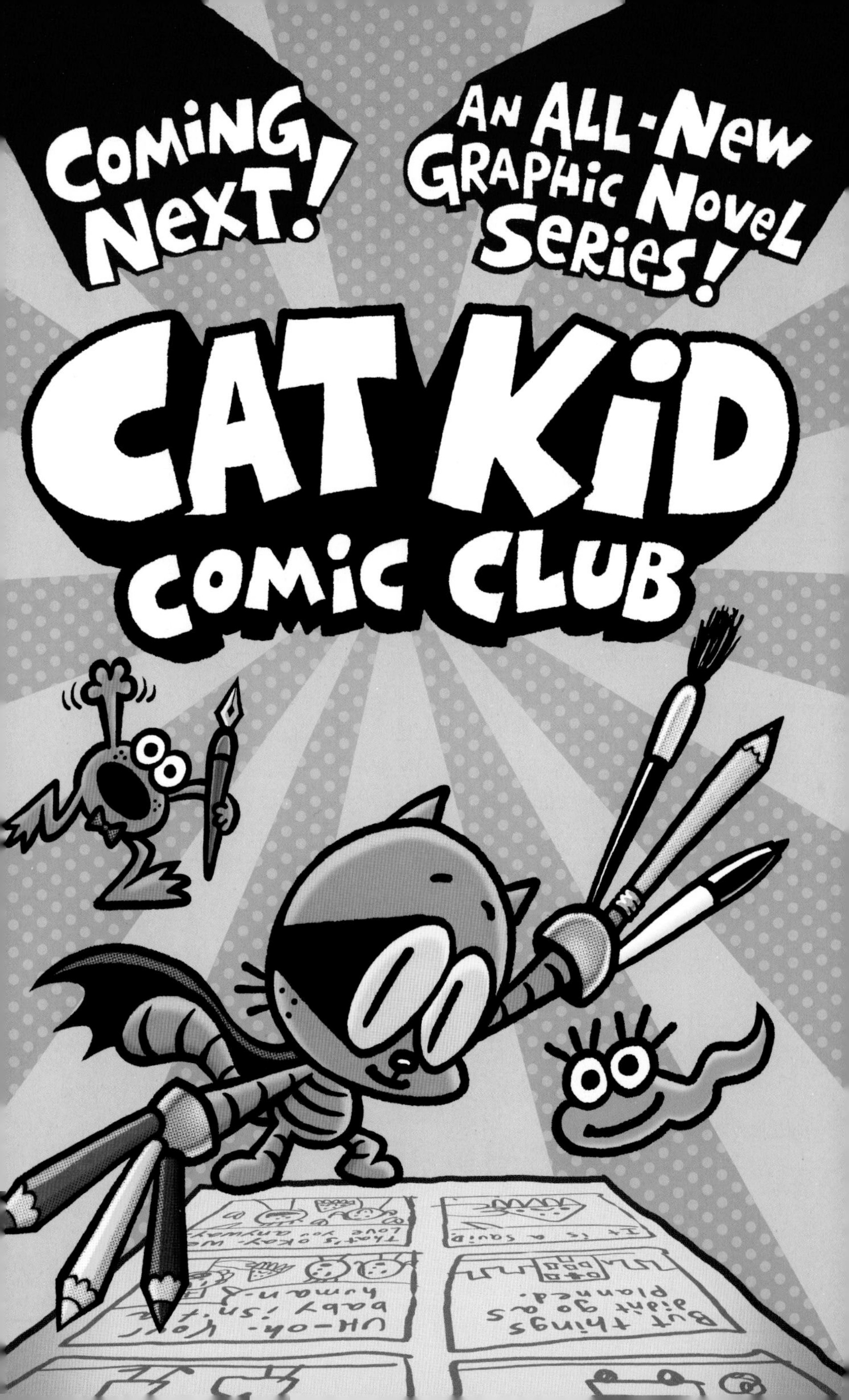

Coming Next!
An All-New Graphic Novel Series!
CAT KID
COMIC CLUB
That's okay- we love you anyway
It is a squid.
But things didn't go as planned.

GET READING W

TH DAV PILKEY!

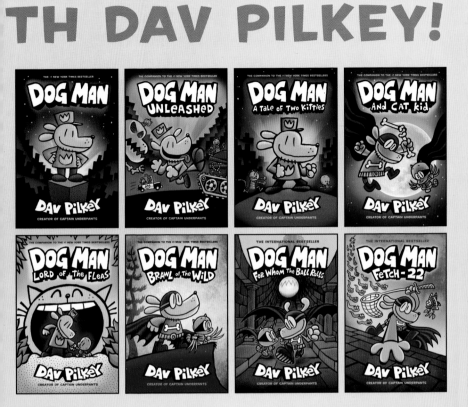

ABOUT THE
AUTHOR-ILLUSTRATOR

When Dav Pilkey was a kid, he was diagnosed with ADHD and dyslexia. Dav was so disruptive in class that his teachers made him sit out in the hallway every day. Luckily, Dav loved to draw and make up stories. He spent his time in the hallway creating his own original comic books — the very first adventures of Dog Man and Captain Underpants.

In college, Dav met a teacher who encouraged him to illustrate and write. He won a national competition in 1986 and the prize was the publication of his first book, WORLD WAR WON. He made many other books before being awarded the 1998 California Young Reader Medal for DOG BREATH, which was published in 1994, and in 1997 he won the Caldecott Honor for THE PAPERBOY.

THE ADVENTURES OF SUPER DIAPER BABY, published in 2002, was the first complete graphic novel spin-off from the Captain Underpants series and appeared at #6 on the USA Today bestseller list for all books, both adult and children's, and was also a New York Times bestseller. It was followed by THE ADVENTURES OF OOK AND GLUK: KUNG FU CAVEMEN FROM THE FUTURE and SUPER DIAPER BABY 2: THE INVASION OF THE POTTY SNATCHERS, both USA Today bestsellers. The unconventional style of these graphic novels is intended to encourage uninhibited creativity in kids.

His stories are semi-autobiographical and explore universal themes that celebrate friendship, tolerance, and the triumph of the good-hearted.

Dav loves to kayak in the Pacific Northwest with his wife.